THIEF

OF Hearts

L.H. COSWAY

"How can I begin anything new with all of yesterday in me?"

-    Leonard Cohen.

For the ones we've lost who live on in our hearts.

One

If you ever want to experience the true depths to which humanity can sink, go live in a ground-floor flat in any major city.

It was three a.m. on a school night, and I'd just been woken by the sound of someone shuffling around outside my bedroom window. I groaned and blinked my eyes open, sitting up and rubbing the bird's nest that was my hair. Grumpily, I wondered who was out there this time.

I used to get anxious, worried about what kind of nutter could be hanging around and if they were going to try and stage a break-in.

Now I was just numb to it, willing the person to get whatever they were doing over and done with so I could go back to sleep. Sweet, precious sleep.

When I heard the recognisable trickling sound, I saw red. Acting purely on instinct, I got up, shoved my feet into a pair of boots, grabbed the cricket bat I kept especially for occasions like these, and stomped my way outside.

A middle-aged guy in a suit stood there, pissing into the corner of my building, directly outside my bedroom window like it was his own personal urinal.

"Get the fuck out of here before I do something I regret," I threatened, wielding the bat like a sleep-deprived mad woman. The irritating thing was, other than the fact that he was clearly drunk, he looked like a perfectly normal human being. He wasn't some kind of homeless crackhead who had nowhere else to go. He was someone with a home, and most likely, a job, but more importantly, a bathroom. In spite of all this, he decided that tonight was the night he said *fuck it* to common decency and pissed on somebody's *home*.

As you can probably guess, this wasn't my first rodeo. I'd had a lot of time to stew on the fact that people did the scummiest things when they thought they weren't going to be caught. Unfortunately, this was what you had to put up with when you were drowning in debt like I was. Simply put, nice flats cost money.

The man's drunken, bleary eyes widened, as he quickly put his cock away, tucked tail, and made a run for it.

"You should be ashamed of yourself!" I shouted after him.

There was a deep, dark part of me that kind of wished I'd hit him with the bat . . . just a little. Maybe it'd teach him a lesson. Or maybe I was going mad from lack of rest. I wasn't the best sleeper in the world, and even the slightest noise woke me up.

I stomped back inside and noticed the light was still on in my cousin Alfie's room. Alfie was a creature of the dark, burning the midnight oil as per usual. We'd been sharing our tiny two-bedroom flat in Finsbury Park for the last three years. It was on the basement level of a renovated Victorian house that had been split into separate units. We weren't even technically on the ground floor. We were subterranean. Still, this was one of the more affordable neighbourhoods to rent in London, though strangely home to a disconcerting number of hair shops. Some days I felt like throwing caution to the wind and getting myself some hot-pink extensions.

I could hear chuckling a moment before Alfie came out of his room, holding his hand to his stomach as he practically bowled over with laughter. I scowled at him.

"You were watching from your window."

"That was priceless, Andie, the look on his face. If he wasn't already pissing, I think he might have wet himself."

My scowl didn't fade as I walked into the kitchen and grabbed a bottle of water from the fridge. "Ha ha."

"Seriously, we should hire you out to scare children on Halloween. You could play the role of the crazy old witch."

I gave him the finger as I slugged back a mouthful of water. He came over, sighed, and draped an arm around my shoulder. His attempt at parental soothing didn't exactly work since he was several inches shorter. The kids at school used to call us Little and Large, though I'd always been slim.

"I'm almost finished *Young Girl with Kite*. Do you want to see?"

I nodded and exhaled. "I might as well now that I'm up."

We went inside his bedroom/studio and I tried not to trip over all the crap on the floor. Alfie was a chaotic soul: a painter. Born the only child of two wealthy parents, he'd been able to pursue an artistic calling. Well, that was until his dad was prosecuted for running a Ponzi scheme and subsequently had his assets frozen. These days Alfie survived on rare patronage and sales of his works to a handful of specialist art galleries.

My cousin left the flat mostly to buy coffee and sandwiches from the hipster café around the corner, whose employees consisted solely of six-foot-tall Swedes with white-blond hair. I wasn't sure if these attributes were a job requirement or what, but Alfie always said he found their presence soothing. He also spent a lot of time at his best friend, Jamie's, second-hand bookstore. If it weren't for Jamie and me, Alfie would probably turn into a full-fledged hermit.

I stood in front of the canvas, taking in *Young Girl with Kite* and feeling that sense of awe that often accompanied seeing Alfie's finished works. I took several moments to absorb his mastery before turning and giving him a hug.

"It's beautiful. Every time I think you can't possibly top the last, you go and prove me wrong. You're a genius."

Alfie rubbed at his chin, contemplating the piece and leaving a smudge of brown paint behind. "The yellow is revelatory. It allows your eyes to absorb the leaves on the ground and the kite in the clouds all at once," he said, his voice energised. Alfie was fascinated by colour, could find things in it I'd never even think to look for.

He was the most intelligent person I knew, but it was the kind of artistic intelligence that left you a homeless vagrant on the street, rather than a millionaire CEO. The problem was too much empathy. Alfie could see a story on the news about how Russia was involving itself in the troubles in Ukraine and spend days wallowing over the disaster it might lead to. Whereas I, on the other hand, could see the same story and continue on with my day, wholly oblivious.

Don't get me wrong. I wasn't heartless. In fact, as a teacher I spent most of my days helping others. I had empathy in spades, but I didn't have Alfie's level of intelligence, and trust me, folks, that was a blessing.

"You're right," I told him finally. "And the ribbon in the girl's hair has so much life; the way it moves in the breeze looks like dancing."

Alfie turned to me, his grin wide. "That's exactly what I was trying to achieve."

I returned his smile, gave his shoulder a small, congratulatory squeeze and told him I was going back to bed. On my way out I noticed some paintings stacked by the door. They were copies of old masters, Vermeer and Rembrandt mostly. Oddly enough, reproduction was how

Alfie started out painting. Growing up, his mother liked to decorate their home with replicas of famous pieces, so Alfie used to create imitations. The accuracy was actually kind of spooky. Anyway, after a few years he finally progressed to doing his own original works, but the replicas were how he honed his skills to what they are today.

I turned back to him, nodding at the paintings. "Do you want me to drop those off at a charity shop during the week to clear up some space?"

My cousin rubbed his chin, his signature *I'm considering it* action. "Let me think about it. You know I hate giving stuff away, and those have sentimental value."

"Well, let me know what you decide."

When I woke up to my alarm at seven, the flat was quiet like usual. Alfie wouldn't be awake until well after midday, as was his habit.

I showered, dressed, ate breakfast, and climbed into my Nissan to head to work. I taught an adult education class, designed specifically for those seeking to return to college as mature-aged students. Most of my pupils had been out of school for years, if not decades. The course helped improve their writing and grammar, as well as identified their strengths and/or weaknesses in preparation for higher education.

My class had fifteen students, ranging in ages from twenty-one to sixty, and was held five days a week, from nine to three. Running for six months, the course was intensive. We were only three weeks into the new school year, but already I had my favourite students.

Mary was a no-nonsense cockney in her early fifties, with dyed black hair and ever-present matte-red lipstick. She was at least a few stone overweight, with a penchant for leopard print, and always had the best advice about relationships and paying your council tax. Kian was the youngest member of the class, a goth rocker from Camden who suffered from Tourette's. Despite his purple Mohawk and frequent obscenities, he was one of the kindest, most adorable people I'd ever known.

And then there was Larry, barely over five feet with endless stories about his days on the markets. He used to run a stall selling pirated videotapes, before DVDs and Internet streaming came along and made them obsolete.

They were all there, chatting with the other students and drinking their morning coffee. I entered the class and exchanged hellos, remembering there was a new student arriving today. The information on my schedule said his name was Stuart Cross, and he was thirty years of age, with very little previous schooling. Actually, he'd just gotten out of prison after a two-year sentence. His crime wasn't listed, though, and I had to wonder what he'd been in for.

I was wary of someone new coming in, someone with a record, because in my experience it only took one bad egg to ruin the carefully cultivated atmosphere of friendship and learning. I wanted everyone to feel at ease, to look on this room as a place without judgement, somewhere they could express their dreams as well as frustrations without cause for worry or criticism.

Sometimes it worked, sometimes it didn't. Thankfully, this year I'd been blessed with a class where everyone genuinely liked one another and got along. Hopefully, Stuart would fit in well.

Organising my things and opening my laptop, I pulled up the morning's lesson plan when I heard the friendly chatter quieten down. Glancing up, our new student had arrived, and I had to take a second to catch my breath.

Stuart Cross looked dangerous, in a James Dean, careless-male-beauty, leather jacket wearing sort of way. He was tall, with chestnut-brown hair, hazel eyes and dark, expressive brows. He looked like he drank beer straight out of the bottle and drove a motorcycle.

Mary placed a hand on her hip and smirked as she looked him up and down in a very *I've got your number, Sonny Jim* fashion. I imagined she'd eat him for breakfast if he even gave her so much as a hint he was interested in becoming her boy toy.

And I, well, I couldn't seem to take my eyes off him either. He was just so unexpected. It was like entering Alfie's bedroom and discovering a newly finished painting. He seemed too much for our ordinary, comfortable little classroom.

He made eye contact with me just as he pulled out a chair in the third row and sat, a whoosh of air capturing my lungs. I rubbed my palms on my skirt and leaned forward, about to introduce myself when a student approached him. It was Harold, a small, bespectacled man in his early fifties, who liked everything to be done *just so*. In other words, he was set in his ways, and Stuart was currently occupying his usual seat.

"Pardon me, but I sit there," he said, tapping Stuart on the shoulder.

Stuart rested an elbow on the desk and slowly turned to look at him. "You what?"

Harold cleared his throat. "This is where I sit. I'm sorry, but you're going to have to move."

Stuart let out a quiet chuckle, shook his head, and leaned back to spread his legs. "I don't think so. I've just gotten comfortable, mate."

I frowned and rose from my seat. Making my way past the desks, I felt the others watching as I approached our new student. I stopped just in front of him, briefly placed a reassuring hand on Harold's shoulder and levelled Stuart with a strict look.

"We actually have a set seating plan. Come with me and I'll show you where you can sit. I'm Miss Anderson, by the way. Your teacher."

Stuart took his time raising his eyes to mine, slicing his teeth across his full bottom lip for a second as he contemplated me. I rested my hands on my hips, trying not to fixate on his mouth as I felt a tiny flicker in some long-neglected part of my body.

"All right then, Miss Anderson. I wouldn't want to cause a fuss," said Stuart, standing to his full height and allowing Harold to take his seat. His attitude rubbed me the wrong way, but nevertheless, I led him to the only free seat in the front row. He stepped forward, his chest brushing mine before he sat. I caught my breath for a second; the contact took me by surprise. In fact, it almost felt like he'd done it on purpose.

Yep, I was definitely going to have to keep an eye on this one.

Clicking on my laptop, I opened the file with the discussion points for the morning lesson. But first, we'd have our usual start-of-the-week chat, where my students talked about what was going on in their lives.

"I hope you all enjoyed your weekend," I said. "Did anybody do anything fun?"

The shyer members of the class avoided making eye contact, while Mary spoke up. "My daughter went into labour early on Saturday morning. She had a healthy, eight-and-a-half-pound baby girl. I'm made up."

"That's wonderful news, Mary. Did she decide on a name yet?"

"She's calling her Georgina. I'm off to the hospital later today to bring them both home."

"Well, I'm glad it all went well and they're both healthy," I said and glanced around the room. "Would anybody else like to share something?"

I was met with quiet but it didn't faze me. I knew how hard it was to speak up in situations like these, but I always encouraged my students to do so because it was a great way to build confidence. I never pushed anyone to talk, but I did like to gently cajole. My attention went to our new student.

"How about you, Stuart? Would like to tell us a little about yourself?"

"It's Stu," he corrected, levelling me with his eyes again.

"My apologies, Stu," I replied kindly.

He flexed his hands. "What do you want to know?"

"Anything you're comfortable telling us. I like to think of this class as something of a family. We all support one another, and I'm happy to provide a friendly ear. If you don't want to tell a problem to the entire class, then I'm always available to speak with privately at the end of each day."

His gaze moved over me and I shifted in my seat, not entirely sure why. He made me feel odd, like he knew me already, which was absurd because we'd never met before. He took his time answering, first running a hand over his jaw then rubbing his lower lip with his thumb.

"This isn't a family," he stated, like the idea vaguely offended him.

I tensed. "Yes, I know that. I said it was *like* a family, or well, as close to one as we can get."

"Fuckers!" came a loud expletive, but it wasn't from Stu. Kian had shouted it from his position at the back of the class. His Tourette's had obviously kicked in. I was used to his outbursts and never made a big deal of them, no matter how obscene, but today I wondered if the presence of our new student had put him on edge.

Stu cast an amused glance in Kian's direction then looked back at me. "You gonna let him get away with that language, Miss Anderson?"

His tone was oh so cocky and the challenge in his voice made my cheeks heat. I'd had all manner of students in my time, but none who made me feel quite so flustered. "Kian has Tourette's," I explained. "We all know that nothing he says is meant to insult."

"Sorry," said Kian, scratching his head and I cast him a kind expression.

"I've told you, you don't ever need to apologise."

Stu grinned at Kian. "So, you can get away with calling us all a bunch of wankers and arseholes and we just have to let it fly?"

Kian smiled shyly, still scratching his head. "Yeah, pretty much."

"Well, fuck me."

I levelled Stu with a firm look. "I make an exception for Kian. You, however, are not permitted to use foul language in class."

Stu raised his hands in the air. "My bad."

I sniffed. "Yes well, if we could get back to my original question. Is there anything you'd like to share?"

Stu contemplated me for a long moment, then surprised everyone with his candidness. "I just got out the nick a fortnight ago. Last weekend I made up for lost time. Seeing as how I was just told off for foul language, I won't go into details," he said, baiting me. It was almost like he wanted to piss me off. "I enjoyed myself, though, let's put it that way."

"What were you in for?" Mary interjected, never shy in asking questions.

Stu glanced at her but didn't hesitate to answer. "Stolen car racket. Learned my lesson."

Funny, he didn't sound like it. I wondered if the likes of Stu Cross ever learned their lesson. I was, however, relieved. At the back of my mind I'd been worried his crime might've been violent or sexual in nature. Stealing cars was bad, but at least it didn't lean toward deviant behaviour.

"How long were you in for?" Mary went on.

Now Stu grew tense and a little defensive. "You writing a book, luv? Want to know what I ate for breakfast and the last time I took a shit, too?"

"Just curious. No need to get your knickers in a twist," Mary huffed.

I could tell by the look on Stu's face that he was two seconds away from saying something unfriendly, so I quickly cut in.

"Well, like I said, this class is a judgement-free zone. We've all got a clean slate here."

Stu eyed me for a long moment, like he was trying figure out if I was full of crap. I wasn't. My life was dedicated to helping others nowadays. It was the only way I could keep moving forward.

I cleared my throat. "Anyway, we'd best start the morning's lesson. How are you all finding the book?"

Every month I gave the class a new book to read, assigning them a few chapters a night so we could have a discussion the next day. The first book I'd chosen this year was Thomas Hardy's *Jude the Obscure*. Yes, I'll admit, it was a heavy read, but in my opinion, a worthwhile one. I favoured stories that gave you something to take away at the end, books that brought insight, or a different perspective.

A few years ago I'd recommended the same book to Alfie. When he got to the '*because we are too menny*' chapter, he'd stormed into my room at three in the morning, bawling his eyes out and telling me he hated me for ever suggesting he read it.

I'd always been fascinated by stories like that, where words on a page could make you feel things as strongly as though the emotional trauma was happening in real life.

"That Arabella's some piece of work," said Larry, pulling out his copy and plopping it down on the desk. "Known a few women like her in my time, let me tell you."

"Ah yes, the last few chapters were about Jude and Arabella's wedding," I said as I grabbed my own copy and walked around the desks to hand it to Stu.

"She's a manipulative cow," Mary piped in. "And Jude's a gullible fool for marrying her."

"You can borrow this. See if you can catch up over the next few days," I whispered quietly to him. He seemed uncomfortable as he glanced at the novel. In fairness, he didn't exactly strike me as a bookish type.

"Just 'cos she wears hair extensions and makeup doesn't make her a cow," said Susan, pointing a finger in Mary's direction. She was in her early twenties but had left school at fifteen. She was also one of the most outspoken members of the class. "Women like you are the reason feminism is dead. I bet you go around slut shaming girls just because they like to wear clothes that show off their bodies."

"Hey now, that's not what I was saying at all," Mary defended. "Women can dress any way they like. It's their actions I judge, and that Arabella is taking advantage of Jude's kind nature, pure and simple."

"My first wife was exactly like Arabella. Took me for every penny in the divorce," said Larry.

Mary shot him the side eye. "How many times you been married?"

"Three," Larry answered, like it was a perfectly reasonable number of times to have wed.

I enjoyed listening to where their book discussions usually went, but in this case they were getting slightly off topic. "All right, all right, think about this question. In your opinion, what's the role of Arabella's character in the book?"

"Her role is to be Sue's opposite. If it weren't for Arabella, we wouldn't be able to appreciate quite how lovely Sue is," said Kian quietly before blurting an unexpected, "shit!"

"Good answer," I said encouragingly, and our discussion continued. Stu didn't contribute, and I was a little unnerved by how closely he watched me, unsure if it was simply because I was in his line of sight or if he was trying to suss me out somehow. Anyway, there was definitely some sort of calculation going on.

I just couldn't tell whether or not I should be concerned.

Two

Overdue.
Final notice.
Past due.

When I arrived home that evening, I flicked through the bills that had arrived in the post with the usual mounting sense of dread. The feeling of being overwhelmed was always there, but I'd become adept at ignoring it and pretending it didn't exist most of the time. Unhealthy? Yes. But really, it was the only way to sleep at night.

"I don't like the look of that frown," said Alfie, and I startled. I hadn't noticed him standing by the kitchen counter with a bowl of cereal in hand, so distracted as I was by the strongly worded letter.

"And I don't like the look of that dinner," I countered in an effort to steer his attention away from the dire state of my financial affairs.

I'd married young, barely twenty years old, tied the knot with my childhood sweetheart, starry-eyed and completely in love. Sadly, there was no fairy-tale ending for us. Mark was diagnosed with Non-Hodgkin's Lymphoma at twenty-four and passed away six months later. It was a late diagnosis, and because of the rapid spread of his disease and urgent need for treatment, we'd decided to go private. Hence my current financial state.

In the end I still lost him, my heart irrevocably broken into a million tiny pieces. Nowadays I managed to hold them together with haphazard duct tape and determination. In other words, I focused so hard on helping other people overcome their issues I didn't have to think about my own.

At just twenty-eight, I was in debt to the tune of almost fifty grand and a widow. Instinctively, my eyes flickered down to the diamond that still graced my ring finger.

I couldn't take it off. The very idea was emotionally traumatising. I knew it wasn't a healthy way to deal with my grief, but some days it felt like the only way to keep living my life.

"It's more of a late lunch," Alfie replied. "I only woke up a couple hours ago."

I sighed and dropped my keys onto the counter. "You're going to have to regulate your sleeping pattern soon, Alfs. If you don't, you'll get sick." My voice quavered with emotion. I had so few people left in my life, and I was terrified of losing them the same way I lost Mark.

"Oh, don't look at me like that. You know I can't deal with your sad doe eyes," Alfie huffed, sounding guilty. I immediately felt bad for making him feel bad. It was a vicious circle.

"Don't mind me. It's been a rough day. Actually, would you mind pouring me a bowl of whatever that is?"

Alfie nodded and a minute later we were both munching away in companionable silence. I'd once heard a dietician say cereal held all the nutritional goodness of cardboard, but God, it tasted so bloody good. Carbs and sugar were the food equivalent of getting a hug from a life-sized fluffy teddy bear.

"So, what happened?"

I glanced at Alfie, lost in my own thoughts. "Huh?"

"At work. You said you had a rough day."

"Oh, right, yes. There was a new student, an ex-offender. He claims he was involved in a stolen car racket. Mary gave him a bit of a grilling."

Stu hadn't said much after that initial introduction to the class. In fact, he'd continued to unnerve me with his silent attention. And despite the vague stirrings of attraction I'd felt, something told me his own interest wasn't that way inclined. My gut said he was more interested in my purse than my knickers, and I hated myself for feeling that so instinctively. I never wanted to be judgemental, and I truly believed that everybody deserved a second chance.

Alfie grew still and I instantly regretted telling him about Stu Cross. My cousin could be paranoid at times, and it was one of the reasons he was a virtual shut-in. He suffered from a mild anxiety disorder and trusted very few people, me being one of them. The only reason for that was we'd known each other since birth. Needless to say, Alfie didn't like the idea of me teaching an ex-criminal.

"You didn't give him your surname, did you?"

"Of course I did. All the students know me as Miss Anderson, Alfie. It was unavoidable."

"But what if he looks you up or follows you home some day? What if he becomes obsessed and starts stalking you or something? You can't trust people who've been to prison, Andie. You just can't."

"Will you calm down? He's not going to start stalking me. You're letting your imagination run away with you."

"How can you know that? You don't know what could happen."

Reaching across the counter, I grabbed his hand and reassured him earnestly. "I promise it won't. I'll be careful and make sure no one follows me home. Now, would you like to go visit Jamie before he closes up for the day?"

Jamie was Alfie's best friend, and we were both big fans of his book store, *Novel Ideas*, because it possessed a certain old-timey charm. The place had been handed down through the generations and was originally owned by Jamie's great-grandfather. We'd known him for a few years, and I personally thought he and Alfie got along so well because they were such polar opposites. Unlike Alfie, Jamie was very open to people and experiences, and he lived life with a sort of enthusiastic ferocity you didn't come across very often.

My cousin's eyes lit up. "Yes. Just let me go put some trousers on."

I didn't even find it weird that he walked around in his underwear half the time. I was too used to his ways by now. About twenty minutes later we arrived at Jamie's. We'd called ahead so he had tea and biscuits waiting. Obviously, he was good people.

"How have you been, Andrea?"

Let me get this out of the way. Jamie was eccentric with a capital E. The kind of eccentric who wore a corduroy three-piece suit with an antique gold watch in the breast pocket on a daily basis. Another of his eccentricities was insisting on calling people by their full names. I was always Andrea and Alfie was always Alfred.

"Not too bad."

"Those banks haven't sold your debt off to a third party yet, have they?"

Oh, another thing? He had no compunction about bringing up subjects I'd rather not discuss in polite company. Also, yes, a portion of my loans *had* been sold off to a third party, one that wasn't so polite when demanding I pay back their money. I'd been doing my best to pay as much as possible, but the salary of a further education teacher didn't stretch very far.

"No," I lied, mostly for Alfie's benefit because I didn't want to worry him. I was sure he was already up half the night fretting over the possibility of a Third World War or a catastrophic nuclear event to rival Hiroshima.

"Oh well, you should definitely keep an eye on your repayments. I read in the papers just yesterday about the unethical practices of these collection companies. They're basically loan sharks in all but name."

"I will. Thanks for the heads-up," I said and searched for a way to change the subject. I caught sight of a copy of *Poldark* Season One resting on the counter and asked, "Is that show any good? The female teachers at the college are always talking about it."

Jamie went and grabbed the DVD, holding it out to me. "It's great. I just finished it, actually, so you can have this copy. I wouldn't want you missing out on the topless Aiden Turner scenes. He's the new thinking woman's crumpet, after all."

I laughed and took the proffered case. "I'm sold. Looks like my weekend plans are all sown up."

Jamie winked. "Don't thank me."

We sipped on our tea a moment before Alfie broke the silence. "Andie had a new student join her class today." I could tell he'd been just itching to talk about it. "An ex-criminal, though you know what the statistics say about reoffending."

"There's a twenty-six per cent chance those who get out of prison will reoffend, and an average of three point one offences per reoffender," Jamie provided casually. The man had a mind like an encyclopaedia at times.

"This is what I'm talking about," Alfie exclaimed. "It's not safe."

"Oh, will you please stop with this. He stole cars. If worse comes to worse my Nissan will be taken and the insurance company will have to fork out for a replacement."

"What if that's a lie, though? What if it was something else? He could be a paedophile for all you know."

"Well, if that's the case then he'll have no interest in me."

Jamie let out a light chuckle while Alfie scowled at my logic. "You know what I mean," he griped.

"Yes, I do, and it's nice that you care about me enough to worry, but it's honestly fine. I've met dangerous men before, and Stu isn't one of them. He just picked the wrong path in life. It could happen to any of us."

Alfie didn't look convinced, and even Jamie appeared a small bit sceptical. If I was being honest, I wasn't entirely convinced myself.

**

The following morning trouble arose when I started our daily book discussion. Although, let it be said I was already bothered by the fact that Stu had strolled into the class twenty minutes late with no apology. I made a note to have a word with him about it before lunch, because in my experience, once one person started arriving late, everyone else began to think it was okay to do the same.

"Did you get a chance to start the book last night?" I asked, my question directed at Stu.

His tone was casual as he shook his head. "Nah, too busy."

"Well, you'll need to start finding the time for homework. You're already behind since you've joined us three weeks late. If you leave it too long there'll be no way to catch up."

"I'll see what I can do, Miss Anderson."

That was another thing. He kept addressing me as "Miss Anderson", but not in a respectful way. His tone was almost patronising, like he was trying to get a rise out of me. Obviously, I'd worked with my fair share of difficult students over the years and had an endless supply of patience. Unfortunately, there was something about Stu that already stretched my tolerance level.

I continued on with the morning lesson, quietly working up the courage to call on Stu when the class let out for lunch. The closer it came to twelve thirty, the drier my mouth grew and the clammier my hands became. What was it about this man that made me so bloody flustered?

The bell rang and everyone started packing up his or her things and heading out to the canteen for food.

"Stu, can I have a word?" I asked as he rose from his seat. He stared me down for a long moment, then nodded.

"Course you can, Miss Anderson," he said, the hint of a smirk on his lips. Oh my effing gee. He was doing it again.

"Thank you," I responded, closing my laptop as I waited for the last of the students to leave. When they were gone and only Stu and I remained, a quiet descended. My stupid dry mouth got the best of me, and I couldn't seem to find any words. Stu just stood there staring, waiting for whatever it was I wanted to say to him. His eyes traced my form and I grew stiff, especially when his eyes landed on my ring finger. His attention lingered there for a long moment in something akin to confusion, but I didn't really understand why. Finally, I broke the quiet.

"You were twenty minutes late this morning."

Stu raked a hand over the light stubble on his jaw. "That a problem?"

I cleared my throat. "Yes. Please make sure that it doesn't happen again."

"Will do. Is that all?"

"No," I blurted.

His gaze went to my wedding ring again, before moving up to my lips and then my eyes. I rubbed my palms on my trousers. Stu took a step closer, and the fact that he was standing over me while I was still seated made me feel at a disadvantage.

"What then?"

"You need to do the work I give you, otherwise there's no point in you being here."

He let out sigh now, like he finally understood my irritation. "You're pissed that I didn't read the book."

"I'm not *pissed*. My job is to teach you, Stu. It's my passion, and if I can't help a student fulfil all their potential then there's no sense in either one of us wasting our time. But look, I understand all this must be a big change for you. If you're feeling overwhelmed, just tell me and we'll take it slow. However, if you don't want to learn then I'm not going to force you."

Stu stared at me for a long moment before a small smile graced his lips.

"You know, this is the first time a woman has ever offered to take things slow with me." He tilted his head, his smile turning flirtatious, and I really didn't get why he was trying to avoid being serious. I wasn't there to berate him and I only had his and the other students' best interests at heart. Like I said before, one bad egg could spoil the lot.

"You don't have to deflect. There's no judgement here."

Now he bent to lean his hands on my desk and look me directly in the eye. "I'm not deflecting, Miss Anderson, I'm flirting."

His voice was low and purposefully husky. I fought the urge to roll my eyes. It just felt stereotypical for the young worldly male student to use his wiles to flatter the plain, bookish teacher. Little did Stu know, I was impervious to wiles, nor did I have any real interest in the opposite sex. I hadn't been interested in anyone since Mark, and I couldn't imagine that changing. He had been my world. Irreplaceable.

But you did feel attracted to Stu when he first arrived, a little voice in my head piped up.

And yes, okay, that was technically true, but I put it down to being female, and Stu Cross was the sort of man all women reacted to, whether they were teenage girls or eighty-year-old grandmothers. He had sex appeal; it was as simple as that. Luckily, I was more or less unsusceptible to sex appeal. Sure, he gave me vague stirrings, but I wasn't the sort of woman who dropped her knickers for vagueness.

I let out a soft chuckle. "Here's a life lesson for you, Stu. And I say this with absolutely no malice or hard feelings. The combination of young and female in a teacher does not equal naïve. Pretend flirting with me isn't going to help you pass. What will help you pass is working with me, participating in class, and arriving on time in the mornings. I'll always be respectful toward you, and I hope you'll be respectful to me in return."

I expected him to react one of three ways: embarrassed, apologetic, or hostile. Surprisingly, it was none of those. What he did do was lean closer, granting me a waft of his masculine, woodsy cologne. His gaze never left mine as he replied simply, "And here's a life lesson for you, Miss Anderson. I'm not pretending."

He startled me when he reached forward, took a strand of hair that had fallen free of my ponytail and gently tucked it behind my ear. I inhaled sharply when his fingers brushed my earlobe and felt momentarily speechless. He withdrew and cast me a final heated look, then left the classroom.

Em, what the hell was that?

I remained in place, my heart hammering in my chest as I fought to calm my breathing. I was having all sorts of strange feelings and the reaction alarmed me. I couldn't remember the last time I'd felt so flustered and lost for words. In fact, I barely recognised myself. I didn't act like this, all girlish and fluttery. At least, I hadn't for a very long time.

One thing was for sure: Stu Cross wasn't as predictable as I thought, and even though I was the teacher in this situation, somehow it felt like I'd just been schooled.

Three

After lunch I felt awkward. It was difficult to concentrate on teaching with Stu right in front of me, the memory of his touch replaying over and over in my head. Why was I even thinking about that? I was being ridiculous.

Unfortunately, the fact still remained that was I going to have to talk to him again. This time I wouldn't let him get the last word, and I wouldn't let his *not-pretend* flirting affect me either. At least, I hoped I wouldn't.

At three o'clock when the class let out for the day, I asked Stu to stay back again. He almost looked like he expected it, but more than that, he looked like he'd won something. I took my time packing away my things while Stu waited quietly. When everybody had left, he asked, "Can I help?"

I paused and glanced at the folders I was shoving into my handbag. "Uh, no, I'm almost done."

Stu sat on the edge of his desk, his arms folded and an expectant look on his face. Remembering the error of my ways at lunch, I stood and went to lock up the cabinets behind my desk.

"I like your top," said Stu, his eyes blatantly perusing my chest as I walked back and braced my hands on the top of my chair. I had to glance down because I'd forgotten what top I was wearing. Whether this was due to being flustered or the fact that I never really paid much attention to such things, I couldn't say. It was a simple navy blouse, nothing special. He was obviously still on his pretend flirting kick.

"Thank you," I replied.

"The colour suits you," he went on.

"Again, thank you, but can we talk about what happened earlier? I'd like to clear the air."

"Are you married?" Stu asked, completely blindsiding me.

I frowned. "I don't see what that has to do with anything."

"You're wearing a wedding ring, but everyone calls you Miss Anderson, not Mrs," he went on and I stiffened. For whatever reason, no one at the college had ever called me on the fact that I still wore my ring. Perhaps it was because they already knew my story. It was no secret I was the widowed teacher whose husband died tragically young. I'd learn to ignore the occasional pitying looks.

"I was married. He's passed. And going by Miss is a personal choice. After a while you get a little tired of people asking about your husband and having to explain you're a widow," I said and let out a humourless laugh. "Like right now, actually."

God, what was I doing? I shouldn't even be entertaining this conversation. My personal circumstances were none of his business.

Stu shot me a commiserating look and ran a hand through his hair. "Shit, I'm sorry. I didn't know."

"It was a long time ago," I said, not bothering to correct him on his language this time. I was beginning to think it was a lost cause, encouraging Stu Cross not to swear.

"Can't have been that long," he replied, eyeing me up and down. I didn't look particularly young for my age. In fact, I always tended to look the exact age I was. Still, twenty-eight was young to have lost a husband, I knew that.

"It's been almost four years," I said, again not knowing why I was being so open. Bizarrely enough, there was something oddly liberating about speaking to Stu.

"Four years? What were you, a child bride or something?"

I shook my head. "I married at twenty."

Stu whistled. "That's young."

"It was, but I was always mature for my age."

"And you still wear the ring," he said, his voice very quiet now.

I lifted my hand up in front of me to study the small diamond. It hadn't been particularly expensive, but it had been the most beautiful thing in the world to me the night Mark proposed. In an odd way, it still was.

"Yes, I guess I'm just very sentimental in that sense."

Surprising me, Stu came forward and took my hand in his. I hitched a sharp breath as he slowly slid his thumb down the centre of my palm. Tingles skittered along my spine as his eyes followed the movement of his thumb and he made a low humming sound in the back of his throat. I stood completely quiet and still, partially because I was dumbfounded and partially because I couldn't remember the last time a stranger had touched me.

Had a stranger ever touched me?

Stu Cross was without a doubt the most forward person I'd ever met.

He turned my hand over to reveal the front of the ring. "Pretty," he said, and I nodded before glancing up into his eyes. My heart skipped a beat when I found he wasn't looking at the ring, but at me. Words were unreachable and all I could manage to do was pull my hand from his and take a sobering step away from him.

I stared the floor as I whispered, "Why are you acting like this?"

"Because I like you," he answered simply.

I looked up, studied him closely. Something was off about this entire situation. "No, you don't."

He let out a quiet chuckle. "I've just spent the last two days watching you, Andrea. Believe me, I like you."

"Address me as Miss Anderson, please," I said, fumbling through my mind for a way to put an end to this bizarre moment. How had he known my first name? Perhaps one of the other students mentioned it.

The edge of Stu's lips twitched and he winked at me. "Okay. If that's how you like it."

I shook my head at him. "Don't be cute. I'm your teacher. I'm trying to help you."

He met my gaze squarely. "Do I look like I need help?"

My instinct was to move farther away but I stood my ground. He could be intimidating when he wanted to be. "Sometimes it's the ones who don't look like they need help that need it most."

"I don't need help. I just want to be friends," he said, mustering a very handsome and charming smile. "No wait, that's a lie. I definitely want to be more than friends."

His determination had me flabbergasted. No man had ever pursued me like this, not even Mark. Something was amiss.

"Well, friendship is all I have to offer, Stuart," I said, putting as much authority into my voice as I could muster. "And the flirting will need to stop. Like I said, it won't get you an easy pass. The only thing that will that get you a pass is hard work."

He grinned. "You're sexy when you're laying down the law, do you know that?"

Now I just shook my head in exasperation. There was no talking to him. Maybe he was just a natural flirt and couldn't help himself. Either way, it wasn't going to work on me so perhaps I should just let him have it his way. Still, it was difficult not to return his smile. He really was far more handsome than he had any right to be. Plus, the twinkle in his hazel eyes was pretty much irresistible.

"Completely shameless." I sighed and walked around to the other side of the desk, needing some space from his heady presence. "So, tomorrow I hope we can start over. Please try to fit in some reading this evening and get an early night so you're not late again." When I looked at him this time he was smirking.

"Just gonna ignore the fact that I want you, eh?"

I shook my head, exasperated. "I'm sure my oversized grey slacks get you real hot and bothered, Stuart," I deadpanned. "Now go on, I'll see you bright and early in the morning."

Busying myself gathering the last of my things, I studiously avoided looking at him, hoping he'd concede defeat and leave. *Big* mistake. Before I knew it, strong hands took my handbag and coat and set them back on the desk. Then Stu used his broad frame to corner me into the wall behind my chair.

I stared up at him, my breathing heavy, unsure why I wasn't screaming for help. *But I knew why.* It was the soft, sexy look in his eyes. It was a dangerous look, but not one that could lead to harm, not physically anyway. This was by far the most surreal thing that had ever happened to me. It was like some little Cupid baby had shot him with a love arrow and all of a sudden Stuart Cross was hot for his teacher.

Or perhaps all that time behind bars away from the opposite sex had turned him into a crazed horndog. I mean, when *was* the last time I had been flirted with? Mark and I started seeing each other when we were seventeen, so perhaps I should be asking *had I ever been flirted with?* Surely I was imagining things. Stu made it clear he hadn't wasted any time catching up on what he'd missed out on for two years. So, why me? Was this all just a game, a bit of fun?

The dark look he gave me said it wasn't. In fact, all I saw in his eyes was need.

"I could take or leave the slacks," he breathed, all gravelly. "But those lips and your big brown eyes, now those are what get me all jacked up."

I couldn't look away and there was something in his voice that said he wasn't lying. Well, wasn't this just wonderful. The resident classroom bad boy fancied me. Some days the world really did have a sense of humour. It was like Fred suddenly having a hard-on for Velma when there were a hundred Daphnes he could be shagging.

Levelling both hands firmly on his impressively hard chest (prison workouts?), I pushed him away and stepped aside. I couldn't look at him now, my eyes trained determinedly on the floor as I grabbed my things. My voice wouldn't work either, so, with spectacular awkwardness I shrugged into my coat, hitched my bag up on my shoulder, and walked silently out of the classroom.

And yes, I didn't think I'd ever been so stiff and uncomfortable in my entire life. But I mean, what do you say to something like that? I had no idea how to flirt and was entirely out of practice with men. Furthermore, I'd never known a man like Stu Cross.

And further-furthermore, he was my student. There was no chance in this life or the next that anything could happen between us.

I felt like I was walking on air as I made my way to my car. Fumbling for my keys in my handbag, I glanced around the mostly empty car park. A black Honda Civic idled by the entrance to the college, but the windows were tinted so I couldn't see inside. A moment later the door I'd just exited opened and Stu strode out. He stood there for a second, pulling a packet of smokes from his pocket and lighting up.

Almost as though he sensed my attention, his eyes flicked up and our gazes locked. Something fluttered in my chest for a second but then he turned away, continuing down the steps and climbing inside the Honda.

Huh.

I wondered who'd been waiting to collect him, and it struck me as odd because Stu didn't seem like the sort of man who let other people chauffer him around. Then I remembered he was fresh out of prison. Perhaps he didn't have the money for a car yet, or maybe his licence had been revoked. His crime had been driving related, after all.

I thought on this on my way home, still trying to decide whether or not his interest in me was real or fake. Don't get me wrong, I didn't see myself as ugly, but I definitely didn't get pursued like this. *Was* he pursuing me?

Ugh. I needed to stop thinking about it before I gave myself a headache.

When I arrived back at the flat, Alfie was sitting on the floor in front of the TV, still wearing the same clothes from yesterday. Tears were running down his cheeks as he watched the news.

Alfie was incapable of turning off his feelings when it came to distressing world events. I called it Anti-Bystander Effect. We've all heard accounts of people standing idling by and filming disasters on their phones while others lay fatally injured. Well, Alfie was the opposite of those people. He'd jump into shark-infested waters to save a stranger, and that was no joke. This was another reason he was a shut-in. Alfie was an emotional sponge. The outside world held too much pain for my cousin, because he was just one person, far too small to absorb it all.

I glanced at the TV screen and sure enough a story was being reported about a bombing in Syria, where over twenty people had been killed.

"Alfie," I whispered, and he blinked. He'd been so engrossed in the story that he hadn't even heard me come in.

Letting out a small, watery breath he began wiping his eyes as he got up off the floor.

"Are you okay?" I asked, my voice quiet, gentle.

He nodded but didn't speak, instead taking a chair from the kitchen and carrying it over to the cupboards. He stepped up onto the chair so he could reach the highest cabinet, where he kept some of his paint supplies. I watched as he hurriedly grabbed tubes of paint and various brushes, before getting back down off the chair. Then he disappeared inside his room and shut the door.

I'd lived with him long enough to know he'd retreated inside his artist's mind. It was likely I wouldn't see him for a couple of days now until he'd finished whatever piece he'd been inspired to create.

I guessed I was having dinner alone tonight. Story of my life. I considered popping over to visit Jamie, but then again, I wasn't much in the mood to discuss the details of my personal finances and have him question whether or not I was doing okay. I knew he only asked these things because he cared about me, but sometimes I simply preferred not to think about them.

It was the only way to keep from sinking under the weight and stress of it all.

Four

The week went by and I was relieved when Stu didn't make any more untoward advances. He did, however, make a few random comments during class that seriously confused me. Unfortunately, they were too subtle for me to properly reprimand him on.

You work a projector screen like nobody's business, Miss Anderson.

Pardon?

Just complimenting you on your very fine projection.

And . . .

What does adumbrate mean, Miss Anderson?

It means to summarise or roughly describe.

Oh, right.

Why?

Thought it meant something else.

Cue my *WTF* face. I was beginning to think that despite his very mainstream manly appearance, Stu Cross was a bit of an oddball.

When the following Monday arrived, I checked my schedule and remembered I'd organised for the class to visit the nearby library to borrow some books. I liked to encourage my students to read both fiction and non-fiction, and since they were currently reading *Jude the Obscure,* their assignment today was to select a non-fiction book to borrow.

Everybody seemed enthusiastic when I announced our mini excursion, all except for Stu, who had no discernible reaction to the news. The library was only ten minutes away, and I walked next to Mary and Susan, as the rest of the class followed behind. Stu was directly behind me, talking with Kian, who today had taken quite a shine to the phrase 'cocksucking dickface'. At least it kept life interesting.

I could tell Stu took a subversive pleasure in befriending someone who had free rein to shout expletives at random. Kian seemed happy to have made a friend, which made me glad, too. I just hoped Stu's interest was genuine. So yeah, I was still trying to figure him out.

Despite their differences in age, both Mary and Susan were avid Tinder users and had decided to regale me with dating stories on our walk.

"He seems real nice," said Susan, talking about a guy she'd been seeing. "But he can be a bit of a wet lettuce at times."

"Oh, one of those," said Mary, pursing her lips. "I went out with a bloke like that once. He used to make me take my shoes off before I came inside his flat. I can't be dealing with that."

"Well, the trouble with Keith is that he doesn't want to do anything that involves alcohol," said Susan with a grimace.

"Is that a bad thing?" I asked.

"Yes, very bad. He only ever wants to go to the cinema or out for coffee. I can't get him to come to a pub with me to save my life, and don't even get me started on nightclubs. The problem is, I can't do the deed without alcohol, so sex has been a no-go area. I'm just not confident enough to do it sober."

I tensed up a little at her mention of sex. Not because I was at all embarrassed talking about this stuff with them. My teaching style had always been very casual and easy-going in that sense. The trouble was, Stu was right behind me, and I had the feeling he was listening in on our conversation. I could also feel his eyes on me, wandering

41

over the back of my neck, over my shoulders, down my hips. It was eerie, but I just *knew* he was watching me. Studying. Looking for cracks.

"Well, do you both have to be drunk? Why don't you just drink and let him stay sober?"

Susan shook her head. "No, it has to be both of us, otherwise I'll still be self-conscious because I'll know he's going to remember everything."

"You don't want him to remember you had sex?" I asked, frowning.

Susan threw her hands up in the air. "Hey look! I never said I was normal. This is just how I operate."

I had to admit, insecurity was the last thing I expected of Susan. She just always seemed so confident, never afraid to speak her mind. Though I guessed we were all a muddle of contradictions when it came down to it.

"You've obviously got body issues," said Mary. "Which is ridiculous because look at you. You're only a slip of a thing. But I get it. When I was your age I had a fantastic figure, but I never believed it. I always felt lacking in some way. Then after I hit forty I just didn't give a crap anymore. To hell with all that insecurity bull, I was going to have sex with who I liked, when I liked, and I wouldn't let anyone tell me otherwise." She paused to point at Susan. "You should be exactly the same. Enjoy your life, because it'll be over like that," she finished with a click of her fingers.

"I suppose you're right," said Susan, her confidence bolstered though she still seemed a little sceptical.

Mary winked at her, pleased that her pep talk had proved relatively successful.

I smiled to myself. Seeing friendships blossom between my students was always something I took great pleasure in.

42

And since there was such a mix of age groups in adult classes, I felt like everybody could learn from each other.

"What about you, Miss Anderson?" Susan enquired. "Have you ever tried online dating?"

I grimaced a little and shook my head. "No, I've, uh, never tried it."

"Why not? You should be getting out there like me and Susan, trying all the different flavours," said Mary with a saucy grin, and I actually felt myself starting to blush.

"She's right," Susan agreed then eyed me up and down. "Though I'm not being funny, you'll probably need to get yourself some new clobber."

I glanced at my worn jeans and white shirt. "What's wrong with my clothes?"

"You want the honest truth?" she asked, and I nodded, bracing myself. Susan never pulled any punches.

Taking another look at my outfit, she continued, "Well, no offence, but you dress like a lesbian. And not one of those stylish lesbos with the biker jackets and choppy bobs, but the plain-Jane ones who wear baggy chinos and checked shirts."

I let out a surprised laugh while Mary elbowed her in the side. "Go easy, would ya? She asked for honesty, not to be insulted."

"Sometimes honesty is insulting." Susan shrugged. "You're not offended, are ya, Miss Anderson?"

I smiled. "Not at all. You're right about my clothes. I've always been pretty inept when it comes to fashion."

"You see?" she said, eyeing Mary. "She doesn't mind. Oh em gee! I just had a great idea. Why don't you let us give you a makeover? Then we can help you set up a Tinder account."

"Don't get carried away," I said, chuckling. "I think fashion advice is where I draw the line."

"Oh, you're no fun," Susan pouted in disappointment.

"You should seriously give Tinder a try some time, though," said Mary. "A pretty thing like you needs to be getting out there."

"Please don't," another voice joined our conversation. It was Kian. "Tinder's full of perverts, and you're too classy for unsolicited dick pics, Miss Anderson."

I shot him a smile. "Why, thank you, Kian."

He blushed a little and Susan turned to slap him on the shoulder. "Teacher's pet."

"I'm just trying to give her a more rounded picture. You two are painting it like a single lady's paradise. Wankers!"

"Too right," said Stu, finally speaking up. His deep, masculine voice had a weird effect on me. "People who use Tinder are all a bunch of wankers." Kian chuckled, and they both high-fived. Both Mary and Susan looked unimpressed. I was relieved when we reached the library, because I could tell Mary was just about to confront Stu for basically calling her a wanker.

I swear, sometimes it felt like I was teaching teenagers. Well, at least they made me laugh.

"Here we are," I announced before turning to address everyone. "You have half an hour to find a book, then we'll meet back at the check-in desk at eleven thirty." They all nodded and moved by me while I levelled my gaze on Stu.

"Have you got a library card?"

He shook his head.

"Okay then, come with me and I'll grab you an application form. They'll give you a temporary card so you can check a book out today, then they'll post the permanent one to you in a week or so."

"You shouldn't listen to them," he said as we stepped through the entryway.

I shot him a glance. "To who?"

"Mary and Susan. You don't need to change anything about yourself. You're already sexy as fuck."

I sucked in a breath at his words, so blunt and to the point. I didn't think I'd ever been described quite like that before. It made me feel nervous . . . but a little excited, too. I turned to face him, plastering on a strict look. "You need to learn to stop talking to me like that. I'm your teacher."

He cocked a brow. "So you can talk to Mary and Susan about their sex lives, but I can't tell you how sexy you are?"

I placed my hands on my hips. "Yes, that's exactly right. I'm friends with my students. I'll talk to them about their lives and give advice when needed. The way you speak to me isn't friendly, Stu, and I think you know it."

He shrugged. "I say what I think."

"Yes, well, try to keep some of the things you think to yourself every once in a while."

"Oh, I have been," he said, pausing to slice his teeth across his lower lip. I was beginning to notice it was a signature move of his. "I've been keeping things to myself for over a week. Seems only natural that some of it finally slipped out."

My eyes flickered between his as I shook my head. His persistence was both bizarre and flabbergasting, and yes, a tiny bit flattering, which was why I decided to swiftly change the subject. "God, there's no talking to you. Come on, let's go find you an application form."

Stu was quiet as he followed me to the reception desk. A few minutes later I sat down with him at a table close to the poetry section so he could fill it out. I pushed the form across the table and handed him a pen. He glanced down at both items in consternation before levelling his gaze on me.

"You do it. I hate filling out forms."

"They need your address and a few other personal details," I said, as I noticed Kian scanning books in the poetry section. "It's quicker if you do it yourself." He seemed irritated, possibly by my presence, so I thought I'd go check on Kian. "Go ahead. I'll be back in a minute, then we'll take it to reception to get your temporary card."

Leaving Stu, I approached Kian. He was holding the collected works of T.S. Eliot. "'*This is the way the world ends, not with a bang but a whimper,*'" I quoted and he looked up at me curiously. "It's from *The Hollow Men*, should be in there."

"I've only read *The Wasteland* so far. I like it but it's very long."

I gave a soft laugh and made a gesture with my hands. "I can see that quote on the blurb. *T.S Eliot, fantastic poet, but God, does he ever shut up?*"

Kian chuckled quietly. "Does poetry count as non-fiction? I want to borrow this one and read more of his stuff."

"Sure, go for it. You've got good taste. Eliot is actually one of my favourite poets," I replied and then heard a muttered expletive from Stu. Turning around, I saw him glaring at the form and it made me worry.

"I better go see what's bothering him," I told Kian before making my way back over to Stu.

"What's wrong?"

He lifted his gaze to mine, his dark brows drawn together in frustration. Letting out a gruff breath, he shoved the form across the table and stood from his seat.

"Fuck this shit," he muttered under his breath then strode past me. *What the hell?* After several seconds a thought suddenly hit me. I felt like such an idiot. He said he hated filling out forms and all last week he hadn't submitted any homework. I'd given him leeway because he was new and still settling in, but I should've seen the signs sooner. It was a very real possibility that Stu had trouble reading and writing.

Firming my resolve, I followed in the direction he'd gone, finding him outside the library lighting up a cigarette. He glanced at me, inhaled a drag, then leaned back against the wall. I folded my arms over my chest and met his gaze head-on.

"Care to explain what that was all about?"

He shook his head. "Not really."

I studied him, trying to decide how to broach the subject. "Stu, if you have trouble with reading and writing, you only have to say the word and I'll . . ."

He turned and glared at me. "I can read and write fine." The bitterness in his voice told me he was lying, though whether it was to himself or me I couldn't say. Judging from his defensiveness, I decided now wasn't the time to push the matter. So, I'd put it on the back burner, but it was definitely something we needed to discuss soon if he was going to progress in the class.

I tried a different tack. "Is everything okay at home?"

He blew out some smoke. "Just rosy."

"Are you sure about that?"

"I'm thirty years old, Andrea. My daddy isn't beating on me, if that's what you're wondering," he practically sneered.

I ignored his tone. *For now.* "Are you living with your parents?"

"Oh, Andrea. Fuck off."

"Stu, I overlooked your language inside the library just now, but if you swear at me again I'll have no other choice but to report your behaviour to the dean."

He at least had the decency to look regretful. "Sorry. Look, it's how I talk. I don't mean anything by it."

I sighed. "Well, try not to swear around me, okay? You might be thirty years old, but this is still school. You need to be respectful."

"Got ya."

"So, if you don't live with your parents, where have you been staying?"

"With my brothers."

"Oh, really?" I said, relieved he wasn't all alone. "How many brothers do you have?"

"Three. Lee, Trevor, and Liam."

"And you all live together?"

"Yeah. It's a bit of a full house at the moment, actually. Lee's missus, Karla, lives with us now, and then there's our cousin, Sophie, and her son, Jonathan. Oh, and her foster daughter, Billie."

"Wow, that really is a full house," I said.

Stu nodded. "Tell me about it. I feel like I'm getting under everyone's feet. They got used to me not being there, and now I'm back, taking up space."

"I'm sure they don't see it that way. They're probably just happy to have you home and safe," I said, sad for him. He'd been away for two years and things had changed. It must be difficult to feel like there wasn't a place for you anymore.

"I've been looking into getting a place of my own, but everywhere in London's so bloody pricey. And it's a pain in the arse trying to find work when you've got a record. Lee has his own restaurant, and he's offered me a job doing the books, but I dunno, feels like charity."

I was surprised to hear his brother owned a restaurant, especially given Stu's criminal history. Usually, crime ran in families, but not always. "The books?" I asked, impressed, especially considering my suspicions about his reading and writing. Perhaps things weren't as bad as I thought. "Have you done accounting work before?"

He took the final drag of his smoke then stubbed it out with the toe of his boot. Sending me an arch look, he replied, "Sure, none of it technically legal though."

Realisation hit me. So, by "the books" he meant cooking the books. I really hoped his brother's restaurant wasn't a front business for something more sinister. Stu must have read my mind because he went on, "Lee's place is all above board. He's given up the old life."

"Ah, I see. And you?"

"What about me?"

"Have you given up the old life, too?"

It took him a few beats to answer. "Course I have."

I wasn't too sure I believed him. Stu let out a low chuckle. "You've got a very expressive face, Andrea. Like a fucking billboard."

I pursed my lips at his persistent use of profanity *and* my first name. It felt like a losing battle. Still, his statement made me self-conscious as I glanced away. Was I really that transparent?

"You don't believe I've given up thieving, and that's okay. You're right to be leery of me. I mean, look at me. If ever there was a shifty-looking geezer, it's me. But listen, even if I wanted to get back into that racket, where would I find the time? I have to have perfect attendance on this course as part of my parole."

"There are plenty of hours in the evening to be getting up to no good," I said, placing my hands on my hips. Stu's eyes glinted and a smirk shaped his hips. The innuendo in my statement hit me right after I said it.

"There sure are, Andrea," he said, taking a step toward me. His eyes traced my form as his voice lowered a notch. "There sure are."

I tugged on my shirt collar, warmth suffusing my cheeks. How could a man's gaze seem so carnal, as if he was defiling me with just a look? Even worse, why did it both thrill *and* terrify me?

Five

Most of my students had gathered in the reception area to borrow their chosen books. Had thirty minutes passed already? There wasn't going to be enough time for Stu to fill out the form now. Though maybe that was for the best until I got to the crux of his reading issues.

"Come on," I told him. He was still standing uncomfortably close. "We need to get back to the college."

Ignoring the heated look he gave me, I went to join the students and a short walk later we were back in class. There was only an hour left before lunch, and I planned on using that time to set up a Facebook group we could all use to interact with one another in the evenings. Given it was always a questionable area interacting with students on social media, I'd obtained permission from the department head.

However, since I was teaching adults as opposed to children, it was allowed. In the past I'd used the college's online forum for such things, but I found nobody really bothered checking in. By creating a group on Facebook, a site many of my students used daily, I found participation was almost ninety per cent higher.

Of course, I didn't make it compulsory, because I knew not everybody used social media, but I just wanted the option to be there should anyone need support with study or homework.

"I don't have a Facebook account," said Larry, speaking up. "Too many of my ex-wives are on there, and I don't want to see pictures of the new blokes they've shacked up." His grin told me he was trying to be funny.

"That's quite all right, Larry. If you want I can help you set up an account, but if not you can always contact me by email if there's an urgent matter you need to discuss. You were all given my address in your orientation folders the first week of class."

"I never got one of those," said Stu, levelling his gaze on me. A sliver of awareness trickled down my spine. It seemed to be happening every time we made eye contact now, and I really didn't know what to make of it.

"Oh, that's right. It's because you started late. I'll put a folder together and have it ready for you tomorrow morning. Does anyone else have any questions?"

Nobody spoke up, but Kian did shout out a certain C word, which I obviously wholeheartedly disregarded. I knew it must have been incredibly difficult living with his condition. Though he was in treatment and most days he did incredibly well keeping his Tourette's under control.

"Okay," I said, walking through the room and handing out laptops. They were old and the software was in serious need of an update, but you could still use them to go online. That was the main thing. "When you log on to your accounts you'll be able to find me under Andrea Anderson. If you click on the *friend* button, I'll accept your request and then I can add you to the study group. I've posted the rules to the top of the page so you can all familiarise yourselves with them."

Everybody got to work quietly, and I returned to my desk to find a good number of friend requests had already popped up on my screen. There was one that stood out most, making my heart beat erratically as I stared at his picture.

Stu Cross.

Why did he have to be so good-looking? It really was unfair. He stood in front of a car on a rundown residential street, his arms folded as he smiled at whoever was taking the picture. He wore a black T-shirt and jeans, the gun show very clearly on display.

For some reason it felt odd that he had a Facebook account. He just seemed too rough and ready. I couldn't picture him sitting in front of a computer, checking his friend requests or commenting on the latest viral post. Hovering the cursor over the request, I finally hit accept and my heart rate sped up further. Why did this feel like stepping over a threshold that I couldn't turn back from?

As soon as the deed was done I started to wonder if he'd check out my page. Although, I didn't have very many personal photos or anything like that. There were a few from my holiday last year to Mauritius with Mum and Dad, and a few random ones from various social gatherings over the last few months. There were also a couple older ones of Mark and me that I'd never been able to bring myself to delete. Of course, there were none of Alfie. He expressly forbade posting any pictures of him and said he'd disown me if I did.

Needless to say, he wasn't the biggest fan of social networking. Neither was Jamie. Given that my two closest friends didn't use Facebook, my page was pretty boring and inactive.

I tried resisting the urge to have a peek at Stu's page, but my willpower barely lasted five minutes before I clicked on his profile to snoop. I was such a weak-willed human being.

Scrolling down, I saw that most of the posts on his wall were from other people, a lot of them congratulating him on his early release. I found it weird, but then again, I wasn't from that world. *So why was I so interested?*

I avoided answering that question the same way I avoided thinking about my debt. Seemingly, it was my coping method in many areas of life.

Aside from a few funny memes, I couldn't really find any posts he'd written himself, and it further piqued my concerns about his writing. Obviously, he must've been able to read somewhat if he was on Facebook in the first place, but the question was how much.

There were a lot of family pictures he'd been tagged in, and well, his brothers were certainly an attractive bunch. Stu was definitely the best looking, with his dark hair and eyes. The rest of his brothers had lighter hair and piercing blue eyes. He was also the tallest, and studying them all together, I thought he might be the eldest, too.

I startled when somebody spoke, immediately shutting down the page. Seriously, you'd swear I'd just been looking at porn.

"Miss Anderson, I haven't received any invite to the group yet," said Harold with a hint of impatience. He didn't like to be left waiting for things. I noticed Stu shoot him an arch look and remembered the first day when I'd had to quell a potential argument between the two of them over seating.

"I'm sorry, Harold. I got caught up sending an email," I lied. "I'll get on those invites right away."

"Or he could just wait for you to be finished with what you're doing," said Stu, one arm resting casually on the back of his chair.

"It's already been five minutes and the bell is going to ring for lunch any second," Harold complained, which only functioned to bother Stu further.

"And she's in charge," Stu countered. "So quit being a whiny little bitch and wait until she's ready."

"Stu!" I exclaimed, while several of the other students gasped their surprise at his aggression. Sure, Harold wasn't exactly a favourite in the class, but no one would ever think to speak to him like Stu just had. "That's quite enough," I continued, my voice hard. The bell chimed right after I said it and everybody stood from their seats, probably relieved for an excuse to leave.

"I'll send the invites during lunch, everyone," I called then shot Stu a pointed look. "Stay back a minute. I need a word." It felt like I was constantly holding him back to have words, but I just couldn't let behaviour like that slide. *He wasn't my first student to have teething problems while adapting to classroom etiquette, yet I was undecided whether it was his upbringing or perhaps arrogance.*

"That was completely uncalled for," I said once everyone was out of the room.

"What? I was only saying what everybody else was thinking. That bloke is constantly complaining about shit. Someone needed to call him on it."

"Not like that, Stu. That's not how we speak to each other in this classroom. It's about respect, not name calling. You're breaking the rules of behaviour."

He scrunched up his brows. "Just because I called him a whiny little bitch? I'm sure he's been called worse."

"Harold is fifty-seven years old and about half your height. He's also been out of the education system for almost forty years. You can't imagine how scary that is for a person. He basically has to learn *how* to learn all over again from scratch."

"We've all been out of school for a long time, Andrea. I know exactly how it feels, but I don't go around complaining about every little thing."

"That's because you're stronger than he is. Try to have a little empathy, Stu. Stepping into someone else's shoes will help you see that we're all struggling, and that way you'll learn tolerance. You can't just go around telling people off because they deal with things in different ways than you do."

He ran a hand through his hair, swearing under his breath. "I just don't like him talking to you like that, okay? It's disrespectful."

Now I laughed. "Coming from someone who's disrespected me countless time in the past week."

"I haven't disrespected you. I just talk to you how I'd talk to anyone. And I think you're gorgeous, so . . . yeah, when I like a bird I tend to be a little full on. Sorry. I also haven't been around women for a long time, so I'm kinda rusty." His expression turned self-conscious, which oddly looked good on him.

I couldn't seem to hide my blush at his compliment, even if I did dislike being referred to as a 'bird'. "If what you said on your first day is to be believed, then you didn't waste too much time getting reacquainted," I teased, trying to lighten the mood.

His gaze flicked up, his hazel eyes turning dark and introspective. "Yeah. Right."

It felt like I'd struck a nerve, and I immediately felt bad for making light of his time in prison. I frowned. "That comment was in poor taste. I apologise."

Stu's hand went from his hair down to rub at his jaw. It was a very nice jaw. I couldn't help noticing. "Don't apologise. I just, what I said that day was bullshit. I was peacocking or whatever they call it. Truth is, I haven't been with anyone since I got out. Haven't had an appetite for women at all, really. It's kind of depressing."

I didn't bring up the fact that he'd been hitting on me pretty hard since day one. Instead, I asked, "Why do you think that is?"

His tone was self-deprecating. "Prison fucked my head up, probably."

I approached the desk where he sat and pulled up a chair, my heart clenching for him. I couldn't even imagine what prison would be like. "Did something happen to you while you were in there?" My voice was soft.

Stu arched a brow. "Do I look like the sort of bloke that 'something' would happen to? Fuck no, Andrea. But I saw it happening to others, and more. Every time I close my eyes at night, I see it. Makes me feel sick."

I stared at him; the look on his face told me he wasn't lying. In fact, this was probably the most real he'd been with me so far. "The college has a counsellor, you know. If you ever want to talk to someone." I thought it was a good idea. Maybe he'd even be more comfortable telling the counsellor about his reading and writing.

His head whipped up. "Why can't I talk to you?"

"Of course you can talk to me, but I'm not a counsellor, Stu. I can lend an ear, but I'm not qualified to give advice."

"And ear's all I need."

"Okay, then. Do you mind if I eat lunch while we talk? I'm starved."

"Go ahead."

He watched as I went to grab the food container from my bag and I thought it'd be rude to not offer him anything, so I asked, "Do you want to share with me?"

A small smile graced his lips as he shrugged. "Sure."

I sat down next to him again and placed the food on the table, dividing it up between us as I spoke. "So, you'll need

57

to apologise to Harold. But you have to promise you won't act out in class again. The college has strict rules, Stu, and the dean expects compliance. I'll make an allowance this once but I won't be able to do it again, otherwise people will become suspicious."

Stu got a flirtatious glint in his eye, his voice lowering as he teased me. "Will they think we're fucking after hours, Miss Anderson?"

I narrowed my gaze, trying to ignore how my belly fluttered in response to his use of the F word. I wasn't a prude, but Mark and I had never *fucked* as such. We had always made love. I swallowed and tried to keep my voice steady.

"Don't be a smart-arse, or I'll take back the olive branch I just extended."

He raised his hands in surrender. "My bad. I'll keep this smart-arse locked up tight."

My lips twitched but I just about managed to keep my smile at bay. "See that you do."

Stu grinned, and his eyes traced my features. "You run a tight ship, huh?"

I picked up one of the sandwiches and took a bite. Taking my time to chew and swallow, I finally replied, "That's right, so you should consider following my rules from now on."

The rest of my thoughts I left unspoken. The thing was, I had a feeling if I didn't run a tight ship with Stu Cross, it was possible I'd find myself falling overboard very quickly.

Six

Outside the college at the end of the day, I saw Stu approach the same car as before, the one with the tinted windows. *White Room* by Cream was blasting from the stereo and this time the driver was standing outside drinking a bottle of Lucozade. He was tall, with pale skin, brown hair, and startlingly blue eyes. Looking more closely, I recognised him from Stu's Facebook pictures. He was one of the brothers, and I had to admit he was even better looking in real life.

I was just a few feet behind Stu as he took the guy's hand and they did one of those very street handshake/shoulder bump greetings. Keeping my head down, I pretended to be typing on my phone as I passed.

"Andrea, hey!" Stu called.

When I acted like I hadn't heard him he only spoke louder. "Miss Anderson. Come over here a minute, would ya?"

Unfortunately, I wasn't far enough away to pretend I hadn't heard him a second time, so I looked up and plastered a smile on my face. It wasn't that I didn't like Stu. In fact, despite all the many reasons why I shouldn't, I probably liked him a little *too* much. It was just that the more I allowed myself to get to know him, the more problematic our relationship became.

The effect he had on me was unexpected, and in an odd way it felt like I was being unfaithful to Mark just by having these . . . feelings.

Hey, I never claimed to be a rational human being.

"Hi, sorry, I uh, didn't see you there," I said, rubbing my hand down the front of my coat as I glanced between the two men. Stu wore a smirk that told me he knew I'd been ignoring him, but he didn't look offended.

"I wanted you to meet my brother, Trevor. Trev, this is my teacher, Andrea."

Trevor had the sort of blue eyes that constantly shone with mischief, forever concocting plans and schemes.

"It's Miss Anderson, actually. Nice to meet you, Trevor," I said, holding out my hand.

"You, too," he replied, shaking with me before glancing at Stu. "She likes to keep things professional, eh?"

"She thinks she does. She'll learn," said Stu, but I didn't really get what he meant.

"Okay, well, I'll see you tomorrow, Stu. And again, it was nice to meet you, Trevor."

I immediately started walking but Stu's voice stopped me. "Wait a sec. You need a lift?"

Trying to hide my grimace, I turned back. It was just my luck that the day Stu offered me a lift home was also the day I'd decided to take the tube to work instead of driving.

"Oh no, that's quite all right, but thanks for the offer," I replied and saw his eyes scanning the lot.

"Can't see your motor anywhere," he said, taking a step closer to me.

"Yeah, I got the tube this morning."

He was already pressing his hand to the small of my back and guiding me over to Trevor's car before I had the chance to protest. "Well then, I won't take no for an answer. We'll have you home in half the time."

"Honestly, Stu, I don't think . . ."

He pressed his fingers deeper into me, the action stealing my words. Why did he always have to smell so good? "Listen, you did me a solid today. Let me return the favour."

I was momentarily consumed by his dark eyes as he continued to manoeuvre me. Before I knew it I was sliding into the back of the car with him.

Um, why wasn't he getting in the front?

Trevor echoed my sentiment as he cocked a brow at his brother. "What am I, your bloody chauffeur?"

Stu just ignored him, scooting right in next to me. Everything felt too close as both men slammed the doors shut and Trevor pulled out of his parking spot. Stu's thigh rested against mine, which there was absolutely no need for. Sure, he was a big guy, but he wasn't that big. Trevor eyed me through the overhead mirror.

"So, where to?"

I swallowed thickly, my heart fluttering at the idea of handing over my address. It felt like all of Alfie's paranoia was suddenly my own.

"Oh, you can drop me off at Finsbury Park tube station. I live close by."

"Nah, we'll take you to your gaff. Looks like it could be rain," said Stu, nudging me with his shoulder. I wished he'd stop touching me. I wasn't used to it, which was why it made me go all mushy and ridiculous.

I hesitated another few seconds and Trevor let out a low chuckle. "I don't think she wants you knowing where she lives, bruv."

My throat went completely dry as Stu turned his body to face me. Also, let it be noted that his arm was resting along the back of the seat, just shy of my shoulders. I was more or less surrounded by Stu Cross, and I had to admit that even if my brain was wary, my body was overjoyed. Glancing to the side I found him studying my profile.

"That true, Andrea?"

I shook my head and protested a little too profusely. "Of course not. I just don't want you going out of your way."

"We're not. Like I said, I want to return the favour, so tell him where we're headed."

Trevor piped up, a twinkle in his eye. "Return the favour? What did I miss?"

"None of your business, so shut up and drive."

"Can't drive with no destination."

Stu reached out and grabbed my knee, giving it a squeeze. I felt the touch zing right between my legs and wanted to slap myself for the reaction. *Why was I suddenly growing a libido after years of nothing?*

"Your address, luv."

"My name is Andie."

"Andie's a bloke's name," said Trevor.

"I told you to shut it," Stu barked.

"I was only saying."

"Yeah well, don't."

"I live on Queen's Drive," I blurted, if only to end their bickering.

Trevor grinned. "Aw shit, babe. I didn't think you'd actually tell us."

"Just drive, dickhead," Stu growled, growing irritable now.

"But she should know about your problem, bruv, just in case you fall off the wagon."

I looked at Stu. "What's he talking about?"

"He's acting the prat. Don't listen to him."

Trevor eyed me through the overhead mirror again. "You want to know what he was really put away for? The stolen car racket is a load of bull. You see, Stu actually has a thing for breaking into women's homes and stealing their underwear. It's a . . . what do you call it? A fetish. Can't help himself. And now that he knows where you live, well . . ."

I knew he was making it up when he winked at me. I wanted to laugh because Stu looked like he was about to throttle his brother.

"You're fucking hilarious, Trev. See how I can't stop laughing," Stu deadpanned.

"Tell me about it. I should have my own show. I'd make a mint on TV."

I let out a chuckle and Stu's eyes returned to me, focusing in on my smile. His lips curved slightly, but he held his own smile at bay. I was overly aware of how his hand still rested on my knee. When Trevor focused back on the road, Stu's thumb moved, brushing back and forth over the fabric of my trousers. I hitched a breath and he shifted closer, which really wasn't necessary because he was already in my personal space.

"I enjoyed our lunch," said Stu, dipping his mouth so he could speak at my ear. "Can we do it again tomorrow? My treat this time."

I turned my head, my eyes drawn to his for some inexplicable reason. Our mouths were way too close. "But you're already paying me back by giving me a lift home." My voice was barely a whisper.

"I'll bring the food. I like talking to you," he said, ignoring my previous statement.

Needing some space, I slid my arse across the seat so I was practically plastered against the window. He had me penned in and there was literally nowhere else to go. All he did was move with me, and I inwardly sighed because there was no winning in this situation.

63

So, I sat it out, folding my arms across my chest and staring at the passing scenery, thankful the stereo was on to drown out the silence. A minute later Trevor's phone rang, and he put it on speaker before proceeding to chat away with one of his friends. I barely heard what he was saying, because I was too aware of Stu. His smell. The feel of his body next to mine. The way he watched me as I continued to pretend I didn't notice.

The journey felt like it took forever, especially since Stu seemed to have taken a vow of silence. Trevor was still on the phone to his friend when we pulled up to my flat. Stu got out first, coming around to open my door for me. As I emerged I saw the curtains twitch in the living room. *Great.* Alfie was spying.

"Thanks," I murmured, unable to meet Stu's gaze. The car journey had been way too intense, especially the quiet portion.

"No problem. See you tomorrow, Andrea," he said, his deep voice caressing my name.

"Yeah, see you," I said, hitching my bag up on my shoulder and turning abruptly to open the gate. He knew where I lived now, and there was something both powerless and electrifying about it.

I could feel his gaze on my back all the way to the front door. It was only when I got inside the flat that I felt I could breathe again. Unfortunately, it only lasted a moment before Alfie was in front of me, his arms folded, and an accusatory look on his face.

"Who was that?"

I shrugged and went to hang up my coat. "A friend."

"Hmmm. I didn't know you had friends like that."

"Like what?"

"Friends who look like they just stepped off a Guy Ritchey film set."

"Oh Alfie, I'm really too tired for this today."

"That was him, wasn't it? The ex-criminal? That man looked exactly as you described your new student, and I think it'd be a bit of a coincidence that you suddenly made a new friend who's practically his clone."

"He's not dangerous," I said and moved past him into the kitchen. All I wanted to do was cook dinner and pour a glass of wine. I really didn't have the patience to indulge my cousin's paranoia.

"Even so, I've never seen you get a lift home from a student before. This isn't like you."

He was right. It wasn't like me, but I didn't have the emotional energy to delve into why I was acting so out of character. Sure, Stu had been determined to give me a lift home, but it wasn't like I couldn't have put my foot down and declined. If I was being completely honest with myself, I'd *wanted* to take the lift. Some deep, dark, very unprofessional part of me enjoyed his attention. Nevertheless, I wasn't prepared to admit any of this to Alfie.

"He offered me a ride and it would've been rude to say no. That's all there is to it."

"He could be grooming you."

I cocked an eyebrow. "Grooming me for what?"

"I don't know. For something illegal. Maybe he wants you to be his drugs mule, or to put your name down as guarantor for a mortgage he's going to skip out on."

I barked a laugh at that. Honestly, where did he come up with this stuff?

"It's not funny," he huffed.

"I know it's not. I'm just tired. Can we eat dinner and leave the worrying out of it for one night?"

Alfie pursed his lips, glanced at the floor, then nodded his head. At least he was aware of how trying his personality could be at times. And yeah, maybe I would be more worried about Stu's interest in me if I wasn't already drowning in financial woes. The money I owed tended to take up the majority of my head space, leaving no room for anything else.

I pulled the band from my hair, letting it fall around my shoulders as I opened the fridge to search for food. "I take it that you've finished your painting, since this is the first I've seen of you in days."

Alfie let out a breath and went to sit down at the table. "Yes. My bedroom door's open if you want to go see." I slid a glance his way and noted the frenetic energy about him. He always got like this when he finished a new piece. For some reason he was never satisfied that it was actually good until I told him so. I was like his very own live-in art critic.

I nodded to him, poured myself a glass of Merlot and headed for his room. There were paints, paintbrushes and bits of stained cloth covering almost every available surface. The air was so thick with the smell of resin I was surprised Alfie hadn't gotten high off the fumes. *Although, that could explain his high energy . . .*

First I cracked open the window, then I turned to study the piece and my breath caught in my lungs. The canvas showed the wreckage left after a bomb, piles of concrete and rubble stacked high. The eerie stillness after a disaster.

The entire piece consisted of varying shades of grey, except for a single beacon of light. A red ribbon lay vibrant but lifeless on a shattered brick, its owner nowhere to be found. It was the same red ribbon that had been in his last painting, the one of the little girl with the kite.

There was something about the stark meaning that had me sitting down on the bed for a moment to let it sink in. Alfie could be one of the most difficult people in my life, but it was moments like this that made it all worthwhile. Emotion clutched at my throat as I realised that Alfie painted pictures that were like books, sad books like *Jude the Obscure*. They told a story, made you feel things.

I glanced back at the painting, suddenly seeing something else and my heart pounded. The picture wasn't all that it seemed at first glance. It required taking a step back, just a little more distance, to see what it really was. It didn't depict just one thing, but two. Up close you saw the wreckage, but take a few steps back and you saw the face of the girl from the other painting. Pure genius.

Movement caught my eye. My cousin hovered in the doorway, awaiting my feedback. I ran my fingers beneath my eyes and rose from the bed. Grabbing him around the shoulders, I pulled him into a hug, no words forthcoming. But none were needed. He'd seen my reaction. He knew it was good.

"I took inspiration from the Sistine Chapel," said Alfie once I let him go. "A lot of people believe that Michelangelo concealed images of the human anatomy within the painting as a sort of subversion to the Catholic church. If you look at the fresco of The Creation of Adam, it's actually shaped exactly like the human brain."

"Really? I've never heard of that."

"It's true. He might've been a painter and a sculptor, but he was also an anatomist. I wanted to achieve that sort of juxtaposition in my own piece."

"Well, I think you've outdone yourself. You're going to have a lot of people interested in buying this painting, Alfie. I just know it," I said and looked over his shoulder at the stack of old replicas still hadn't been moved. "Are you keeping those?"

Alfie glanced to where the paintings sat, looking torn. "I don't want to give them away."

I walked over and picked up the one at the top. It was a copy of *The Abduction of Europa* by Rembrandt. Turning it over, I noticed the wood used to stretch out the canvas looked very old. There were even cracks in the paint, as though Alfie had been trying not only to replicate the piece, but also make it appear like the original.

"Where did you get this wood?" I asked, running my fingers along its knots and dents.

Alfie's expression turned guarded and he appeared uncomfortable with the question. "I got it from a chest of drawers I bought at an antique fair years ago."

I glanced at him. "And you chopped it up to use for your paintings. Why?"

"Does it matter?"

I shook my head. "Not really. I was just wondering why you'd go to the trouble."

He scratched his neck. "You know me. I get weird ideas sometimes."

"Well, you're right there. Anyway, can I keep this? I've been thinking I need something new to hang on my walls."

Alfie hesitated a moment then shrugged. "Sure. Have it."

I smiled and came forward to kiss his cheek. "Thank you. It's really beautiful."

***

The following morning I arrived to class early, having compiled the requested orientation folder for Stu. I also brought along a non-fiction book to see if he'd be interested, *The Selfish Gene* by Richard Dawkins. I'd decided to try a new tack by offering to help him read it, rather than going straight for the jugular and suggesting extra tutoring sessions to bring his reading up to standard. I suspected he'd only turn me down and get defensive like before.

I was also trying to gauge where his interests lay. Politics, art, economics, literature. I'd find his sweet spot eventually. If he enjoyed this book, I'd recommend more science-based works, and if not, I'd try a different subject.

That was the nice thing about teaching a class of only fifteen students. It gave you the time to discover each person's strength, and encourage him or her in that direction.

A few people started to arrive, Kian among them. He came straight up to my desk, his eyes alight beneath the thick black eyeliner he wore.

"Morning, Kian," I said, smiling at him as I organised the math worksheets for the morning lesson.

"Morning," he replied, shifting on his feet like he wanted to tell me something. "Wankers!"

"How are you?"

"I'm good, really good. I was up half the night reading the book I got yesterday. I think I'm in poetry love."

I smiled, making a mental note to recommend similar poets to him. I'd officially found his sweet spot. "I take it you're now a fully-fledged Eliot fan."

He nodded. "Pretty sure my next tattoo is going to be a quote of his."

"Oh," I sat up straighter, interested because I was also a big fan, "which one?"

Kian rubbed at his lips. "Hmm. It's a toss-up between *'There will be time. There will be time'* and the last verse of *The Hollow Men*."

"Ah! The one I quoted to you yesterday? That's my favourite, too."

We both shared a smile before a shadow fell over my table, and I glanced up to see Stu had arrived.

"Hey Stu! Fuck! How's it going?" Kian greeted him.

"All good, buddy," Stu replied and turned his attention to me as Kian went over to chat with a few other students.

I cleared my throat. "I have your folder here, the one you asked for yesterday."

Stu glanced over at Kian, who was now out of earshot, then back to me. "Goth boy's got a crush on you."

I sputtered a laugh. "Who?"

"Kian. He likes you. Can't you tell?"

"You're imagining things," I said, handing him the folder. "I'm old enough to be his . . . older sister."

Stu chuckled. "Older sisters are hot. And I'm not imagining things. It's actually pissing me off if I'm honest."

"Oh yes, because being hot for teacher is your thing, right?" I joked. "Wouldn't want anyone stealing your thunder. Honestly, Stu, you can drop the act now. It's getting old." Even as I said it I wasn't sure if I believed it. The way he looked at me said he was attracted, but that could be faked, right?

"Oh Andrea, there's so much you're gonna learn," said Stu in a low, sexy voice.

I focused on the papers I was organising, trying to ignore the shiver his words induced. "Fine. Don't drop the act then. It's your own time you're wasting."

He didn't respond, just kept on staring at me in a heated way that made my shirt feel too tight. The tension had me rambling. "I mean, honestly, we're basically the same age. It's not like there's even a taboo. This isn't high school. You're not a seventeen-year-old girl and I'm not an attractive twenty-something male history teacher."

"No, I'm a thirty-year-old ex-convict and you're an attractive twenty-something adult education teacher. Still feels like a sexy taboo to me," he said with a wink and a smirk. I decided I'd already indulged this line of conversation far longer than I should have and stayed quiet.

Stu took the folder back to his desk, and it was moments like these where I questioned my decision to seat him so close to me. *To the front of the classroom.* Only three feet away . . . from me. *Shit.* I really needed some distance between us or I was going to spontaneously combust. Watching him out of the corner of my eye, I saw him flick through the pages and wondered if he'd ever be brazen enough to use my email for a non-class related subject. Was there a part of me that wanted him to . . .?

Nope, not going there.

Once everybody had arrived, I stood to give the class a quick lesson in basic algebra. Mathematics wasn't a main component of the course, as it was more literature and history based, but I did like to at least touch on everything to round out the experience. I handed out some worksheets, and they were all quiet as they completed it. I noticed even Stu was busy. It didn't last long though, and after only a minute or two he set his pencil down and pushed the worksheet aside.

I glanced at him, asking quietly, "Is everything okay? Do you need me to go over the equation with you again?"

Stu shook his head. "Nah, I'm finished."

"You finished the entire worksheet?" I asked, my mouth falling open slightly. It typically took students twenty to thirty minutes to answer all ten questions.

"Yeah, no offence but it was a piece of piss."

"Are you for real?" Susan whispered from the desk next to Stu's. "I'm only on question two."

Stu shrugged. "I'm good at this sort of thing."

Susan shot him a jealous look then turned back to her own work. I rose from my seat and went to collect Stu's worksheet. I felt him watching as I scanned the paper, stunned to find he was telling the truth. He'd completed the entire thing in less than five minutes and every single answer was correct.

"Have you taken any maths lessons before?" I asked and he shook his head.

"No, I'm mostly self-taught, but honestly, that worksheet is kids' stuff. Why don't I give you something *harder*? Sorry, I mean, why don't you *give me*?" he replied, a grin on his face like he was baiting me.

I didn't rise to the innuendo, though it did make my mind momentarily wander. I imagined that had been his intention. Instead I went back to my desk and rifled through my drawer for a new worksheet, this one containing some fairly difficult quadratic equations.

I handed it to him and he gave a little scoff as if to say, *this all you got?* Ignoring his attitude, I went and sat down again, all the while watching him work out of the corner of my eye. If anything, I was fascinated, especially considering how he used to do illegal accounts. If I could just get him to use his skill in a more productive way, there was no limit to what he could achieve after the course ended.

Again he finished in record time and again I was flabbergasted by the accuracy of his work. Not a single answer wrong. Had I just found Stu's subject? The only problem with him having a talent for equations was that I wasn't equipped to teach him anything more than the basics. He was clearly on another level and would need someone more adept at the subject in order to be properly challenged.

An idea niggled at me. My dad was a mathematics professor at King's College here in London. I knew that if I asked him he'd be more than happy to tutor Stu after hours . . . but did I want to introduce him to my dad? For some reason it felt like a step too far. Too personal.

When I looked up I found him watching me, almost like he sensed my thoughts. I'd been chewing on my lip so hard I tasted blood. Stu lifted an eyebrow in question but I just looked away, going to collect the worksheets from the rest of the class.

When the bell rang for lunch I noticed Stu hanging back, and when he approached my desk with a food container and a flask, I knew I had to set some boundaries.

"So I'm not gonna lie, my brother Lee put all this together for us. He's got mad skills in the kitchen. I can't cook for shit."

"Stu, what you are doing?"

He frowned. "I told you I'd bring lunch today."

"And I told you the lift home was a perfectly reasonable way to return the favour."

Setting both the flask and the container down on the table, he eyed me shrewdly. "That's how it's gonna be, huh?"

"Stu, I'm happy to spend time with you if it's coursework related. I'll even lend an ear if you're having personal issues, but I think we both know that's not what's going on here." I paused and glanced down at the packed lunch. "Is that sushi?"

Stu smirked. "Oh, now she's interested."

"I'm not interested. I was simply surprised by your choice of cuisine. You don't look like the sushi type."

His smirk transformed into a grin. "Well now, that's just racist."

"Don't be a smart-arse. You know what I meant."

Stu ran a hand over his jaw. "Like I said, my brother made it. He's a chef, has his own restaurant and everything. You should stop by sometime."

I tensed up. "Thank you for the offer, but no."

"There you go again, making assumptions. Just because I might be a shifty fuck, doesn't mean my family is, too."

"I never said they were. Or you for that matter."

"You don't need to. Your face said it all, Andrea. Though you should know that Lee's married to a copper. Can't get any more law abiding than that." He paused to eye my reaction and I didn't know what to say. I couldn't deny the information surprised me.

"Come by the restaurant this weekend. It's Trev's birthday. We're throwing a big shindig or what have you. It'll be fun, good chance for you to let your hair down."

The look he shot me had tingly goosebumps rising on my skin. Desperate for some way to break the moment, I bent over and pulled the Dawkins book from my bag, handing it to him.

"This is for you, since you didn't get the chance to borrow a book from the library. I was thinking we could read it together during class while the other students are doing written work."

Stu didn't look at the book. Instead he stared at me, his expression hard. I felt like I couldn't breathe and regretted bringing up the subject. But I couldn't just let him continue as he was, sweeping his problems under the rug and ignoring them. Finally, he broke eye contact and glanced at the cover. His mouth was a straight line as he shook his head, then placed it back on my desk. "Not my thing, sorry."

"How do you know it's not your thing? You haven't even looked at the blurb."

"I can just tell," he replied, scooping up the lunch he'd brought. "Listen, if you don't want to share this then I'll head off. No need to shove shitty books at me to try and scare me away," he grunted before turning and stalking out of the classroom.

I sat there, mouth agape as he slammed the door behind him. My stomach twisted into knots as I dropped my face into my hands and rubbed at my temples. His unhappy expression said it all. By trying to discuss the matter in a roundabout way, I'd offended him. Well, crap.

Seven

"So, any plans for the weekend?" Susan asked as she helped me stack some folders into the cabinet behind my desk. Most of the class were busy making a start on the new assignment I'd given them, but I could tell Stu was eavesdropping. After his abrupt departure at lunch, I wondered if he was still pissed at me.

"My friend Jamie is having an author visit his bookstore to do a reading and I offered to help out," I replied.

"Wow, no offence, but that sounds mega boring, Miss Anderson."

I chuckled. "It's not boring at all. This guy wrote a book about the Persian Wars. You should read it if you ever get the chance. I find the whole thing fascinating."

"Oh my God, it gets worse. I think you just about put me to sleep there."

I heard a little snicker come from Stu's direction and now knew he was definitely listening. Well, at least snickering was better than the scowl he'd given me at lunch. Turning to Susan, I smiled, because for some reason I had a fondness for the way she liked to playfully rib me. Unlike Stu, who I still had suspicions about, being cheeky was just Susan's way. "Did you enjoy the movie *300*?" I asked.

"Yeah, *obviously*. Tell me a woman who doesn't want to stare at Gerard Butler's oiled-up CGI abs for ninety minutes."

"Well, that film tells the story of the Battle of Thermopylae, where a small force of Spartans and their allies fought against the giant Persian army to defend against invasion. There's a chapter in the book that gives a more realistic overview of it. I always find it interesting to pick out the alterations made when transforming history for the big screen."

Susan rolled her eyes. "Yeah, I'm still bored."

I wagged my finger at her. "A curious mind makes life interesting, Susan. You shouldn't always dismiss things before they've had a chance to wow you. If you do, you'll miss everything that's wonderful in the world."

"Maybe my idea of wonderful is just different to yours. Ever think of that?" She cocked a hip, all attitude.

"Okay, true. But if you go around living your life indifferent to new experiences, you're going to have a grey life. Wouldn't you prefer it to be a rainbow?"

Susan shot Mary a look like I was some hippy-dippy crazy woman. "Here she goes again, philosophising."

Mary chuckled, shaking her head and continuing with her assignment.

"It's my job to help you open your minds," I said, addressing Susan again.

"Yeah well, you know what they say about that," said Larry, joining our chat. "If you open your mind too much, your brain might fall out."

Smiling, I replied, "That's why you only have to open it a little. You'll be surprised what you'll learn with just the tiniest smidgen of curiosity."

"Curiosity killed the cat though, didn't it, Miss Anderson?" Larry went on unhelpfully. Sometimes I wondered if he just liked the sound of his own voice.

"Are you just going to keep throwing sayings at me today, Larry, or are you going to get on with your assignment?" I questioned firmly.

"I was only saying," he huffed, lifting his pen and turning back to his work.

Sensing someone's attention, I glanced to the side to find Stu studying me. I held his stare, wondering what he was thinking. A shiver trickled over my skin, the same awareness he always seemed to provoke. I wore a sleeveless shirt and his eyes traced the bare skin on my arms, the hollow of my throat. Feeling too exposed, I shrugged on my cardigan and excused myself to the bathroom.

The man frazzled me, even when he didn't say a word. How I was going to survive the next five months?

***

"Herodotus is by far my favourite classical author. Sure, he might've been a tad creative with the truth, but you have to be if you want to entertain people. I mean, everything else seems flat and lifeless in comparison to his *Histories*," said Jamie. I was helping him open cardboard boxes full of books in preparation for the author reading and signing he was hosting today.

"Hmm, I quite like Aristotle, and I was always very interested by the teachings of Hippocrates," I replied, and he screwed up his face in disgust.

"Oh *God*. When suffering from insomnia at university I'd read *The Nicomachean Ethics* and it'd send me right to sleep. And Hippocrates? Aren't you at all offended by his theory of the wandering womb?"

I laughed, pulling out a stack of books and placing them on the table. "You mean how he thought the female monthly cycle and accompanying mood swings were caused by the womb becoming displaced and knocking around inside the abdominal cavity?"

"No, the other wandering womb theory," Jamie deadpanned. "Of course that one."

I shrugged. "Not really. All through history people came up with lots of wacky ideas. We have to make mistakes in order to get to the truth, after all."

"Well, I can't argue with you there," said Jamie, pausing to glance over my shoulder. "Where's your cousin gotten to by the way? He told me he'd be here to help."

"He's running late because he was up half the night working on a new painting."

"Another one? I thought he just finished a large piece."

"He did. It seems the muse has been upon him lately."

"Well, he's the finest artist I've ever had the pleasure of knowing. I suppose it's best to just leave him to his process," said Jamie.

I nodded my agreement and then there was a knock on the shop door. Peeking through the window, the author and his assistant had arrived. Jamie went to let them in while I continued unpacking the books.

A few minutes later Alfie showed up, and I watched as he and Jamie spoke earnestly about a story that had been on the news that morning. If I was honest, I secretly held out hope there might be something romantic between my cousin and his best friend. Unfortunately, from what I'd observed of Jamie, he didn't date often. And although he was always very straightforward and open about things, I suspected something was holding him back. Perhaps he thought he'd scare Alfie away if he expressed his true feelings.

My cousin had had a few boyfriends over the years, but none in the last fifteen months at least. I couldn't tell if it was because he liked Jamie and was holding out for him, or if he was simply too preoccupied with his art.

About an hour later the shop was all set-up and people were starting to arrive for the reading. I was busy manning the service counter while Jamie schmoozed with the author and Alfie sat in a corner sketching something on a piece of torn paper. I'd always found it fascinating how he could be struck by inspiration anytime, anywhere, and he'd have no choice but to use whatever materials were at his disposal.

My attention drew away from my cousin when somebody approached the counter. Glancing up, I caught my breath because Stu Cross stared back at me.

"H-hello. What are you doing here?" I greeted, a frog in my throat.

"I came for the reading," Stu answered casually, a sexy smile gracing his lips. "After I heard you getting all jazzed up about it in class yesterday, I thought I'd come see what the fuss is about."

His explanation sounded genuine, and I perked up at the idea that he might actually be interested in classical history. Usually my passionate speeches fell on deaf ears, so there was a certain triumph in knowing I'd gotten through to someone. Mostly though, I was happy because it meant he was interested in reading—or least trying to read—a book. After our conversation yesterday, it seemed like a bizarre turnaround, but I was willing not to question it so long his interest wasn't fake. I mean, what would be the payoff? Perhaps he simply realised how unreasonable he was and decided to make up for it by coming to the reading.

"Really?" I grinned. "That's great. Would you like to buy a copy of the book?"

He lifted a shoulder. "Sure."

"Okay, wonderful," I grabbed a hardback and rang up the purchase while Stu scanned the room. I noticed his attention fix on Alfie for a long moment, but he was probably just curious as to why he had paint all over his clothes.

"Here you go. That'll be £12.99," I said, and Stu handed over the money before nodding to Alfie.

"Who's that?"

"Oh, that's my cousin, Alfie. He's an artist, forever stuck in some creative endeavour," I explained with a smile.

Stu's eyebrows jumped. "Your cousin? Care to introduce me?"

I frowned, remembering how freaked Alfie had been when Stu dropped me off at the flat the other day.

Biting my lip, I answered, "Um, he's not the most social animal. It's probably for the best if I don't."

Stu took a step closer, and once again, the intoxicating scent of his cologne made me a little weak-kneed. *Why did he always have to smell so good?*

"You ashamed of me, Andrea?" he asked low.

My heart pounded, both at his closeness and his question. "You're my student. What's there to be ashamed about?"

"You tell me. All I know is you looked anxious as fuck just now."

"Like I said, Alfie's not great with people, all people. It's got nothing to do with you. Now, would you like to take a seat? There are customers behind you waiting to be served."

Stu stared me down for a moment before going to sit. I watched as he sat a few seats away from two plainly dressed middle-aged men, so completely out of place. Stu wore dark jeans and a T-shirt under his worn leather jacket. Definitely the last person you'd expect to see at an event like this.

The reading would start in just a few minutes, and I was relieved Stu and I wouldn't have any more opportunities to talk for a while. It wasn't that I wasn't happy he was here, showing an interest in an academic subject. It was more that our conversations always tended to veer toward the uncomfortable or awkward, or *sexy awkward*. And I couldn't tell if it was his fault or mine.

Probably a little of both.

When the reading began I took the opportunity to pay a visit to the bathroom, and when I returned, Alfie was waiting outside, an unhappy slant to his mouth.

"What is that man doing here? Did you invite him?"

"He expressed an interest in Persian history," I answered, trying for casual. "I'm encouraging him to be pro-active about his learning." It wasn't exactly the truth, but it was the best I could do. I couldn't tell Alfie that Stu had turned up after eavesdropping on a conversation and discovering I'd be here. If I did he'd blow a gasket. He already thought I was too lax with my personal information as it was.

"He keeps turning up, Andie. Are you sure he isn't stalking you?"

"He's not stalking me. Now relax and go back to the reading. Jamie's spent the last month organising all this, and it'd be nice for him to see you show an interest."

"He's well aware that wars are my most hated aspect of history."

"Your last painting depicted the wreckage after a bomb," I countered.

"Yes, and every moment creating it was agony. Sometimes the things I hate the most make me feel the most, Andie."

"I know. I'm sorry. I shouldn't have said that."

Alfie looked at the floor. "Well anyway, I think I might head home. I don't feel safe with your stalker hanging around."

He said the last part with a hint of sarcasm and I had to wonder if he just didn't like the idea of anyone taking my attention away from him. He could be very possessive of my friendship in that respect. Even when Mark was alive, Alfie and I had been close, but still not as close as we were now. I'd been terribly bereft and lonely after Mark passed and Alfie had been desperate to move out of his mother's house, hence our decision to move in together. Over the years we'd come to depend on one another in different ways, though Alfie definitely depended on me more than I did him. But it was a good fit. For both of us.

"Andrea, is there a john in here I can use?" came a familiar voice and I startled when Stu appeared.

Alfie looked at him with absolute horror in his expression. He seemed to shrink as if he was hiding himself, like Stu had walked in on him naked, towelling himself dry after a shower. Oh, Alfie. Always one to overreact. I guessed Stu now understood what I meant about Alfie being a little odd.

I cleared my throat. "Yes, it's just through there," I said, indicating the way I'd come.

"Thanks," he replied and glanced at Alfie. "Hi, I'm Stu, a student of Andrea's. You must be her cousin."

He held out his hand but Alfie just stared at it like he was offended. His social awkwardness really knew no bounds. In fact, it was making me feel awkward by association.

"You all right, mate?" Stu asked, frowning.

Alfie looked at me, shook his head and began backing away. "I'm going home. I'll see you later." And with that, he left.

I shot Stu a look of apology. "I'm sorry. I told you he's not good with people."

He chuckled. "Yeah. I got that."

Staring at the wall because his eyes were intense this close, I continued, "He's also incredibly paranoid. I, um, I may have mentioned your past to him. He thinks you're stalking me."

Stu's smile grew wider. "How do you know I'm not?"

His response took me off guard as I sputtered a reply, "*Are* you?"

"Nah, but you have to admit it'd be just a little bit sexy if I was."

I rolled my eyes, trying not to let him see how his words affected me. "Sure."

"You know I'm right, Andrea," he said, stepping close and running a hand over my shoulder. It took a concerted effort not to tremble. Until two weeks ago, another man hadn't touched me this intimately since Mark. I felt skittish, affronted. I backed up as far as the wall and levelled him with a stern look.

"Does that voice work on all women?"

His lips twitched. "I'd say it's got about a ninety-five per cent success rate. Why? Is it working on you?"

I scoffed, my denial a little too fervent. "Noooo."

Stu's eyes flicked down to my chest then back up again. He leaned even closer as he whispered, "Then why are your nipples hard?"

I gasped and reared away, glancing down to check. I was wearing a padded bra, and although yes, admittedly my nipples were hard beneath the fabric, they weren't visible.

Stu had baited me and I'd fallen for it hook, line, and sinker.

He winked. "I bet they are."

"They aren't."

He let out a low, sexy laugh and moved by me into the bathroom. "You keep telling yourself that, luv."

I exhaled a breath when the door closed and then went to find a quiet spot amid the bookshelves to calm my erratic pulse. The reading had moved on to questions and answers, as Jamie held court taking questions from the attendees. A minute or two passed before I sensed movement in my peripheral vision. Judging by the faint hint of his cologne, I knew he'd found me.

"Are you hiding?" came his deep, masculine voice, and I glanced up from my place on the floor.

"Just having some 'me' time," I answered, and Stu's brows rose.

"Behind the shelves of a public book shop? Andrea, I didn't peg you for the kinky type."

"You're an incurable smart-arse, do you know that?"

Stu smiled and dropped down beside me, his shoulder bumping mine. "Ah yes, smart-arsery runs in the family. You've met my brother, right?"

I nodded, thinking he was definitely correct on that one. "I have."

A moment of quiet ensued as I stared at the shelves in front of us. Out of the corner of my eye I could see Stu studying my profile, but I didn't dare move. I felt like I was on display somehow, my every thought on view to him. Lacing my fingers in my lap, I tried not to let the quiet affect me but it was a lost cause. It wasn't necessarily awkwardness I felt, but I was definitely uncomfortable.

"You should come meet the rest of my family," said Stu, breaking the quiet, his eyes still on me.

Now I turned to him. "Huh?"

I know, so eloquent.

Stu reached out and began pushing my hair back behind my shoulders. I normally wore it up at work, but today it was down. "It's Trev's twenty-fifth today. We're having a party at Lee's. I like your hair like this."

His offhanded compliment made me blush as I tried to think of the nicest way to decline the invitation. "Thank you. I can't come to the party though. I promised Jamie I'd help him clean up after the reading," I croaked.

Stu's eyes told me he didn't believe that for a second. "I'm sure he'll manage. How messy can things get?"

I swallowed hard. "Pretty messy."

"You're right. I bet those history buffs leave empty beer cans and cigarette butts everywhere," Stu quietly teased, his hands still on my hair as he groomed me. The feeling was heavenly, probably because nobody ever touched me like this. I couldn't help sinking into it.

A smile curved my lips. "It's true. They go a little wild after they've gotten their books signed."

Stu moved ever closer, his mouth at my ear as he whispered, "Do you know what I think, Andrea?"

Goosebumps marked my skin as his breath washed over me. "What?" I replied, so quietly I was surprised he heard.

"I think you're a dirty little liar."

He startled a gasp out of me when he tongued my earlobe into his mouth and gently sucked.

I should have pushed him away, jumped to my feet, proclaimed my indignation. But I did none of those things. *Couldn't* do any of those things. Instead I sat there, eyes closed and frozen to the spot as I sank into him and he continued to do magical things with his tongue.

Breaking away, he murmured, "I like you. Come to the party."

"O-okay," I breathed. *What the hell?* I hadn't meant to say that. It just slipped out, my body running ahead of my mind. For the first time in years I felt unchained from my inner worries, and all because Stu Cross had sucked on my earlobe.

Figure that one out, because for the life of me, I couldn't.

Stu's mouth smiled around one last suck on my earlobe before he pulled away, standing and offering me his hand. I took it and he yanked me up to standing, my chest bumping his in the process. My heart was beating an erratic rhythm again and I couldn't seem to find my voice.

Finally, I managed. "Actually, um, maybe I shouldn't . . ."

Stu placed a finger over my lips and involuntarily, I shivered. "You said you'd come, no going back now, Miss Anderson," he teased, his hold still tight on my hand. "Do you have a bag with you? A coat?"

"Yes, just behind the counter," I answered and Stu guided me over, grabbing my things for me before I realised what he was up to. I caught Jamie's eye just before Stu led me outside. My friend wore a quizzical expression as if to ask, *who is that and where is he taking you?*

Of course, I didn't have time to answer. A black Toyota with a bright orange stripe along the bottom was parked just around the corner, and when Stu pulled the keys from his pocket I admit I was surprised. *This was his car?* It was certainly eye-catching.

"Me and my brothers all have a background as mechanics," he said, as though to answer my unspoken question. *Where did you get this?* "Lee and Liam fixed this beauty up for me while I was inside. It wasn't quite ready by the time I got out, which is why Trev's been picking me up. She's all fixed now though, runs like a dream, too," he said, sliding his hand over the hood almost reverently.

"I take it you're a petrolhead then," I replied, and he shot me a grin.

"You have no idea. Get in."

I hesitated, still trying to think of a way to get out of going, even though part of me was dying to spend the evening with Stu. "Are you really sure you want me to come? None of your family know me. They might not like it if a stranger just shows up."

"That's not true. Trev's met you, and it's his day so that's all that matters. The rest of them will get to know you." The next part he muttered under his breath. "Whether they like it or not."

Placing his hand to the small of my back, Stu reached forward to open the passenger side door and ushered me in. Before I knew it he was helping with my seatbelt and then we were off.

I was on my way to meet Stu Cross's family. *How the hell had that happened? And why did I feel more excited than anything else?*

Eight

"This feels a little bit like a kidnapping," I said to Stu on the drive. "How on earth did I let you talk me into this?"

He flashed me a devilish grin. "Got a magical tongue. Works every time."

I shook my head, trying not to let him see the effect that grin had on me. My body was literally buzzing with awareness, because the man was right. His tongue was magical.

"This is so wrong. I could get fired for this, you know."

Stu's grin grew even wider. "How? We haven't broken any rules. Yet."

I couldn't help but laugh. "You're a bad influence."

"I hope so. Maybe I can influence you into letting me do more tongue stuff," he said and winked.

I shook my head, a fizzy feeling of excitement in my belly. I couldn't remember the last time I'd been so spontaneous. And I quite liked watching Stu drive, the way he moved his body. It was certainly a new experience to be driven by a man. Alfie had never learned, and Mark and I didn't own a car when he was alive because we'd both lived within walking distance of our work. It was something we'd always planned to do. After he died it was a bittersweet challenge to go it alone.

God, I missed him. Spending time with Stu reminded me how much I enjoyed having a man around, a partner in crime to do everything and nothing with. A little pang struck my heart.

"Where'd you go?" Stu asked, glancing at me then back to the road.

I shrugged and fiddled with my hands in my lap. "Just thinking about stuff."

"Stuff?"

"My husband, Mark. He never learned how to drive. He always planned to but then, I don't know, fate had other plans, I guess."

Stu's look was empathetic as he turned the steering wheel. "I'm sorry. Do you miss him a lot?"

"Some days more than others."

He nodded and a silence fell between us. After a moment Stu spoke again. "I was only fourteen the first time I got behind a wheel. I was a cocky little shit, thought I knew it all. Me and my brother Lee took our uncle's Ford Fiesta and went for a joyride. I nearly crashed the thing, but Lee was a natural from the start, came out of the womb knowing how to work a gear stick."

"I guess that's like people who pick up an instrument and just know how to play."

"Like a driving virtuoso?" Stu asked. "He always was the clever one, got all the talent, too."

The way he said it made me curious. He sounded almost . . . self-deprecating. I wondered if it stemmed from his reading difficulties, but I was wary of broaching the subject again after last time. I needed to wait for the right moment. "Oh, I'm sure he didn't get all the talent. Is he as good with numbers as you are?"

Stu lifted a shoulder, looking vaguely uncomfortable. "I'm all right."

"You're probably better than you know. You just need the right teacher."

He glanced at me sideways. "Not you?"

I shook my head. "I've got a basic understanding, but I'm no expert. My strong suits are literature and history."

"Ah, got ya."

Again, I thought of my dad, how he could guide Stu. If he was as talented as I suspected he might be, then he needed the right kind of cultivation.

"You're thinking about something. What is it?" Stu asked, his expression curious.

"How do you know?"

He reached out and tipped my chin. "You chew on your lip when you're thinking, and your forehead crinkles up."

I shifted in my seat, feeling self-conscious. "I do? I never noticed. And I was thinking about maybe introducing you to my dad."

Stu chuckled. "Hey, slow down, gorgeous."

I flushed at him calling me gorgeous, unable to look him in the eye for a second as I slapped him lightly on the shoulder. "Not like that, you goof. My dad is a mathematics professor at King's College. I think he'd be interested in meeting you."

Stu returned his attention to the road, his smile disappearing. "Nah, you're all right."

"Don't you want to see if you can get into university? If you meet my dad and he thinks you have potential, he could help you with your applications."

"Don't put yourself out, Andrea. I'll never go to uni. The only reason I'm doing this course is because it's a requirement for my parole. This isn't *Good Will Hunting*."

His answer made my stomach twist. He just sounded so resigned to never being anything other than an ex-criminal, and it made me sad. "So then what will you do when the course ends?" I asked quietly.

Stu flexed his hands on the steering wheel and stared straight ahead. "I'm sure I'll find something."

He sounded like he didn't really care much either way, which made me even sadder. I knew how difficult it was to break out of the social strata you were born into, how stuck in a mindset people could become. The thing was, ever since Mark died, I considered it my calling in life to help people achieve their potential. I'd spent almost a year in a deep depression, had taken a leave of absence from my old job teaching sixth-form English. Mark had been a social worker when he was alive, and even though he'd only been doing the job two years before his diagnosis changed everything, he'd still managed to make a difference for so many people. He had the biggest heart.

Once I pulled myself out of my depression I felt like it was my duty to continue his good work, so I changed career paths and started teaching adult courses instead. Teaching teenagers often felt like force-feeding, but in adult classes you had a group of people who genuinely wanted to learn, to make a difference in their lives. It was what gave me purpose, kept me going. I guess that was why Stu presented such a predicament. He wasn't in my class because he wanted to be there. He was in it because he had to be, and that put me in a difficult situation, because sometimes I felt like he didn't want my help.

Stu parked just down the street from his brother's restaurant, a bistro-style eatery called the Grub Hut. Somebody had hung pink balloons and purple party streamers outside and it made me smile. I didn't imagine those were Trevor's favourite colours. Stu's family must have a wicked sense of humour.

"Lee's idea," said Stu, placing his hand to the small of my back again. "Like I said, smart-arsery runs in the family."

"Yes, I can see that," I said as we stepped through the entryway. I felt a little underdressed in my jeans, Converse, and pale yellow T-shirt. All the men wore shirts and slacks, while the women wore party dresses.

"Everybody's dressed up," I whispered to him, feeling self-conscious as I tugged on the hem of my top.

He shot me a warm look and his eyes briefly scanned my body. "Leave yourself alone. You look gorgeous."

Both the husky compliment and the warmth of his breath made me a little wobbly.

Stu's brother Lee was the first to approach us. Again I recognised him from Stu's Facebook pictures. He wasn't as tall as Stu, in fact, he was an inch or two shorter than I was, but he was attractive in a way you didn't see too often. It wasn't that he was particularly handsome or anything, but there was a confidence in the way he held himself, a certain wisdom in his light blue eyes that was infinitely appealing.

He looked surprised when he saw me with Stu, his shrewd gaze going back and forth between us.

"Who's this?" he asked. The concern in his voice had me tensing up.

"My friend, Andrea. Andrea, this is my brother, Lee."

Lee cocked an eyebrow. "Your friend?"

"That's right."

Not wasting a moment, Lee pulled his brother aside to talk privately. The thing was, they'd only stepped a few feet away and I could still make out what they were saying.

"I ain't seen you with a *friend* since before you got out, Stu. In fact, you told me you had no interest. So what's going on?"

"My interest came back."

"Bullshit."

"Fuck off, Lee. Sometimes I think you forget I'm older."

"I haven't forgotten shit. You've not been the same since you came home. We've talked about it. It's too soon for you to be with anyone, and we both know it."

My stomach twisted at the comment, a pang of sympathy hitting my chest. *Why* hadn't Stu been with anyone? Had prison traumatised him somehow? And if that were the case, then why was he interested in me?

"Jesus Christ, you're as bad as your missus these days. Relax and enjoy the party; I'm going to grab a beer."

With that Stu left his brother and returned to my side, taking my hand and leading me through the restaurant to a small bar at the back.

"You heard all that, didn't you?" asked Stu, not looking at me as he walked around the bar, grabbing a glass and pulling himself a pint.

"I did."

"Lee worries about me is all. Most of my life I kind of flaked out on being the eldest, so he took on the role. Now I've seen worse than him and he thinks I'm going to fall apart at any minute. It's getting on my tits."

"Why would he think that?" I asked as Stu finished pulling his pint.

"What'll you have? Wine? I make a mean Long Island Iced Tea."

"The cocktail sounds good," I replied, needing alcohol to get me through this weird day. "But you can quit avoiding the question."

Stu went to work grabbing ingredients for my drink, his brows drawn into a thoughtful line. "The day I got out I had a bit of a meltdown. Now Lee thinks it's gonna happen again any minute. He doesn't seem to realize how irritating it is to have someone constantly hovering, waiting for you to snap or break apart. He also thinks I'm not ready for a relationship, which is why he's being all frosty knickers around you."

"I thought it was because he knows I'm your teacher. Did Trevor tell him?"

"Course he did. Trev couldn't keep a secret if his life depended on it." There was an edge to his words.

"Well, you do know there's no relationship between us other than friendship, right?" I went on, and he shot me a cynical look.

"You're too fond of my tongue for that to be true, luv," he said and winked at me just as a curvy brunette came and joined us. She had a little boy with her, and he was wearing the most adorable blue dungarees.

"Grab me a glass of white, would you, Stu?" asked the brunette as she fixed the boy's hair. "There, absolutely gorgeous," she continued, pinching his cheek and making him giggle. He was probably only about two or three. She smiled when she saw me sitting next to her.

"Hi, I'm Alexis," she said, introducing herself and holding out her hand.

"Andie," I replied as I shook with her. "I'm a friend of Stu's."

I noticed her eyes widen a fraction as she replied somewhat disbelievingly, "Really?"

"Be nice, Lex," Stu warned as he set a glass of wine down in front of her then continued mixing my cocktail.

"What? I didn't say anything."

"Your face said it all."

"Well, can you blame me for being surprised? I've never known you to have female friends, and no offence,

95

but Andie here seems way too classy for the likes of you," she said, mildly teasing.

I didn't know where she was getting classy from, since she was wearing a fitted black dress and I was wearing the sort of clothes most people did their gardening in. Perhaps it was my accent she thought fancy.

"Yeah, yeah." Stu waved her off before his eyes fell on me. "Lex and I used to go out."

"About a million years ago," Alexis put in.

"She thinks she knows what I'm all about."

"That's because I do. And this girl is way too good for you. I can tell with just one look."

I was momentarily uncomfortable to discover this woman was Stu's ex, but then I felt someone tug on the hem of my T-shirt. The little boy was smiling up at me.

"Hello." I grinned. "What's your name?"

After I spoke he grew shy, burying his face in Alexis's shoulder. It was pretty much adorable. "This is my son. His name is Oliver."

"He's gorgeous," I said, while inside I began to wonder if he was Stu's. It was a sobering thought and must've been written on my face because Stu said, "He ain't mine, if that's what you're wondering."

"Oh, I wasn't—"

"Face like a billboard, I already told you."

I blushed and Alexis chuckled. "And thank God for that. I think we'd end up killing each other if we had to raise a child together."

Stu shook his head in good humour then set my cocktail down in front of me. I thanked him and took a sip.

"I'll be back in a sec. Just want to say a quick hello to Trev," he said, and I watched as he went to join a group of guys who were surrounding the birthday boy.

"So, are you really just friends?" Alexis asked once Stu was out of earshot. She sipped on her wine, her son still on her lap. He kept stealing shy glances at me, which again, was adorable.

"Yes, well actually, I teach at the college he attends. He has to take part in my class as part of his parole. I'm trying to help him but it's difficult. Whenever I try to discuss anything serious he just changes the subject. If I'm being honest, I'm not entirely sure why he asked me here today."

Alexis took a moment to absorb everything I'd just told her. Then she shook her head. "Typical Stu. I hope you don't mind me being blunt, but he probably wants in your knickers. He tends to think with his cock first, then his brain. Don't get me wrong, the bloke's got a heart of gold, but he can be a bit full on when he fancies someone. Seems to me you've got his attention, and take it from someone who knows, he doesn't give up easily."

"Oh, I'm not sure about that. At first I thought he might be trying to sweeten me up so I'd let him pass the class without putting the work in. Now . . . well, now I don't know what to think."

Alexis mulled it over. "No, I think he likes you. He's got that look in his eye. Haven't seen it in a while. Truth be told, he's not been himself since he got out of prison. We've all been worried."

I took another sip of my cocktail. Stu was right; he did make a mean Long Island Iced Tea. "How so?"

"He's been quiet, introspective. If you knew him before, you'd know that wasn't like him. Stu's never been a deep thinker."

I thought that was a little unfair, but I didn't comment on it. "Well, I'm sure prison changes everyone," I said finally.

"True." Alexis nodded just as a redhead pulled up a stool next to her.

"Hi," she said, introducing herself to me. "I'm Karla. Lee's wife. He mentioned you're a friend of Stu's?"

I could tell by the way she didn't even say hello to Alexis that she was on a mission for information. Lee must've put her up to it.

"That's right," I said, keeping my cards close to my chest. I didn't know these women, didn't know their intentions.

"And you're his teacher?" Karla went on. I opened my mouth to say something but she interrupted me. "Don't bother denying it. Trevor's already filled us in. Little thing you should know about this family. Trev's the one that can't keep his mouth shut, so don't go telling him anything you want to keep on the down-low. Anyway, is it okay for you to see your students? Isn't that sort of thing frowned upon?"

Wow, she was certainly direct. I tensed and took a sip of my drink for courage before replying, "Yes, it's heavily frowned upon. In fact, I'm not allowed to date my students at all because it's a conflict of interest. But Stu and I aren't together. I see a lot of untapped potential in him, and I want to help him cultivate it."

"Seems like you're going out of your way to do that," said Karla, studying me in a detached, almost clinical way.

"Oh my God, would you leave the woman alone?" Alexis asked, giving me a look of apology. "I'm sorry about my friend. She's a policewoman. Interrogations are a force of habit."

"I just want what's best for Stu. Lee's worried he's heading down a destructive path. He barely talks to him anymore, and when he does he's grouchy. None of us want him put away again, and we certainly don't want him getting into a relationship that could be bad for him."

"You're one to talk," Alexis teased, but I was still hung up on the whole 'destructive path' thing. Were they really that worried he'd return to crime? "When you started seeing Lee you were a police constable and he was still stealing cars for a living."

This caught my interest, my attention going to Karla, who shot Alexis an annoyed look. "Thanks, Lexie. Just go right ahead and air all my dirty laundry in public, why don't you?"

"Don't act like you don't deserve it. You're grilling poor Andie here like she's a flipping murder suspect."

Karla grimaced. "I am, aren't I?" Then she looked to me. "I'm sorry, I'm being horrible. You seem lovely, really. I suppose I'm worried for you as much as Stu. You don't want to put your job in jeopardy, believe me, I've been there."

"Is Stu really acting that differently?" I asked in concern.

Karla chewed on her lip. "This is going to sound mean, but before he went away nothing really seemed to faze him, and I think it was because he never really thought about things too deeply. I mean, if something bad happened he'd get sad for a little while and then move on. But nowadays he's been moping, snapping at everyone, basically acting like a depressive when before nothing could ever touch him."

I frowned as I thought on it. He never seemed particularly depressed in class, but maybe I just wasn't looking closely enough. Maybe I was too frazzled by his advances to notice.

"Can I get your number?" I asked Karla. "I'll keep an eye on him, and if I see him acting strangely I'll give you a call."

She nodded eagerly, and we swapped phones to type in each other's details. I was relieved that we'd just switched back a minute before Stu returned, his gaze moving between Alexis and Karla in suspicion before his eyes landed on me.

"You hungry?"

"Um, sure."

He came and helped me down off my stool. "Come on, Lee's serving up the food. I hope you like Mexican. It's sort of his speciality."

"I love it." I smiled and he led me over to a long table where everybody was sitting down to eat. Stu introduced me to his youngest brother, Liam, who looked like a less hardened version of Lee. Apparently, he was following in his sister-in-law's footsteps and joining the police. Stu informed me proudly that he'd just finished his training and passed all his exams with flying colours. We shook hands and exchanged hellos and then Stu ushered me into a seat. The food was delicious, tangy and spicy, and I wondered when I last sat amongst such boisterous chatter.

Stu's arm rested against mine, and though I probably should have, I didn't move. I enjoyed his touch, as much as it was bad for me. Because Karla was right. Putting my job in jeopardy wasn't worth it, especially since I had a mountain of bills to pay.

If I lost my job due to any kind of scandal, I'd become unemployable, and then I'd have to file for bankruptcy. The very idea threw a cold bucket of water over my burgeoning feelings for Stu.

A little while after dinner, Lee emerged from the kitchen with a massive cream cake, twenty-five candles stuck on top, and we all sang *Happy Birthday* to Trevor, who clearly relished the attention. The man didn't have a shy bone in his body.

Looking around the table, one thing was for certain: this was a family that loved each other dearly. It warmed my heart to know that Stu belonged to a group of people who cared about him a lot. *How could he feel he wasn't welcome?*

"You ready to head?" Stu asked, his breath hitting my neck as he leaned into me.

"I think so. Alfie will be wondering where I am." As soon as I said it I pulled out my phone, and sure enough there were several missed calls and messages from my cousin, asking me where I was. I suspected Jamie hadn't had the chance to tell him I left with Stu yet, because if he had I'm sure his texts would've been far more panicked.

"Let's go then." Stu took my hand. All three of his brothers, plus Karla and Alexis, seemed fixated by the action. I wanted to let go but Stu held on way too firmly. It was almost like he was trying to make a point. Perhaps he was aware of his sister-in-law's meddling earlier in the day.

"You've got a great family," I said on the drive home. Stu had been silent for a couple of minutes and I'd started to grow tense.

"Yeah, they are; they're great," he replied, but he sounded miles away. Where had he gone inside that head of his?

"Well, I'm really glad you invited me today. I had a lovely time," I went on, running my fingers up and down the edge of my seatbelt. Several moments of quiet passed.

"You ever wonder if maybe you're not such a good person?" Stu asked, breaking the silence.

Where on earth had that come from? I wasn't sure how to respond. "Not really. I try to do good every day."

He glanced at me, interested. "Yeah?"

I nodded. "I suppose I'm in the perfect environment for it. Being a teacher puts me in a position to help. I guess it'd be more difficult to be good in other professions."

"I'm not a good person," said Stu. "And even if I had a job like yours, I'd probably twist it, turn it into something bad, find a way to exploit people. You shouldn't trust me."

His tone took me by surprise and I grew concerned. "Where's all this coming from?"

He shrugged. "What Alexis said today was true. You're too good for me. I think it took her saying it for me to realise."

"I'm far from perfect, Stu. All of us are. And you are a good person. If you weren't you wouldn't be warning me off right now. You'd be taking advantage."

His handsome eyes slid to mine, glints of gold shining in the hazel. "That's the thing, I want to take advantage of you, Andrea. I want to so badly, in so many ways."

His statement struck me as odd, because yes, there were sexual undertones that set my nerve endings abuzz, but there was something else, too. Something that had my fight or flight impulse kicking in, telling me I should keep my guard up.

"Do you always get so introspective after a few drinks?" I asked in an effort to lighten the mood.

"No, if I was drunk right now I wouldn't be driving. I'm trying to warn you to stay away from me. I'm not good for you, Andrea. Please remember that, because the next time I try to touch you, if you let me, I won't stop."

His words sunk in, a shiver spreading through me, and not the pleasant kind. Mark had never made me feel this way, possibly because there had been no mystery to him. He was light, honest and kind, a completely open book, while Stu was mostly closed off. There were thoughts inside his head I wasn't sure I'd ever decipher, and though there was a part of me that desperately wanted to figure him out, there was another that said I should heed his advice and keep my distance.

I just wondered if I was strong enough.

Nine

An entire week passed, and Stu barely spoke a word to me. He sat in class every day, completed the assignments, but never approached me in the way he had before. I wasn't sure why, but I got the feeling he was wrestling with some kind of internal struggle.

It concerned me.

That wasn't the only thing that was troubling me though, because now that he'd submitted some written work, I knew for certain that he suffered from some form of dyslexia. It wasn't that he couldn't read or write, but unlike when we were studying maths and he was faster than everyone else, when the class had written work to complete he was always far slower. His sentences were disjointed and awkward, his syntax off, and he repeatedly misspelled common words.

I'd tried several times to talk to him about it, but every time I did he put up a wall. He purposely made himself unapproachable, silent and unsmiling, and I was at a loss as to how to deal with him.

I spoke with my head of the department about possibly providing extra tutoring sessions, and she was all for it. I even asked for advice from Mrs Merrion, the college's guidance counsellor, and she suggested maybe inviting not just Stu to the sessions, but one or two other students who could use help with their writing, too. This was to ensure he didn't feel singled out. She was right, because although they didn't struggle as much as Stu, Mary and Susan could do with some extra tutoring as well.

Today I was taking the class on a field trip to the National Gallery in Trafalgar Square as part of their art history module. The admission was free and I liked to encourage my students to make the most of every educational resource available to them. I was hoping that sometime over the course of the day, I'd summon the courage to talk to Stu again. Perhaps he'd be more inclined to listen outside the classroom environment.

Everyone was on top form, happy to be spending a day out of class. We completed the short walk to the tube station, and I was aware of Stu trailing behind. Unlike the rest of the students, he didn't seem very enthusiastic about the trip.

When we boarded a carriage, I took a seat in between Mary and Kian, while Stu stood next to the opposite window directly across from me. I wore a loose blouse and a long skirt since the weather had picked up. Stu's gaze travelled down my body, provoking a sense of awareness. He didn't say anything though.

"We should do this all the time," said Kian with a grin. "I love going out and about with you lot. Feels like I'm back at school."

Mary shot him a look. "It wasn't too long ago that you *were* at school."

"Yeah, but this is better because there aren't any bullies or dickheads. I can just be myself."

I smiled at him, glad that my class was a place where he felt comfortable.

"How can you enjoy this?" said Stu, addressing Kian. Hearing his voice took me off guard because he'd been so silent lately. "I feel ridiculous walking around in a group of grown adults like we're a bunch of five-year-olds."

"Nobody's forcing you to be here," said Mary, clearly annoyed. "In fact, we'd probably all be better off if you weren't. You've been going around with a face like a smacked arse the past week, and I for one am sick of looking at it."

Stu stood up taller. "Did I ask for your opinion?"

Mary folded her arms and levelled him with a hard stare. "No, but you're getting it. We're all looking forward to a nice day out and you're being a moody little prick. Seriously, if you were my son I'd give you a good clip around the ear."

"Mary," I said in reprimand, and she shot me a look that said, *he was asking for it.*

Stu's lips twitched, and I couldn't tell if he was going to laugh or say something unkind. In an effort to quell the tension, I stood and gestured for him to follow. "Come with me. I need a word."

He followed me to the end of the carriage, where there were less passengers and we could have a private conversation. Several of my students watched us curiously, but I wasn't worried about them becoming suspicious because I often spoke in private with class members when they were having issues or acting out of turn.

I gestured for him to sit before taking the seat next to him.

"What's going on with you?" I asked, eyeing him in concern. "You've been behaving differently."

He folded his arms, kicking his legs out and crossing one ankle over the other. "Been keeping my head down. Something wrong with that?"

"Not at all, but you aren't just keeping your head down. You've been gloomy. Are you sure there isn't something that's been bothering you?"

Stu plastered on a fake smile. "Nothing at all, Miss Anderson."

I studied him then looked away. Being so close to him had me tensing, like my skin was too tight for my body. My voice was quiet when I spoke again. "I don't believe you."

Stu turned to face me, his eyes raking over me in a blatantly sexual manner. "You been missing my come-ons, is that it?"

My heart sank. I hated when he deflected like this, trying to make me feel uncomfortable so I'd drop the issue. I also hated that it was working. I let out a sigh, not knowing what to do with him. A few moments of quiet passed before I summoned up the courage to broach a new subject.

"How have you been finding the assignments? Any difficulties?"

His face turned hard. "Nope."

I studied him, chewing on my lip because his refusal to discuss his problems truly bothered me. You could lead a horse to water . . . For so much potential in Stu to be untapped was beyond frustrating for me. *How could he be so indifferent to wanting more for himself?*

"I've been thinking of doing some extra tutoring sessions for those in the class who'd like to work on their grammar and writing skills. Both Susan and Mary have expressed an interest, and you're welcome to join us," I said, testing the waters.

"No thanks."

"Are you sure?"

"For crying out loud, Andrea. Will you just say what you're thinking instead of beating around the bush for once? I can't write for shit, and my reading is even worse. I know it, and I know you know it. I just don't care."

What he said angered me, like really fucking pissed me off. His refusal to work, to accept an offer to grow, was a travesty against himself and I couldn't stand it.

"You're so . . . so difficult sometimes, do you know that?"

Strangely enough, his expression softened at my show of temper. "I told you not to waste your time on me. I'm not worth it."

"Well, I disagree."

"That's only because you don't know me."

"I don't know you because you keep a wall up, never letting anyone in. I see it when you interact with the others. Whenever any of them try to befriend you, you give them nothing. You don't even talk to Kian anymore, and I can tell he's upset by it. He likes you. I think he actually looks up to you." It bothered me mostly because I'd witnessed him interact with his family, and although he was probably the most reserved of all his brothers, there'd been obvious warmth in him. I saw in his eyes that he loved them, that he valued their friendship, too. So I knew he was capable of being someone other than who he was right now.

Stu let out a scoff of derision. "Because I'm such a fucking role model."

"You're more than you think, Stu. You're strong, striking to look at, not to mention you practically ooze cool. To a young guy like Kian, that's everything. You should talk to him again. He probably thinks he's done something to upset you."

Exhaling heavily, Stu ran a hand down his face, staring out the window as blackness whizzed by. Then he turned to me again. "He's not done anything. I'm just dealing a lot of shit right now."

"So there is something that's bothering you?" I said, trying to keep my voice soft and non-judgemental.

Stu's eyes wandered back and forth between mine, the intensity in them provoking butterflies. He really was incredibly attractive. Sometimes I had to remind myself that he was my student and not some male model who'd lost his way and found himself in *my* adult education class.

"You never give up, do you?" he said, voice low. "Relentless."

I blinked, about to say something in response when Mary called down from the other end of the carriage that we'd arrived at our stop.

I stood and gave Stu a serious look. "We'll continue this another time, okay? Even when you've given up on yourself, I won't give up on you."

He seemed to grow uncomfortable at my words, staring the floor as he nodded then followed me off the train. The walk to the gallery didn't take too long, and when we got inside I guided the class around, making stops at the paintings we'd be studying so that they got the chance to see them in the flesh.

I paused when we arrived at Leonardo Da Vinci's *Virgin of the Rocks*, allowing them a moment to take it in before I gave a little background info. "This piece would've been completed sometime in the early sixteenth century. It shows the Madonna with an infant Jesus and John the Baptist, alongside an angel. See the wings?" I asked, pointing to the right of the painting at the figure in the blue cloak. "There are actually two versions of this piece, one here and one in the Louvre, this one being the later version. The National Gallery bought it in 1880, and it has been here ever since."

I spoke enthusiastically, but I could still see a few of my students weren't really interested, while others, notably the older ones, were paying avid attention. Often it was difficult to convince my younger students to appreciate art unless there was some kind of nudity involved. It seemed an arse or a pair of boobs would always garner an audience, no matter if the picture was hundreds of years old.

"Okay, well, this is the final piece on our curriculum. You're free to go wander around and check out the rest of the gallery yourselves, so long as you meet me back at the lobby in an hour."

They all nodded and off they went, while I made my way to the cafeteria to grab a coffee. I waited in line then went to find somewhere to sit. As soon as I found a free table the chair across from mine moved and Stu plopped down onto it.

"Everything okay?" I asked.

He nodded. "I've just been to see that Van Gogh painting, you know, the one with the sunflowers that people are always harping on about."

I took a sip of my latte. "Oh?"

"Bit of a let-down if I'm honest. I don't get what all the fuss is about."

I laughed. "I always preferred *Starry Starry Night* myself."

A moment of quiet passed as Stu rubbed the stubble on his jaw. "How much do think someone would get for those sunflowers anyway?"

"What do you mean?"

"Like on the black market. If someone were to steal the painting, how much would it fetch?"

I shrugged. "I've no idea. Millions, probably."

Stu shook his head. "Seems like madness, to pay that much just for a bit of art to hang on your wall."

"Well, it's not just a bit of art, Stu. The works on display here are a part of history. They say so much about the time they were created, about the artist who painted them, and that makes them priceless."

He eyed me seriously, chewing on his lower lip, his gaze calculating. "You ever wondered what it would be like to steal something so valuable?"

I gave him a funny look. "Can't say that I have."

"Really? So you've never imagined a scenario where you've robbed a bank, or I dunno, stolen diamonds or some shit, and had all your money worries just float away."

I glanced at him, my hands cupping the coffee mug as I shifted in my seat, self-conscious. Little did he know, I had money worries far bigger than he would probably imagine. "Well, maybe, but it's not like I'd ever act on it. You might get rich quick, but then you'd have other things to worry about. I wouldn't want to live my life constantly looking over my shoulder, wondering if I'd be caught for what I'd stolen."

Stu's gaze was steady on me, his elbows resting on the table as several thoughts flickered in his eyes. "I never used to worry. You know, when I stole."

"Never?" I found that hard to believe.

"I suppose I grew desensitised. When you've been stealing since you're a kid, it just becomes a way of life. It was more like a job than anything else. Me and my brothers got away with it for so long that we thought we were invincible. At least I did. Then it all fell apart and I learned I wasn't. Far from it, in fact."

There was an odd note of nostalgia in his voice, almost like he missed it. Not the stealing, *per se*, but the sense of invincibility, of thinking he'd never get caught.

"I guess you live and learn," I said, lifting my mug and taking a long gulp.

Stu's eyes shone with some sort of hidden knowledge and I wondered where all this was coming from. The subject matter was certainly odd.

"But that's just it, Andrea," he finally continued, "some of us never learn at all."

Ten

My conversation with Stu played on my mind. His words echoed in my head, bringing with them a sense of unease.

But that's just it, Andrea, some of us never learn at all.

There were so many things the statement could mean, the most obvious being that he hadn't learned his lesson from his time behind bars. Did that mean he was going to start breaking the law again, or that he had already?

I hated the idea of him falling back into that life and wanted to do everything in my power to keep it from happening, which was why I picked up the phone and called my dad. Would Stu accept guidance from someone else?

"Andrea, honey, to what do I owe this pleasure?" came his happy voice as he answered.

My dad was the sort of man who was forever in a good mood. My mum, too. They were pretty much the most perfect couple ever to exist in my eyes. So completely in love even after all these years together. Maybe that was why they were so endlessly cheery, because of their love for each other. It was the same as what I had with Mark, and a part of me would always mourn the fact that we hadn't had years and years together like my parents. Sometimes I succumbed to sadness, but I tried not to fall too deep. I'd had a true and wonderful love once. Perhaps that was enough.

"Hi Dad, I actually called to ask a favour, but how've you been? Is Mum well?"

"We're both as fine as can be. Now what do you need?" he replied kindly.

"Well, I've this student. He comes from a very disadvantaged background and is actually just out of prison. I suspect he's dyslexic but he has a real talent for maths. It could be just that he's above average, but I think it might be more than that. I think he could be truly exceptional with the right teacher."

"And you'd like me to assist?" Dad finished, guessing my intentions.

"Yes, if you're up for it. He wasn't in prison for anything violent. He used to steal cars, but he's gone straight. I just worry that if left uncultivated, he'll slip back into his old ways. If you can mentor him I truly believe he could qualify as a mature student for a university course somewhere."

"Well, I have to admit, I'm intrigued. You know I love a good underdog story," Dad said, a smile in his voice.

"That's why I love you."

"I love you, too, honey. Now listen, I just had an idea. Here's what we're going to do . . ."

***

My hands felt clammy the following day in class as I handed out worksheets containing a complicated algebraic equation. I told everyone it was a competition, and that whoever was first to solve it would win £10. It was my dad's idea, of course. He could be such a big kid sometimes.

Obviously, the competition was a ruse. Stu was the only one with a chance of winning, but my dad wanted to see how he fared. If he could solve the equation, or perhaps come close, then it proved he had aptitude. After that, all I had to do was convince him to come meet my dad and attend regular tutoring sessions over the coming months.

Piece of cake, right?

Perhaps not.

As soon as I told the class their challenge, Stu grew suspicious. I could tell by the set of his mouth and his narrowed gaze. I plastered on an innocent expression and sat back down at my desk, setting the timer on my phone for twenty minutes.

After a while I shot a furtive glance in Stu's direction, relieved to find he had his head down, his pen scribbling away. When the twenty minutes were up, I discreetly took a picture of Stu's work and texted it to my dad. His response came quickly.

Dad: We're onto a winner. Bring him by the house later.

Shuffling through the papers, I saw that although they made decent efforts, nobody else had come close to getting it right. Clearing my throat, I announced to the class, "It looks like Stu's the winner. You can come collect your prize at the end of the day."

"Well done, Stu!" Larry congratulated.

"Shit!" Kian yelled. "Sorry, I mean, congrats, man."

"Thanks, buddy," said Stu, his shrewd eyes landing on me. He smelled a rat, I could tell. Now even my neck was sweaty. I'd never make a good magician. People could see my tricks coming a mile off.

"Damn, I could've done with that ten quid," said Susan.

"That's you and me both, hon," Mary commiserated.

"Miss Anderson, can we do a competition for who's the most fabulous next?" Susan asked, all sassy. "Because I'd definitely ace that shit."

"Language, Susan."

"Sorry."

"Forgiven. And maybe we'll make the competitions a weekly event, though I'm not sure I can afford ten pounds every time."

"If there's no cash on offer then I'm not interested," Mary said with a cheeky grin.

"How about a night off homework? Would that tempt you?"

She smiled wide. "It might."

"All right, well, I'll see what I can do. Will you all take out the art history workbooks I gave you and open to page eleven?"

I busied myself with the next lesson, trying not to look in Stu's direction again. I could feel his mounting suspicion like a physical thing. By the time class ended for the day I was a nervous wreck, worried he was going to outright refuse my dad's offer of tutoring the same way he'd refused mine.

"So, where's this ten quid I've been hearing about?" he asked, approaching my desk once the room had emptied out.

I picked up my bag and rummaged for my wallet before pulling out a crisp ten-pound note and sliding it across the desk. When Stu went to pick it up I held on. His eyes flicked to mine.

"There's just one condition."

He smirked and let go of the money, rising to his full height and folding his arms across his chest. "I thought there might be."

"Please don't get mad, but I talked to my dad about you. He's the one who gave me the equation."

"So it was a test?"

"Sort of. But I promise it was only because I have your best interests at heart."

Stu's eyes hardened as he stared at me, but then, unexpectedly, they softened. "You're very lovely, Andrea, but I promise you, I don't deserve it."

"Just give it a shot, please. For me? You do realise that the percentage of people who could've solved that equation on the first go without any prior learning is tiny, right? *Minuscule.* You're special, Stu, and incredibly lucky to have been born with such a mind."

He shifted from foot to foot, clearly uncomfortable with my compliment. I wondered if anyone had ever really praised him like this, or encouraged him to develop his skill.

"Look, I'll give this tutoring thing a try, but if I don't like it then you have to leave it at that. No pestering me to keep at it, are we clear?"

"Clear as crystal. So, are you free now? My dad is really looking forward to meeting you."

Stu lips twitched. Clearly he found my eagerness terribly amusing.

"Yeah, I'm free. I'll follow you in my car."

About forty minutes later we arrived outside my childhood home. Stu scoped the place out when we got there, his eyes scanning the street.

"Nice neighbourhood," he said as he came around to meet me.

"It is. I was very lucky to grow up here."

"No offence, but where you live now seems like a bit of step down," he went on, raising an eyebrow.

His comment made me tense. "Yeah, I, um, I'm not in the best position right now, financially speaking. It's all I can afford at the moment."

"It's a basement, right? Even I think that's depressing, and I live in a shithole."

I frowned. "Now you're just being rude."

"I speak my mind, luv, always have. You ever thought of doing something to make more money? Something that would help you pay for a better flat?"

"Of course, but what could I do? I work full-time. It doesn't leave much room for anything else."

He eyed me closely, weighing his words. "What if I told you there was a way you could make a lump sum in just a few weeks? Would you be interested?"

I narrowed my gaze at him. "Stu, where are you going with this?"

The conversation was an eerie reminder of what we spoke about at the art gallery. It made me feel like he was suggesting something illegal. Stu's eyes moved back and forth between mine, measuring, calculating. Whatever conclusion he came to, it seemed he'd decided I wasn't prepared to play ball.

"Nowhere. Never mind."

I didn't like how he just dropped the subject, because although I was wary, I was also curious. I wanted to know what all these cryptic conversations were about, and why he was having them with me of all people. However, if I'd learned anything about Stu so far, it was that there was no point pushing him to explain himself when he didn't want to.

"Okay, well, come on. Let's go inside and I'll introduce you to my dad."

Now he wore a cheeky grin. "Do I get to check out your old room, too?"

I pointed a stern finger in his direction. "No. Definitely not."

We stepped through the gate, past my mum's hydrangeas and to the front door where I knocked twice.

When Dad appeared, he wore his favourite grey jumper, and his brown eyes shone as he smiled and welcome us inside.

"You must be Stu," he said, his voice friendly, excited even. Dad always loved the prospect of a new protégé. "I have to say, it's been years since I've come across a student who managed to complete that equation after the first try. You have no idea how thrilled I am for the chance to tutor you."

"Well, it's uh, it's nice to meet you, Mr Anderson," said Stu, his posture a little stiff and his words awkward. He obviously wasn't used to professor types like my dad.

"Please, call me Jim," Dad said, leading Stu into his study.

"I'll leave you two to get to work," I called after them. "I'm going to go say hi to Mum."

"Yes, of course. Are you staying for dinner?" Dad asked.

"I wouldn't miss it," I told him fondly.

After a cup of tea and a catch up with Mum, I left her to finish preparing dinner and oddly enough, went to have a look around my old bedroom. It must've been Stu's mentioning it that put the idea in my head. The space was mostly used for storage now. An old exercise bike sat abandoned in the corner. Dad had bought it a few years ago but stopped using it after less than a month. There were also a few boxes of wool that belonged to Mum. Whenever anyone she knew was having a baby, she always knitted something for the newborn—mittens and socks and such.

I sat down on the bed, remembering my teen years when I'd first met Mark and we'd fallen head over heels for one another. I'd lost my virginity on this bed, spent countless nights in his arms while my parents slept just down the hallway, completely oblivious to my overnight guest. Life was so much simpler back then.

I was startled out of the memory when someone knocked lightly on the door. Turning around, Stu stood in the doorway, his hand braced against the wood.

"Oh, hey," I said, my voice breathy. "How did the tutoring session go?"

He lifted a shoulder, the gesture noncommittal. "Good."

"Just good?" I asked, seeing a light in his eyes that hadn't been there before. He was excited but trying to hide it.

Stu shot me a look. "Fine. It was better than good. You were right. I've learned more from your dad in the last hour than I have on my own in thirty years."

I smiled, delighted. "I'd say that's a success, then."

"Yes, Andrea, it's a success," said Stu, stepping into the room and approaching the bed. I shifted back a little, my thoughts going fuzzy the closer he got. We were in a bedroom, a bedroom full of memories. It felt too much. Too private. The pores on my forearms drew tight.

"I bet you were a real bookworm as a teenager," said Stu, running his finger along the shelf that held my old collection. He came to stand before me and I glanced up.

"What makes you say that?"

"You know stuff."

I let out a chuckle at his comment. "Very true. I do know a lot of stuff."

"Is that why you decided to become a teacher?" he asked, slicing his teeth over his lower lip as he studied me. I felt conscious of every inch of my skin, the air thickening between us.

"No, actually, believe it or not, when I first graduated from university I had every intention of going into marketing. I got an internship, did it for six months, and decided it wasn't for me. So, I enrolled in a teacher training course and never looked back."

Stu's brows drew together. "I bet if you'd stuck with marketing you'd be on a much better salary."

I shrugged. "Probably, but it had no soul. I find teaching far more rewarding. I get to make a real change in people's lives, instead of spending my days trying to figure out ways to make them buy more stuff they don't need."

Stu chuckled. "Yeah but, maybe that way you wouldn't be living in a crapshack basement flat. There's an upside to everything."

I shook my head. "Not necessarily. I could own a swanky penthouse but if I was miserable in my heart then it might as well be a hovel. Teaching makes me happy. It feels right, even if I am living in a 'crapshack basement flat'" I said, throwing his own words back at him. Stu let out a quiet laugh before levelling me with a stare, his expression oddly tender.

"You remind me of my brother, Lee. He's always putting the rest of us before himself. I didn't understand it for a long time," said Stu, running a hand through his hair as he came to sit next to me on the bed. The mattress dipped and my skin tingled when his arm brushed mine.

"But you do now?"

Stu stared out the window. "Yeah, I do now. It was supposed to be Lee, you know. He was supposed to be the one to go to prison. Little bastard was prepared to fall on his sword like always, take the flack for the rest of us. And you know what? In the past I would've let him, but something changed in me. I was sick of sitting back and letting him take one for the team. No matter what way you want to spin it, I was a coward, hiding behind my fucking little brother of all people. So I stepped up. I went behind his back and made sure it was me who got sent down instead of him. He was angry at me for a long time. In a way I think he felt powerless. I'd taken away his ability to protect us by putting myself on the chopping block."

I stared at him, taken aback by his story. "That was a very selfless thing to do."

He shook his head. "Nah, I was just taking what had been coming to me for a long time. Anyway, I'm out now and that's all that matters, but my point is, you and Lee are alike. You'd rather live a life for others than for yourselves, and it's not right. You should live your own life, Andrea. Just because someone you loved got stolen from you too soon doesn't mean it's over. There's so much more out there for you."

His voice was tender as his gaze dropped to my lips, his eyelids hooded. My lungs felt bereft of air as his meaning sank in. And I hated to admit it, but I was shocked by his sentiment. I knew Stu wasn't stupid, but I hadn't thought him capable of seeing so much of me either. *Just because someone you loved got stolen from you too soon doesn't mean it's over. There's so much more out there for you.* He understood me on a level deeper than I ever could've expected and it was sobering.

"I never realised I was so transparent," I breathed, my cheeks heating under his attention.

"You're not. I've just been looking real close."

Heat encapsulated me as Stu's gaze darkened. My tongue dipped out to wet my lips, the action involuntary. I was staring at his collarbone, too shy to meet his eyes. "How close?" I whispered, finally glancing up at him.

122

All the air left me as he reached out, his big, strong hand cupping my neck. I felt like I was under water, struggling to breathe.

"This close," he whispered, right before his mouth descended on mine.

Eleven

Stu's kiss was hot and electric. I couldn't move, couldn't pull away. And believe me, my brain was yelling at me to do so, but my body had other ideas. My body wanted Stu Cross to taste every inch of me until I was warm and sated.

He didn't kiss me tenderly, instead he kissed me hard, his tongue plundering inside my mouth like a man starved of oxygen only I could provide. It was disconcerting, because although we'd just shared a pretty intense moment, I didn't feel like it warranted such *hunger*. Then a thought hit me. Despite how he'd bragged during his first day in class, Stu hadn't actually been with a woman since he'd gotten out of prison. He'd confessed as much the day I'd shared my lunch with him.

I was his first kiss in over two years. And God, was he kissing me.

Wow.

His hand wrapped around my throat, the action making me shiver. His fingers felt hard and soft at the same time, giving just enough pressure to make me tingle all over, but not enough to hurt me. His lips were warm and wet, his scent incredibly masculine. When I shifted my weight, turning my body into the kiss, he groaned into my mouth and I trembled.

I've never been kissed like this.

Mark's kisses had been sweet and tender, beautiful in their own right. Stu's kisses were fierce and hungry, like he had a fire burning under his skin and only my lips could put it out.

"Open your legs," he breathed, breaking the kiss long enough to push me onto the bed and climb between my thighs. I felt his hardness press against my inner thigh and grew instantly wet. Stu wasn't the only one who hadn't been intimate in a long time. In fact, I had him beat by more than two years. Perhaps that was why everything felt so much more intense than I expected. Every sweep of his tongue, every press of his fingers on my throat had me wanting to open for him, let him take whatever he wanted, however he wanted it.

It was only when I heard my parents chatting downstairs that I came back my senses. Yes, parent chatter was the perfect bucket of ice-cold water to throw over any sexual situation. I drew away from Stu, my breaths coming hard and fast. My entire body felt warm, ready for something it had forgotten it even wanted. Stu's eyes were still closed, and he seemed lost in me, drugged by our kiss. He pulled me back under him, his mouth finding mine again.

"Wait, wait, stop," I gasped, my mind at war with my body yet again.

"Andrea," he murmured. "Just let me—"

"I can't," I said as his mouth lowered to my jaw, planting kisses that sent a pleasurable sensation down my spine and made me moan. "My parents are downstairs. You have to stop."

Stu groaned and let his face drop to my chest, his nose brushing the top of my breast. How I wanted to feel his mouth there, his lips, tongue . . . teeth. Honestly, where had all this desire come from? Had it been building up for years, silently wait for its time to unleash?

His eyes were still dark, still full of need and want, even as he withdrew from me, our moment of bliss cut short. I knew it was the right thing to do. Being with Stu was not only bad for my heart, it was bad for my career. I could lose my job if anybody ever found out.

"Let's go back to yours," he said, his voice pure gravel.

"We can't. Alfie will be there. We live together." I was using my cousin as an excuse, I knew that, but it was all I could think of on the spot. I needed to pull the brakes.

"Come back to mine then."

I let out a small squeak of a laugh. "That's an even worse idea. You said yourself your house is packed to the rafters."

"We'll be quiet then," he said, running his hand along my shoulder, down my arm.

"Stu, I'm surprised my parents didn't hear your groans just now. If you're that loud just kissing, then I can't imagine how you'll be doing . . . other things."

Now he smirked. "Oh yeah? Care to find out?"

Before I could respond my mum called up the stairs that dinner was ready. I looked to Stu as I asked quietly, "Are you staying to eat?"

His smirk widened. "Course I am."

Wonderful.

"Okay, well, please behave yourself."

"I always do."

I scoffed at that, then rose from the bed and led him down to the dining room. I did my best to smooth out my top and fix my hair, but somehow I still felt dishevelled, like my parents would be able to tell what I'd done with Stu just by looking at me. I was being paranoid, of course, because neither of my parents noticed a thing.

In fact, dinner was less awkward than I anticipated. Mostly because my dad chatted away to Stu about what he planned on teaching him in the coming weeks, and I filled my mum in on how Alfie was doing. My parents cared a lot about my cousin, but given his hermit-like ways, he didn't come to visit them very often. Or let them visit him for that matter. I knew it hurt their feelings, but I always tried to reassure them that it wasn't anything personal.

Alfie simply didn't maintain contact with many people, and a lot of the time it was because he was so wrapped up in his art. Also, we weren't actually blood relatives, since Alfie's mum was adopted into my mum's family after my grandparents discovered they couldn't conceive any more children. This was why my aunt was so different. She'd spent her early childhood in foster care and it made her very ambitious. Determined never to be poor again, she'd married Alfie's dad, who came from wealthy stock. She didn't foresee how he'd get caught in a fraud scandal, resulting in him losing all his money.

"Let's go back to yours," Stu whispered over my shoulder as we left my parents' house and made our way to our respective vehicles. My thoughts of my cousin's family were cut short when his body pressed into mine from behind.

"I told you, Alfie will be there," I replied.

"I'm sure he won't mind. Actually, I've been hoping to try again with him. We didn't get off to the best start."

"Don't be offended. He's like that with everyone except for Jamie and me. My cousin is one of the hardest people to get to know."

"Well, I'd still like to try," said Stu, and there was a determined note in voice that made me curious.

"Why?"

He lifted a shoulder. "He seems interesting."

"He is interesting, but I'm not sure you two would get along. You're very different kinds of people."

Stu's lips drew into a tight line and he seemed annoyed with what I'd said. "What's that supposed to mean?"

"It means exactly what I said. You and Alfie are polar opposites, plus, he's incredibly paranoid. He doesn't let new people in very often, and if I brought you to the flat he'd get freaked."

"So what do you do when you want to bring a man home? Sneak him inside while your cousin is asleep, then ship him out before he wakes up in the morning?"

"No," I answered before thinking it through. "I don't bring men home."

Stu came around to face me, his expression disbelieving. "Never?"

"Never," I said, feeling a blush creep in. A moment of quiet ensued.

"So . . . eh, when's the last time you—?"

"Oh my God, I'm not discussing this with you. I'm getting into my car now, okay? I'll see you in class in the morning." I felt self-conscious. He knew how long it had been since Mark's passing. Would he laugh at my celibacy or be understanding about it?

"Come on, Andrea. Don't just run off when things get personal. I'm trying to get to know you."

When I reached my car I opened the door, threw my bag into the passenger seat, then turned back to Stu. "That's just the thing, you shouldn't be trying to get to know me at all."

I slid into the car before he could respond, closing the door and slotting my key in the ignition. I was on edge as I pulled away from my parents' house. In my driver's side mirror, I saw Stu standing on the street, his frustration evident in the way he clenched his fists.

I'd let things go way too far tonight and it wasn't his fault. Even though he was older, he was still my student. I was in a position of power over him and it was wrong to let him kiss me. I should've stopped him, should never had let things progress that far. But I'd been incapable of resisting. His touched had stoked a fire in me that had lain dormant for years, and it felt almost freeing to let it out, like I'd been waiting all this time for the right person to bring it out of me. Was Stu that person?

No, he couldn't be.

My hand started to tremble as my attention fell to my ring finger, where my wedding band sat, like always. My shirt sleeve was rolled up, revealing the end of the tattoo I got a year after Mark passed away. I felt like I needed to commemorate him in some way, so on the inside of my left forearm I had a small M shaped into a heart surrounded by pretty flowers. I'd caught Stu staring at it once or twice, but he never asked me about it. Perhaps he knew it was too personal.

Even distracted by the tattoo I couldn't get his kiss out of my head and I felt awful, because even though he was gone, I felt like I'd betrayed the man I'd loved since I was seventeen years old. And that was the most disconcerting part of all.

***

A fresh batch of overdue bills arrived the following morning. I shoved them into my bag on my way out the door, too afraid to leave them in the flat in case Alfie found them. My cousin was blissfully unaware of how bad things had become and I planned to keep it that way.

When I arrived at college, I immediately spotted Stu's car a few spaces away from where I parked. The fact that he was here made me nervous. We'd both acted completely inappropriately last night, and I was scared of him telling someone. My stomach tensed at the very idea.

As I approached the entrance, I saw him leaning against the wall smoking a cigarette. Our eyes locked and we both moved at the same time, reaching for the door handle. Our bodies collided, knocking my handbag off my shoulder and sending my bills spilling out onto the ground.

Crap.

It was just my luck that the most visible one had a big red OVERDUE stamped on the envelope. Stu bent over to help me pick them up, and I knew he could see it. A deep sense of shame washed over me. It was ridiculous, because it wasn't like paying for your deceased husband's medical bills was anything to be ashamed about, but I felt it all the same.

"Here," said Stu, handing me the letters. I shoved them back into my bag, glad when he didn't comment on them.

"Thanks."

Hurriedly, I made my way inside, feeling uncomfortable. All that morning, I felt jittery. Was he staring at me because of the kiss or the bills? I kept dropping things and making mistakes all the way through until lunch. When the bell finally rang, I felt like I needed some air and decided to take a little walk around the grounds.

About fifteen minutes later I returned to the classroom and found Stu waiting for me. No other students were around and I hovered in the doorway, wary of his presence.

"Do you need something?" I asked.

Stu's gaze was intense. His hazel eyes first traced over my face then wandered down my body. My outfit was plain and conservative, but the way he looked at me made me feel naked. Like he could see everything, visualise it in his head even though he'd never actually seen it.

My throat went dry.

"I want to talk to you, Andrea. Come in and shut the door," he said, his voice commanding. It was like we'd switched roles and all of a sudden he was the one in charge. On instinct I did as he requested, closing the door and stepping inside the room. I took a seat at one of the desks and waited for him to speak. When he didn't say anything for a long moment, I grew even more antsy.

"For crying out loud, just spit it out," I blurted, unable to take any more silence.

"You need to introduce me to your cousin," Stu answered. "Properly this time."

I furrowed my brow, not understanding. This was the last thing I expected him to say. If I was being honest, I thought he was about to proposition me, especially after the way his eyes raked my body.

"Alfie? Why?"

"I'll explain everything once you introduce us, but it has to be today. I've been stalling and now I'm running out of time."

I frowned at him. "Stu, what the hell are you talking about? What do you mean, 'running out of time'?"

"Once you introduce me to Alfie I'll tell you everything. I promise."

The forcefulness in his voice got my back up. Standing, I placed my hands on my hips and levelled him with a hard stare. "I'm not introducing you, so you can leave now. You're not permitted to be in this room during your lunch hour."

"Andrea, don't be difficult, please. I'm just trying to protect my family." His tone was softer now, cajoling.

"Stu, I'm won't be able to understand anything you're saying until you explain yourself fully. So either tell me what's going on or get out. I don't have time for games."

"Fucking hell," he swore, pacing now as he raked both hands through his hair. I watched him, deeply concerned by how odd he was acting. Was this what Karla had meant about unpredictable behaviour? Gone was the flirt. Here was the serious ex-con brother-in-law she'd been worried about. I remembered I still had her phone number, but wasn't sure whether or not I should use it.

Finally, he stopped pacing and stood still, his eyes intent on mine. "My being in your class isn't a coincidence. That's why I've been telling you not to invest your energy in me. I'm piece of shit."

"Stu, what the—"

"Once you hear what I have to say you'll agree with me. All along I've been here under false pretences. It's not a condition of my parole. I enrolled with the college of my own free will, all with the intention of getting to know you."

His words sent an eerie chill down my spine, his sometimes-golden eyes turning a flat dark brown. "Why?" I whispered.

"Because you're the only way I can get to your cousin."

Now I was trembling. "Again, what does Alfie have to do with any of this?"

"I came here fully prepared to use you, Andrea," Stu continued, avoiding the question. "But then I got to know you, and fuck, I decided you were too good to be used. I decided I wasn't going to do it anymore. The problem is, I don't have a choice."

He appeared distraught, and although I was disturbed by what he was saying, I still wanted to comfort him. I was at a loss to explain it. Closing the distance between us, I took his hands in mine.

"Tell me," I breathed, my heart beating double time.

"I think we should both probably sit down. It's a complicated story."

I nodded and we each took a seat. Stu pulled his keys from his pocket, fiddling with them as he spoke, not meeting my eyes.

"Since we were kids, me and my brothers worked for a dangerous man. His name was McGregor, and he was the one who got us into stealing cars in the first place. Fast forward a decade and Lee decided he wanted out for all of us. He had a hand in putting him behind bars. It meant we could get free of the life; otherwise he never would've let us quit working for him. But when our thieving came back to haunt us and I got sent down, I was put in the same prison. McGregor had it in for me from the beginning, wanted to use me to send a message to Lee. My first week in there I got the shit kicked out of me by five other blokes, spent ten days in the infirmary recovering. I knew those ten days were my last, and that as soon as I was out I was a dead man."

"Oh my goodness, Stu," I gasped, horrified.

"Belmarsh had two kings. McGregor was one of them and the other they called the Duke, 'cause he was a posh prick. He was also an absolute sociopath, which was why he'd climbed his way to the top of the ladder so quickly. Anyway, the day I got out of the infirmary, I got called to the Duke's cell. He offered me protection from McGregor in exchange for my loyalty. I didn't have a choice. It was life or death, so I chose life.

"McGregor was killed soon after by another inmate, but I was still stuck with my promise to the Duke. He made me do some shit I'll never forgive myself for, and I went to a very dark place for a while. Then, when I was given my release date, the Duke started spouting all this crap about a job he wanted me to do for him when I got out. I told him I was going clean, that I'd promised Lee, but he was having none of it. Said that if I refused the job he'd send people to hurt my family." Stu paused and lifted his eyes to mine. They shone with moisture and I was taken aback by his show of emotion. "That's where you and your cousin come in."

"But how?" I breathed.

Stu started fiddling with his keys again. "The Duke knew of your cousin. He'd heard about a Rembrandt he forged once. Said you'd never tell it apart from the original. Long story short, luv, he wants me to convince Alfie to paint another."

"Another replica?" I asked, baffled. *How had this person even known about Alfie's replicas? He only ever painted them as a hobby.*

"Yes."

"For what?"

"For a robbery."

I barked a laugh. "This is a joke, right? Some sort of prank?"

Stu's gaze sharpened, his breathing deep and even. "I'm not joking, Andrea. In fact, I've never been more serious in my entire life."

"So that's why you needed to meet me, to get to Alfie," I said, suddenly understanding. It was quickly followed by another revelation: the only reason Stu had been coming onto me so hard was because *he had to*.

You're already sexy as fuck. A lie. *But those lips and your big brown eyes, now those are what get me all jacked up.* A lie. It made so much sense I almost felt like laughing again. Of course he wasn't into me. I was so far from his

134

level it was ridiculous. But still, it hurt, because the fact of the matter was, even if his attraction had been fake, mine hadn't. I'd genuinely liked him, more than liked, and now I felt like a fool.

"That's about the size of it, luv," Stu sighed.

I pushed my hurt feelings aside and plastered on a brave face. "And just imagining that Alfie actually agrees to do the painting, then what? Who's supposed to pull off the robbery?"

Stu stared at me for a long moment, his expression torn. Finally, he replied, "We will."

Now I did laugh, shaking my head in disbelief. "*We* as in me and you? I don't think so."

"I saw your bills, Andrea. I know you're drowning in debt."

"That doesn't mean I'd break the law to pay them off. My God, that's what all that talk was about at the gallery, and again at my parents' house. You were trying to suss out how far I'd go."

"He'll hurt my family. My *family*. They're all I've got, and I'd go to the ends of the earth to protect them. This isn't about how far you'd go. It's about how far I'd go, and I don't think there's anything I wouldn't do to keep them safe."

"That's incredibly admirable, Stu," I said, my voice still hard. "But I'm sorry, I can't help you. You need to go to the police. Talk to Karla, even."

"The police can't help with this. You have no idea how powerful he is. That kind of power overrides the law."

"If you do this and get caught, you'll only get more time. You know that, right?"

He stared at me, his expression blank. "It's a chance I have to take."

"Well, I won't be taking it with you. I'm sorry, but I just can't."

Stu didn't respond, instead he turned and left the room, his shoulders drawn tight. He was angry with me, that much was clear. But what else could I do? We weren't Bonnie and Clyde. As far as I was concerned, the world of theft and art heists was the stuff of movies and crime novels. It wasn't real, not to someone like me.

And it certainly wasn't a world I ever wanted to be in.

Twelve

Stu didn't return to class that afternoon, his empty desk a stark reminder of what he'd revealed to me earlier in the day. I could still hardly believe it, and I had so many more questions. Like, did he know I had money troubles before he'd chosen to befriend me? And what exactly did this robbery entail? Who was he stealing from, and where?

The fact that he'd targeted me, that he'd known who I was before we'd even met made me feel vaguely ill. Of course, I couldn't deny that the idea of being debt free, of being able to live my life without bills and constant repayment worries, sounded like heaven. But it wasn't as though I could just randomly pay off my debts without explaining where my sudden windfall had come from.

It just seemed like so many details of his proposal hadn't been thought through.

As though to punctuate my current situation, I arrived home to find a money collector standing on my doorstep. He was tall and broad, wearing a brown leather jacket and worn jeans. I couldn't tell what age he was from behind, but if I were to guess I'd say late forties. I hid behind the bushes out front (not my finest moment) as he lifted the knocker and continually banged on the door. Alfie was clearly ignoring him, though he wasn't known to answer the door to strangers, especially ones who looked like this.

I walked to the end of my street and waited until he was gone. I only made a move after he pulled away in his car, looking pissed that he hadn't gotten to speak to anyone.

"Andie! There was a man at the door for over twenty minutes, and he looked shifty. He shoved this through the letterbox before he left," said Alfie when I finally entered the flat. He handed me a sealed envelope with my name on it. I didn't have to open it to know what kind of threats lay within.

"It's okay. Nothing for you to worry about," I said as I tiredly made my way into the kitchen. Alfie watched as I poured myself a glass of wine then took a seat by the counter. I was exhausted. This day felt like it was never going to end.

"It was a money collector, wasn't it?" said Alfie, his voice soft. "I'm not stupid. I know what they look like. Do you need a loan? I can give you some money when I sell my next painting if you need it."

"No, Alfie, this isn't your problem," I replied. "It's mine. I'll figure something out." Alfie's rent money already came from his painting sales, so I wouldn't dare ask him for more. He had to live, too.

"But how? Aside from winning the lottery, there isn't much you can do."

"I know," I said, staring glumly into my wine glass. "I know."

"What about your parents? Surely they must have some money set aside."

I shook my head. "They've already given me a lump sum. I won't ask them again." Stu's voice echoed in my head, his offer sounding more and more appealing by the minute. If only it didn't frighten me so much.

"You're thinking of something. What is it?" said Alfie, his gaze perceptive.

I slid my eyes to his, chewing on my lip as I considered telling him everything. In the end, I went with, "I had a weird day."

"How so?"

"You remember my new student?"

"You mean the one you disappeared from Jamie's shop with on the weekend? Don't think he didn't fill me in."

I shook my head. Those two were like a pair of gossiping old ladies sometimes. "He invited me to his brother's birthday party. I didn't want to be rude."

"He's your student, Andie. It's not rude to refuse an offer like that. It's called being professional."

I scrunched my face up at his disapproval, feeling sorry for myself when I blurted, "There's more to it, you know. He befriended me for a reason."

It must've been the wine giving me loose lips. The alcohol was hitting me hard because I hadn't eaten since breakfast. The whole thing at lunch sort of stunted my appetite. "It was all because he wanted to meet you. He was using me."

Saying the words made it hurt more. My chest felt strangely empty and I realised just how much I'd enjoyed Stu's interest. It had awoken something in me both old and new, something I didn't think existed anymore. Now I knew it was all an act. Of *course* it was. I was such a fool, blinded by his handsome face and smooth come-ons. Stu must've thought I was completely naïve falling for his charms, especially since all the while he had an ulterior motive.

Picking up my wine glass, I downed the rest of its contents and poured myself another.

"I don't understand," said Alfie, his voice wary. "Why would he want to meet me?"

"Because he wants you to paint him a replica. A piece he can use in a robbery. And he knows about my debt, that's why he wants me to help him. He's trying to tempt me with the prospect of being able to pay it all off. You were right all along. I should've listened to you. He wasn't to be trusted, but like a naïve fool I let myself believe he was a genuine person." *That he liked me.*

I was rambling now. Alfie straightened on his stool, his posture stiff as he eyed me. "Okay, Andie, start from the beginning and leave nothing out. I want to know everything he said, word for word."

So I told him about Stu's proposition. When I was done we both fell silent, lost in a sea of our own thoughts. I had no idea what Alfie was thinking, but then he finally spoke. "I have to tell you something."

I eyed him, curious. "Go on."

He let out a long breath and reached for the wine, pouring himself a glass. It was unlike him because he didn't usually drink, which made me wary of what he was going to say.

"Do you remember when we were teenagers and my dad lost all his money?" I nodded. "Well, after Mum threw him out she was beside herself because we were going to lose the house. Then she remembered my talent for forgery and talked me into painting a piece that we could sell. I was young and impressionable, and Mum had me convinced we'd be living on the streets if I didn't do it, so I agreed."

I stared at him, speechless. "How come you never told me?"

Alfie took a long gulp of wine. "I was afraid you might tell someone and that Mum and I would get sent to prison—"

"Alfie, I'd never—"

"I know you wouldn't, but I've always been such a worrier. In the end we only sold three paintings, but it was enough to save the house. That's why the Rembrandt you took for your bedroom is stretched on wood that dates from the seventeenth century. I used to practice with all sorts of materials to try and create pieces that could pass for the real thing. There are so many details that could expose art as fake and you have to know every single one."

"I . . . I don't know what to say," I breathed, astounded. It was like he'd lived a secret life I knew nothing about. I was starting to wonder if today was just one bizarrely surreal dream.

"I only created the art. I never had any contact with the dealers. Mum took care of all that. I still have no idea who she used to sell the paintings to, but she knew a lot of wealthy people from the years she spent married to dad, attending galas and company parties. Maybe one of them was the guy Stu met in prison, or someone he knows. It would explain how he knew who I was. I've always worried those paintings would come back to haunt me one day and now they have."

I placed a reassuring hand on his shoulder, not knowing what to say. Another long few minutes of silence passed between us. We were both lost in thought again.

When Alfie spoke he sounded nervous. "The man who came knocking today, he didn't look friendly."

"No," I said in agreement. "I don't imagine he did."

"He's going to come back."

"I know."

"And when he does, it wouldn't hurt to have someone just as scary on our side, someone like Stu Cross."

At this I swivelled to face him. "What exactly are you suggesting?"

"Okay, don't go crazy but I'm . . . I'm suggesting we do it."

I opened my mouth to speak, to ask if he was on crazy pills, but he held up a finger to shush me.

"Let's face it, Andie, on your salary you're going to be an old woman before you pay off all that money, and the interest is just going to keep piling up and up. I don't want that life for you, always looking over your shoulder for dodgy loan sharks. And besides, I've already pulled this off before. It meant my mum and I weren't thrown out onto the streets. If this time it means you won't have to file for bankruptcy then I'll paint whatever he wants, but I won't let you help him with this robbery. In exchange for the replica, he'll give us enough to pay off your debt, and the money will be considered payment for my artwork. We have plausible deniability. All I know is that a patron contracted me to complete a piece. I don't know anything about a robbery and neither do you. It's foolproof."

"Alfie, I'm not sure it's going to be that simple."

"If he wants me to work for him then he's going to have to make it so."

His confidence bolstered me slightly. Trust my cousin to find strength in the surreal, while normal, everyday occurrences scared him half to death. I stared at him for a long moment, trying to figure out if he was really serious about what he was saying. His brown eyes met mine, never flinching.

Crap, he *was* serious.

"Let me sleep on it," I said, trying to buy myself some time.

"No, call him now. Tell him to come here and we'll discuss the particulars."

"Alfie, slow down. I haven't decided if I want to do it yet. I need to think everything through first."

"If we leave it until the morning I'll change my mind, I know I will. I'm always far more adventurous at night. So please, call him. Otherwise I'll lose my nerve."

Swallowing a mouthful of wine, I replied, "I don't even have his number."

"There must be a way for you to contact him. Does he have an email?"

I snorted, amused by the idea of Stu Cross having an email account. Even in this day and age, he didn't seem like the type. Then I remembered we were friends on Facebook. Without thinking I pulled out my phone, logged in and shot off a message.

Andrea Anderson: Can you come by my flat? We need to talk.

It was probably a silly idea. I mean, I doubted he even used the account that much, let alone checked his messages. But then, to my utter surprise, after a couple of minutes I got a response. My palms grew clammy, mostly because I really hadn't expected him to reply.

Stu Cross: On my way.

My heart started to pound, and my lips became dry as the reality sunk in.

"He's coming over," I told Alfie, my voice more air than sound.

He nodded, sounding almost as nervous as I did. "Good. This is good."

"I'm going to take a shower."

Knocking back the last of my wine, I went inside the bathroom and shut the door. Standing under the warm spray, I endeavoured to scrub away my misgivings. If Alfie, a man who was literally paranoid about everything and trusted no one, thought this could work, then maybe it wasn't so far-fetched.

After I'd scrubbed my skin raw, I got out and dried off, hearing a knock on the door as I slipped into my bathrobe. He was here. My pulse sped up again.

Alfie let him in, and I heard a murmured conversation going on as I stepped out into the living room.

"Andrea," said Stu, his gaze moving from my wet hair, down my bathrobe-clad body before coming back up to my face. I had to wonder what was with the small backpack he had with him.

"Andie's filled me in on your proposal," said Alfie, his arms folded as he took a seat on an armchair.

"Right," Stu replied, nodding as his attention moved back and forth between the two of us. He looked like he thought he was being ambushed, like maybe the police were going to spring up from behind the sofa.

"Sit, please," Alfie went on, gesturing to the couch. Stu sat and I went to perch on the edge of Alfie's armchair.

"We're prepared to help you, but first, we have a few conditions."

Stu gestured with his hand. "Go ahead."

"My conditions are as follows: One, I'll complete the painting but Andie is to have no part in the robbery. Two, you'll pay me a pre-agreed-upon sum for services rendered. You'll act as my patron and I your artist. As far as anyone else is concerned, I know nothing about what you intend to do with my work. Three, once the transaction is complete, you'll leave us alone. We don't want to see you ever again once all this is over and done with."

A trickle of unease hit me at the idea of never seeing him again.

No, Andie, that is a good thing. Stu Cross is not healthy for you.

Stu raised an eyebrow. "That it?"

Alfie nodded, his expression stoic.

"Well," Stu began, "if Andrea isn't helping me with the job, then she won't get any money, and what I'm prepared to pay you for your work will be a fuck of a lot less."

"How much are we talking?" asked Alfie.

"A hundred K."

"What!" I exclaimed, my mouth falling open. "Just how much is this painting worth?"

Stu looked to me, his eyes falling to my chest where my bathrobe revealed a hint of skin. I quickly shifted it higher, trying to ignore the goosebumps his attention brought on.

"The Duke's buyer is prepared to pay a mill for it. I get £200,000 and my family's safety, you get £100,000, and the Duke gets the rest."

Alfie snickered a laugh. "I'm sorry, but the Duke? I thought this couldn't get any worse and then you go and throw a nickname like that into the mix."

Stu just stared at him, giving no discernible reaction to his amusement.

"So," my cousin continued, "a million pounds, eh? What painting exactly am I supposed to be replicating?"

"A Rembrandt," said Stu. "I hear he's your speciality. The painting's called *The Storm on the Sea of Galilee*."

Alfie barked a laugh. "I think someone's been pulling your leg, darling." Stu raised an eyebrow at the endearment. My cousin was totally channelling Jamie right now. Maybe that's where his confidence was coming from. "That piece has been missing since 1990, after it was stolen from the Steward Gardner museum in Boston. It's one of the most notorious art heists in modern history."

"Yeah, but that's just the thing," Stu replied, leaning forward and resting his elbows on his knees. "We're not stealing it from a museum. We're stealing it from the person who has it now."

Alfie's mouth shaped into a grin. "The plot certainly does thicken. You do realise that the FBI has been hunting down the thief for over two decades? I mean, people have written books about this robbery. Are you entirely sure this isn't another fake?"

"Look, mate, I'm just a bloke doing a job for another bloke. I don't know shit other than how I'm gonna steal it. After that, my work is done. I could give two fucks if it's the genuine article or not. And look, I know what you're thinking. You're thinking I'm too thick to pull this off."

"On the contrary," Alfie cut in. "In spite of what Hollywood would have us believe, the majority of art thefts aren't undertaken by sophisticated criminal masterminds with dapper fashion senses, but quite the opposite. In fact, a lot of these thieves know little to nothing about art. They do it for the money. Take the Stewart Gardner robbery for instance. The robbers actually cut the paintings from their frames. Cut them from their frames! Anybody with a love or appreciation for art would never dream of doing such a thing. There were also far more valuable pieces they could've taken, which indicates they were either working with a shopping list of sorts, or they didn't actually know what they were looking at. The latter being more likely. So, when you think about it you're a perfect fit."

Stu frowned at him, his mouth set in a firm line. "You know what, I can't tell if you're trying to reassure me or mugging me off."

"Neither. I'm merely trying to inform you of the facts."

I turned to my cousin, wanting to know more. Admittedly, I'd never heard of this notorious robbery, but then again, art was Alfie's field. "What do the authorities know about the people who originally stole it?"

Alfie rubbed ponderously at his chin. "If memory serves me correctly, the thieves entered the museum dressed as police officers and stole thirteen pieces altogether. The empty frames that the paintings were cut from still hang on the museum walls. When Isabella Gardner, the owner of the museum, died, she put it in her will that if any of the art was ever changed, the entire museum would be handed over to Harvard for liquidation, hence why they remain in place."

His words caused my skin to prickle, the significance of it, the history. Alfie levelled his gaze on Stu. "What I want to know is, who has the Rembrandt now, and how exactly do you plan on stealing it?"

Stu cocked an eyebrow. "You said you wanted nothing to do with that side of things, so maybe you should just focus on your part of the job."

"But don't you want my advice? Not to toot my own horn, but I'm pretty much an expert in this field. I can point out the holes in this plan 'the Duke' has given you."

Stu eyed him dubiously. "You ever stolen before?"

"Well, no, that's not what I meant. I'm not an expert in thievery, but I am an expert in people who appreciate art because I'm one of them. The person who owns this painting must surely be an art lover to risk imprisonment just to own such a piece. I'll be able to tell you what makes him tick, as it were."

Stu gripped the back of his neck, his expression thoughtful. "You've got a point there."

"So fill us in," Alfie urged.

Stu opened his mouth to speak but I cut him off. "Wait. Maybe we shouldn't know any of that side of things," I said, eyeing my cousin. "Plausible deniability, remember?"

Alfie's expression sobered. He actually looked a little disappointed. "You're right. As much as I'm dying to know the ins and outs of all this, we should keep ourselves in the dark as much as we can."

Stu didn't say anything. Instead his hazel eyes fell on me and I could feel the heat of it. A moment of awkwardness ensued and Alfie cleared his throat.

"Well, if you don't mind I'm going to bed. This has been a tiring night."

"Wait," said Stu. He picked up the small backpack he carried in with him and handed it to Alfie. "This is from the Duke. There are pictures, film and a USB drive with three-hundred-and-sixty-degree photographs of the painting as it is now. He had one of his men break into the owner's house to get it all so you can imitate the wear and tear that you can't see in regular prints."

"Well, wasn't that kind of him," said Alfie, eyeing me before continuing on to his bedroom. "It looks like I've got a painting to get started on."

I could've cursed him for leaving me alone with Stu. The tiny hairs on the back of my neck stood on end, and not because I sensed danger. Well, at least not the kind that could cause physical harm. The fact of the matter was, I was embarrassed and annoyed, and quite frankly, royally pissed off. Stu's gaze wandered over me again, his mouth almost tipping into a smile.

"Nice bathrobe."

"Oh please, the jig is up now. You don't have to keep pretending," I huffed, folding my arms defensively.

One dark eyebrow rose. "Pretending?"

148

"You must think I'm an idiot," I went on, my cheeks heating. I hated how attractive I still found him, sitting there with his tousled hair and effortless male beauty. He didn't even have to try and quite frankly it was infuriating.

"Course I don't. Why would I think that?"

"Because I fell for your act. I had no clue the only reason you were . . . you were in my class was to get to Alfie."

"Andrea, of course you wouldn't suspect me. It's not like it's the sort of thing that happens every day. I'm the one who's at fault."

I sat up straighter, folding my arms. "I'm well aware you're at fault, and I want to hate you right now for dragging my cousin and me into all of this." I wanted to, but I couldn't, because at the core of his actions was a love for his family. I felt so torn.

Stu's expression hardened. "It's not like you're not getting anything out of it. You're getting a hundred grand. So don't act like I'm the only one who benefits here."

"Yes, well, why couldn't you just be up front about it? There was absolutely no need for you to pose as a student and then pretend to like me. You could've simply approached me and told me your story. I'm not an unreasonable person. In fact, I'm probably more reasonable than most. I would've tried to assist if I could."

At this he scoffed. "Like fuck you would. You'd have been straight on the phone to the coppers, so let's not pretend otherwise."

I didn't reply, because deep down I suspected he was right. He let out a sound of irritation and stood. I levelled my hands on my hips and endeavoured to maintain a hard expression. I wouldn't be a soft-hearted, gullible fool with him anymore.

149

His gaze was unwavering, but then he just shook his head, muttered something unintelligible to himself and then headed for the door.

Before he left he turned back around, giving me one last irritable glance. "You'll be seeing me, Andrea."

Then the door closed and he was gone.

"Well . . . shit," I muttered to the empty room.

Thirteen

I woke up the next morning full of regret. This was due to the fact that I'd stayed up half the night polishing off that bottle of wine and looking through old photos of Mark and me. I used to be into keeping albums, but ever since he passed I'd barely taken any pictures. It was like that part of me died with him, the part that wanted to store precious memories.

Some days I wished so hard for him to still be here, so hard that my entire body hurt. My throat felt like a lump of raw, abused meat and my stomach constantly ached.

Yesterday was one of those days, and it was the reason I arrived at work ten minutes late with a hangover and blotchy eyes from crying myself to sleep. Usually, if I could keep my mind focused on every day, practical things, I could avoid feeling this way. Unfortunately, yesterday and last night had been all kinds of crazytown and I lost the run of my emotions.

"You're looking a little worse for wear, Miss Anderson," Mary commented with a grin. "Late night, was it?"

I knew she meant well, thinking I'd been out enjoying myself. Little did she know, it had been a party of misery and loneliness for one. Plastering on a brave face, I replied kindly, "Something like that."

Mary winked at me and I continued inside the classroom, stumbling and almost falling over my own feet when I saw Stu in his usual seat. He turned and caught me by the elbow, preventing my fall. His touch brought on the usual tingles and his eyes shone with concern but I was having none of it. What the hell was he even doing here? Now that his true intentions had been revealed, I didn't think he'd continue attending class. *And to think I'd introduced him to my dad for his insight.*

I just didn't see what he thought his being here was going to achieve. Perhaps he simply wanted to prolong my discomfort.

"I take it you all finished the final chapters of *Jude* last night?" I said, clearing my throat as I opened my laptop. I strongly suspected that Stu hadn't read a single page, which was sort of the reason I'd said it. Maybe I was being mean-spirited, but I thought he deserved a little discomfort, too. Most of the class called out that they'd finished but Stu remained silent. I addressed him directly.

"Stu, I know you started late, but did you get a chance to fit the book into your busy schedule?"

Yes, I said the last part with a hint of cynicism, but it couldn't be helped. I was wounded and needed to reassert myself. Stu stared at his desk then brought his dark gaze to mine, scratching his head self-consciously. A pang hit me right in the chest and I instantly felt bad for putting him on the spot. Of course he hadn't read it. It was a four-hundred-page book and he had difficulty with reading and writing. I was an awful person.

"Yes, I, uh, I did, actually," he said, surprising the hell out of me. So much so my mouth fell open, my disbelief written all over my face.

"You did?" I asked.

He ducked his head, his voice going quiet. "Took me longer than most, I'm sure, but Lee's been helping me with my reading."

My heart pounded, because even though I was still angry with him, the idea of him going out of his way to read the book, to get help from his brother, was just too admirable. Why couldn't he be horrible and let me enjoy hating him for a while?

"And did you enjoy it?" I went on, trying not to let my voice convey how touched I was.

"I'm not sure if 'enjoy' is the right word, Miss Anderson, but I definitely felt like it made me see things differently. Guess I could relate to the whole being dirt-poor thing. Actually, there was a lot I could relate to."

"Really?" I went on, curious. "What else?"

Stu glanced around the room, then shot me a look as if to ask, *why aren't you asking anybody else questions?* The answer was rather simple, really. I wasn't asking anyone else, because in spite of all the reasons he shouldn't, Stu fascinated me.

"You have the whole Christminster thing. That's supposed to be Oxford or Cambridge or something, right?"

I nodded and gestured for him to continue.

"Well, I feel like to Jude, Christminster represents everything that's good. It's his goal to get there and become a student, but he's so far away from it, it almost feels impossible. I think we all have a Christminster, this thing we want more than anything else, and it's what keeps us moving forward. If we didn't have that, a goal, a dream, there'd be no point to keep going. Because who wants to work their fingers to the bone for minimum wage day in and day out without something to look forward to? If we knew for definite that we weren't going to get to Christminster, then we'd all just give up."

I stared at him, taken aback by his words and how deeply he'd thought about this. And considering the difficulty Stu had with this area of his learning, what he'd just come out with felt like a real breakthrough. I smiled at him, my disgruntlement momentarily forgotten. As a teacher, these were the sorts of moments I lived for.

"You're right. That's a fantastic point, Stu," I said and turned to the rest of the class. "Now, would anyone else like to contribute?"

For the rest of the day Stu didn't approach me. He didn't stick around at lunch and he didn't try to provoke me in class. In fact, he was acting like he genuinely wanted to be there, and I wondered if his continued attendance had something to do with the robbery. But then, how could it?

I was busy correcting papers when the final bell of the day rang and everybody started getting up to leave. After a few minutes the room fell quiet and I thought they'd all gone, which was the reason I let out a startled yelp when Stu suddenly spoke.

"Andrea."

"For crying out loud, Stu," I said, clutching my hand to my chest. "You frightened the life out of me."

His lips twitched and it looked like he was trying to hold in his laughter. "Sorry."

"It's fine. What do you need?"

Now his expression grew serious. "I wanted to talk."

"About?"

"About us."

I swallowed, returning my attention to the papers I was correcting. I made sure to put as much dismissal into my voice as possible. "There is no us, Stu."

"That's bullshit, Andrea."

I blinked at him. "I think you'll find it isn't. And don't talk to me like that. I'm your teacher."

"Oh, come on. Don't act like you're bothered. Susan swears in class all the time and you never give her stick for it."

154

"It's the spirit in which it's done, Stu. When Susan swears it's good-natured. When you swear it's aggressive."

"That's only because you frustrate me."

At this I slammed my hand down on the desk. "I frustrate you? That's a laugh. You're the most frustrating person I know."

"For God's sake, what do you want from me? I told you I'm sorry. I even read that bloody book for you even though it took me forever. I'm really trying here."

"That's what I don't get. Why are you trying? Why are you even still attending class? You said yourself the only reason you enrolled in the first place was to get to me to get to Alfie. Well, mission accomplished. Your presence is no longer necessary."

His expression wavered ever so slightly, almost like my words hit a sore spot, and I instantly wanted to take them back. But I couldn't. I had to stand my ground, show him I wasn't a pushover.

Stu stepped closer, leaning forward to take the pen from my hand and shove the papers out of the way. "You talk like I came up with all this on my own and I didn't. I was put up to it. If it were down to me I never would've used you like I did."

His features were etched with regret, and yet there it was—the truth. He'd used me. He'd probably only read *Jude* to alleviate his guilt, to prove to himself that he wasn't such a bad person.

And there was me thinking he had an actual interest in expanding his learning.

My head hurt, the final remnants of my hangover and dealing with Stu making it ache.

"Look, I'm tired. I can't do this right now," I said, rising from my seat and frantically shoving my things into

155

my bag. "I still don't understand why you're coming to class, but whatever. If you want to learn I'll teach you. But like I said, there's no us. There never will be."

Stu's gaze hardened as I gestured for him to leave. Silently, he turned and left the classroom. As I locked up I felt emotion catch in my throat but I did my best to tamp it down until I got home. Once there I could let out all my pent-up emotions.

Stu's car was still parked outside as I left but I couldn't see him. The glare from the sun blocked out his windows, and butterflies flitted in my stomach at the idea of his unseen, watchful eyes.

I was antsy the entire way home, wondering about Stu, a million questions swirling around inside my head. Had I been too harsh? Or had I given him exactly what he deserved?

My fluster meant I was out of my car and almost to my front door before I saw him. The very same man from yesterday had coming knocking again, but this time he was facing me. I stood frozen to the spot as I dropped my keys in fright. They fell to the ground with a loud clatter.

The first thing I noticed were his black shark-like eyes. Seemed oddly fitting that he worked as a money collector.

"Andrea Anderson?" he asked, his voice hard. Yep, there definitely wasn't going to be any messing around with this one.

"I, um . . ." I mumbled, unable to find my voice.

The man withdrew a leather-bound folder from under his arm, opening it up and flicking through some papers. I felt like using this opportunity to make a run for it, but then again, I doubted he'd have trouble catching up to me. When he found what he was looking for, his eyes scanned back and forth and I swallowed, my mouth dry as sandpaper. Inside my chest my heart beat like a rabbit on crack.

Why was this happening to me today of all days? When I just wanted to shut myself inside my room, eat chocolate, and have a good cry.

He let out a low whistle and lifted his gaze to mine. "You're two months behind on your repayments. I need to collect £1375 by the end of tomorrow or we'll be upping your interest by another two per cent." At this he closed his folder with a definitive whump and shoved it back under his arm.

My mouth opened and shut several times as I tried to find words. "I don't have it right now, b-but I'll have it in a couple of weeks. I'll have every penny I owe in just a couple of weeks," I promised him. Stu hadn't given us a time frame for the robbery, but it had to be happening soon, right?

"Forgive me if I find that hard to believe," said Shark Eyes, his expression cynical.

"It's the truth, I swear. I'm set to inherit some money from a relative," I lied.

"Oh yeah? Me, too. I'll be getting a big windfall once my uncle Rupert Murdock pops his clogs. Come on now, do you think I don't hear this bullshit every fucking day? You come up with the cash before five p.m. tomorrow evening or your interest goes up, Miss Anderson. It's that simple."

"But please, it's just not possible," I said, my voice pleading.

He glanced over my shoulder to where my car was parked out on the street. "That your motor?"

I nodded before thinking it through.

"Bet you could get yourself a couple grand for it. See? Problem solved."

"I can't sell my car. I need it to get to work." And really, I didn't want to. I loved driving, loved the freedom it provided. It was one of my few pleasures in life and I wasn't prepared to give it up. Not yet, anyway.

"Public transport is a wonder these days," he said, taking a step toward me. His face was hard, not a shred of empathy in his expression. I couldn't remember the last time I'd felt so small.

"I won't sell it. I told you. I'll have the money very soon. I'm not lying."

His stance grew threatening as he continued to advance on me, leaving barely an inch between us. My gut quivered, because he practically oozed intimidation. I guess that's why this was his job.

Glaring down at me, he spat, "Sell the fucking car and have the money by tomorrow, babe, or your interest goes up. No compromises. I'm not gonna fall for that innocent doe-eyed bollocks you're trying to peddle." His words were cutting and I flinched away from him. He honestly sounded like he was two seconds away from roughing me up.

"You want to repeat that, mate? This time to someone your own fucking size," came a familiar voice. When I turned and saw Stu standing behind me, his expression was furious. Quick as a flash he wrapped his arm around my middle, pulling me back and away from the loan collector. When he'd set me firmly behind him he stood face to face with Shark Eyes, staring him down. Though this guy had width on his side, Stu had height, plus what I'd always suspected to be the kind of athletic muscularity only prison could provide.

"This is between me and Miss Anderson," said Shark Eyes. "So why don't you piss off and stay out of it."

"I'm not going anywhere, so why don't you piss off, yeah? Go get your jollies threatening some other poor defenceless woman."

Shark Eyes pointed at me. "If she doesn't pay up, things are only going to get worse for her, whether she has a dumb-shit little guard dog on her side or not."

"Leave," Stu grunted, his entire body coiled tight. I could tell his patience was already wearing thin and watched as he repeatedly clenched and unclenched his fists, ready for a fight. The fact that he was defending me when he didn't have to gave me an odd swishy feeling in my stomach.

"I'll leave when I'm good and ready."

"You'd better be good and ready in three seconds because I'm about to give you some help."

Shark Eyes grunted as he looked Stu up and down, deciding whether or not he was worth it. He must've decided he wasn't because a second later he gave another grunt, shot me a final threatening look, and stalked away from my flat.

As soon as he was gone I let out a relieved sigh, slumping back against my front door as I willed my pulse to slow down. I'd never endured a confrontation like that before. Up until now, I'd only received threatening letters and phone calls from my bank. This was new territory, and I was completely unequipped to deal with it. I'd been brought up relatively privileged, had spent the majority of my life quite sheltered, really.

Perhaps that's why Stu took facing off with Shark Eyes in his stride. He hadn't been sheltered, had experienced real hardship. Threatening confrontations were probably a daily occurrence for him in prison.

He stood silently next to me and I could feel his eyes looking me over, searching for cracks. He probably thought I was going to break down any moment, and believe me, I wanted to. I wasn't normally so weak, but everything had just been piling up lately and I'd been internalising so much of it. It was only natural that the floodgates would burst open sooner or later.

But no, not here, not in front of Stu Cross. I could wait for privacy, until there were no judging eyes present, just my four bedroom walls and my pillow to comfort me and soak up my tears.

"You all right?" Stu asked, laying a hand on my shoulder, his voice soft.

And just like that, as though all I needed was a sympathetic word and a light touch, I broke. In spite of my determination to put up a strong front, all my pent-up sadness, feelings of inadequacy, fear of losing everything, utter indignation erupted, and I was helpless to do anything about it. Tears rolled down my cheeks as I turned away from him and dug in my handbag for some Kleenex. All I found was a crumpled napkin. I used it dab my eyes in an effort to hide my tears. Unfortunately, there was nothing I could do to cover up the sniffling.

"Ah fuck, come here." He wrapped his arm around my waist again and pulled me into his warm chest. "Hush, I've got you," he whispered as he turned me and I buried my face in his neck, unprepared to let him see my blotchy cheeks.

Stu's hand drifted comfortingly down my back, coming to rest at the base of my spine. There he started to rub soothing circles as his other arm held me to him. It felt so good to be held by another human being that I simply sank into the embrace, helpless to resist the comfort.

"You're okay, I've got you," Stu murmured, his lips in my hair as he pressed a light kiss to the top of my head. Tingles radiated down my spine from his voice alone. I could lose myself in these arms. *How was I still this attracted to him when I knew it wasn't reciprocated?*

He smelled so good. I couldn't help inhaling his masculine scent. There was something incredibly comforting about it, something that made me feel protected. I paused, hoping he hadn't noticed me practically nuzzling his neck. But he just continued rubbing circles, letting me cry it out. After another minute or two I drew away, suddenly feeling self-conscious. Earlier today we'd fought. I'd been horrible to him and here he was defending me against threatening money collectors and holding me as I cried. I didn't feel like I deserved it, even if he had used me before.

His hazel eyes looked me over as I dabbed the remaining wetness from my face. I couldn't look at him, and instead stared at the ground as I asked quietly, "Why did you come?"

"I didn't like how we left things."

I glanced up, studying his expression and seeing nothing but remorse.

Stu raked a hand through his hair. "Andrea, listen I—"

"Do you want to come in for tea?" I cut him off, feeling too raw to continue standing on my doorstep with a red post-crying face.

"Yes," he answered, his voice still soft. Maybe he thought that if he spoke normally I'd break down again. Now that my crying jag was over I felt *more* embarrassment creeping in.

Busying myself with picking my keys up off the ground and opening the door, I led him inside the flat. The distinct tones of Rachmaninov echoed from Alfie's room so I knew he was busy at work. He always listened to classical music when he painted. Seemingly hearing us come in, the music shut off and my cousin emerged from his room.

There was dark blue paint in his hair and his fingers were stained black. I took this to mean he'd started working on the piece for Stu. He also had his laptop tucked under his arm, which made me think he'd come out to show me something. Really though, I was glad of his presence, because I felt like I needed a buffer. My emotions were too close to the surface.

Alfie looked between the two of us, his concerned gaze falling on me the longest. "Andie, is everything okay? You look upset."

Before I could answer Stu spoke. "There was a piece-of-shit money collector outside coming the hard man with her. I ran him off."

"Oh," Alfie exclaimed, his hand going to his heart. "Was it the same man from yesterday? I'll admit I was too scared to answer the door when I saw him."

"Yes," I said, nodding, "it was the same guy."

"Well, in that case I suppose thanks are in order," he said to Stu somewhat warily. "I'm not sure what Andie would've done if you hadn't been there."

I huffed at this, not liking the insinuation that I was a weak, defenceless little woman, even if admittedly, I had been a tad weak and defenceless.

"No worries," said Stu, noticing my tense posture. Sure, I'd just been crying my eyes out, but it wasn't like I wouldn't have survived the encounter if it weren't for him.

I just wouldn't have had a soothing shoulder to cry on afterwards. No big deal.

A moment of quiet ensued as I went to put the kettle on and Alfie perched himself on a stool by the counter. Stu went and took a seat by the window, his face etched with thought. *What on earth was going through his mind now?*

"Pssst," Alfie whispered over the noise of the kettle, gesturing for me to come closer.

"What?" I mouthed.

"Don't you think we should help him? Not to be mean, but he doesn't strike me as the sharpest tool in the shed. This Duke character could be setting him up. We should let him tell us his plan for the robbery, like I offered last night."

I frowned just as Stu spoke up. "I can hear you, you know."

Alfie wore a sheepish expression. "Sorry."

"And just so you know, I'm not as dumb as I look."

"You're right, I apologise," said Alfie, appearing embarrassed. "I'm afraid I fall victim to stereotyping from time to time. And you're right, just because your muscles are big doesn't mean your brain is small."

Stu tilted his head from side to side, like his neck was tense. "People always make the same assumption about me. I'm used to it." The way he spoke made my chest ache, and I wished I could go over and give him a hug. Had people always judged him on the way he looked?

"Yes well, most people are small-minded," I said. "They don't realise that there are many different kinds of intelligence."

"And that right there is why you're such a wonderful teacher," said Alfie. "You can find a talent in everyone."

163

Stu's gaze heated as he watched me and I shifted from foot to foot. His expression gave me butterflies. I busied myself making us all tea as Alfie turned to ponder Stu.

"So, would you like my advice?"

"Your advice?"

"About the robbery. If I'm honest, I'm quite eager to poke some holes in this plan of the Duke's. In my opinion the best schemes are plotted when several heads knock together."

Stu rubbed his thumb across his lips, an action I founded strangely mesmerising. So much so that I almost spilled the milk I held, catching myself just in time.

"You sure you won't start going hysterical on me again? Last night was dramatic enough," said Stu, eyes wary.

"I promise. I might not like it but I've made my peace with the situation. For better or worse, we're all in this for the long haul."

Stu eyed him a moment as I set Alfie's cup down in front of him then carried the other over to Stu. Our fingers brushed when he took it, reminding me of how good it felt when he'd rubbed my back so soothingly. And yes, how good it felt when he'd kissed me at my parents' house.

"The Duke's getting out in a month. That's why he needs the money. He plans on hotfooting it over to the Seychelles where he can spend his days in the sun and his nights bedding all the East African beauties he can get his hands on."

"How delightfully extravagant and predictable," Alfie sighed and I gave a light chuckle.

Stu's expression warmed at my laughter and I glanced away shyly, focusing on my teacup. "Well anyway, the

164

bloke we're ripping off is actually an old acquaintance of the Duke's, goes by the name of Renfield."

"As in Dracula's thrall?" Alfie scoffed. "That's an unfortunate surname to get stuck with."

"Renfield's a big deal, some kind of hedge fund millionaire and apparently a crazy art fanatic. He's had the painting in his private collection since the early nineties, when he supposedly purchased it from the thieves who pulled off the museum heist. The Duke caught wind that Renfield was relocating from London to the United Arab Emirates. Trouble is, he's going to have a hell of a time moving his collection of stolen art and antiquities across the pond. That's where I come in."

I frowned past a sip of tea, my stomach churning as I listened to Stu speak. The whole thing just felt too real now Alfie and I were being held privy to the actual plan.

"The Duke used his contacts to have me recommended to Renfield as a specialist trafficker. I've got to pose as some bloke whose job it is to transport contraband across country borders. I've been in contact with him for a while now, but we won't meet in person until next week. That's where I'm going to have to convince him I'm the real deal."

"And if you don't?" I put in, scared for him. I had no idea what kind of nutcase this Renfield might be.

"Then the whole thing is screwed, I imagine," said Alfie before Stu could reply.

"Pretty much," Stu agreed.

"So, if my skills of deduction prove correct, what you plan to do is transport the Duke's items while replacing the real painting with my fake, yes?"

"Yep."

"But what if you get caught?" I asked anxiously. "Even after you swap the paintings you still have a bunch of stolen art to transport all the way to Dubai or wherever he's moving to. That's a big risk to take."

Stu scratched his jaw, his expression torn. "The Duke says he's organised for me to travel on a cargo ship that goes fucking everywhere before ending up in Malaysia, and from there I take another ship to Dubai, where Renfield's men will collect the items."

"Sounds a little too simple, if you ask me," said Alfie, his expression thoughtful. "I've a feeling you'll have a much bigger problem getting into the UAE than this Duke is letting on. And of course he won't care because he'll have his painting by then. I'm sure I'm right when I say you don't want to go back to prison, especially not some Middle Eastern prison where quite frankly you'll stand out like a sore thumb, not to mention you don't even speak the language."

Stu thought on this a moment before speaking. "So what you're saying is I need to be one step ahead, right? Maybe I could pay somebody to transport the goods for me. Somebody who actually comes from the Middle East and understands what they're dealing with."

"Precisely," said Alfie.

"Yeah, but how can I trust they'll follow through?"

"Simple. You don't pay them until the job is done. I might be an artist but I'm the son of a businessman. Growing up for me was a series of deals that my father was constantly in the middle of."

Alfie's voice grew detached for a moment. He never really spoke of his childhood because those years had been privileged but lonely. Also, even before they lost all their money, his dad had cheated on his mum countless times,

166

turning her into a paranoid wreck. I was surprised Alfie lasted so long under her roof, since she wasn't the easiest woman in the world to live with.

"Think I'm gonna have to call in some favours, find someone who's desperate for the money and willing to take the risk," said Stu, his expression thoughtful.

"That's probably the wisest action to take. I certainly wouldn't put myself through the risk of completing the journey."

My heart clenched at Stu's predicament, and though I was still trying to convince myself I was angry with him, I worried. I worried what would happen if he couldn't find someone to take on the job, because in my gut I couldn't stand the idea of him going it alone.

"Oh, before I forget," said Alfie, opening up his laptop. "I made an interesting discovery today while studying the images the Duke provided."

Both Stu and I came to stand by him as he pulled up a picture file that showed a 3-D image of *The Storm on the Sea of Galilee*. Alfie zoomed in on the cracks in the paint. "When I did this before I never had actual images of the original like this. It's fascinating the things that can't be seen in ordinary prints. I've always known that unlike paintings done on wood panels where the cracks run in somewhat straight lines, on canvas it's the exact opposite. The cracks form in concentric circles, with a secondary network of finer cracks that radiate from the centre and join the circles together like a spider-web."

He paused and zoomed again, this time rotating the image at an angle. "And see here, the cracks actually appear to be elevated. Fortunately, I have a few methods of replicating this effect so it shouldn't be too difficult. My new discovery though, are these tiny little black and brown pinhead spots at the edges of the painting." Now he zoomed to the far left of the piece. "All day I've been trying to figure them out, and with a bit of research online I managed to discover what they are." He paused as though for dramatic effect.

"Well, what are they?" I asked.

"Ancient fly droppings!" Alfie exclaimed as though it was the most marvellous thing ever.

"Lovely," Stu deadpanned and I gave a light chuckle.

"That's kind of disgusting," I said and Alfie frowned.

"Oh, you're no fun. I wish Jamie could be in on this with us. I'm sure he'd be just as excited as I am."

"Excited about fly poo. What is the world coming to?" I joked.

"Well, I for one am looking forward to figuring out a way to replicate them," said Alfie, sticking out his tongue at me. I smiled and walked over to the fridge.

"I think I'll make something to eat. Anybody hungry?"

"Oh yes, I'm starved," said Alfie, rising from his seat and heading for the door. "Call me when it's ready."

Stu eyed his departing figure, a single brow raised. "He always treat you like that?"

"Like what?"

"Like you're his mum."

I laughed. "You mean because he lets me cook for him? Believe me when I say nobody wants Alfie loose in the kitchen. He might be a genius with a paintbrush, but my cousin could manage to burn a ham sandwich."

Stu let out a quiet chuckle and stood, crossing the room to stand before me. I swallowed, my throat dry at his proximity. I turned and opened the fridge to check what food we had in, trying to ignore the awareness he provoked.

"Are you staying to eat?" I asked shyly, not meeting his eyes. I could feel his heat as he approached again, this time standing behind me.

"I should get going," he replied, voice low.

I nodded. "Okay, I guess I'll see you in class then."

"See you in class, Andrea," Stu whispered right before he pressed a kiss to the back of my neck. I closed my eyes, the sensation overpowering even though it was only a kiss. By the time I turned around to face him he was already gone.

It was a shame his presence still lingered.

Fourteen

The rest of the week passed by and Shark Eyes never came back, probably because he didn't want another encounter with Stu. But since I hadn't managed to come up with the money I knew my interest rate had gone up. I just hoped this whole thing with the robbery worked out, because otherwise I was screwed. I could see myself having to move back in with Mum and Dad, selling my car and anything else I owned of worth.

Each day Alfie worked on his painting. Stu still attended class, which was odd. I didn't get it, nor did I understand the kiss from the other day. He wouldn't have done it if he wasn't attracted to me, right? But then, why had he been so distant ever since?

Aside from during class, he hadn't spoken to me at all. Now it was Saturday and I was spending the morning in the back garden we shared with the two other flats above us. The sun had decided to make an appearance, so I was making the most of it by marking papers outside. There was knock at the front door, and I heard Jamie announce his presence when Alfie let him in.

Twenty minutes later, there was a second knock, and that had me puzzled. Admittedly, we didn't really get guests aside from Jamie, but maybe my parents had decided to pay a visit. Smiling at the idea getting to see Mum and Dad after the week I'd had, I quickly set the papers under my sunhat so they wouldn't blow away and headed inside.

I stopped in my tracks when I entered the hallway and saw Stu standing at the door with Jamie.

"Why, Andie, would you look at who decided to pay a visit? It's Brad Pitt's decidedly broodier younger brother," he declared loudly and I winced a little.

Stu glanced at me, his expression perplexed. He looked nothing like Brad Pitt, but I suspected that was the only handsome male celebrity Jamie could recall off the top of his head. It went to show just how long it had been since he'd picked up a gossip rag.

"Well, don't just stand there," Jamie went on. "Come in."

Stu stepped inside, and I grew conscious of the fact that I was wearing cut-off jean shorts and a blue string vest. Since I had longer legs than most, I felt a little bit too bare.

"I came to see how that, uh, thing is coming along," said Stu, his gaze wandering over my aforementioned bare legs. His throat bobbed as he swallowed.

"No need to be cryptic," said Jamie, waving his hand in the air. "Alfie's told me all about your arrangement and my lips are sealed."

Stu appeared agitated by the idea of Jamie, a virtual stranger, knowing about the robbery. He opened his mouth to say something, but I grabbed his hand and pulled him down the hallway and into my bedroom before he could speak. I heard Jamie chuckling and muttering, "Well, that's one way to get a man in your bed."

I closed the door and turned to Stu, still clasping his hand. Our mouths were literally inches apart and a heady sensation washed over me. "He doesn't know about the robbery," I whispered and his expression instantly relaxed. "Alfie told him one of your brothers is a Rembrandt fanatic, and he's painting the piece as a surprise birthday gift."

Stu grinned at that and so did I. I'd met his brothers. They weren't the sort of men who were into Rembrandt. After a second the mood changed. Our smiles fell but our eyes stayed connected. Stu's gaze turned hot and needful and it made something flutter in my chest.

"How've you been?" he murmured, moving his thumb along the inside of my wrist. Neither one of us let go, and I wondered if he enjoyed the feeling of being skin to skin as much as I did. Sweat pebbled my forehead, both from the unseasonably hot day and Stu's effect on me. My body responded to his on instinct.

"Good. Busy," I croaked as he moved an inch closer. His eyes wandered to my lips, which suddenly felt dry so I licked them. Stu's expression turned pained as he endeavoured to look away. Now his gaze was on my collarbone, studying my bare skin.

"I don't think I've ever seen you in so few clothes," he said, a strain in his voice.

"It's sunny," I replied.

"You've got the most flawless skin," he continued, his gaze moving to my chest. My boobs weren't small. They weren't gigantic, either. They were just sort of . . . medium. Though for some reason they felt bigger now as Stu ogled them, almost as if they were straining to break free.

"Um," I said, biting my lip. Words were never my strong suit when Stu was near.

He braced one hand against the wall at my shoulder, his thumb still brushing the inside of my wrist. How could I feel that one touch all the way between my thighs? This man had some sort of magic.

"Do you ever think about that kiss at your parents'?" he asked huskily, dipping his head to trace his lips across my jaw. A small, embarrassing noise escaped me that I wasn't sure how to label.

"Um," I said again. Seriously, brain, could you come up with something more than single syllable nonsense right now?

"I do," Stu went on, his tongue dipping out to taste me. My head fell back against the wall, granting him more access. Stu groaned and started kissing my neck in earnest, sucking and biting. His lips felt like heaven, and I was already wet. How quickly things escalated. Stu pressed his hips into me. *Shit, he was hard.* His mouth travelled across my neck, along my earlobe and to my mouth. When he kissed me it was soft and explorative. I didn't stop him, didn't want to. Desire had won this round.

Reaching down, he lifted my thigh and hitched it around his waist. I gasped into his kiss, allowing him to slip his tongue in and taste me. I loved the feel of his soft licks, how his tongue danced with mine.

Stu pulled away, going to kiss my neck again before moving down to my cleavage. He mouthed the top of one breast, then the other, and the moan that came out of me sounded foreign. I didn't realise I was still capable of such a sound.

"Your tits are gorgeous," Stu breathed, kissing and licking them. When he gave them a little bite I yelped. His answering chuckle was low, hitting my right in the pit of my stomach. "I spend half my time in class staring at them, the other half I spend wondering what your nipples look like. You drive me insane, Andrea."

I moaned again and Stu grunted, pinching my hardened nipple through the fabric of my top. "I love that sound," he said. "You've no clue how long it's been since I've heard a woman make that sound." His voice was practically a growl now, more animal than man. I strained against his erection where it pressed firmly between my thighs. I could tell he was . . . substantial. The thought actually had me blushing.

"Stuart, are you coming to see this painting, or what?" Jamie called from Alfie's bedroom, his tone full of mischief. Mortification hit me as I wondered if they'd heard us, but then I remembered Alfie had the radio on. I just hoped it drowned out the sound of . . . whatever that just was.

"If we ignore them they'll leave us alone, right?" Stu asked irritably.

"Unfortunately, it'll only make them more determined. You should go."

"I don't want to," he grunted, standing back to his full height and brazenly dropping his hand between my legs.

"Stu!" I yelped, stifling a gasp.

"I want to stay and taste this," he continued, massaging me. I hadn't been touched like this in such a long time that I was embarrassingly close to orgasm. If he applied any more pressure, I was in danger of coming and he'd barely done a thing.

Stu swore and moved away, turning to face the window for a second as he willed his erection to go down. I busied myself fixing my hair back into place and made an effort to calm my laboured breathing. A minute passed, maybe two, and then Stu moved by me out the door. I didn't get why he wouldn't look at me, but I hoped it was because it'd make it harder for him to leave. I closed the door and moved into my room. Flopping down on my bed, I pressed my face into my pillow to muffle a groan. I'd never been so aroused in my life, not even with Mark. *That* thought was sobering.

Our relationship had always been more friendship based than sexual. We were just seventeen when we first met and became fast friends. Our friendship blossomed into love, rather than lust becoming love. Don't get me wrong, we had a fantastic sex life, but I never felt that hot itching need beneath my skin that Stu gave me. Again, guilt set in. A part of me thought I shouldn't be feeling this way. If my love for Mark was as pure and true as I thought, then how could I possibly want Stu? Maybe it was all just lust. Lust could make even the tamest person act out of character, and I was still wrapped up in its madness.

I lay there, my hand resting on my lower belly, where my top had ridden up a little. My nerves were frazzled and wondered if I should allow myself a little relief. What harm could it do? Moving my hand under the waistband of my shorts, I slid my fingers beneath my underwear and touched myself. I was embarrassingly wet.

Stu's muffled voice sounded from Alfie's room as they carried out a conversation. I let it wash over me as I stroked my tender flesh and imagined it was his fingers. I had a vision of him coming to me after class, locking the door and kneeling before me. I'd be wearing a skirt and he'd push it up, burying his head between my legs as he went down on me with his skilled tongue.

I moved two fingers inside myself, using my other hand to circle my clit. My hips jutted forward, practically in the air as I strained to come. My movements got faster, harder, until a fresh swell of moisture coated my fingers. I buried my face in my pillow once more as I orgasmed so intensely I wanted to scream. The fantasy in my head combined with Stu's voice just one room away was a heady combination.

This wasn't something I normally did. Sure, I got myself off every once in a blue moon, but it was more of a bodily function rather than a necessity. Being turned on by a real live person was certainly new territory for me.

175

I lay there for long minutes, feeling sated yet wanting more. *Wanting him.* I knew it was wrong but I just couldn't help myself. It wasn't a choice, it just was. Moving off the bed, I opened my wardrobe and grabbed a cotton jumper, pulling it on over my vest. My nipples were still hard beneath my bra, and the feel of the fabric sliding over them both aroused and frustrated me.

After paying a quick visit to the bathroom, I knocked on Alfie's door and stepped inside. My cousin was hard at work, stabbing the paintbrush into the canvas with passionate abandon. Stu sat at the worktable by the window with Jamie, funnily enough engaged in a game of Go. Jamie was fanatical about this Chinese board game akin to chess. He actually attended Go tournaments from time to time and I always lost whenever I played him.

Glancing at the board I was surprised to find that Stu currently had the upper hand. The objective was to surround as much territory as possible using black and white pebbles. In this particular case, Stu was the black pebbles and Jamie the white.

"Hey," I said and Stu's attention fell on me. His eyes traced my body then focused intently on my face. I flushed, feeling like he could tell from my expression what I'd just been up to. He stared a long moment, his eyes dark and heated, but that could've just been because of what had transpired between us earlier.

"Andrea, it seems I've finally found a worthy opponent," said Jamie, smiling from ear to ear. He always loved a challenge. "Stuart here is quite the natural."

I looked at Stu. "You've never played before?"

He shook his head. "No."

"In that case you're doing incredibly well."

176

His lips curved into a smile while Jamie's attention returned to the board, pondering his next move.

I tugged on the end of my sleeve as Stu continued to study me. "You okay?" he asked.

I nodded, perhaps a little too fervently. "Of course, why wouldn't I be?"

It took him a moment to answer. "You look . . . flushed."

"It's just the weather. I'm fine," I said, waving him off.

"So, Stuart," said Jamie, and I was relieved he decided to speak if only to divert Stu's attention away from me, "do you mind if I ask about your time in prison? I have to admit I'm morbidly curious."

Obviously, my relief was short-lived. This was typical Jamie. The man had been born without a filter.

"Maybe some other time," said Stu, shifting uncomfortably in his seat.

"Oh, don't be shy. I've had a few run-ins with the law myself over the years. I knew all those unreturned library books would catch up with me eventually," he joked.

"How about I make us all something to drink?" I said in an effort to change the subject. "Anybody thirsty?"

"I'll take a juice," said Alfie, not moving his eyes from his work.

"Sure, whatever you have is fine," said Jamie with a smile.

"I'll help you," Stu offered, about to get up from his seat but I waved him off.

"You stay and continue your game. I'll only be a minute."

When I returned with four glasses of orange juice the men were in the middle of a conversation that had Stu saying to Jamie, "Come on, even you have to admit she's sexy."

I paused by the door, not entering yet because I wanted them to continue talking and suspected they'd stop if I came in, like a domestic version of the 'waiter pause'.

Jamie's eyes glinted with mischief as he answered pointedly, "Well, everything else aside, being that I fancy men, I'm not exactly her target audience."

A small moment of awkward silence fell before Stu spoke. "Ah, right. Didn't pick up on that."

"Not your fault," Jamie went on. "People can rarely tell. I'm more Rock Hudson gay than Liberace gay."

Alfie scoffed, his paintbrush held in mid-air as he shot Jamie a look. "That's a laugh. You're Oscar Wilde gay and we all know it.

Jamie gave him a playful glance. "Well, at least I'm not Alan Turing gay."

"Hey now, be nice," Alfie frowned. "Our intelligence might be matched, but don't curse me to poor Turing's fate."

"You're right, that was mean," Jamie allowed.

"So you're both . . ." Stu cut in, his words falling short.

"Raving homosexuals?" Jamie provided. "Why yes, dear."

I stifled a laugh at him calling Stu 'dear' and stepped over the threshold into the room. As suspected, all conversation hushed when I entered. I still wondered who Stu had been referring to as 'sexy' but it wasn't like I had the nerve to ask. After handing out the refreshments I took a seat on Alfie's bed, while Jamie and Stu returned their focus to the board game.

I looked around, realising that I never really spent much time in Alfie's room if I wasn't there to provide a critical eye for his art. It was a lot bigger than mine, but I let him have it because he worked from home. All I really needed was a bed and somewhere to store my clothes and I was happy. My attention fell on the stack of paintings in the corner, more specifically the one at the top. Alfie had painted me numerous times in the past, but this one I'd never seen before.

I sat with my legs crossed at the water's edge at my parents' holiday home in Lake Windermere. The painting was based on a picture they'd taken when I visited with them almost two years ago. My hair hung long down my back as I stared out at the water, my face in profile.

"Stuart was just admiring that one," said Jamie, his voice breaking me from my thoughts.

"Oh," I breathed, eyes going to Stu, "you were?"

He shrugged, actually looking embarrassed, but that couldn't be right. "Yeah, it's . . . nice."

"Oh, come now," Jamie tsked. "You said it was a little more than nice just a minute ago."

I blushed as realisation hit me. Had Stu been calling *me* sexy? I'd been so twisted up over the idea of him faking his attraction just to get to Alfie, but what happened in my room earlier wasn't fake. It had been too raw, too messy and spontaneous to not be real.

I sipped on my orange juice, trying not to blush. Every once in a while, I felt Stu's eyes on me, but I didn't look at him. I was too edgy, too needful. If I looked at him now I'd be liable to jump him in front of both my cousin and one of my closest friends. After a couple of minutes, I excused myself to go and finish correcting my papers. The men were far too ensconced in their activities to notice me leaving, and I breathed a sigh of relief to have some distance from Stu.

I felt so conflicted around him.

On the one hand, I was incredibly attracted to him, both physically and cerebrally. He was gorgeous to look at and, more often than not I liked how his mind worked. But on the other hand, his past was so incredibly different to mine, the circles he moved in unnerved me, and the fact that he entered my life with dishonest intentions was cause for concern. In fact, no, it was a whole lot more than just that, but my feelings of lust seemed to be mingling with my anger, making it incredibly difficult to figure out how I felt at all, really.

Over an hour passed and none of them had yet to emerge from Alfie's bedroom. I knew how absorbing the board game could be, and imagined Jamie was relishing the challenge Stu presented. His natural talent for the game showed his tactical aptitude, which was yet more proof of my theory about different kinds of intelligence. Stu might struggle reading books and completing written assignments, but he was leaps and bounds ahead of the pack in other areas.

When I returned to Alfie's room my cousin was lying on the bed, his arm thrown over his face and his breathing deep and even. I would've thought he was asleep if it weren't for the way he was mumbling to himself, something about finding the right shade of blue-black. The painting wasn't anywhere near finished, but I could definitely see it taking shape.

"Did you know that Go dates back over five thousand years?" asked Jamie while Stu stared at the board, his dark brows drawn together as he contemplated the pebbles. "The first written record of it is contained in an annal dating from the fourth century. Think of the sheer historical significance, the simplicity of a game that is at the same time incredibly complex. It's quite fascinating."

"You talk a lot," said Stu, casting him an irritated look. "And I know what you're doing. I've got the edge and you're bricking it. You're trying to make me lose my concentration."

Jamie shot him a look like butter wouldn't melt. "Why, I'd never dream of doing such a thing."

Stu smirked and shook his head, finally reaching for a pebble and making his move. Jamie swore loudly and Alfie chuckled, sitting up from his reclining position.

"You lost. I can't believe it."

"Oh hush," said Jamie. "I'm well aware of Stu's victory. No need to rub it in."

"Yes, but this is definitely a first. We should take a picture."

"No thank you, Alfred. There's absolutely no need for photographic evidence of me losing to a novice."

"I'm kinda regretting not putting some money down," said Stu smugly. I smiled to myself, because it was nice to see him happily interacting with two of the most important people in my life.

"I was thinking of ordering in some pizza. Anybody want some?" I asked and was met with three resounding yeses. Even Jamie appeared soothed by the prospect of bread and melted cheese. I went to place the order while the others congregated in the living room. As I was setting out plates and cups Stu came up behind me, lowering his mouth to my ear.

"I can't stop thinking about you."

"You could've fooled me. I thought you might've forgotten my existence you were so absorbed in your board game," I teased.

"It wasn't like that. I needed a distraction," he answered quietly, his hand going to my stomach and gently caressing. "Didn't like leaving you like that though."

I turned my head a little. "Like what?"

"All horny and gorgeous. Such a fucking waste."

His husky whisper made me tremble as I recalled that my arousal didn't exactly go to waste. But no way was I telling him about that.

"What are you thinking about?"

I shrugged. "Nothing."

"Don't lie. Your head went someplace just now. Where was it?"

I was blushing bright red. "Honestly, you're imagining things." I twisted out of his hold and walked to the other side of the kitchen to grab some knives and forks. Not that we needed them. Nobody ate pizza with utensils. What I needed was distance.

Stu caught me by the wrist just as I set them on the counter, twirling me back around to face him. His eyes traced my features as he took hold of my chin so I couldn't turn away again. After a moment I knew he saw the truth because he swore under his breath.

"Fucking *hell*."

His head dropped to my shoulder, where he seemed to take a few calming breaths. The next time he looked at me his eyes were dark and full of sin. "Do you have any idea what I would've given to see that, Andrea?" he whispered huskily. "God, I can just imagine you with that gorgeous hair spread across the pillow, your hand between your legs, making yourself come just for me."

Every pore on my body drew tight, his words plunging me into a moment of desire and unleashed need. I opened my mouth to say something, another denial most likely, when the front door buzzed. The pizza was here and I was literally saved by the bell.

Fifteen

Stu left shortly after we finished the pizza. I was touched when he insisted on paying the delivery man, especially considering he was probably just as broke as I was. Throughout the meal he barely took his eyes off me, causing my skin to prickle with awareness. Alfie and Jamie chattered away about the Go tournament Jamie planned to host at his shop in a few weeks' time.

The following day at work was a nightmare, not because any of my students were acting out, but because of Stu. I could feel his eyes caressing, stroking, worshipping every inch of my skin without a single touch.

It was exhilarating and nerve wracking all at once.

As soon as it was time for the mid-morning break, I left to use the bathroom and my students went in search of tea and coffee as per usual. The college had a small coffee stand in the lobby, alongside several vending machines. Most people preferred to get it fresh from the stand, but often the queue took forever.

On my way back from the staff bathroom I glanced up. Stu was walking towards me, determination in his gait. I barely had time to react when he took my hands and pulled me into the nearest open doorway. As luck would have it, the door led to a small filing room that one of the caretakers must've left open.

"How long until break is over?" he asked breathlessly, his mouth at my neck as he began kissing his way up to my earlobe.

I lifted my hand, glanced at my watch and replied, "About seven and a half minutes."

I felt his smile rather than saw it. "I can work with that."

"What—"

"Hush. Let me do this. I've been thinking about you all morning."

There weren't any windows and the lights were off. A small sliver of daylight trickled through the gap between the door and wall, but it didn't illuminate much. Still, I understood Stu's intention when he knelt before me, his hands going to the waist of my jeans. I caught his deft fingers in mine, preventing their movement.

"Stop. We can't," I whispered, my heart hammering at the idea of being caught. I was well aware of how wrong this was, of how being with Stu broke the rules of my employment. But being with him in the moment felt so good and the pleasure made me weak. He made me forget myself and that was scary. *I'd never felt this way before.*

Stu stared up at me, his features still so handsome even in the dark. "If you really want me to stop, I will," he said, leaning in and pressing his face to my crotch. I stifled a moan at the foreign yet blissful sensation. His eyes met mine again as he continued to nuzzle me, "Tell. Me. To. Stop."

I sighed and slouched back into the wall, helpless to resist. Stu's deep chuckle hit me right in the pit of my stomach. His hands returned to my waistband, undoing the fly and pulling my jeans down to mid-thigh. I really should've worn a skirt today. All thought fled my mind when Stu pressed his mouth to my underwear, moving his lips and creating a pleasurable wet heat.

He slid my knickers to the side, moving a finger teasingly down my centre.

"Seven minutes," I reminded him breathily and he chuckled some more.

"So bossy, Miss Anderson," he chided, clicking his tongue before diving in and doing something . . . else . . . with . . . it. He sucked my clit into his mouth and my hand went to his shoulder to steady myself. For the first time in my life my knees felt too weak to hold my body up.

"How fast do you think I can make you come?" he asked, his voice laced with arousal. Pressing his mouth to me, he sucked again and I wanted to scream. What he did to me felt so good, but at the same I was aware of how close we were to the classroom. My students would be making their way back any minute and if anyone discovered us I'd be fired on the spot.

Fear was a heady thing, it seemed.

I hardly recognised myself from the rule-following person I usually was. It was concerning *and* liberating.

Stu circled my clit with his tongue, applying the perfect amount of pressure. He pulled one leg from my jeans and lifted my thigh, my ballet flat falling off in the process. Then he slid my thigh over his shoulder so he could go deeper. He sank two fingers inside me and I cried out, unable to hold it in. My heart pounded, wondering if somebody passing by had heard.

"You've no idea how sexy you look right now," Stu growled. "Come for me, Andrea."

I gasped when the movement of his fingers sped up, his tongue matching the pace as he built to a mind-numbingly pleasurable crescendo. I gripped his shoulder, fisting his T-shirt and biting my lip to prevent any more noises from escaping.

Stu made a humming sound in the back of his throat, his eyes alight with desire, like he was enjoying the act far more than I was. I came with a harsh intake of breath, pleasure gripping me as Stu wrung out every last tremor.

He kissed my sex, then nuzzled my inner thigh, humming his appreciation yet again.

"So fucking sexy," he said, his grin wicked as he teased me. "That was quick, too. Think we might have broken a record."

I was shivering all over, still on a high. Stu lifted the hem of his T-shirt, revealing a set a toned abs that I couldn't take my eyes off. When I met his gaze he was still grinning as he used the fabric to wipe his mouth. The action combined with the eye contact was oddly arousing. I lowered my leg from his shoulder, my limbs pure jelly, and quickly pulled my underwear and jeans back up. Glancing at my watch I noted we were a minute or two late. Not the end of the world, but it was going to look suspicious if we both arrived back at the same time.

"You go," said Stu. "I'll follow in a few minutes. Just try not to punish me too hard for being late."

I swatted his arm and laughed softly. He caught my chin and pulled my lips in for a kiss. I tasted myself on his tongue, something I never thought I'd find sexy but I did. When he let me up for air he gave me playful slap on the arse as I stepped into the hallway.

All of a sudden I was nervous again, glancing left and right to make sure nobody saw me exiting the file room. I had just enough time to pay a quick visit to the bathroom to clean myself up and then hurried back to class. My students sat around chatting, barely noticing my lateness. I approached my desk and sat down, calling for them to settle as I brought up the history lesson I planned last night. We were studying the French Revolution and the rise of Napoleon.

I'd started a discussion in the class's Facebook group, so I had the page up on my laptop. When the door opened and Stu entered, Susan immediately piped up, "Well, would you look who it is, Johnny-come-lately. I think you should give him detention for tardiness, Miss Anderson."

I shot her a smile. "If I give Stu detention for being late, then I'll also have to give you detention for being a smart-arse."

Susan smirked and made a show of zipping her lips while Stu took his usual seat. When our eyes met I flushed. I could smell him on me, could still taste myself on my lips from his kiss. It felt a little obscene, yet my skin tingled all over.

I focused on the lesson, trying not to look Stu's way as much as possible. The man had just made me come with his mouth and fingers. How was I going to avoid looking at him when all I wanted was more?

Things quietened down when I handed out some assignment questions for everybody to work on. When I returned to my seat I saw a conversation window had popped up with a message from Stu. My heart skipped a beat.

Stu Cross: Ur beautiful.

My eyes instinctively lifted and I found him staring at me, his gaze intense. Flushing even redder now, I tried to think of a response but nothing came to me. He sent another message.

Stu Cross: U taste beautiful 2.

I swallowed thickly, not glancing up this time as I typed a reply.

Andrea Anderson: Stop messaging me.
Stu Cross: Can't help it.
Andrea Anderson: Try.
Stu Cross: Ur blushing.
Andrea Anderson: I'm not.

Stu Cross: 4got how much I loved eating pussy.

I lifted a hand to my neck, self-consciously rubbing my skin as if that was going to help matters. When I looked at Stu this time his head was bent over his laptop as he typed. A moment later I got another message.

Stu Cross: Gonna make u blush everywhere.

Worrying my lip, I felt like everyone in the room was going to know what he was saying to me, somehow figure out what we'd done. I needed to logout so he couldn't message me anymore. Kian was sitting right behind him, and if he saw the conversation I didn't know what I'd do. At the same time, I was struck with the urge to send one final message. I agonised over it for a couple of minutes before finally biting the bullet.

Andrea Anderson: I have feelings for you.

Andrea Anderson: Do you have feelings for me?

The moment I hit *send* I regretted it. I felt like a teenage girl, worrying over whether or not her crush liked her back. The change in me was disconcerting. Just weeks ago I knew who I was. I was a teacher. I was a widow. I'd loved one man with all my heart, and I'd lost him. I'd thought that love was enough for one lifetime, as if *that* part of me was done. But now, everything was changing. I felt new and sad, happy and regretful, excited and guilty. So many overlapping emotions.

Glancing back at my laptop screen, I saw Stu hadn't replied yet and I couldn't bring myself to look his way.

God, this was awful.

Unable to take any more I slammed the device shut and tried to focus on the lesson again. I walked around the room, providing help with the assignment to those who needed it. Not once did I approach Stu, too scared of what I might see.

Pity. Rejection.

This could all just be sexual for him. Basic attraction. On an emotional level he might not feel anything for me at all. At lunch I left the classroom before most of the students, hurrying to my car and hiding there for the rest of the hour. My phone practically taunted me, urging me to check my messages and see if he'd responded. I was too much of a coward though, and instead ate my sandwich and read yesterday's newspaper that I'd left on the back seat.

There was no way I'd emerge from my car until certain there'd be students in my classroom. Sure enough, most of them had returned from lunch, Stu among them. He was chatting with Kian, his back turned to me as I entered. The other students were the buffer I needed. He couldn't say anything in front of them. At least, I hoped he wouldn't.

When the day drew to a close I started to concoct an exit strategy. How could I get out of the classroom without colliding with Stu?

In the end I latched on to Mary and Susan, chatting with them about how they planned to spend their evenings as a method of avoidance. I could practically feel Stu's irritation like a tangible thing, but I continued to ignore him. On the drive home I decided I'd pay my parents a visit and eat dinner at their place. After a quick pit stop at the flat to take a shower and change my clothes, I set out for their place. Alfie was holed up in his room, oblivious to my comings and goings.

"Andrea! What a lovely surprise," said Mum, answering the door to me. She wore a light floral dress and I could tell she'd recently gotten her hair done.

"I hope you don't mind me stopping by."

"Not at all! But you should've brought Alfie with you. I haven't seen him in months."

I gave her an apologetic look. "You know how he is. It's difficult to get him to leave the flat at the best of times, never mind visit family."

Mum frowned, leading me into the kitchen. "Those parents of his really did a number on him."

"Mum!"

"You know I'm right! Madeline was always a very cold woman. And Raymond was even worse, always working, never home, cheating on Madeline with every new floozy that came along," said Mum, lifting the glass of wine she was clearly in the middle of enjoying when I knocked.

I had to admit, I sort of loved it when she went all gossipy. I enjoyed hearing scandalous stories about all my aunts and uncles who had always seemed like such boring, staid grown-ups to me as a kid.

Mum smacked her hand to her head like she just remembered something. "Oh, by the way, your student is here, the one your father's tutoring. They're just inside the study having a lesson now. I invited him to stay for dinner again. He's very handsome, don't you think?" Her eyes sparkled, and I sensed some form of matchmaking in the air.

Little did she know, her efforts weren't needed. Still, the news that Stu was here at the house had my nerves spiralling. Why couldn't I just spend a quiet evening at my parents' house without any emotional entanglements? It was my own fault though. I should've remembered it was this day last week that I first brought Stu over to meet Dad.

"He's my student, Mum," I said as she pulled a glass from the cupboard and poured me some wine.

"Oh sure, but only for another few months. Besides, your dad and I have been worried about you. You're still so young, Andrea," she said, her eyes turning sad as she glanced momentarily at my ring. Most days I forgot it was even there, an unseen comfort blanket. I slid my hand onto my lap, hiding it from her view.

"We all miss Mark very much," Mum went on. I wished she'd stop with the sad eyes, because she was making me sad and I didn't need misery lobbed on top of my already frazzled emotions.

"I miss him, too," I replied quietly, lifting the glass and taking a sip.

Mum studied me, her wise old eyes too perceptive for their own good. Before she could say more, voices sounded from the hallway and a second later Dad and Stu came into the kitchen. I sat by the island, eyes downcast as I tried to think up an excuse to leave. If only Alfie could call me right now with some emergency, I'd love him forever.

"Come in, you two," said Mum. "I hope everybody's in the mood for shepherd's pie."

"Ah, my favourite," Dad exclaimed happily while Stu took the stool beside mine. I didn't have the courage to meet his gaze.

"Would you like a lager, son?" Dad asked. He was big into trying out fancy European brews.

"That'd be great, thanks," said Stu, his voice making my stomach flutter. The memory of him going down on me was still too fresh in my mind.

"How'd the lesson go?" Mum questioned, one leg crossed over the other as she perched on a stool and delicately sipped her wine. My mother was a tiny woman. I'd taken more after my dad's side of the family in that sense.

"Wonderfully," said Dad. "He's coming on in leaps and bounds. Andrea, I've actually been speaking to Stu about applying to one of the undergrad courses at the university. Do you think he'll be able to qualify as a mature student?"

"Sure. There'll be a mountain of forms, and he'll have to pass all his end-of-year exams first, but I don't see why not," I answered, chancing a peek in Stu's direction to find him watching. Yep, still as brooding and darkly handsome as ever.

"You see," Dad went on, spirited, "we'll make a mathematician out of you yet."

"Jim just wants you in the club so you can teach and attract more women into the field," said Mum, and I shot her a look. Seemingly my mother got flirtatious with a glass of wine in her. Stu grinned.

"Hey now. I'm the only hunk in your life," Dad complained jokingly as he went to wrap his arm around Mum's petite shoulders and kiss her cheek. Normally, I found their love for one another endearing, but today I just wasn't in the right frame of mind. Especially with Stu sitting next to me. My phone continued to burn a hole in my pocket. I was still avoiding checking to see if he'd answered my question.

"Okay, you all go sit down and I'll dish up the food," said Mum, waving us over to the dinner table.

"Can we talk later?" Stu whispered while Dad was out of earshot.

I pretended I hadn't heard him. Probably not my finest hour, but it had been yet another in a long line of weird days. Mum carried the plates over, providing me with something else to focus on. Stu and I stayed relatively quiet while my parents chatted away throughout the meal, completely oblivious to the growing tension.

When we finished eating I immediately offered to wash up. Stu looked irritated that I was still avoiding him. And yes, I was being immature, but I was mortified for Christ's sake. I felt like a teenager, wishing I could erase an embarrassing drunken text. The only difference was I'd been stone-cold sober when I sent those messages.

I noticed Stu checking the time before agitatedly running a hand over his jaw. It was clear he had somewhere he needed to be, and I was relieved. He likely had to go soon. To my dismay he stood and followed me to the sink.

"You wash, I'll dry," he grunted, his shoulders knit with tension.

Since Mum and Dad were still in the room he couldn't confront me for avoiding him. Unfortunately, that saving grace was lost when they both retreated to the living room to watch TV.

"What's up with you?" Stu asked once they were gone, his voice all growly.

I turned on the tap, plastering on a neutral expression. "Nothing."

"Are you upset about today? Do you . . . regret it?" he questioned further, his brows furrowed. I turned off the tap, bracing my hands on the edge of the sink.

"Of course not."

"Then why are you being such an ice queen? You barely looked at me in class and even now you're acting strange. Was it the messages? Because I promise, nobody will ever see them. In fact, I'll delete them right now if it'll make you happy."

He started pulling his phone from his pocket. I let out an exasperated breath and twisted to face him. "You don't have to do that. I'm just embarrassed, okay? That's why I'm being weird."

194

He slid his phone back in his jeans as he frowned at me, then his features softened when my meaning sank in. "Luv," he murmured, coming to cup my cheek, "you've absolutely nothing to be embarrassed about. You've got a gorgeous little pussy. I loved every second of having my mouth on it."

"Stu," I gasped. His dirty words made me blush and I glanced shyly at the door, worried Mum or Dad might overhear. The volume was loud on the TV though, so I knew it was unlikely.

I cleared my throat. "Let's, um, let's get these dishes sorted and then we'll talk, okay?"

"Sure, Andrea, whatever you want," Stu replied, dipping down to capture my lips in his. His kiss was brief and I turned back around to focus on the task, my lips tingling the entire time. When we were done we went and said goodbye to Mum and Dad, and I promised them I'd try to convince Alfie to come visit with me next time.

As soon as we were outside Stu grabbed my hand, interlacing our fingers and leading me over to his Toyota. I had no choice but to follow.

Sixteen

"Let's take my car. I'll drive you back in a little bit."

"If you're busy we can do this another time."

Stu's grip tightened. "Nah, we're good. I can multi-task."

He had me strapped into the passenger seat before I had the chance to ask, "Where exactly do you need to be?"

Stu started the engine and pulled away from the kerb, his jaw firm. He actually seemed a little stressed. "I need to do some recon. This is the only time this week I know Renfield's going to be out of his house."

"You're taking me to scope out the house of the man you plan to steal from?" I exclaimed, not happy in the slightest. "Stu, let me out of this car right now. I'm not helping you break into someone's home."

"Relax," he urged, bringing his hand to rest on my thigh. "I'm not breaking in anywhere. I just need to get a feel for the place, see what I'm dealing with. And I want to do it while he's out so there's no chance of anyone spotting me. There's no danger, Andrea. We won't even be getting out of the car."

"How do you know he won't be there?"

"There's some big charity hoopla going on tonight. The Duke told me about it. Said Renfield never misses an event."

"Oh," I breathed, my nerves subsiding a little. If Stu said there was no danger, then I trusted him. In a way it was completely unearned, but it was just how I felt in the moment. I couldn't explain it. "Well, where does he live anyway?"

Stu shot me a grin. "Hampstead 'I'm too rich for my own good' Heath."

I laughed because it was true. I was pretty sure half the celebrities in London lived in Hampstead Heath. A little while later Stu parked his car down the street from a moderately sized Georgian house, though given the location it probably cost as much as a mansion anywhere else. He'd picked a spot shrouded by trees, to avoid security cameras capturing the licence plate on the car.

Killing the engine, he turned to face me. "So, are we gonna talk this out, or what?"

I shifted uncomfortably. "Don't you have some scoping to do?"

"The scoping can wait. I want to know what's bothering you."

"I'm fine, honestly. I was just being weird earlier. If you knew me, you'd realise I'm prone to bouts of weirdness."

Stu squeezed my thigh, his voice warm yet commanding when he said my name. "Andrea."

He wasn't buying my bullshit, I guess. I needed a new tactic. "So, the painting is right in there, huh? Feels weird that we're so close yet so far."

"Luv, stop being an oddball and just talk to me," Stu urged, his patience wearing thin.

"I'm not being an oddball. I'm just marvelling at the fact that we're mere yards away from countless stolen antiquities. I wonder if he has any Ancient Egyptian artefacts in there. I've always been fascinated by hieroglyphics."

"Right, that's it," said Stu, reaching over and unclipping my seatbelt. I yelped when he gripped me by the waist, lifted me up and placed me firmly on his lap. I scrambled to escape but it was no use. He was far stronger. The only exercise my muscles ever got was lifting coffee mugs and holding up paperbacks for prolonged periods as I read.

Before I knew it he had me straddling him, his warm hands gripping each of my thighs to hold me in place. "Now, let's talk," he said, his tone commanding.

I swallowed when his hands started moving slowly back and forth, caressing me. A tendril of desire coiled tight in my belly at the simple motion.

"This isn't the best position for a casual chat."

"Nothing casual about us. Now talk."

"I told you, I'm embarrassed," I said, eyes downcast.

"Because of what we did at the college."

I shook my head. "Not just that."

"Then what?"

"The message," I mumbled shyly.

Stu let out a breath and lifted a hand to snag my chin. He pulled me forward and pressed a soft kiss on my lips. "Now why the fuck would you be embarrassed about that? Never be embarrassed about telling your man how you feel, Andrea. I fucking love that shit."

I gaped at him, his words making my chest ache.

Your man.

"What?"

"I said," he enunciated, "I fucking *love* that shit. I love that you have feelings for me. Do you have any idea how frustrating it is? I have to sit feet away from you every day, listen to you speak, witness you be patient and caring to every single person in that class, even though if you ask me, there are some who don't deserve it. Every day you're deeper under my skin, and I have no clue how deep I am under yours."

His thumb came up to brush my lips, and I trembled at both his touch and his declaration. "You're under my skin,

Stu. I think you have been since the first day you stepped foot in my class."

He stared up at me, his thumb still whispering back and forth over my lips, his other hand inching closer and closer to my inner thigh. His features were softer now, almost like my words were a relief to hear.

"Can I tell you something?" he asked, his voice low. I nodded and his thumb briefly skimmed the inside of my mouth. I wanted to sigh, because it made me think of other acts, things I wanted to do to him.

"When I got out my brothers took me to a strip club. In the past I would've been over the fucking moon," he admitted and I smiled a little. "But that night I felt so numb. Everything about the place depressed me. I felt like I was broken, that there must've been something about my experience in prison that killed that part of me. Aside from being with my family and the need to take care of them, everything else seemed empty. I was determined to get this job done for the Duke so I could finally be free of my past and just focus on what mattered. But women? Yeah, I could take or leave them."

"It's no surprise that prison changed you," I whispered. "I can't imagine what it must've been like."

"It was shit, but I'm used to shit," said Stu. "It wasn't the harshness; I could deal with that. In fact, being behind bars is probably more real than life outside. We're stripped down to our baser natures—dog eat dog. It's a lot more honest that the shifty bullshit that goes on in the outside world, people hiding behind their money, behind computers, behind the façade of decency. I hated everyone, hated the cowardice.

"The thing about having experienced prison is that you come out and you start thinking everyone else should have to experience it, too, and not because they need to be punished, but because they're all so soft it's scary. If society ever broke down they'd be the first ones to go. But then, I walked into your class, totally focused and prepared to use you, and you changed my mind."

"How?" I whispered, my eyes flickering back and forth between his. I got the feeling Stu wasn't ever this open, not even with his brothers. He was always so self-contained that I didn't think being vulnerable before someone else would even be on his radar.

"You made me realise that softness is necessary. That we need both. People who are kind and who help others are needed, but so are people who are hard, toughened by experience. If everyone was like me, the world would be a shitty place. We'd all just be starting fights and kicking the crap out of one another. People like you give people like me a soft place to fall. Otherwise we'd just be cold and hard. That's how I was before I met you."

My heart clenched, the honesty and emotion in his words hitting me right in the chest.

Leaning forward, I kissed him, because I couldn't find the right thing to say.

"Nobody's ever seen me like you do," Stu went on, whispering now. "Not even my brothers."

"You see me, too," I replied, my voice shaky. "Like no one else does. What you just said means everything."

We stared into each other's eyes for a long moment, my need for him building by the second. The front seat of his car was too small a space to contain us and I felt just about ready to burst.

Stu shifted his body, reaching down and pulling his phone from his pocket. The movement caused a friction between us that made my breath whoosh out. He smirked knowingly and swiped his thumb across the screen. A second later he held it up to me.

"Here."

I took the phone and glanced down, seeing our conversation from earlier, only this time there was a response to my question.

Stu Cross: Yeah. 2 many feelings, luv.

The simple answer made my chest ache. I felt so raw and exposed, yet relieved and overjoyed at the same time. Slipping the phone back to him, I pressed my lips to his, kissing him with a renewed hunger. This situation was far from perfect, but it was real.

Stu Cross made me feel alive. So much so that it took him coming into my life to make me realise I hadn't been living. I'd been imprisoned in the past, hiding behind a future that was lost to me.

The kiss grew hungrier, our lips seeking, tongues colliding. Then a loud noise made me jump back and bang my head on the roof of the car. Stu chuckled and pulled me to him, rubbing the top of my head as I grimaced. The noise had been two cats having a fight, hissing and mewling at one another behind the trees.

"Come here," Stu murmured, pulling me back to him and pressing his mouth to my temple. We stayed like that for a few minutes, quiet. Stu ran his hands up and down my back, dipping lower and lower each time. It was odd, but I felt at peace. Here we were, more or less on a stakeout. It was the least likely place to feel comforted, but he just made me feel safe.

I could tell he was still alert, still watching the house even as he held me. I wondered what he saw, if there was anything that suggested this job wasn't worth taking the risk. In my heart of hearts, I really wished for him to back out, to tell the Duke he couldn't be blackmailed. But I knew he wouldn't. There were more people at stake here than just us. And for better or worse, we were in this together now.

"I won't be in class on Wednesday," said Stu, breaking me from my thoughts.

I pulled back to look at him. "Why not?"

"Got a meeting with Renfield at his place," he answered, nodding to the house. "I'll have to convince him I'm the real deal."

I frowned, not liking the sound of that. "On your own?"

He nodded, his expression deceptively blank. I'd come to recognise it as a sign he was uneasy.

Stu stroked a hand down my hair. "No other choice, Andrea."

I studied him a moment, taking in his features and feeling a sudden burst of protectiveness. "I'll come with you," I blurted.

Now Stu was the one frowning. "You will not."

I stroked his dark hair away from his forehead. "I'm not letting you go alone."

"Oh yes, you are. And anyway, he's only expecting me. If I show up with some bird on my arm it's only going to look suspicious."

"Hey," I said, suppressing a smile, "I'd prefer it if you didn't refer to me as 'some bird', thank you very much."

Stu gave me a sexy smirk. "Yeah, you're right. You're too classy for that."

"My point exactly. My fine breeding will see you well when you meet with Renfield. I'll bring an air of sophistication to the dealings," I said, only half joking.

He studied me now, and I could tell he was considering it. "You know what, you've actually got a point there."

"So you'll let me come?" I asked, hopeful. I knew it wasn't a good idea putting myself in harm's way, but I cared too much for Stu now. I needed to be there to make sure nothing bad happened. Just because this Renfield lived in a fancy house in a wealthy neighbourhood, didn't make him a good person. And I couldn't help hearing Stu's earlier words. *People like you give people like me a soft place to fall. Otherwise we'd just be cold and hard.* I wanted to be his soft place, his *safe* place, more than I wanted anything else.

Amid all my attempts to the contrary, my heart had latched on to Stu and I cared about him too much to let him go it alone.

He let out a long, exasperated sigh. "Yeah, Andrea, even though I know I'm probably going to regret it, you can come."

Seventeen

"So, remind me again. Where exactly did Jamie get these clothes?" I asked Alfie as I studied myself in the mirror. I wore a tight black pencil skirt and a white blouse, courtesy of Jamie, oddly enough. I hadn't found anything suitable in my wardrobe to wear to the meeting with Renfield.

"He dressed up as Dita Von Tease for Halloween last year," Alfie explained, like it was the most normal thing in the world.

"What?" I chuckled. "How did I not know about this?"

"You were visiting your parents."

"And what about the wig? Doesn't Dita Von Tease have black hair?"

"Oh yeah, the wig was from the year beforehand," Alfie informed me casually. "Sandra Dee."

I sputtered a laugh of disbelief. How had I not realised that Jamie was so fond of dressing up as a woman? And there was me thinking he was eccentric for wearing a three-piece suit on a regular basis. I straightened out the blonde wig, then went to collect the blue contact lenses I'd picked up from a nearby pharmacy yesterday. Pulling my eyelids back, I quickly popped them in, having taken lessons on how to do it from the girl at the pharmacy. *Can't say I'd want to put contacts in every day.* Once finished, I studied myself in the mirror. My transformation was complete.

"You look weird," said Alfie, taking in my altered appearance.

"Weird good or weird bad?" I asked, anxiety kicking in. Why had I volunteered to do this again? Right. Because I was an idiot.

"Weird good. The contacts and the wig look surprisingly natural, but I still think this is a terrible idea. If

Renfield cottons on, then the entire plan goes out the window, and you can kiss goodbye to being debt free."

I'd told Alfie a bit of a white lie. He thought Stu needed me with him to pose as his business partner. That I didn't have another choice. My cousin was still entirely oblivious to my newly developed feelings for my student. It only added an extra layer of anxiety to my already frazzled nerves. He was going to blow a gasket when he eventually found out.

"What did you tell Jamie I needed the outfit for?" I asked, a little dismayed by the fact that everything fit me perfectly. Either I was big boned or Jamie had decidedly feminine measurements. I hoped for the latter.

"I said you'd been invited to a fancy dress party for a work colleague's birthday and wanted to go as Blondie. Don't worry, he doesn't suspect anything untoward. No offence, but we don't exactly come across as hardened criminals."

Well, he was right there. I swiped on some red-tinted lip gloss just before there was a knock at the door. Sliding on my black heels, which I thankfully already owned and didn't have to borrow from Jamie (a woman needs to keep some dignity), I went to answer the door. When I did my breath caught because Stu stood on the doorstep, looking like an Armani model. Just like me, he'd undergone a transformation in the hopes of not being recognised further down the line should the robbery go south.

Stu wore a fitted navy blue suit, white shirt, a slim black tie and horn-rimmed glasses.

Actually, I take back the Armani model comment. He looked like a spy from the fifties, a very, very sexy spy.

"Um," I said, looking him over as I chewed on my lip, "come in."

"Andrea?" Stu asked, taking in the wig and the contacts, and well, the entire outfit really. "You look . . . you don't look like you."

"That's the intention."

"Is it weird that I'm a little bit turned on?" His grin was wicked.

"Yes, very weird," I said past a nervous chuckle as a flutter went through me.

"Well, I am. I didn't expect your disguise to be so . . . believable."

"Some of us decided to put more of an effort in than using the old Clark Kent trick," I teased as he stepped inside the flat, his chest brushing mine in the narrow doorway. I glanced over his shoulder, surprised to see a silver BMW SUV parked outside.

"Is that yours?" I asked, gaping at the car.

"Nah, called in a favour from a friend. Need to return it by five. It's just for appearance's sake. Renfield will be expecting someone with money."

"Oh."

Stu smirked. "You like it?"

"Um, yeah."

Now he winked. "If we have time later I'll take you for a little spin."

My cheeks heated at the insinuation as I led him into the living room where Alfie waited.

"Somebody scrubs up well," he said, eyeing Stu, almost as surprised as I'd been. A brief thought struck me. *Did Alfie find Stu attractive?* I realised that even after all these years, I had no idea what his type was. Though in fairness, Stu Cross in a suit had to be everybody's type.

Okay, so maybe I was a tad biased.

"Right so, let's get this straight. You two get in and out quickly, no sticking around for a glass of five-hundred-pound Scotch after the meeting. In fact, don't accept any alcohol whatsoever. I know how these types operate. They'll be plying you with vodka, all the while there's water in their glass, and you're telling them all your secrets."

"Don't worry," said Stu, glancing at himself in the mirror over the mantelpiece. "I'm not Freddy McGonagall. I know what I'm doing."

"Freddy Mcwho?" asked Alfie, puzzled.

"Freddy McGonagall was my cellmate. Also Britain's dumbest criminal, though in fairness, he was a junkie at the time, so you can't really blame him for the dumb part."

"What was his crime?" I asked, strangely curious.

Stu scratched at his stubble. "He used to take out low-end hits to pay for his drugs. Set out to do a job high as a kite, took a bloody taxi to the location, boasting to the driver all the way there that he was going to kill some well-known gunrunner. In the end they got him from fingerprints on the bullets. Silly prick loads up his revolver with his bare hands then slips on a pair of leather gloves afterwards, wouldn't want to leave any evidence, after all."

"Oh my God, that's so tragic it's almost funny," said Alfie.

"World's full of 'em." Stu sighed.

"Yes well, we'd better get going," I cut in, glancing at the clock.

I was antsy to get a move on, even if we ended up arriving early. Really, I just wanted to get the whole thing over and done with. Stu approached me, his gaze soft as he lifted his hand as though to cup my cheek and ease my anxiety. Instinctively I stepped away to avoid it, conscious that Alfie was still in the room. Stu frowned, a brief look of frustration marking his features.

"After you," he said, voice tight as he gestured for me to lead the way. I grabbed my handbag and went outside, the cool air soothing my frazzled nerves.

"Sorry about that," I apologised when he opened the passenger side door of the BMW for me. "Alfie doesn't know about us yet, and I'm not ready to tell him."

"No worries," Stu replied stiffly.

My gut sank at the realisation that I'd hurt his feelings. He started driving and I just wanted to climb astride him and kiss him until he forgave me. A pity it'd ruin my makeup. I pulled open the overhead mirror to check my appearance, unable to remember the last time I'd worn so much foundation and eyeliner. It was good though. I looked like a completely different person, unrecognisable from my usual self.

"Stop fussing. You look perfect. Do you remember our story?"

I nodded. "Yes. I'm the business manager, you're the hands on the ground, as it were."

"Exactly. Anyway, just let me do most of the talking. If we're lucky, Renfield will be too distracted by how tight your blouse is to realise the bullshit I'm peddling." Now he shot me a smirk, and I was relieved he wasn't still pissed at me. "Let's just hope he prefers blondes."

"Don't all men?"

Stu shook his head, his expression heating. "Like brunettes myself, always have."

I blushed and focused on the road ahead. When we arrived at Renfield's my nerves really kicked in. *How was Stu so calm?* I found an unopened bottle of mineral water in the glove compartment and knocked back a long gulp. Stu squeezed my knee.

"You're going to be fine," he murmured, his deep voice reassuring me more than anything else could.

We exited the car and approached the house, where we had to be buzzed in. What I assumed was the modern-day version of a butler opened the door to us, wearing a dapper suit with a red tie.

"Mr Kennedy and Miss Jordan," the butler greeted in an overly posh accent, using the fake names we'd given. "Mr Renfield has been expecting you."

"How do," said Stu, cheekily tipping his imaginary top hat to the guy. Was he seriously taking the piss right now? The butler just about managed to hide his displeasure. I shot Stu a wide glance but he only winked at me. Then I got it. This was exactly how he should be acting. After all, if we were making jokes then we couldn't possibly be nervous, right? Couldn't possibly have anything to hide.

We were led into a large study, the walls lined with bookshelves. Renfield stood from his chair and came to shake our hands. I didn't know what I'd been expecting, but he looked very normal, like any ordinary fifty-something-year-old man on the street. Though his clothes were clearly expensive.

"Mr Kennedy," he said, shaking with Stu. "And Miss Jordan, it really is a pleasure to meet you both."

Stu and I spoke simultaneously.

"It's a pleasure to meet you, too."

"Likewise."

A moment of awkwardness ensued, Renfield glancing between us. I plastered on an expression as if to say, *happens all the time*, and our host quickly moved things along.

"Please, take a seat. Can I offer either of you a drink? A little tipple, maybe?"

I shared a quick look with Stu, both of us remembering Alfie's warning.

"No, thank you," I declined, plastering on a bland smile.

"Yeah, I'm good, too. But thanks," said Stu.

"Well then, I suppose we should get down to business," Renfield declared, clasping his hands together. "Miss Jordan, I believe you'll be taking care of planning the transportation and route, while Mr Kennedy here will be doing the groundwork. Now, I have it on good authority that you're both the best in the field, but can I please have full disclosure? Have there ever been any hiccups in the past? I only ask because the cargo I wish to have transported is very precious to me and I want to know of any possible issues in advance so we can plan to avoid them."

"We're generally fine leaving the port. It's arriving at Port Klang and transferring onto the next ship where the trouble could come in. I've got men on both ships, and a friend at customs in Dubai who'll grant me clearance," said Stu.

"We've completed over fifty transfers to the United Arab Emirates in the past two years," I felt compelled to add. "All of them without a hitch."

Renfield's attention came to me, his shrewd gaze taking me in, and I immediately regretted opening my mouth. "Forgive me, but you look vaguely familiar, Miss Jordan. Have we met before?"

I tensed, unsure where this was coming from. We definitely hadn't met before. Either it was an interrogation technique or in my current guise I resembled someone he knew.

"I don't believe so," I answered.

"Are you quite sure? Your accent is from Surrey, correct? I have a lot of acquaintances in that area. Perhaps our paths have crossed at some soiree or other."

I gave a soft laugh, though it was completely fake. "Perhaps."

"Who's to say when libations have been taken, am I right?" Renfield chuckled. I sort of wanted to laugh at his use of 'libations' in regular conversation. The only time I ever came across that word was when I was reading the classics.

"I can hardly remember my own name, never mind the folks I've met after one too many glasses of wine," he went on, obviously finding himself completely hilarious. Stu's eyebrow rose slightly.

"Oh, I've been there myself a time or two," I said, humouring him.

Renfield smiled at me widely, his face taking on a look of interest that I didn't immediately recognise. It was only when his eyes travelled along my breasts, lingering on my hips that I realised he was checking me out. Stu glanced between us, seemingly coming to the same conclusion. His posture stiffened.

Renfield leaned forward slightly. "Tell me, Miss Jordan, do you enjoy art?"

"Oh, very much so."

"Do you have a favourite artist, or a favourite style, perhaps?"

"I'm quite fond of the impressionists, Cezanne in particular, though technically he was a post-impressionist," I answered.

211

"Ah yes, when it comes to the impressionists I'm a purist, I'm afraid. It's Monet all the way," said Renfield, laughing boisterously. I chuckled and feigned amusement. Stu was staying strangely silent, and I could've been mistaken but I thought he was a little irritated at how Renfield was flirting with me.

"Are you a fan of cubism? I have a Picasso in my collection that I'd love to show you sometime."

"Oh," I said, pretending to be flattered, "that would be amazing."

"Is that one of the pieces you want us to transport?" Stu asked, his voice holding a note of derision. I stiffened, hoping Renfield didn't pick up on it.

"No, no, the Picasso will be travelling with me. The purchase of that piece was all above board. It's my other more precious cargo that I'll be entrusting you with," he answered, his gaze almost dismissive. When he looked back at me he was smiling again, all charm. "Now, might we discuss the matter of payment? I know, such a pesky topic when we could be chatting about our beloved artists, but I would like to come to an agreement on a figure."

"Of course," I answered as he picked up a pen and a piece of paper and scribbled something down. He slid it across the table to me. I picked it up and tried not to gape at the sum. He was going to pay us one hundred thousand pounds, or more specifically, he'd be paying whoever Stu convinced to do the job. Our money would be coming from the eventual sale of the painting.

I wondered why the Duke didn't plan to take any of Renfield's other pieces, but then, that was the beauty of the con. Rembrandt was probably the only artist in his collection that Alfie could successfully imitate, their styles being so similar. Renfield would probably never discover that the painting he owned was a fake, and if he did it could be years down the line.

I passed the paper to Stu and he nodded. "Looks about right."

"Wonderful," said Renfield. "Now, are you sure you both won't join me in a drink to toast a successful arrangement?"

"I'll take a whiskey if you have it," said Stu and I resisted the urge to nudge him and remind him of Alfie's warning. There was a calculation in his eyes, though, which led me to believe the drink was purposeful. Renfield's attention came to me, that flirtatious grin back in place. "And you, Miss Jordan?" he asked expectantly.

"She'll have a whiskey, too," Stu answered for me. I wanted to grimace because I hated dark liquors, but I didn't want to kick up a fuss and continued smiling my false smile. Renfield opened his cabinet, pulling out three glasses alongside an expensive-looking bottle of Scotch. He poured some for each of us and we toasted before taking a sip.

Ugh, I didn't care how much it cost, it tasted disgusting. Where was a spittoon when you needed one?

"By the way, Miss Jordan, or can I call you Rebecca?" Renfield enquired, sidling up to me. He was several inches shorter, but unlike most men he seemed pleased by the fact. Over his shoulder I saw Stu shooting him a narrowed-eyed glare, lifting his glass to his mouth and knocking it all back before discreetly pouring himself another. Since Renfield was so focused on me he didn't notice. I widened my eyes infinitesimally to try and urge him to act normal.

"Of course you can," I replied.

"And you can call me Kenneth," he continued. "Rebecca, the offer to view my Picasso still stands. In fact,

I'd like to take you out to dinner sometime, too. What do you say?"

I opened my mouth, then closed it, trying to come up with a polite way to decline.

In the end I didn't have to because Stu spoke for me, pointing his glass in the direction of my wedding ring. "She's married."

Damn, he really needed to stop sounding so angry or this whole meeting was going to go belly up pretty quickly.

"My apologies," Renfield exclaimed. "I didn't realise. Since you go by 'Miss' I just assumed—"

"No, it's my fault. I'm newly married, and I still haven't gotten used the whole 'Mrs' thing yet," I joked. "I'm sure it'll stick eventually."

"Yes, yes, let's hope," said Renfield, tipping his glass to his mouth with a vague look of disappointment. This was *so* weird.

Renfield left my side and went to return the Scotch bottle to the cabinet. While his back was turned Stu plucked my still-full glass from my hand and downed it in one. When he was done he gave it back to me, and I had to admit I was impressed by his ability to down it so quickly. I was also glad not to have to drink it myself.

When Renfield brought his attention back to us I placed my empty glass down on the table and thanked him for the delicious drink.

"It really has been a pleasure to meet you," I said.

"We'll be in touch with dates and times for the transportation," said Stu as Renfield led us to the door.

"Very well. And it was a pleasure to meet you both, too. Rebecca, if you ever get bored with that husband of yours, you know where to find me," he said, casting a final appreciative glance my way. It made me feel a little ill, if I was being honest, and it wasn't until we got to the car that I felt like I could breathe again.

Eighteen

Stu pulled away from the house as I undid the first two buttons on my blouse, feeling too hot. I also leaned forward, using the overhead mirror as I carefully removed my contact lenses, because they'd started to itch. After that we were quiet for a couple of minutes and my nerves slowly subsided.

"I can't believe we pulled that off," I said finally.

He didn't respond, his jaw firm as he stared dead ahead. I thought maybe he was just trying to concentrate on driving, but then I noticed the stiff line of his shoulders and the way he fisted the steering wheel.

"Stu, are you all right?"

It took him a moment to answer. "Pervy old bastard had his eyes all over you," he grunted.

My stomach tightened at his tone. I didn't like it when he was angry.

"Well, you did say you hoped he'd be distracted by my outfit, and it worked to our advantage in the end, didn't it? He believed us."

"Doesn't mean I've not still got half a mind to go back there and punch him in the face for coming onto you like that. I mean, I was sitting right there."

"Stu. It's not like I could do anything about it. We needed to keep him sweet."

"You kept him a little too sweet, if you ask me."

"Oh my God, now you're just being ridiculous. And what was with you slugging back all that whiskey? Didn't we agree we weren't going to accept any offers of drinks?"

"It would've come across dodgy if we said no. You have a drink once the deal is done, that's how it works."

"But you didn't just have one drink, you had at least three. I'm not even sure you should be driving."

He scoffed at this. "I'm nowhere near drunk, luv. I would've had to down the entire bottle for that."

His dismissive tone got my back up, and I folded my arms across my chest. Stu's eyes followed the movement, lingering on the open buttons on my blouse. I made a show of doing them back up. His jaw worked as he focused back on the road.

"If I hadn't cut in, would you have taken him up on his offer?" he asked gruffly.

"Are you being serious right now? He's old enough to be my father."

Stu shrugged. "Some women are into that. I'm sure Renfield would be more than happy to pay off your debts in exchange for a few nights with you."

I gaped at him, outrage building. "That's it. Let me out of the car. I'll make my own way home."

He ignored me and kept on driving.

"Stu! I mean it. Stop the car right now. I won't sit here and listen to you talk to me like that."

"No."

I huffed out a breath. "Why are you acting so jealous? You don't honestly believe I have any interest in Renfield, do you?"

"He can offer you a fuck of a lot more than I can."

Was that insecurity behind his aggression?

"Well, it's a good thing I'm not interested in people for what I can gain from them. Although the fact you think I can be bought says a lot about how you see me," I replied, my voice hard. His insinuation seriously infuriated me.

At this he let out a long, exasperated sigh. "That's not . . . shit, Andrea, that's not how I see you."

217

"Then why did you say it?"

He ran a hand over his jaw. "Because I'm a dickhead."

I didn't say anything to that, because quite frankly I agreed with him. Stu continued driving, our argument at a standstill. I honestly couldn't tell if he really believed I was flattered by Renfield's interest, or if it was simply his jealousy making him speak out of turn. After a few minutes I realised he wasn't going in the right direction for my flat.

"This is the wrong way. Where are we going?"

"Said I'd take you for a spin."

"Well, I don't want to go for a *spin* anymore. I want to go home."

"Too bad."

"Stu, turn this car around right now or I'm going to start shouting."

"Just relax."

"No, I won't relax until you apologise for how you spoke to me just now."

We were driving through a leafy area, one of London's many parks, but I wasn't familiar with the neighbourhood. Stu let out a growly sigh and pulled the car to a stop in an empty spot, shrouded from view by a number of bushes and tall trees. I didn't see anyone about, but I imagined there'd be dog walkers and joggers happening by sooner or later.

"I'm sorry. I just . . . I hate it when other men look at you." He sighed, and it sounded like it took a lot for him to admit it.

I was sure my expression portrayed my bewilderment. "Well, it's a good thing men don't look at me very often, and when they do it's only because my outfit is so tight it's fit to burst, and I'm wearing a blonde wig."

I thought injecting some humour into the conversation might lighten things up a little. I was wrong.

"That's bullshit. Kian's constantly staring at you in class like a lovesick puppy. Gets on my nerves."

"Not this again. Kian likes me as a teacher and I like him as a student. There's nothing more to it. Besides, I thought you two were friends."

"Yeah well, sometimes I want to tell my friends to stop mentally undressing my woman."

I sucked in a breath, not knowing whether to continue being angry or to melt at him calling me his woman.

I wanted him.

But I also wanted to throttle him.

Admittedly though, I wanted him more than I wanted to throttle him.

And honestly, the way he looked at me made me feel weak. I felt like I was his and it had happened practically against my will. It was like waking up one day with red hair when you'd always been a blonde. You're at a loss to explain how it happened.

He let out a gruff breath and dragged a hand through his locks, not looking at me as he spoke. "I feel like I'm not good enough for you sometimes, and seeing that posh prick flirt with you just hammered it home."

"Stu, that's ridiculous. You need to quit thinking that way. You also need to realise that I'm not interested in "posh pricks" like Renfield, I'm interested in you. Only you. And you're definitely good enough."

At this he unclipped both our seatbelts and pulled me to him, deftly dragging me onto his lap just like when we were in his car the other night. Only now we were in a BMW and there was a lot more room.

"You're not invisible like you think you are," he whispered, eyes holding mine intensely. "You're beautiful. So beautiful. I *see* you."

His fervent words took me off guard. He reached up and pulled off my wig before freeing my hair from the clip beneath. It fell long and heavy around my shoulders. "I see every gorgeous inch of you. Hold still," he ordered, placing his hand around my neck to keep me from moving. His fingers dug into my throat, making me feel oddly vulnerable. With his other hand he caressed my cheek then tucked a strand of hair behind my ear, the touch reverent. He tipped my chin up so I was looking at him. "And these eyes are my favourite," he went on, whispering now. "Never hide them, Andrea."

My entire body tingled, my skirt hitched so high around my waist that my underwear was exposed. Stu's breathing was fast, his arousal evident in the hardness that pressed against my inner thigh.

Again, I wanted him.

"You're so infuriating," I said, but my voice held no anger anymore, only desire.

"And you're sexy. Come here."

Stu took my chin, pulling my mouth to his for a hard, possessive kiss. My pulse skyrocketed. One half of me wanted to tell him to stop, to let me get back into my seat so he could drive me home. The other half—*the half that was winning*—wanted his hands all over me. We kissed like two people starved for air. I gripped his shirt, then started undoing it button by button. Once I had enough of them free I slid my hands over his chest, feeling every hard, muscular inch of him.

His mouth smiled around our kiss. "Gonna let me return the favour, luv?"

I shivered at the idea of him feeling me like I was feeling him right then. My breasts ached for it. "Yes, touch me. Please."

220

Stu squeezed my hips, running his fingers up my thighs before bringing them to my blouse. He had it open in seconds, and before I knew it he'd unclipped my bra and my breasts were bare.

"Perfect," he murmured, moulding them with his hands and pinching my nipples. I grew slick and ready, a delicious friction building between my underwear and his trousers. I moved my hips, rubbing against his hard length a little more aggressively than I intended. In spite of the larger front seat, my backside hit off the dashboard, pressing on a button and causing the radio to come to life. *Hounds of Love* by The Futureheads blared from the speakers.

Stu chuckled but he didn't let me pull away, even though I was a little embarrassed. The song was weirdly appropriate, the volume so loud it was surely going to attract attention, even with all the windows closed. I tried to reach for the buttons to turn it off but Stu pulled me back to him.

"Leave it," he growled, like he couldn't stand the idea of breaking our kiss for even a second. He cupped either side of my face and kissed me with such passion I felt it all the way to my toes. Fast guitar music filled the car as he slid his tongue deep into my mouth, tasting me, claiming me. I trembled, my hands gripping his shoulders now as I continued to rut against him. Stu broke the kiss to stare up at me in awe, his eyes taking all of me in.

"Christ, look at you."

"Stu, I need—"

He put a finger to my lips. "Hush, I know."

After that we were nothing but commands and fevered grabbing.

His hand gripped my hip, the other massaged my breast.

"Kiss me."

I slid my fingers up and down his length and brought my mouth to his.

"You're so hard."

He palmed my arse and slid his fingers past the elastic of my underwear.

"And you're so wet."

"Faster."

"Like this?"

"Yes."

"Need your mouth, luv."

More kissing, tongues, wet heat, friction. I hurried to undo his fly and pull his erection free, feeling his hot silky skin for the first time.

"Give me . . ."

"Need to . . ."

"Wait."

Heavy breathing. Hands fumbling.

Pressure.

Pressure.

Such lovely pressure. The music continued to blare around us, but I was too lost in him to care. People might be able to see us, still, neither one of us cared. We were need and desire and emotions entangled. His cock slid against my sex and we both moaned simultaneously.

"Stu."

"No."

"Stu."

"I said no, Andrea."

I bit my lip. "Please."

"I fucking . . . I fucking don't have . . . Oh God, quit doing that for a second," he panted and shifted me in his lap, then leaned forward to reach for the glove compartment. I kissed his neck, loving how his skin pebbled beneath my mouth while he rifled through his friend's stuff, searching for a condom.

"Terry, you fucking legend," he swore then came back to me, a small foil packet in his hand. I didn't stop kissing his neck as he reached between us, vaguely aware of him tearing the packet open with his teeth. Jesus, that was sexy.

He slid the condom down his length and dragged my mouth away from his neck so he could kiss me properly. His tongue was hard and unrelenting. I lifted my hips so he could position himself beneath me. I gasped and bit his lower lip when his cock nudged inside me the tiniest bit. My eyes were closed but I opened them to find him watching me, soaking me in. His gaze was fierce, wild, his need for me clear as day. He continued to watch me as I lowered, letting him fill me completely.

I cried out, unable to contain the pleasure of how amazing he felt inside me. The fact that it was still bright out, that we were in the middle of a public park where anyone might happen by felt electric. I didn't ever think I'd get off on exhibitionism, but with Stu I wanted things I never did before.

"You're tight," he breathed.

"You're just big," I countered, and he chuckled.

"I've never seen you look more beautiful, Andrea," he said, his voice worshipful as his gaze turned dark, his next words erotically carnal. "Ride me."

I didn't break eye contact as I started to move my hips. Stu plucked one nipple, then the other, sending delicious bolts of pleasure through me. I was so wet, so turned on, that I felt like a different person. Someone wild and free.

"That's it, faster, luv, you're perfect, you feel perfect."

Stu's words spurred me on, and I started to realise he was quite adept at talking dirty. He gripped my hair, winding it around his fist and giving it a little pull. "Do you know how hard I'm gonna fuck you when I get you in my bed?" he whispered.

My only response was a whimper. He yanked on my hair again, harder this time.

"I'll get you on all fours, spread you so fucking wide . . . don't stop, keep moving, fuck me, Andrea. I'm yours. Jesus, your pussy was made for me. I'm close. Are you close?"

Sweat pebbled his forehead. I bounced on his lap, speeding my movements, feeling more and more confident the dirtier his words became.

"Bet nobody knows what a dirty little thing you are," he continued hoarsely, his gaze turning unfocused. "This is all for me, yeah?"

His tight grip on my hair was the perfect edge to the pleasure of him filling me. The way he devoured me with his gaze made me feel beautiful and sexy and fierce.

Stu let go of my hair and reached for my clit. "There you are," he murmured, such tenderness in his eyes. "There you are. Will you come for me, luv? I want to feel you come on my dick. *Fuuuck.*"

Stu rubbed circles into my clit, swearing profusely all the while. I knew he was seconds away from coming but he was holding back. He wanted us to peak together. As soon as he knew he had me, his cock twitched and he spilled inside me. My orgasm hit me fast and intense, and I couldn't remember ever coming so hard. I felt boneless, falling into his arms as tremors encapsulated my body. We were both quiet, only the sounds of the radio and our heavy breathing filling the car.

Stu ran his hand up and down my back, his touch soothing. As I came down from my sex high, I startled and looked out the windows, scared I'd find some voyeur outside watching us. But there was no one. Stu had picked a wonderfully secluded spot, even if he didn't predict exactly how far things were going escalate. I mean, neither had I, and I was kind of reeling from the fact that we'd just had sex. It was certainly spontaneous.

"You okay?" he asked and I nodded, my face buried in the crook of his neck. I never wanted to move. He chuckled. "Gonna take a little nap, are ya?"

I smiled. "Maybe."

"One day I'll fall sleep inside you, Andrea," he whispered huskily. "Just not today."

His words struck a chord, because really they should've terrified me. I barely knew the man, but he was inside me and it was *amazing*, and I loved the idea that sometime soon he wanted to be that intimate with me. *With. Me.* My heart felt alive.

I kissed him once on the collarbone then reached for my bra where it lay on the passenger seat. Stu went about buttoning up his shirt as I did up my blouse. Jamie's wig had somehow found its way to the back seat. Gently, Stu lifted me off his lap and I climbed onto the passenger seat, fixing my underwear and skirt back into place.

I couldn't believe we'd had sex.

I couldn't believe we'd had sex in a car, in broad daylight.

Stu Cross definitely had an unprecedented effect on me. I'd never broken a single rule before I met him, never mind the actual law.

When we were done fixing ourselves, he cast me a sexy look as he pulled out of the park, biting his lower lip as he murmured, "Look at you. Christ, I could go again."

I blushed. "Shut up."

"Don't get shy on me now, luv. You just stole my post-prison virginity cowgirl style."

A surprised chuckle escaped me. "I don't think you were ever a virgin, Stu."

"Whatever. You're sexy, Andrea. You should own it."

I blushed and focused my attention out the window. When we arrived at my flat I expected him to stay in the car, but he didn't. He followed me inside where Alfie was anxiously pacing around the kitchen, like he was waiting to hear whether or not he got the lead role in *Joseph*.

"Where have you been? I've been calling non-stop. I thought something awful happened."

I stepped by him and went to grab a bottle of water from the fridge, knocking half of it back in one long gulp. Who knew car sex could make me so thirsty? Stu took the bottle from me, never breaking eye contact as he tipped it to his own lips and drained the rest.

I shivered.

"Wait, *did* something awful happen?" Alfie questioned, eyeing the two of us in concern. "Andie, what happened to your disguise?"

Well, crap.

Nineteen

My pulse raced, my eyes going wide as I fumbled for an explanation. I must've looked completely dishevelled. "The, um, the wig was making my scalp itch, so I took it off on the way back. And the contacts made my eyes too dry, so yeah, I took those out as well."

"Oh, right. Well, how did the meeting go? Did you pull it off?"

"Without a hitch," said Stu, his gaze meeting mine for a second. I wouldn't exactly say the experience was 'hitch-free', especially with how jealous he got when Renfield flirted with me. But I suppose it could be considered successful since the man believed us to be genuine. I almost felt guilty for conning him, but then I remembered all the stolen art he owned. He was hardly innocent.

My cousin was watching me closely and I could tell he was suspicious. Maybe my cheeks were still flushed, or perhaps I was displaying some other outward sign that I'd just had sex with Stu Cross. I. Just. Had. Sex. With. Stu. Cross. Incredible, exhilarating, spine-tingling sex.

Thankfully Stu's phone started ringing and Alfie's attention was drawn away from me.

"Trev, how's it going?" he answered and then listened to his brother speaking on the other end of the line.

"Oh yeah, sounds good. I'll be home in a bit. Have to return a motor to Terry Teabag before I head back. Yeah, yeah, okay. See you then."

He hung up, sliding the phone back in his pocket. My cousin pursed his lips, and I could tell by his expression that he was amused. He wanted to say something but was holding it back. I frowned at him, kicking his foot with the toe of my shoe.

"What's wrong with you?"

An amused chuckle escaped him. "Oh, come on. Terry Teabag? That's the most hilarious name I've ever heard." Stu folded his arms and cocked an eyebrow. Alfie shot him a gleeful look. "I'm sorry, but I have to ask. Why do they call him Teabag?"

Stu's lips twitched. "Guess."

Alfie stroked his chin ponderously. "Hmm. Let me see. Does he always leave the bag in after he makes a cup of tea?"

Stu shook his head, almost smiling.

"Oh! I've got it. He stole a crate of teabags off the back of a truck one time and gave them away for free to everyone in the neighbourhood."

Now Stu chuckled. "Seriously? No."

"Wait, wait, I'll get it eventually. Okay, is it something sexual?"

"Alfie!" I exclaimed, horrified.

Stu's chuckle deepened. "No, you numpty. He doesn't like teabags. They freak him right out."

Alfie frowned. "That's it?" Stu nodded. "Well, that's rather disappointing."

"Everyone 'round my way has nicknames like that. You've got Tall Warren, only five foot one. Chipper Fred, works the local chippy. Tommy the Taxi, drives a taxi. Ballbuster Mick, got in a fight once and literally busted some bloke's balls."

My cousin held on to his stomach he was laughing so hard. "Oh my God, stop, I can't breathe," he exclaimed.

I had to admit, I was giggling myself. That last one was pretty funny. Stu shook his head, obviously not finding it all quite as hilarious as my cousin. His eyes came to me. "Can we talk?"

I swallowed and gestured to the hallway, leaving Alfie to continue his amused laughter solo. "What is it?" I asked quietly, glancing up at Stu.

"We're having a barbecue and a few beers at ours tonight."

"Oh?"

"You should come."

The way his voice dipped on the last word made me tremble slightly. I chewed on my lip and dug my heel into the floor. "Well, um . . . I'm not sure if . . ."

Stu gripped my upper arm. "Andrea, quit overthinking everything and just agree to have dinner with me and my family. It's really not that complicated. Please."

It was the 'please' that had me nodding my head before I could properly weigh the decision. "Well, I suppose I could pop by, but I won't be able to stay late. I already had to call in sick to work today and I can't do it again."

Now he smiled wickedly. "Don't worry, I'll make sure you get to work in the morning."

I folded my arms across my chest. "Stu, I'm not staying over."

He winked. "We'll see."

"Stu—"

"Look, I'll be back in a while to collect you. Wear something nice," he said, dipping down to press a quick kiss on my lips and then he was gone. I realised how quiet the flat was once the door slammed shut and fretted over whether or not Alfie had heard us. But then I went inside the kitchen and found him staring out the window, lost in his own head. He blinked when I opened the cupboard to search for a snack.

"Is Stu gone?" Alfie asked, his expression sober.

I nodded.

"You don't think he was offended by me laughing, do you? I feel like he might think I was mocking where he comes from, their way of life."

"He didn't think that, Alfie. It's fine."

"I just realised after you both left how condescending I came across, but it wasn't intentional. If anything, I envy him a little."

"I thought you were wary of his background."

"Well yes, in the beginning I was, but I can see now he doesn't intend us any ill will. In fact, I kind of like having him around. I feel like if anything bad happens we've got a big muscled action hero on our side to swoop in and save the day."

I laughed at this, but at the back of my mind I was thrilled that Alfie was thawing towards Stu. I'd never seen him take to a stranger before. Even when I first started dating Mark, Alfie had taken a long time to accept him.

"And why would you envy him?" I asked, curious.

Alfie lifted a shoulder. "I suppose I just would've preferred a deprived upbringing to what I had. At least he had his brothers. They could support one another."

I gave his shoulder a small squeeze. "If you hadn't had the upbringing you did, then you wouldn't be who you are today, and I quite like who you are, Alfie."

He sniffed and nodded, then without another word disappeared inside his bedroom. When he was gone my nerves returned, remembering I'd agreed to go to Stu's house for dinner. Trying not to fret on it, I took a shower and put on my nicest pair of jeans, alongside a silk camisole and a light cream cardigan.

I was sitting by my laptop, checking some lessons for work the next day and letting my hair air dry when a knock sounded at the door. I knew it had to be Stu, but I just hadn't expected him back so early.

He'd changed out of the suit and now wore his typical ensemble of T-shirt and jeans. I much preferred him like this. Leaning down, he kissed the edge of my mouth. Butterflies took charge of my stomach.

"You ready?"

"Yes, just let me grab my things."

A few minutes later we were in his car on our way to his house. I noticed the neighbourhoods getting dingier as we travelled, which reminded me how the rich and poor lived in such different circumstances in London. I'd always been somewhere in the middle, not quite rich, not quite poor. In more recent times I certainly knew how it felt to be stretched thin financially, but it wasn't like I'd ever gone hungry. Feeling nervous, I chewed on my fingernails, wondering what sort of welcome I'd receive.

"Do your brothers know I'm coming?" I asked, my voice betraying my nerves.

Stu nodded. "Yeah, but don't worry. I told them you're just a friend." He reached over and took my hand in his, his thumb rubbing just beneath my ring. "Besides, if anyone asks you can just say you're married."

A self-deprecating laugh escaped me. "I guess having emotional attachments to objects has its benefits."

"Hmmm," Stu murmured, his expression contemplative.

"What?"

He seemed to weigh his words. "Do you ever think you'll feel ready to take this off? Maybe put someone else's ring on there?"

My posture stiffened at his question, my stomach churning. It was far too early for him to be asking me questions like that. I pulled my hand out of his hold.

"I don't know," I answered quietly.

Stu didn't say anything, but I felt him looking at me for a long moment before he settled his attention back on the road. When we reached his house I was just about ready to burst from the awkward silence, relieved to get out of the car. I looked up and down the street, trying not to judge how rough it looked. Stu pulled his keys from his pocket and opened the front door. I stepped inside, and the smell of barbecued meat drifting down the hallway made my mouth water.

Unlike most of the street, Stu's house was actually incredibly well looked after. Everything was new and modern, and it looked like the entire place had been gutted out and renovated. We bypassed the living room to enter a large, open-plan kitchen. It even had an island and one of those range-style cookers. Large sliding doors led out to the back garden where it appeared all the family had congregated.

"Stu!" Trevor called, the first to spot us. "Come over here and tell Reya I'm right. Joker would kick Dare Devil's arse any day of the week."

Stu placed his hand to the small of my back, his heat soothing even though I suspected he was still annoyed with me, and led me over to Trevor and his friend.

"Sorry, Reya, but I have to side with my brother on this one. It doesn't matter what character you put him up against, Joker always wins."

"Oh whatever. You two are biased," said the woman. She was about my height, with long golden brown hair and similarly coloured eyes. I thought she might be Spanish, or maybe Italian.

"Hi, I'm Andie. Stu's friend," I said, introducing myself.

"She's Stu's teacher," Trevor butted in, elbowing Reya in the side and shooting her a wink. She returned it with a look that told him to quit being a smart-arse. I liked her already.

"Oh well, it's nice to meet you. I'm Reya," said the woman just as Trevor threw his arm around her shoulders.

"She's my best buddy, aren't ya ReyRey?" He grinned widely, and she narrowed her gaze.

"How many times do I have to tell you to stop calling me that? You know I hate it."

"And that's why I'll never stop." He grinned before leaning in and licking the side of her face. Uh, *okay*. Reya squealed her displeasure and Trevor scarpered. She chased after him but he effortlessly jumped up onto the high wall at the back of the garden, like some kind of ninja.

"The next time you do that I'll string you up by the testicles," she shouted. "Don't think I won't."

Trevor blew her a kiss. "Sure, sure, you love my testicles too much to ever do them harm."

"First of all, gross. Second of all, wanna try me?"

I glanced at Stu. "Are they always like this?"

He shrugged, his expression a little distant, even if his hand still lingered at the base of my spine. "Depends on what mood Trevor's in."

"How did he manage to get up there so easily? I've never seen anything like it."

"He's a traceur. We all are, actually. Or well, I used to be. I'm too old for all that nowadays, haven't got the legs for it."

233

"Forgive my ignorance, but what's a traceur?" I asked, embarrassed I didn't know.

"It's someone who practices parkour. Ever heard of free-running?"

"Oh! Yes, I have. Those people are incredible. You used to do that?" I had to admit I was impressed.

Stu glanced away. "Yeah, when I was younger. Fucked my knee up in prison, so my legs can't take the impact anymore."

"Don't listen to him. He's just gotten lazy in his old age," came Lee's voice. I turned to see him holding a spatula and wearing a chef's apron. Just behind him was a fancy-looking barbecue, burgers sizzling away over the coals. He gave me a nod. "All right, Andie? You hungry?"

"Very."

"Good. And it's good to see you again. Sorry I was a nasty prick last time. Had my wires crossed."

"Oh, um, no worries," I replied, not knowing what he meant about having his wires crossed.

"Come on, let's get a drink," said Stu, his breath hitting my ear as he led me over to a deck table where the rest of his family were enjoying themselves. "You want me to fix you up another cocktail? Same as last time?"

"No, that's okay. Just give me whatever you're having."

"So long as it isn't whiskey, right?" He winked.

I remembered him taking my glass at Renfield's, drinking it for me. That had actually been quite a sexy move. And now I couldn't stop looking at his lips.

"Right yeah, can't stand the stuff," I said, a little too breathily.

Stu shot me a heated look, like he knew what I was thinking. Then he grabbed me a beer, before proceeding to re-introduce me to his family members. There was his youngest brother, Liam, Lee's wife, Karla, and their cousin, Sophie, and her two kids, Billy and Jonathan. I waved hello to everyone, smiling all the while and trying not to forget their names. Trevor and Reya came to join us, having called a truce to their bickering.

Reya took the seat on the other side of me, and I noticed she smelled really nice, like vanilla pods. It must've been her perfume. Trevor sat on her other side, continually ribbing her in the same way he'd done before. I felt a little awkward when Stu went to help Lee with the food, sipping on my beer and just letting everyone else chat around me.

"I'm pretty sure she isn't," I heard Stu saying to Lee.

"Just go and ask her," Lee urged.

"Fine," Stu grunted. "Andrea, you aren't a veggie, are ya?" he asked while Lee snickered at him, crooning, "Oooooh, Andrea, is it? I'm fairly sure her name is Andie, ya posh prick."

Stu got him in a headlock for a second. "I call her Andrea, so shut it."

His attention came to me again once he was finished roughhousing with Lee. I shook my head. "No, I'm not a vegetarian."

He turned back to his brother. "See, I told you."

A few minutes later the food was served, and Stu returned to his seat next to me. I didn't speak much, but that was mainly because everyone here was so chatty that I could hardly get a word in. I startled when Stu put his hand on my thigh midway through the meal, mainly because I hadn't been expecting it. His fingertips were dangerously close to my inner thigh, and all of a sudden I wasn't hungry for food anymore.

I flicked my gaze to his, widening my eyes as a message for him to quit touching me. He didn't look at me, but his lips twitched once so I knew he was aware he was pushing his luck. Still, it didn't stop him from moving his fingers back and forth in a caressing motion. They danced briefly over the apex of my thighs, and I sucked in a harsh breath.

I swallowed, glancing across the table to find Lee studying me. For a second I thought he knew what was going on under the table, but I realised I was wrong when he spoke, his curious blue eyes on my ring.

"You married, Andie?"

My throat went dry as sandpaper. Finally, I summoned up the will to reply. "Oh, no my husband passed away."

Lee's expression sobered as he swallowed a gulp of beer, his gaze going to Stu for a second. For some reason he didn't look happy.

"I'm sorry," said Karla, her voice soft. "Was it recent?"

I knew why she asked that. Obviously people would think Mark's death wasn't too long ago if I was still wearing my ring. I shook my head, embarrassed. "No, it's been just over four years."

An awkward silence filled the table, and believe me, when you were dealing with a bunch as loud as the Cross family, silence was certainly unusual.

"How'd he go?" Lee asked, his arm around his wife's shoulders as he levelled me with a concerned look. It was almost . . . protective.

"Cancer. Lymphoma," I answered and then downed a long swig of beer.

"My condolences. Cancer's a fucking shitty way to go."

I let out a breath. "Yeah, it is."

Everyone was watching me then, which was probably why I felt the urge to escape. Rising from my seat, I said, "I'm just going to use the bathroom."

Stu made a move to follow me. "I'll show you where—"

I stayed him with a hand. "It's fine. I'm sure I can find my own way."

"First door at the top of the stairs," said Lee, and I shot him a thin but grateful smile. When I was safely ensconced in the bathroom, I leaned back against the door and exhaled deeply. My face was red, and my heart was beating too fast. I couldn't take their pitying looks. I hated it when people felt sorry for me. It often made me feel sad all over again, made me wish he was still alive.

I stared down at my hand and twisted the ring around and around in a way that soothed my nerves. Why couldn't people just accept the fact that I still wore it? It was just a piece of jewellery and it wasn't like me wearing it was causing anyone else harm.

But then I thought of Stu in the car and how he'd been upset by my response to his question about wearing someone else's ring in the future. Maybe I was hurting him and I didn't even realise it. But surely Stu wasn't thinking that far into the future with us. He barely knew me, and I didn't really know him either. Was this about the ring and its place in my life, or the future I had never considered before? *Could I remove it? Would I consider another man's ring on my finger?*

I ran my hands under the cold tap, took a few deep breaths, then headed back downstairs to re-join the others. I could hear their voices as I entered the kitchen, and when my name was mentioned I paused just shy of the doorway to listen.

"She's clearly vulnerable, Stu, and seems like a good person. I just wouldn't like to see her get hurt." This was Lee.

"I'm not going to hurt her," Stu grunted his reply.

"How do you know? You haven't been yourself for a while now. You're vulnerable, too."

"Fuck off."

"Don't swear in front of the kids," Sophie scolded.

"Sorry, but he needs to mind his own business," Stu said.

"You're my brother. You are my business. And maybe she's not the only one I'm worried about. You've been through the ringer yourself. What if she hurts you?"

"She won't, because like I already told you, we're just friends. Now can you please shut up? She'll be back down any second."

"Fine, but we're not done discussing this," Lee said.

"Did you make your baked Alaska for dessert?" Karla asked, clearly trying to distract her husband.

"Course I did," Lee answered. "I know it's your favourite."

I waited another minute or two before stepping out into the garden to make sure they didn't suspect me of eavesdropping. I was still self-conscious though, especially since it seemed Lee could see right through my façade. But how did he think I could hurt Stu?

"You all right?" Stu asked quietly as I sat back down beside him.

I nodded. "I'm fine."

He studied me, his eyes tracing my features. "My family can be a nosy lot when the mood takes them. Don't feel like you need to answer their questions. Just do like I do and tell 'em to eff off."

I giggled softly at this and Stu smiled, seemingly happy he'd made me laugh. The rest of the meal wasn't so bad, and no one else asked me any personal questions. About two beers later I was sitting with Karla, Reya, and Sophie. The brothers took turns shooting hoops at the basketball net affixed to the wall at the other end of the garden. There was some kind of wager going on, but I was too busy chatting with the girls to know what was at stake.

Sophie, who had just put the kids to bed, was telling us about the guy she was currently seeing. "He's just . . . so lovely," she beamed. "And he doesn't seem at all put off by the fact that I have children because he already has one of his own from a previous relationship."

"That's probably because he's older. Older men are more mature in that sense. It's the young ones that freak out over stuff like that," said Karla.

"Yeah but, you're married to a younger man," said Sophie. "And it's all worked out well enough for you."

"Lee's younger than you?" I asked, intrigued.

She shrugged. "Only by three years. And besides, there were never any kids between us. It's a whole different ball game when children are involved."

"Oh, come on. Lee might as well have been a father of three when you first met," Reya joked, grinning. "I still think Trevor has the mental age of a four-year-old sometimes."

"Ugh, don't even get me started," said Sophie. "You didn't have to grow up with the boy. He was worse when he was kid, more energy than five Jack Russell Terriers combined."

This made me laugh, and I lifted my beer and drained the last of it. I hadn't noticed him approach, but suddenly Stu took the empty bottle from me and pulled me up from my chair. The girls were still engrossed in their chat and didn't notice him pull me away.

"Where are you taking me?" I asked as he led me inside the house.

"Thought you might be interested in seeing my bedroom."

"Um, no, not really," I replied even though my belly was all-aflutter at the idea of being alone with him. I was less inhibited now I'd had a few drinks.

He chuckled, the sound low and sexy. "You keep telling yourself that, luv."

Leading me upstairs, he pushed open the door to a small bedroom. There was only a neatly made-up bed and a chest of drawers for furniture, nothing else.

"Wow, now I get it. I couldn't possibly leave without seeing this shining example of interior design," I teased.

Stu slammed the door shut then flung me back against it. "Somebody's feeling mouthy," he whispered. "Let's see what else you can do with that smart tongue of yours."

His lips crashed against mine, hard and unrelenting. I moaned and fisted my hands in his T-shirt, pulling him close so his body practically moulded into mine. He gripped my backside, gave it a firm squeeze then lifted me effortlessly off the floor. I wrapped my legs around his hips and his erection pressed into me, the friction sending bolts of desire shooting through my system. How could I be so hot for him already? We'd just had sex mere hours ago and yet here we were, desperate for each other again.

Stu carried me over to his bed, dropped me down on the mattress and made quick work of unbuttoning my jeans. He slid his hand inside my underwear, fingering my wetness as his mouth crashed into mine again. I gasped when his thumb rubbed my sensitive clit, arching my spine with need. A little whimper escaped me when he broke the kiss, his hand leaving me as he rose to his knees and stared down at me.

"Let's take a look at you," he murmured and proceeded to undress me piece by piece.

I lay there, my every pore tingling, as Stu pulled off my jeans and my top. When only my knickers remained, he was still fully clothed, his gaze raking possessively over my body.

"This isn't fair. Why haven't you taken anything off?" I complained as I held my arm across my breasts, self-conscious.

"I told you, I want to look," said Stu, grabbing my arm and pulling it away from my body. "And stop hiding. There's not a single part of you that isn't perfect."

"Stu?"

"What is it, luv?"

"I want to look at you, too."

At this his mouth shaped into a pleased smirk as he grabbed the hem of his T-shirt and lifted it above his head. "Well, it'd be mean of me to refuse, now wouldn't it?"

"V-very mean," I agreed, feeling breathless as I took in his body. I didn't think I'd ever seen anything sexier than a topless Stu Cross reaching down to undo his belt buckle. His arms were toned and muscular, his abs ripped and leading down to a delectable V. *He. Was. Incredible.* It had been different in the car, because there was less room and we'd still had half our clothes on. Now we were in a bedroom, getting completely naked and I suddenly felt like a nervous virgin or something. Ridiculous.

Though saying that, only one other man had ever seen me naked, so maybe I had a right to be nervous.

"Andrea," said Stu, a note of concern in his voice.

"I'm fine."

"You look like you're about to do a runner."

I bit out a shaky laugh. "You're just very, um, fit. I'm feeling a little self-conscious of all my jiggly bits."

Stu grinned and reached for my hips. "I love all your jiggly bits." Dipping his head down, he sucked one of my nipples into his mouth. "Especially these ones," he continued, mouthing my breast.

I laughed again, this time louder. When Stu bit lightly on my nipple my laugh transformed into a moan. He licked a line across my breast, his gaze intense as we made eye contact. I trembled.

"Let's get these off," Stu whispered huskily as he reached for my knickers and slid them down my legs. He knelt between them, his gaze devouring me before he bent and pressed a kiss to my inner thigh. He kissed all the way up my body until our mouths met again. After that we were a tangle of lips and teeth and limbs. I was breathless when we broke apart. Stu reached over to the chest of drawers beside his bed and pulled open the top one.

A second later he was tearing open a condom and sliding it down his length. My tummy quivered at the sight of him. His brows drew together in concentration, his abs bunching and contracting as he moved. When he was done he braced his hands on either side of my head and stared down at me. My legs were spread wide around his hips and I felt his cock nudge against me. I wanted him inside.

His gaze was tender when he pushed into me, slowly filling me inch by inch. My breath whooshed out when he was embedded deep. He went still, his eyes closed as he held himself above me. A low expletive left his lips and then he started to move. I tried not to be too loud, still aware of all the people downstairs. But God, I wanted to scream when his thrusts sped up. It was all too much.

Our gazes locked and something passed between us, some unspoken emotion I couldn't decipher. I felt my channel clench around him, my body close to orgasm. Stu grunted as he pounded me so hard I was surprised the bed wasn't banging against the wall. When he came it was with a low growl, his mouth finding mine, and his tongue sliding in. The kiss was slow and sensual as he rode out the rest of his orgasm. I moaned when he pulled out of me, and his breathing was choppy. He flopped down onto the bed and dragged me on top of him.

"Move up here," he ordered and my stomach did a flip-flop.

"W-what?" I sputtered, my cheeks heating at the command.

"On my face," he went on and I swear I blushed from head to toe.

"Stu, I—"

"You heard me, luv. C-mere," he said breathlessly. I could tell by his expression that even though he'd just come he was still worked up. *Lucky me.*

Before I could stop him Stu grabbed my hips and shifted my body until I was doing exactly what he'd asked. I yelped and gripped the headboard to steady my balance. Stu pressed his face to my sex, his mouth hot and wet as he tongued me. I cried out, sensitive after the pounding he'd just given me.

Glancing down I saw him watching me, absorbing my every reaction. I hissed when his teeth grazed my clit, and the way his lips curved in amusement told me it had been intentional.

"You're a bastard," I said past a moan.

He only smirked, still going to town on me with his mouth. Every part of me fizzled with pleasure, and when his tongue slid inside me I had to bite my lip to keep from screaming. He was way, way, way too good at this, especially considering he was so out of practice. His fingers dug into my hips, holding me in place. His tongue was on my clit again now, swirling in a circular motion as my stomach tightened and my thighs tensed.

I was close, so close.

"Fuck," I swore. "Stu, I'm—"

He said something but it was muffled by the fact that his face was still pressed to my vagina. The vibration was what sent me over the edge, and I came so hard my body bucked. Stu's groan echoed through me, and he continued licking until every last tremor subsided.

I dropped down onto the bed and snuggled into him, burying my face in his neck because I was embarrassed now. I couldn't believe I'd just done that, that I'd let *him* to do that to *me*.

Stu flipped us so we were spooning, one hand cupping my breast, the other spread out over my stomach. I felt owned by him, every part of me possessed. The thought was sobering. He sucked my earlobe into his skilled mouth then whispered, "Go to sleep, luv."

I wanted to. In fact, there was nothing I wanted more than to drift off into a contented slumber wrapped up in his arms. I didn't realise how much I missed being in bed with a man, being held by him, until this very moment. But I couldn't stay. I already felt too raw, too exposed with him after the day we'd had. I also had to go home because if I stayed out all night Alfie was going to wonder where I'd been. It was a pity I didn't have any close female friends so I could pretend I was spending the night at their place.

Grown women could still have sleepovers, right?

I allowed myself a couple of minutes to enjoy lying next to him before I tried to make a move.

"No chance," Stu grunted, his lips in my hair. "You're staying."

"I can't," I whispered and his arm tightened around me.

"Got plans to wake up and fuck you again. Don't mess with my plans, Andrea."

How did he manage to make that sound charming? It was a true talent.

"If I don't go home Alfie will worry."

"So shoot off a text and tell him not to wait up."

I shook my head and twisted around to face him. "You don't understand. Alfie can't know about us, not yet. He doesn't do well with change. I need to pick the right time."

"You're not his parent. You shouldn't need to pussyfoot around him."

"That's not what I'm doing. Alfie's just not like everybody else, and I'm one of the few people in the world he feels safe with."

Stu wore a serious look. "What's his deal anyway?"

I rubbed my shoulder and sat up. Stu followed suit, his warmth pressing into my back. When I didn't say anything for a long moment he spoke quietly, "It's okay. You don't have to tell me."

"No, no, I want to, it's just . . . Alfie's always been an artistic soul, almost like he operates on a different plane than other people. That temperament was exacerbated as a result of his upbringing."

"Did his old man knock him about or something?"

I shook my head. "No, nothing like that. To be honest, his dad wasn't really present in his life much. Raymond was always working or out spending time with his revolving door of mistresses. His cheating turned Alfie's mum into a paranoid wreck and my cousin had a terrible time of it living with her. After a while her paranoia transformed into coldness and Alfie spent a lot of his childhood without any warmth or parental love.

"She took a lot of her unhappiness out on him, always bossing him around, treating him like her own personal servant. For years I tried persuading him to move out, but he was too under her thumb. Then after Mark passed I finally managed to convince him to come and live with me. Nowadays he keeps very little contact with her, and it's for the best. I know it might not seem like it, but he's so much more balanced now that he doesn't have to see her all the time. It's not that she's a particularly bad person, she's just not good for my cousin."

"I can understand that. Some people are like black holes; they suck out all your energy. And I get why you're protective of him. He's your family."

A breath escaped me, and I was so relieved he understood Alfie's and my relationship. "So you're not mad I can't stay?"

"No, Andrea, I'm not mad," he whispered and bent to press a kiss on my lips.

"Thank you."

We were quite for a few moments before I spoke. "Stu?"

"Yeah?" His hand stroked lazily back and forth across my stomach.

"What was it like growing up here?" Now that we'd been intimate, I felt like I wanted to know everything about him. It was like I had this unquenchable hunger inside me. I mean, the inside of his house was clean and modern, but I had to wonder if it had always been that way. Most of the street looked fairly rundown.

He pondered his answer a while. "Sometimes it was brutal, especially after our Mum died. We were all still kids at the time, and our old man hadn't been on the scene for a long while, so we were more or less on our own."

I gasped. I couldn't believe I hadn't known his mother was dead, but he never spoke about his parents and I'd never asked. "But didn't social services step in? A bunch of kids with no parents can't just be left alone like that."

"Our aunt, Sophie's Mum, let on that she was taking care of us."

"And was she?"

"Nah, but she had no problem spending the social welfare money she got for it."

"That's awful," I exclaimed.

"That's life, Andrea. And we survived well enough. We might've had to break the law to do it, but we survived."

I hugged him close, my heart hurting for him and his brothers, for the little boys they once were. Now I understood how he'd ended up in prison, how he'd gone down the wrong path in life. It was survival, pure and simple. I wished I could somehow go back in time and pluck him from that situation, care for him and his brothers like they should've been cared for.

"My upbringing was the complete opposite," I said, my voice quiet. "I never had a care, never wanted for anything. Thinking about how life was for you, I feel like I took it all for granted."

"You were a kid. All kids just accept their reality, whether it's good or bad."

"Maybe. It just really hurts me to think about you having to steal when you should've been out playing football with your friends or I dunno, going to the cinema and stuff."

Stu gave a tender chuckle. "We still did that, too. It wasn't all bad you know. It just was."

A quiet fell between us and Stu's fingers wandered to my inner arm to trace my tattoo. "When did you get this?"

I startled slightly, because I often forgot it was even there. "Just a few weeks after Mark passed. Alfie was actually the one who suggested it. I was staying at my parents' house, barely getting out of bed, not eating. I think he thought it would be good for me to do something to commemorate him, something permanent that would symbolise how he still lived on in my heart. So he drew the design for me on a piece of paper. It was beautiful, so simple and lovely. And he was right. Every second the ink was going into my skin made me feel better, less lost."

Stu didn't speak, just continued tracing the tattoo, and somehow I felt like he understood. He accepted my past, and though he'd questioned me about my ring earlier in the day, I felt like now, in this moment, he didn't feel threatened by it. If I hadn't experienced everything I had, if I hadn't been married to Mark, I wouldn't be who I am today.

We stayed like that for a long while, just lying in one another's arms and savouring the feeling of connection. Finally, Stu shifted us into a sitting position, his voice tender when he spoke. "Go get some clothes on, and I'll give you a lift home."

"Stu."

"What is it, gorgeous?"

"Thanks for listening to me, and for telling me about your childhood." I paused, a smile tugging at my lips. "You're kind of a great guy."

He shot me a cocky grin. "You're only realising this now?"

I threw a pillow at his head.

Twenty

Someone knocked loudly on my bedroom door, irritatingly waking me up from a lovely, lovely dream. Stu had dragged me into the storage cupboard at the college again, only this time he used his hands to bring me to orgasm.

I sat up in bed, grumpily flicking on my lap and checking the time on my alarm clock. 3:47 a.m. I was going to murder my cousin.

"What do you want, Alfie?" I called. "I can't even think about how early it is right now."

There was a pause and the sound of him hopping nervously from foot to foot. "Well, technically you could say it's late rather than early . . ." he said sheepishly as I climbed out of bed and threw open the door. I was so tired I could only manage to open one eye.

"Just spit it out," I said crankily.

Alfie was practically buzzing with energy as he blurted. "I finished it. It's done."

"Finished?"

"The painting. Stu's painting. It's finished, and Andie, oh my God, it's . . . I feel like it might be brilliant, hell, I feel like it might be amazing but I've been staring at it so long I can't tell anymore, and I need you to look so you can tell me I'm right."

I held up a hand to cut off his never-ending words and then rubbed at my eyes. "Okay, I'm awake. Let's go take a look at this knock-off."

"It's a replica, Andie, not a knock-off," Alfie grumped.

I grinned sleepily and he folded his arms on a huff. "Fine, I guess I deserved that for waking you up. You'd swear I'd just interrupted you from a dream about a Charlie Hunnam striptease."

Now I grinned, because my dream had been *so* much better than that. Two weeks had passed since I had dinner with Stu and his family. Two weeks of stolen kisses and hurried sexual encounters where we were both so eager to fall into one another we barely had time to catch our breath. My skin constantly tingled with the anticipation of when we might get to be together next, the danger that we might get caught. Most evenings he'd wait at the end of my street in his car and then we'd go take a drive somewhere. And by *drive* I meant . . .

My thoughts were cut short when I stepped inside Alfie's bedroom to find a masterpiece on his easel. I stood frozen in place, aghast at the accuracy of his work. It didn't just look like the original, it looked *old*, like I was staring at a piece that had existed for hundreds of years. Alfie hovered close by, anxiously awaiting my feedback.

"Well?" he said, biting his lip. "Do you think it'll pass for the real thing?"

I didn't answer him and instead walked farther into the room, glancing between the fake and Alfie's laptop screen, where the photograph of the original was displayed. I was still amazed by how you could zoom in and out and inspect every single detail, see every tiny crack in the oil paint. I kept looking from one to the other, trying to pick out differences but coming up short.

It was flawless.

Whatever methods Alfie had used to recreate the aging of the paint truly astounded me.

"I can't believe it. Alfie, it's identical," I said finally, and he let out the loudest sigh of relief I'd ever heard. Sometimes I wondered how just one person could hold so much unspent nervous tension inside their body. It almost felt like he was vibrating with it.

My cousin sagged down onto the bed, his clothes and much of his hands smeared with paint. He threw his arm over his face as he muttered. "Thank God."

I sat down next to him to properly take in the piece. It wasn't just flawless. It was magnificent. Dark, deep blue sea curled up into a violent pale wave. The ship tilted in its struggle to stay afloat as Christ and his disciples faced the raging storm. The waves were so vivid it almost felt like I could feel them bashing against the wood of the vessel, the sails billowing in the wind. Above there is a hint of yellow light where the clouds are beginning to part, anticipating Christ's command for the storm to subside.

After a few moments Alfie sat up and we both just stared at it. Soon my awe of my cousin's talent turned to worry. The piece was complete and now the next stage of the plan had to be put into action.

And I, well, abruptly I felt like I was suffocating with the finality of it all.

Too wired to go back to sleep, I showered, got dressed, and worked on my laptop as I mentally prepared myself to tell Stu the painting was ready. The date hadn't been set for the transportation of Renfield's cargo yet. He was still under the impression that Stu and I, or more specifically, Mr Kennedy and Miss Jordan, were ironing out the last few details.

Now that the painting was done there was no longer any point in delaying things.

I was still on edge when I arrived to work. Lots of students were hanging out in the lobby, chatting and drinking their morning coffees when I spotted Stu amid the crowd. His eyes met mine and he smiled tenderly, his gaze softening. This was how he looked at me all the time now, and it made my heart feel too many things.

I felt like I was falling for him, but given the strong, lustful pull toward one another it was hard to tell the difference, to make sense of my feelings.

"We need to talk," I said when I approached him, my expression sober.

Stu got the message loud and clear and silently followed me to my classroom. The place was still empty, none of the other students having arrived yet. I let Stu go in by me before I closed the door, leaned back against it and exhaled a deep breath. He eyed me curiously.

"The painting's finished," I blurted. "Alfie completed it early this morning."

Stu's eyes flared, a moment of quiet passing as he ran his hand through his hair and turned to face the window. "Fuck."

"I know."

He turned back around. "I have to make some phone calls. I'll probably miss class today."

I nodded. "Yes, of course, that's fine. Do what you've got to do."

He came to stand before me, gripping my upper arms. "Andrea, listen, if anything goes wrong, you and Alfie had nothing to do with any of this," he promised. "If the police come asking questions, you tell them you don't know anything, do you hear me? And you have my word that I'll never breathe a word of your involvement."

"Stu, you're talking like you're going to get caught. The plan is foolproof. Nothing bad is going to happen," I said, willing myself to believe it. Things had changed. They weren't the same as they were when Alfie and I first agreed to help him. I had feelings for him now, real, strong feelings, and I couldn't stand the idea of him going back to prison.

"I know that. I just need to make sure you understand. Even on the off chance that the shit hits the fan, I'll make sure your name is kept out of it. I'll make sure you're safe."

My heart clenched, my stomach in turmoil at his words. I swallowed and looked at the floor. "What about the guy you hired to do the transfer? Are you sure you can trust him?"

Stu's expression was stoic now. "I can trust him. Don't you worry about that. Just . . ." he exhaled, his voice gentling, "just be my soft place to fall. I need you, Andrea."

Be my soft place to fall. I need you. If only he knew how much I needed him too now.

My breathing turned erratic, my heart pounding faster. I wanted to say something to express what I felt inside, but before I could utter a word he bent and pressed a kiss to my lips.

"I guess this is where shit gets real."

Twenty-One

I barely slept all week knowing the robbery was imminent. There was a lump in my throat and a brick in my gut that I couldn't seem to shift.

"So, today's the day?" Alfie asked anxiously. He eyed me sitting by the kitchen window, staring outside as though searching for the answer to some unknown question.

"Yep," I replied, lifting my mug and taking a sip of tea. Ugh. I'd been lost in my head for so long it was cold.

"When will we know if he got the painting?"

I glanced at the clock. "In a couple hours."

"And where is Stu planning on storing the piece before he hands it over to the Duke?"

"I'm not sure. He didn't say."

"You never thought to ask him?"

"Alfie, why all the questions? It shouldn't be any concern of ours where the painting is kept so long as it's safe."

My cousin hopped anxiously from foot to foot, chewing on his lip as though he wanted to say something but was unsure how I'd react.

"Oh, just spit it out," I urged. I was way too stressed to humour his weirdness today.

"Well," he began tentatively, "I mean, I feel like I'll regret it the rest of my life if I don't at least ask, but . . . um, what I mean to say is, I was wondering if you could convince Stu to bring the painting here first. This will probably be my only chance to ever see it in the flesh, and I'd just like to spend a few minutes alone with it."

It was his earnest expression that did me in. Alfie was a lifelong lover of Rembrandt, so I understood how much it meant to him to see the real painting. After all, he'd spent weeks labouring over the replica. The least we could do was allow him a few brief moments to appreciate the original.

My features softened as I told him, "I'll call Stu and see what he says. But if it's too risky I won't push the matter. You'll just have to accept that it's not possible."

Alfie's grin spread wide across his face as he hurried over to give me a hug. "Thanks, Andie. I won't forget this."

One long phone call later (Stu took some convincing), we sat down in the living room and waited for him to arrive with the piece. Only ten minutes passed when my phone rang and I practically dove to answer it, thinking it was Stu calling to say something had gone wrong. But it wasn't him. It was Karla. For some reason seeing her name on the screen had my heart pounding fast. I remembered how we'd exchanged numbers all those weeks ago, but why was she calling me now?

Had she found out what Stu was doing today? The fact that she was a policewoman only made matters worse. Alfie eyed me curiously as I took a deep breath and answered the call.

"Hello?"

"Hi Andie," Karla replied. She sounded stressed. "I hope you don't mind me getting in touch, but Stu and Lee had a massive fight this morning, and we're really worried about him."

"Oh. What sort of fight?" I put my hand to my chest and anxiously rubbed.

"It actually happened out of nowhere. Lee asked him if he wanted to go play a game of football with a few of their mates and Stu said no. When Lee pushed him to come he literally just snapped and lost his temper. He stormed out of the house angry, so Lee and I followed him to try and make amends. He won't answer our calls, either. We thought he was going to go see you but then he stopped into a car rental company and drove off in a transit van."

Oh, God. This was bad. This was so, *so* bad.

"Um, well, he never came by my place," I said, trying to keep my voice steady.

"Yes, we know that. We followed him to a really fancy residential area in Hampstead Heath. He just went inside one of the houses."

This wasn't just bad. It was catastrophic. Lee and Karla couldn't be at Renfield's. They were going to ruin *everything*. Before Alfie could ask what was going on I ran to my bedroom and shoved some makeup and Jamie's blonde wig into my handbag. A second later I was out of the flat, the door slamming shut behind me as I hurried to my car.

"Do you have any idea what he's up to?" Karla went on. "Because this has dodgy written all over it."

I coughed and tried to think of an explanation. *Make something up,* my brain urged, *anything*. Why was I so bad at lying? "Oh yes, actually, that's my uncle's place. He's moving and Stu offered to help him with his furniture."

"Are you sure?" She didn't sound convinced.

"Yes. I'm on my way there right now, because I, uh, I offered to help, too." God, could I sound any more nervous? The way my voice echoed back to me told me I was on speakerphone.

"I'm going over," I heard Lee mutter. "Something doesn't add up. Look at all the security cameras."

"Don't go over," I blurted, my pulse racing as I put my foot on the gas. "My uncle, he's well, he's very paranoid. That's why there are so many cameras. If you just wait a few minutes until I get there, I'll go inside and get Stu for you. But I promise, there's nothing to worry about."

Karla let out a long sigh, and I couldn't tell if she was buying my story. I hated that I had to lie to them, but today was the worst day they could've picked to follow Stu. We needed everything to run as smoothly as possible, and if Renfield saw them he was liable to get suspicious and call the whole thing off.

"Okay, we'll wait for you," said Karla. "But we're not leaving until we talk to Stu. Lee wants to make sure he's okay."

"All right, see you in a bit," I replied and hung up. I chewed on my bottom lip and put my phone on hands-free to dial Stu. I'd been so stressed by Karla's call that I hadn't even realised I'd been talking and driving at the same time. Frustratingly, all I got was Stu's voicemail. His phone was off. Wonderful.

I got stuck in traffic halfway there, though at least it gave me enough time to throw on some makeup. When I finally arrived, Lee and Karla were parked just across the street. I cut my engine and hurried over to them. Lee rolled down his window and I bent to speak, trying to keep a calm façade. "Hi you two. I'm just going to run over and get Stu. My uncle's a little, um, eccentric. He doesn't like strangers in his house so it's probably for the best if you stay out here."

Lee eyed me like he was trying to figure out why I was acting weird. "That's some rich uncle you've got."

I nodded and plastered on a smile. "Yes, it's too bad he's not big into sharing the wealth."

Karla was quiet, which only made my nerves worse. She was too shrewd not to notice something was up, especially considering what she did for a living. I just hoped my false breeziness was convincing.

I cleared my throat. "Right, well, I'll be back in a minute."

I walked across the street to Renfield's, first stopping just shy of the security cameras and out of sight of Lee and Karla so that I could pull on the wig and slip on some sunglasses to cover my eyes. My hair had been up in a bun so the wig slid on easily enough. I just hoped it looked okay because I didn't have a mirror on me to check.

This was officially the most surreal day of my life.

When I pressed the button to be let in, I was immediately answered by the butler. I told him I needed to see 'Mr. Kennedy' and that it was urgent. He quickly buzzed me through and I entered the walled garden and driveway. Stu was busy loading carefully packed boxes into the transit van. Several questions flashed across his face when he saw me, and his accusing expression spoke volumes.

What the hell are you doing here?

I swallowed and calmly approached him, wary of a few other members of Renfield's household staff puttering about. Keeping my voice as quiet as I could, I said, "Lee and Karla are outside. After your *fight* with Lee, they followed you here. Was today really the best day for your temper to be let loose?"

Stu's features hardened as he took in what I said. He opened his mouth to say something, but before he could speak Renfield stepped out of his house. He looked delighted to see me.

"Miss Jordan, or should I say *Mrs Jordan*? What a pleasant surprise," he greeted and stepped forward to take

259

my hand in his. He lifted it to his mouth for a kiss then lowered it. "What brings you here?"

After he asked the question I noticed the steel behind his smile. He was suspicious, and he had every right to be. *Come on, brain, don't fail me now.*

"I just found out that there's a police check on the original route I planned for Mr Kennedy to take to the port," I said. It was the first excuse that sprung to mind. "I tried calling him to advise on a different direction to take, but I couldn't get through. I apologise for just turning up at your home like this, but it was the only way to warn him."

"Ah," said Renfield, rubbing at his jaw as his suspicion subsided. "Well, I'm very lucky you took the initiative to come in person, otherwise we might've found ourselves in a terrible spot of bother. Please, come inside and have a drink with me. I'd like to thank you for saving our bacon."

"Oh, well, I . . ."

"She's got a meeting she has to go to. Isn't that right, Mrs Jordan?" Stu cut in.

I nodded. "Yes, that's right. Actually, I'm late. I'd better hurry."

"Of course. I won't keep you then. It was a pleasure to see you again, Rebecca," said Renfield.

"You, too," I smiled.

"I'll walk you out," said Stu just as Renfield turned and went back inside his house. My heart pounded all the way to the gate. Stu placed his hand to the small of my back and his touch eased some of my nerves. Once we were out of view I quickly pulled off the wig and shoved it back in my handbag before Lee saw us. Both he and Karla got out of the car when we approached.

"So you're following me now?" said Stu.

"You lost your rag with me this morning for no reason. What was I supposed to do?"

"Well, don't stalk me for a start."

Lee let out a gruff breath and ran a hand through his hair. "Look, I know it was wrong of me, but I've been worried. You know I have. And then you turn up at a place like this. What did you expect me to think? How was I to know Andie had some rich uncle? You have to admit, it's looks suspicious."

I saw Stu swallow, and I knew he felt guilty. He clearly didn't want to lie to Lee, but he had to. It was the only way to keep his family safe. I didn't know what I expected him to say, but he surprised me when he suddenly blurted. "I'm sorry. I know I've been acting like a moody bastard and you don't deserve it. It's taken me a while to get my head on straight after being inside, but I promise you things will be different from now on."

Lee frowned, but I could tell it was more because he was feeling emotional and didn't know how to deal with it, especially since he had an audience. Karla and I made eye contact and I thought we were both feeling the same way, like maybe we should give the brothers some privacy. At the same time, I was aware that we couldn't stand out here for much longer without causing suspicion.

Without a word, Lee stepped forward and pulled Stu into a hug. "No need to be sorry, bruv. I love you." He drew back, and I felt a little like I might well up. In spite of the urgency of the situation, that had been a heart-warming moment.

"I'll always have your back, Stu."

Stu gave his brother a serious look. "And I'll always have yours."

With that they hugged it out once more time before Lee and Karla got back in their car and drove off. I stood on the sidewalk with Stu, who had gone very still and very silent.

Taking his hand in mine, I asked, "Are you all right?"

"I don't like lying to him."

"I know, but after today you'll never have to again."

He exhaled heavily, his gaze tender when it met mine. "Yeah, you're right. I suppose I better finish this fucking job then, eh?"

I squeezed his hand and pressed a quick kiss to his lips.

"Finish the job, and then come home to me," I whispered.

I was in my car, buckling myself in when I realised how important it was that he do just that. *I needed him to come home . . . to me.* I wasn't sure what I'd do if anything happened to him and the thought was sobering.

Twenty-Two

The next few hours were some of the most nerve-wracking of my life. Stu was out of contact as he took care of switching the paintings and then passing the rest of the cargo on to his man at the port. After explaining to Alfie everything that went down over at Renfield's, I drank copious amounts of coffee and chewed off half my fingernails. I practically leapt up from my seat when at long last there was a knock on the door.

Stu stood on the step and I'd never felt so relieved to see him all in one piece. He was handsome as ever, though he did appear a small bit out of breath. In his hand he held a thin leather case, which I presumed contained the painting.

"Is that . . . did you . . . was everything . . .?" I rambled, my nerves getting the best of me.

"Relax, Andrea, it's done. Everything went off without a hitch," Stu reassured. "Well, after my brother decided to show and almost mess up everything, that is."

I exhaled and motioned for him to come in. Stu stepped past me and inside the flat. I closed the door. Alfie stood and clasped his hands together, his posture practically humming with anticipation.

"I can't express how grateful I am that you're allowing me this opportunity, Stu. You don't know how much it means to me."

Stu stepped forward and handed him the case, his expression kind as he approached my cousin. "Just be gentle with the old girl. She's not as young as she used to me."

Alfie didn't even register the joke, too preoccupied with the precious cargo. *He didn't need to be told to be careful.* He took the case with barely concealed reverence, his palms outspread and facing upward as though he were holding a holy relic. He cleared his throat. "I hope I'm not pushing my luck, but do you mind if I view it alone? I'm afraid I might embarrass myself and tear up in front of both of you."

Stu and I exchanged a glance. I knew Alfie wasn't trying to do anything shifty; he was simply an art lover and this was a special experience for him. Luckily, Stu got it because he smiled and replied, "Sure, mate, take it inside your room and do your thing, but I need to leave in ten minutes to meet with the Duke and make the exchange."

Alfie nodded his understanding and quickly slipped down the hall to his room. I glanced at Stu. "You're meeting with the Duke? I thought he was still in prison."

"He got out a few days ago."

"Oh. Well, are you sure it's safe?"

"I can take care of myself, Andrea," he answered, evading the question. I started to worry.

"You should let me come with you, just in case. He won't be able to try anything if I'm there."

Stu cocked an eyebrow. "What do you think he's gonna do? Kidnap me? All he cares about is the painting. So long as I hand it over I'm good as gold."

"But he still owes you money after he sells it. What if he decides he'd rather get rid of you than hand over the cash? Stu, I don't know what I'd do if anything happened to you," I said, my voice shaky with emotion.

He moved across the room and pulled me into his arms. "Stop worrying. The Duke's a man of his word. So long as I hold up my end of the bargain, he'll hold up his."

I buried my face in the crook of his neck, but for once, I didn't feel calmed. Just because Stu trusted this guy didn't mean I did. I simply couldn't believe that a man who would lower himself to threatening the safety of somebody's family could be trusted.

Stu pulled me closer, hugging me tight as we waited for Alfie to emerge from his bedroom. He inhaled deeply, smelling my hair. His lips brushed the top of my ear and a tendril of desire stirred within me despite the current circumstances.

A minute later Alfie returned, silently handing the case back over to Stu, his words solemn. "Thank you. You're proven yourself a kind and selfless person today, Stu Cross, and I won't forget it."

Alfie's emotional words took me by surprise, and the way he looked at Stu told me he truly meant them. He considered him a friend now—one of us. And for someone like Alfie to accept and trust Stu, well, it spoke volumes. Stu's face reddened a little, like he was just as touched by Alfie's sentiment as I was.

"I owed you," he replied. "I couldn't have pulled this off without you. I'm just the muscle. You're the brains." He paused and then glanced at me before whispering, "She's the heart."

Everything seemed to still and I couldn't seem to get my pulse to slow down. Everything inside me wanted to grab him and kiss him until we were both breathless, but now wasn't the time. A moment passed before Stu looked away. He clipped open the case and took a quick peek inside. He smiled when he looked to Alfie again. "No offence, but you can never be too careful with these things."

Alfie held his hands in the air. "Oh, none taken. I completely understand."

Stu exhaled a long breath and stood up straight. "Right, well, I'm off. I'll call you once I'm done to let you know everything went as planned."

My stomach quivered as I watched him leave the flat, a painting potentially worth millions in his possession. As soon as the door closed I grabbed my coat and car keys.

"Where are you off to in such a hurry this time?" Alfie questioned.

"I'm following Stu. He might trust this guy, but I don't. I need to be there in case anything bad happens."

"And what are you going to do if it does? Take them all on with your mad fighting skills?" Alfie scoffed.

I shook my head, already out the door and halfway to my car. Alfie followed me, not prepared to let me go so easily. "I'll figure that part out when I come to it."

"No, you won't. You shouldn't be doing this, Andie. It's a terrible idea."

I slid into the driver's seat while Alfie got in and strapped on his seatbelt. I stared at him. "What are you doing?"

"I'm coming with you so I can stop you from doing anything stupid."

At the end of the street I saw Stu's car pull away. I started up my engine and immediately followed, making sure to stay a fair distance behind so he didn't realise he had a tail.

"I'm not going to do anything stupid," I huffed.

"And I don't believe you. You've been acting out of character these past few weeks. Who knows what kind of unpredictable decisions you could make?"

"I have not," I protested.

"Oh really? Shall I list all the ways you've been acting strange?"

"No, thank you."

Alfie started listing anyway. "Number one, you allowed yourself to get close to a student outside of work. Number two, even though we agreed you wouldn't be involved in the robbery you still went to that meeting with Renfield, which was ridiculously stupid but you wouldn't listen to me."

"Stu needed me—"

"I'm not finished," Alfie said. "Number three, you wanted to go with Stu to meet the Duke even though it would make you an accessory to the robbery. And number four, you've been having sex with your student, which, I must say, is probably the most stupid part of all."

Fuck.

I gasped in shock before turning to glare at him. "You knew."

"Of course I knew. I'm not the stupid one here."

"Stop calling me stupid."

"All right, I'll amend my wording. Perhaps misguided is better."

"I'm not misguided either. I genuinely care for him."

"Well, yes, that might very well be true. And believe me, Andie, I get it, the guy is a perfect specimen of male beauty, but once all this is over and he has his money he could disappear. Go anywhere. Then you'll be left nursing a broken heart. I'm not trying to be cruel here. I'm only saying this because I care about you. You're my family and I don't want to see you hurt."

I bit my lip, because at the back of my mind I'd worried the same thing. Would Stu leave me once the excitement of our secret relationship wore away and he had his money? Was he simply keeping me sweet so that in turn

I'd continue to encourage Alfie's cooperation with the heist?

Too many questions. I felt a migraine coming on.

"I can't believe you knew and didn't say anything," I muttered quietly, feeling self-conscious now.

"Andie, the most oblivious person in the world couldn't stand in a room with you two and not realise you were sleeping together. Your chemistry is off the charts."

"Don't say that. What if my other students have noticed? Oh God, this is awful." If I wasn't driving right then I'd bury my face in my hands.

My cousin reached over and softly squeezed my arm. "Listen, maybe I was exaggerating a little. If they haven't said anything by now, they probably don't know. If they did there'd be rumours. No one can resist the urge to spill a juicy bit of gossip like that."

"If you're trying to make me feel better, you're failing miserably."

"I'm sorry. Sometimes I say things all the wrong way. I get out of practice with people when I'm stuck indoors painting all the time."

I shook my head, quiet for a moment before replying, "Don't apologise. You know what? You're right. I am stupid. If even a hint of my relationship with Stu got out, I'd be fired. What the hell have I been thinking?"

"I doubt your brain had much say in the matter," said Alfie.

I shot him the stink eye.

"What? Too early for jokes?"

"Way too early."

Focusing my attention up ahead I realised we were on the same street that housed Lee's restaurant. Was Stu meeting the Duke here? It didn't make sense. A moment later he emerged from his car, walked out onto the road, and hailed a taxi.

I followed the cab and soon we were driving towards central London. We passed through the West End, then, to my surprise Stu got out at Trafalgar Square. This was where I'd brought the class on their day trip to the art gallery. It was a busy hour and there were lots of people around. I parked outside an old pub across the street as Stu passed through the crowds, his eyes constantly scanning the area.

"Well, at least he had the wits to organise to meet him in a public place," said Alfie. "It's not like the Duke can pull anything dodgy here. There are too many people."

"You'd be surprised," I said, still on edge.

A red double decker-bus went by, momentarily blocking our view. I panicked when it passed and I couldn't see Stu anywhere, but then exhaled when I spotted him lowering himself to sit on a step. He checked his phone, looked from left to right, and then he just . . . waited.

Several minutes passed and there was still no sign of the Duke.

"Looks like our man is late."

"Either that or Stu's been stood up," said Alfie.

What did this mean? "I'm sure he'll be here soon."

But I was wrong. Twenty minutes later Stu stood, his jaw tight and his posture portraying his unhappiness. Whatever was going on here, something wasn't right. He strode past groups of tourists looking at maps and taking photographs, his tall form striking a formidable figure. Alfie and I were quiet as we watched him, and then, almost like he sensed our attention Stu looked up and spotted my car.

"Oh shit," Alfie swore. "We've been made."

269

"Crap, crap, crap." I twisted my keys, prepared to make a swift exit and then deny everything later down the line.

Who? Me? At Trafalgar Square? Couldn't have been. I was home correcting papers in my pyjamas all evening. Lots of people have this car. It could've been anyone.

Unfortunately, my hands were shaking and it took me longer than normal to start the engine. Before I knew it Stu was standing in front of us, his gaze furious. I swallowed past the hard lump lodged in my throat. A second later he climbed into the backseat, slamming the door shut behind him with a loud thud.

I glanced at him nervously through the overhead mirror.

"Drive," he ordered.

I drove.

The tension was so thick that both Alfie and I were too afraid to breathe a word. Stu was intimidating when he was angry. He ran a hand down his face, his features etched with stress as I drove in the direction of my flat. We'd suffered at least fifteen minutes of tense silence when Stu finally spoke.

"What the hell were you thinking following me? I told you I didn't need you there."

I white-knuckled the steering wheel, trying to come up with an excuse and falling short.

"Would you believe us if we said we just so happened to be in the area?" Alfie asked in an effort to diffuse the tension. Stu glared at him, and he zipped his mouth shut.

"I was worried about you," I managed finally.

"And I told you there was nothing to worry about. For fuck's sake, Andrea, the Duke didn't show. Do you know what this means?"

270

I glanced at him through the mirror, swallowing tightly as I shook my head.

"It means he spotted you. It means he knows I told you more than I was ever supposed to. I've been trying to keep you both safe, and you've fucked everything up."

"Hey, don't talk to her like that!" Alfie butted in, his features drawn in a frown.

Stu's dark eyes cut to my cousin. "I'm pissed off and I'll express it how I like."

My cheeks heated. "Look, it's done now so there's nothing we can do to change it. I messed up and I'm sorry . . ."

Stu leaned forward, his shoulders rigid. "You don't understand. He's not just going to let this fly. He doesn't like loose ends and that means he's going to try and do something to tie them up."

"You mean, to tie us up?" Alfie questioned nervously.

Stu exhaled and dropped back into the seat. "I can't protect you from him."

I looked at him through my mirror again and our eyes locked. It was then that I saw how powerless he felt. He'd been in control but I'd gone and ruined all that. Now everything was up in the air. I really was stupid, always thinking with something other than my head. This time it had been with my soft foolish heart.

"We need to come up with a plan. A story to explain everything away and gain his trust again. Do you have a way of contacting him?" I asked and Stu looked at me like I was being naïve.

"I've got a number," Stu replied, "but look, I think you just need to stay out of this from now on. I'll figure something out."

271

I opened my mouth to say something but came up short. I was at a loss for words yet again. When I turned onto our street and stopped the car outside the flat, I turned off the engine and we all just sat in silence for a minute. Our brains were working overtime to come up with a solution. It was only as I was lost in thought that I noticed the suspiciously out-of-place gentleman standing at the end of the street.

He was big and muscular, but he wore a suit. He looked like he should be working security for the government or something. When I glanced through my side mirror I saw a similarly dressed man at the other end of the street. This didn't bode well.

"Stu," I whispered, afraid that even halfway down the street they might hear me.

He didn't answer so I whispered louder. "Stu!"

His tired gaze flicked to mine. "What is it, Andrea?"

I cocked my head ever so slightly to indicate both gentlemen. Alfie made a move to turn in his seat but I grabbed him and urged him not to look. Stu let out a whispered string of expletives.

"All right, this is what you're going to do," he ordered, his mouth barely moving as he spoke. "Start the car back up real slow and get us out of here as quick as you can."

I nodded and brought my hand to my keys. I was shaking. I started the engine and put my foot on the gas. Just as I pulled out onto the road I hit the brakes and let out a startled yelp, because one of the men was now standing directly in front of my car. I tried to reverse but the other was standing behind it. They both had shoulders so wide they might as well have been brick walls.

"Throw the keys out the window," one of them shouted. I looked to Stu, his face angry yet resigned.

272

Finally, he nodded and I did as the man requested. My keys hit the ground and the man picked them up. "Now all of you get out of the car and head inside. You've got a visitor."

I'd never been so nervous in my entire life. Alfie looked just as terrified. This wasn't our world. We didn't belong here. Stu was the only one who didn't look frightened. If I was honest, he looked like he was weighing his chances of taking on both men in a fight. He must have decided the odds were against him because he didn't initiate any violence.

I took Alfie's hand in mine as we headed for the door of our flat. It was already open. The lock was bashed in and the door ajar. We both took a step inside and entered the living room, Stu close behind us. I sucked in a breath when I saw the entire place had been ransacked. My gaze travelled over our trashed living room before we all stopped short. My heart pounded as I stared at the dapper gentleman lounging casually on our worn-out sofa.

He wasn't a stranger. In fact, I recognised him instantly.

Perhaps this was our world, after all.

Alfie dropped my hand and took a hesitant step backward, his voice hushed as he whispered, "Dad?"

Twenty-Three

"Alfred, my boy, it's been a long time. My, look how you've grown," said Raymond, his gaze sharp as he took in his son.

I did a quick mental calculation. Alfie hadn't seen his dad since he was seventeen when he was prosecuted and sent away for committing fraud. That was over a decade ago. I heard my cousin's breathing quicken as he clutched my hand again, his grip so tight it was almost crushing.

"Get out," he said, voice quiet.

"Well, that's no way to greet your father," Raymond chided.

"Get out, please get out," Alfie went on, louder now. He started to hyperventilate and I quickly realised he was having a panic attack.

"You need to leave," I ordered, channelling as much authority into my voice as possible. Raymond, or should I say 'the Duke', chuckled, a hint of cruelty behind it. "Oh, I'm not going anywhere."

"Can't you see that he doesn't want you here?" I shouted, my protective instincts kicking in. "He doesn't want to see you, so just go."

"Andrea, don't . . ." Alfie pleaded and I immediately regretted my outburst. Obviously, he didn't want us having a domestic with his dad in front of Stu and the two suited men standing in the doorway.

Speak of the devil . . . Stu's every muscle was coiled tight. In fact, I'd never seen him look so furious. The funny thing was, he didn't look surprised. Not. One. Bit.

He'd known.

274

Quick as lightning my hostility found a new target. "You knew!" I exclaimed hoarsely, my voice catching with emotion. "You knew all along, didn't you?"

Suddenly, everything made sense, how 'the Duke' knew so much about us, how he targeted us from the very beginning. Betrayal. It was an ugly, painful sore to experience, but that's what I felt. I had trusted Stu. I had trusted his thoughts, his promises. I had trusted him with my heart. And he did this. *How could he?*

Alfie's dad must've found out that we'd been living together for the past few years. Furthermore, he knew how resistant Alfie was to new people and that the only way for Stu to meet him was through me.

Alfie gasped and turned away from his dad to face Stu. His expression was horrified. "Did you?" he asked in a tiny voice. His feelings were hurt, and it was in that moment that I realised just how fond Alfie had grown of Stu. He might've denied it if asked, but I could see he'd considered him trustworthy, a friend. I'd never seen him look so betrayed and I didn't know who I was angrier for: me or my cousin.

Stu cleared his throat, his expression torn as his brows drew together. "Let me explain—"

"There's nothing to explain. I should've known you were hiding something. You've been lying to us from the start."

"Andrea, I couldn't tell you. You have to believe me."

"I don't want to hear it. Just leave," I growled, turning to Raymond. "Both of you can leave. I don't even know why you came here."

"Andrea, darling, sit down and be quiet," Raymond ordered, standing from the couch and walking towards Stu.

"I take it that's the painting," he went on, eyeing the case eagerly.

Without a word Stu handed it to him and Raymond grinned as he ran his fingers over the leather. He carried it to the coffee table, set it down and then sat again. He flicked open the locks and exhaled a breath once he saw the painting.

"Magnificent."

I couldn't argue with him. I eyed the piece, completely identical to the one Alfie had painted. Raymond ever so gently touched his fingers to the canvas.

"D-don't do that," Alfie stammered and his father shot him a cynical glance, placing his fingers more firmly against the paint as though in challenge. "There might be something on your skin that could corrupt the canvas," Alfie went on.

"I think you'll find my hands are perfectly clean, Alfred," Raymond replied.

"Don't be a prick," said Stu, and Alfie's dad's gaze cut to him.

"I'll thank you to keep quiet. You're hardly in a position to tell me what to do." He paused, his attention sliding to me. "It seems you went above and beyond the call of duty in regards to what I sent you here to achieve."

Stu opened his mouth to speak but Raymond held up a hand. "Don't bother. It's clear to me you allowed yourself to develop feelings for my niece. How tragic. And there was me, thinking I'd found a heartless hardened criminal to do my bidding."

"Fuck you, *Raymond*," Stu swore, the way he said his name dripping with disrespect.

Raymond chuckled a mirthless laugh. "Are you testing me, son?"

"Why can't you just leave?" Alfie interjected. My cousin was still hyperventilating. I wrapped an arm around his shoulders and whispered for him to take slow, deep breaths. Then I narrowed my gaze on Raymond. "Why did you even come here? You could've collected the case from Stu earlier without the need to drag us into it."

"Ah, but I've had my men following young Stuart all morning, you see. And I'm sure you can imagine my surprise when they told me he made a stop here of all places instead of coming directly to meet me. Something was amiss."

"Is that why you ransacked our flat? Nothing was amiss. Alfie wanted to see the painting since he's been working day and night to replicate it. It was the least he deserved for all his hard work."

Raymond dismissed me with a glance, his attention going to his son. "Still so sentimental."

Alfie wheezed a shaky breath. Raymond rolled his eyes heavenward and I wanted to punch him in that moment. It was his fault Alfie's mum was a neurotic wreck all through his childhood, and it was his fault they were left with nothing and my cousin had to paint counterfeits in order to save their house. He wasn't a father. He was nothing.

"For crying out loud, Alfred, calm down. You'd swear I was holding a knife to your throat. If it's the money you're worried about you can relax. I'm a man of my word. I'll pay you everything you're owed once the sale of the painting is finalised."

"You can stuff your money. We don't want it," I barked, letting go of my cousin to face his dad head-on.

"Oh darling, of everyone in this room you're the last person who should be refusing a payout."

I gaped at him. "Look at you, still so obsessed. This has nothing to do with money. This has to do with you leaving your wife and child penniless and desperate. He never wanted to see you again, and he never should have to. Now you're exploiting him for your own gain. You're a worthless excuse for a father."

Raymond huffed a careless laugh. "It's not my fault he's always been soft."

"It's exactly your fault. You were too busy working so hard to defraud people out of their money when you should've been raising your son. As far as I'm concerned they never should've let you out of prison."

"Well, luckily that's not your decision to make," said Raymond, his attention falling to Alfie again. "Aren't you even going to say anything, son?"

Alfie glanced up coldly and shook his head.

"Good Lord, still as soft as ever."

"If not being soft means being like you then you can keep it," Alfie finally muttered.

"Ah, he speaks."

"You've got your painting. You can go now. I have nothing to say to you."

"Well, now you're just being rude. I was hoping we could talk about old times," Raymond replied sarcastically. With a short huff of dissatisfaction, he closed over the case and locked it shut. He cast both of us one final dismissive glance before he stood and brushed down his slacks.

"Stuart, I'd like a word in private if you don't mind."

Stu's eyes met mine briefly. I could see the apology in them but I didn't want to hear it. A second later he followed Raymond outside. My heart felt like it was breaking apart piece by piece.

Everything between us had been a lie.

278

I'd told him all about Alfie's childhood, and he hadn't said a word. He'd known it was his dad behind all this, and he'd known exactly what a careless bastard the man was *and he hadn't said a word.*

As soon as they were gone Alfie deflated, tears streaming down his face as he silently cried. I pulled him into my arms, holding him close and whispering that everything was going to be all right, even though I knew it wouldn't. Stu's betrayal aside, seeing his dad again after all these years was going to set him back. He'd been doing so well since leaving his mother's house and his troubled childhood behind, but now he was back there, lonely and helpless.

Vulnerable.

My cousin was a man made of glass, naturally sensitive, and always so close to shattering. It sounded like a bad thing but it was why I loved him. It was what made him so unique. Unwillingly, my thoughts travelled backwards, as something Stu once said to me rose forth.

You made me realise that softness is necessary. That we need both. People who are kind and who help others are needed, but so are people who are hard, toughened by experience.

Why was it his words I was remembering right then? His words that were helping me make sense of everything. Raymond was wrong to think Alfie's softness was a weakness. It was what allowed him to create things no one else could, art that made people *feel.*

His weakness created his strength. I just wished mine could be considered one, too. Unfortunately, my open-heart hadn't achieved anything beautiful this time. It had brought me hurt. Alfie, too.

A few minutes passed and then I heard car doors slamming and engines starting up outside. I relaxed a little to know Raymond was finally leaving, even if he had left our flat turned upside down. Slowly, I helped Alfie to his room where he quietly climbed into bed and pulled the covers over himself. I rubbed soothingly at his back for a little while until I heard his breathing even out and knew he'd fallen asleep.

I'd unintentionally brought betrayal into his life and it made me feel truly awful.

As quietly as I could manage, I closed his door and went about putting the flat back to rights. If I could just focus on that task, maybe I could ignore how I was falling apart inside.

The last few weeks meant nothing.

Stu had just been using me. *Again.*

I stopped short when I walked into the living room and he was sitting on the couch.

My hand went to my heart as though to shield it. "Why are you still here?"

Stu got up and came towards me. I backed up all the way to the other side of the room. His gaze was pleading, but I didn't let it get to me. "Just let me help you clean the flat. It's my fault the Duke's men wrecked the place. I never should've brought the painting here. That's why he turned everything over. He thought we were trying to hide something."

"Yes well, you never should've done a lot of things, but there's no changing that now. And will you please stop calling him the Duke? It sounds ridiculous. It always sounded ridiculous. He's a horrible little man and you should've been straight with us from the beginning about who was actually behind all this."

"Andrea, I couldn't tell you. He was blackmailing me, remember? He didn't ever want either of you to know it was him. He was going to take the painting and sell it and you'd never be any the wiser."

"Oh, so that makes it better?"

"At least Alfie wouldn't have had to go through seeing him. He's clearly having some kind of a meltdown."

"Alfie is none of your concern anymore."

"You don't own him."

"No, but I protect him. He's my family and he never trusts people, *but he trusted you.* He considered you a friend. The worst part is that I'm the one who brought you into his life, and I'm the one who encouraged him to spend time with you. Now he's suffering and it's all because I let you into our lives."

He took a step toward me but I held up my hand. "Don't. Don't come any closer."

"I promise if I could go back and change things I would."

At this I bit out a humourless laugh. "No, you wouldn't. Because if you did things any differently those men would've been paying a visit to your home instead of mine, and they wouldn't have left at throwing a few bits of furniture around."

"Exactly. My hands were tied."

I frowned, my words stuttering, "N-no y-you still . . . God, I don't even understand how you and Raymond were even in the same prison. He was prosecuted and sent to an open prison for white-collar crimes."

"He got on the wrong side of one of the other inmates. This guy had a lot of sway with the higher ups and he didn't want the Duke, I mean Raymond, around anymore, so he had him transferred," Stu explained.

I gaped at him. "Is that even legal?"

"Half the stuff that goes on in prison isn't legal. That's what happens when you house a bunch of criminals together."

"Yes well, I'll know not to trust one in the future," I said harshly, folding my arms across my chest.

"Andrea, please."

"No, Stu, I don't want to hear it. All I want to do right now is salvage what I can of my furniture, make sure my cousin is okay, and then go to bed. I don't want to talk to you. I'm sick of talking."

He mimicked me when he folded his arms and stood completely still. "I'm not going anywhere."

"Well then you're going to have a long night ahead of you."

I moved by him and went into the kitchen, ignoring him completely as I went about collecting the broken cups and plates and putting them in a black bin liner. Warm fingers covered mine. "Let me help," Stu urged.

I pulled the bag from his hold and turned away. He let out a long, tired sigh as I kept busy cleaning. I heard movement in the living room and knew he was cleaning up in spite of me telling him I didn't want his help. *Of course he wouldn't listen.* By the time I had the kitchen back to rights the living room was almost good as new. I still couldn't face him though. Instead I went to my bedroom and locked the door. A few minutes later there was a gentle knock.

"Andrea, let me in."

"Go away."

"Please, don't . . . don't do this."

"I didn't do this. You did this."

"I didn't have a choice." His voice was scratchy, and in spite of myself my heart panged. He was hurting too but I couldn't let myself feel any sympathy. *His* family was now safe. *He* was a liar. I had to remember how he'd deceived me.

"I said go away," I finally managed, trying to keep my voice steady even though all I wanted was to break down. I cared for him so much and now everything was ruined. Even if he truly was sorry I'd never be able to trust him again. He loved his family, and I didn't hold that against him, not for a second. But the fact remained that for him they'd always come first.

From the beginning I tried not to hold Stu's past against him, but now I knew that I had to. What if some other criminal he knew came along and blackmailed him the same as Raymond had? He'd protect his family before Alfie and me, and that meant I couldn't have him in my life. I couldn't put *my* family at risk. All I had was three people: Alfie, Mum, and Dad. I used to have four but lost one, and I knew I wouldn't survive the pain of losing another. I almost didn't survive the last time. Some days I was still only hanging on by a thin thread.

Hanging on by determination and duct tape.

I refused to live like that anymore. I had to at least learn that I could move forward. Just not with Stu.

"Andrea, let me see your face," Stu whispered but I ignored him. His voice made me want to give in and I had to be strong.

As I crawled into bed I heard him slide down to sit on the floor. He could stay out there all night; I still wasn't opening my door.

Twenty-Four

I didn't hear Stu move for a long time, and after lots of silently shed tears I drifted off to sleep. When I woke it was because my alarm went off, and regrettably I had to get up for work. My heart still felt very broken, and I struggled to leave my room.

I really hoped Stu wasn't still outside.

Very slowly I unlocked my door and opened it. The hallway was empty. I frowned as I glanced at the front door, because the lock wasn't broken anymore. Taking a few more steps towards it I saw it was repaired and knew it had to have been Stu. Again I felt a pang in my heart but I endeavoured to ignore it.

I went to Alfie's room, knocking first before peeking my head inside. I expected to find him asleep but he was up, a new canvas in front of him as he went to work on it with a combination of blacks, yellows, and oranges. Approaching him, I placed a hand on his shoulder but he flinched away from my touch.

"Don't. Please," he whispered, not turning to look at me. "I just want to be alone."

I didn't push him. Instead I nodded sombrely and went to take a shower. It wasn't until I was under the spray that I let myself cry. I thought I couldn't possibly have any more tears left in me but I was wrong. *I hated seeing him in pain.*

The entire drive to work I twisted my ring around and around, an outward sign of my inner turmoil. Thankfully, I was early and none of my students had arrived yet. I wondered if Stu would come today. Half of me didn't want to see him, but the other half didn't want him to give up on his education. I wasn't sure I could handle seeing him every day, but there were plenty of other adult classes at the college he could transfer to.

Just because he'd lied to me didn't mean I didn't still care about him. I wasn't the sort of person who could just turn off their feelings like that. I wanted him to go to university, to fulfil his potential. I wanted him to get a degree and change his life, not be just another statistic of an ex-con returning to crime after serving time.

I wanted him to find his Christminster.

The thought was sobering. How could I hate him for lying yet still want him to find happiness?

Kian was the first to arrive to class. I plastered on a smile I wasn't really feeling and told him good morning. Next was Mary and Susan, and before long all of my students were there, all except one. Stu's seat remained empty until only a minute before the bell rang. The door opened and he strode inside, his shoulders knit with tension and his hair still wet from a shower. I stared at him and his eyes came to mine—so handsome, so golden . . . so sorry.

Now he was here I knew I had to steel myself, especially considering how there were a thousand apologies in his gaze that my heart wanted to give in to. I reminded myself of how Alfie had been last night, of how he'd been this morning. I knew he was going to be like that for weeks, if not months. He'd retreated inside his mind and it was going to be a challenge to get him back on track.

I cleared my throat to make an announcement. "This morning we're going to watch the film adaptation of *Jude*."

"Score!" Susan drove her fist into the air. "I love movie days."

"It's not in black and white, is it, Miss Anderson?" asked Jake, another of my younger students. "I hate black and white films."

"It starts out that way but then turns to colour, sort of like *The Wizard of Oz*," I answered, aware of Stu watching me as I spoke. "It's from the nineties and stars Kate Winslet as Sue."

"Love her," said Mary.

"Ugh, I hated *The Wizard of Oz*," Jake complained.

"Who's Kate Winslet?" Larry asked.

"OMG, I can't believe you don't know who Kate Winslet is." Susan gaped at Larry.

"That's enough," I said firmly. I had to put my foot down before they got rowdy. "I want you to take notes while you're watching and jot down any differences you see between the book and the film," I went on. "Then tomorrow we're going to have a debate on whether or not you think books should be made into films. When you're finished watching it you'll decide whether you're for or against and we'll divide you into two teams."

"I hate debates," said Larry.

"Oh, I love them," said Susan. "I always win."

"There's a difference between winning a debate and being louder than anyone else in the room," Mary teased and Susan stuck out her tongue.

I busied myself setting up the film and then went to dim the lights before hitting play. Unable to handle the idea of Stu watching me in the darkened room, I went to stand by the door as the class focused their attention on the screen. Once I saw they'd all settled down and had fallen into the story I quietly slipped out the door and went to use the bathroom.

Well, I didn't actually need to go. I just needed some air and the staff bathroom was my sanctuary right then. I splashed water over my hands and wrists in an effort to cool myself down, then stared at my reflection in the mirror for a long few moments.

I looked tired, and my eyes were puffy from hours of crying. Just thinking about why I was sad meant they started to water again.

I sniffled and went to grab some tissues from one of the stalls when I heard the door swing open. I didn't want to be caught crying by one of my co-workers, so I quickly dabbed away the wetness. I waited for whoever it was to shut themselves inside a stall, but I didn't hear any locks click. A second later a warm hand came to rest on my shoulder and I didn't have to look to know who it was.

"You can't be in here," I said, still not looking at him.

"The Duke is selling the painting to his buyer this morning. The money will be transferred to Alfie's account by lunch time," he said and I let out a watery laugh. For a second there I thought he'd come to discuss something other than business. I wanted him to be upset about me. About how his lies destroyed us.

But maybe he didn't feel that at all.

"That money is no concern of mine. It's Alfie's. He's the one who earned it."

Stu frowned. "You earned it, too. And you need it more than any of us."

"Get back to class. You're supposed to be watching the film."

"I'll watch it later."

"Stu, get out of the staff bathroom now before I report you for disobedient behaviour." I stood straighter, stepping out of the stall and away from his soothing touch.

His gaze narrowed. "How long are you gonna keep this up?"

"Until you accept that aside from being your teacher, I don't want anything else to do with you."

When he winced slightly, I knew my words had affected him. My throat quivered but I didn't let it show. *Wouldn't.*

"That's a lie," said Stu, his voice low as he advanced on me. I backed up against the sink but he kept on coming forward until our bodies were almost touching. Stu gently took my arms and unfolded them. "Stop trying to push me away. It won't work," he whispered, his voice soft.

I firmed my jaw. "Get your hands off me."

"Never." He took each of my hands in his and laced our fingers together. I was too caught up in his tender gaze to fight it. Stu leaned in, his chest brushing mine, and his scent overpowered me. I'd come to love that scent. *Love.*

I'd come to love everything about him, but in an instant all of that had changed.

"This is the last time I'm going to say it. Go back to class, Stu."

"This isn't the last time I'm going to say it, Andrea, in fact, I'll keep telling you until you finally forgive me. I'm sorry. I've never been sorrier in my entire life."

My eyes moved back and forth between his and in spite of the fact that he'd lied to me before, I knew in this moment he was telling the truth.

"I forgive you," I said quietly.

As soon as the words left my mouth his body sagged and he inched his lips towards mine.

"Thank you," he breathed but I shifted back and moved away from him, my fingers slipping out of his and his lips meeting nothing but air. A confused expression crossed his face.

"Andrea?"

"I forgive you, Stu, but that doesn't mean our relationship can continue. It was wrong of me to let things get this far in the first place."

"But, luv, I need you—"

I held up a hand to stop him from saying anymore, because if he did my strength was in danger of breaking.

"I care about you, I always will, and I hope you'll continue with your studies because I honestly want you to graduate and go on to university. But we can't be together anymore. I'm sorry."

Stu's features hardened. "Why not?"

"Because I can't trust you."

His anger was palpable. I could see it in the way his jaw tensed. "For fuck's sake, you can trust me, Andrea. You know I didn't have a choice. If you were in my position you'd have done the exact same thing."

"I know."

His anger turned to frustration. "Then why the hell are you still holding it against me?"

"I'm not holding it against you. I'm doing this to protect the people I love. I'm sure you know a lot more men like Alfie's dad, Stu. What if one of them decides to blackmail you like Raymond did? I can't take that chance."

"Now you're not even making sense. Nobody's going to blackmail me. This job was my last. I'm going straight."

"You can't know that."

"Yes, I bloody well can. I'll never break the law again; you have my word."

My lip trembled. I hated confrontation but I had to stay strong. Taking a deep breath, I spoke again. "Tell me this, and answer honestly. If someone you knew from prison, or from before you were sent away, came along and said they'd hurt your family if you didn't do their bidding, what would you do?"

Stu raked a hand through his hair, gritting his teeth. "That's not fair, Andrea."

"Answer the question," I whispered.

His body sagged and he stared at the floor. "I'd do whatever I had to."

"Exactly."

And there it was. *I'd do whatever I had to.* Stu may have only spent two years behind bars, but the prison cell provided more than just a place of seclusion. It was a place he had to survive, and thank God he did. But that could never bode well for him and me. *I* wasn't his family. And as much as that actually pained my aching heart, I knew it was now for the best. Alfie needed me, so I would be strong. I would mourn the loss of Stu's care, attention, and focus. But we couldn't survive. I wouldn't survive always living in that shadow of fear.

I moved by him and out of the bathroom, my stomach doing a queasy flip-flop as I returned to class. Everyone was engrossed in the film. I folded my arms and stood by the door, watching Sue and Jude.

Sue was too kind. She was going to get her heart broken.

But Jude wasn't the villain, and his heart would be broken just as badly.

As though to punctuate my inner thoughts the door opened and Stu stalked inside. I swallowed tightly and watched as he returned to his desk. He sat completely still for a few minutes, his posture stiff. When he moved it was to pull a pen and a piece of paper from his bag. He bent over it and started to scribble something down. When he was done he folded the paper up and shoved it in his pocket.

What had he written?

Almost two hours later the movie was over and the class broke up for lunch. I couldn't bring myself to look at Stu so I busied myself sorting through some folders in the filing cabinet behind my desk. I didn't turn back around until the room had grown silent. I just hoped Stu hadn't decided to wait, hoping to hash things out again.

I turned.

The room was empty.

When I glanced at my desk I found a small piece of paper sitting on the keys of my laptop. Without even reading it I knew it was from him. My hand was shaky as I picked it up and carefully unfolded the paper. It contained just one sentence. The words were misspelled but that didn't stop me from understanding the question.

Did you ever stop to wonder if maybe you were my family now, too?

Twenty-Five

My sandwich was left uneaten, my appetite vanished, as I considered Stu's question over and over. I couldn't make sense of my emotions, couldn't decide if I adored him or hated him for making me feel even more mixed up than I was before.

I planned to confront him about the note after lunch but he never showed. In fact, he was absent from class for the entire rest of the week. I didn't realise how much I could miss someone I'd determined to cut from my life. Every morning I stared at his empty desk, forlorn.

Then, after a couple of days, my missing him turned to anger. Because everything else aside, he shouldn't be letting his attendance slip. I couldn't tell if I was hurt more by the fact that he was cutting class or that he'd deceived Alfie and me.

Every day I tried to initiate conversation with my cousin, but it was like trying to talk to a brick wall. All I got from him were one- or two-word answers. On Saturday I called Jamie and asked him to come over. I didn't tell him the whole story, only that Alfie wasn't talking to me and I needed him to try and get through to my cousin.

"Where is the moody little bastard?" Jamie asked as he stepped inside the flat. He had a stack of books under his arm, all tied together with a length of brown string.

"He's in his room. He's barely come out all week."

"Care to tell me why?"

I scratched at my arm in agitation. "His dad got out of prison recently. He showed up here and I can't tell you why but it's my fault. Now Alfie's completely closed himself off."

Jamie hitched the books higher up under his arm. He didn't ask any further questions. "Righteo. I'll see what I can do."

Striding down the hallway, he stopped outside Alfie's door and knocked twice before stepping inside and closing it behind him. I heard muffled voices and was relieved that at least Alfie wasn't giving him the silent treatment as well. I let out a sigh just as my phone rang from where I'd left it on the kitchen counter. Hurrying inside, I saw my dad's name on the screen.

"Dad, hey, how are you?"

"Hello Andrea, I'm quite well. And you?"

I hovered from foot to foot, deciding whether or not to answer the question honestly. "I'll admit, I've been better. Alfie and I have been going through a bit of a rough patch."

I heard rather than saw his frown. "I hope nothing too serious?"

"Um, well, did you know Raymond got out of prison?"

Dad inhaled sharply. "I didn't." There was a pause as I heard him asking Mum the same question. She hadn't known either. "Did something happen?"

"He showed up at the flat, and Alfie's hardly left his room ever since. It's like he's back to where he was ten years ago. Jamie's with him now, so hopefully he'll be able to get through to him."

"Well, would you like me to come over? If Jamie can't help, maybe I can."

"I'm not sure. We'll see how Jamie fares first. Anyway, why did you call?"

"Right, yes," said Dad. "I wanted to ask if everything is all right with Stu? He was supposed to drop by last night for a tutoring session but he never showed up. I tried calling his phone a few times too but got no answer."

I swallowed tightly. "Actually, he hasn't been to class all week either."

"Oh, perhaps he's under the weather?"

"Yes, maybe."

"Well, if you hear anything, do let me know. I've been enjoying our little weekly meetings."

"Will do, Dad. And I'll give you a call tomorrow to let you know how Alfie's doing."

"Very good. Talk soon."

The moment I hung up the phone I started pacing. Stu wasn't just neglecting to turn up to my class, he wasn't going to see Dad either. The idea of him completely giving up on his education bothered me. After I found out about the plan for the robbery and he'd continued coming to class, he told me it was because he enjoyed being there, that he wanted to learn. Well, if he wanted to learn so badly then he shouldn't be giving up just because we weren't together anymore. Hell, I'd organise for him to be transferred to another class if it meant he'd continue with his schooling.

With this in mind, my determination formed. I wasn't just going to let him slip away without confronting him about it. This was more important than him and me, this was bigger. At least, that's what my head and my heart kept telling me. For once they were working in tandem.

I pulled on my shoes, grabbed my coat, and hopped in my car. The closer I got to his house the more my nerves kicked in, and the more I started to wonder if this was a terrible idea. When I turned onto his street I noticed a few teenagers hanging out on the corner. Stu's house was about midway down and it looked like the front door was open. Trevor and Reya sat on two deck chairs chatting and seemingly soaking up the sun since the weather was nice.

Stu's car was parked out front and I saw the hood had been popped. I took my time parking, Trevor and Reya watching me all the while.

When I got out and headed towards them Trevor clamped his hands around his mouth and called, "Oi, oi, how's it going, Teach?"

Something clanged from beneath Stu's car and I heard a few muttered swearwords.

"Hi. Is your brother around?"

Trevor grinned. "Which one?"

Reya elbowed him in the side. "You know which one. Don't be an arse." Her eyes came to me and she nodded toward the car. Now I knew where the disembodied swearing had come from.

"Stu. Your teacher's here and she's looking mighty fine. You'd wanna get your ugly behind out from under there," said Trevor.

I watched as Stu emerged from beneath the car, his white T-shirt stained with motor oil. He held a wrench in his hand as he wiped at his brow with an old rag. He shot Trevor an unhappy look before his attention fell on me, and he gave me a very neutral chin tip.

"What can I do for you, Andrea?"

I fiddled with the ends of my sleeves, and in spite of myself I couldn't help looking at his body. I hadn't seen him all week and now the sight of him had butterflies flitting wildly around inside my chest.

"You've been absent from class all week," I said, finally finding my voice.

"Playing truant, eh, bruv?" Trevor tutted. "I expected better of you."

"Shut it, Trev."

Trevor's mischievous eyes slid to me. "How are you going to punish him, Andie? If you want my opinion, I think you should give him a good old-fashioned spanking."

"Right, that's it. We're going inside," said Reya, grabbing Trevor by the arm and dragging him into the house as she shot me a look of apology. "I'm sorry about him. Sometimes he just doesn't know when to shut up."

When they were gone a silence fell between Stu and me. I glanced up to find him studying me as he used the rag to rub the oil from his hands.

"What happened to your car?"

"Nothing that can't be fixed," he answered, his posture stiff. I wasn't welcome. That much was clear. "What are you doing here, Andrea?"

"I told you. I've come to see why you haven't been to class. And my dad called to say you never showed up for tutoring."

"I'm not coming back," he answered simply and my expression hardened.

"So you're going to give up just like that?"

"No, not just like that. I realised that studying and learning wasn't for me." He eyed me pointedly. "I'm better suited for other things."

"I'm sorry but I call bullshit," I blurted, unable to hold back my temper.

Stu whistled low. "Strong words, Miss Anderson."

"Yeah well, I'm swearing because I'm angry. You're giving up on yourself when you've got so much potential. You're the brightest student in my whole class."

"Is that why it takes me ten minutes to get through a page of a book it takes everyone else thirty seconds to read?" he asked sarcastically.

"How many times do I have to tell you? There are more kinds of intelligence than what the average person perceives. Some people are clever because they study hard. Some people because it's natural intelligence." I gestured to his Toyota. "You can fix a car. I can read a book. You can solve complicated mathematical equations, while I can write a ten-page essay on the Persian Wars. We all have our strengths."

His face showed he was uncomfortable now and my passion deflated. I softened my voice. "Look, I'm not here to force you into coming back. If you genuinely don't want to be in school, then don't be there. But don't lie to me and tell me it's not for you, because I remember how excited you looked the first time I introduced you to my dad. You looked like you'd found something important. Something life-changing."

Stu's gaze seared into mine. "Yeah well, things change."

I stared at the ground. "If you . . . if being around me makes you too uncomfortable, then I can have you enrolled in a difference class. Just please don't quit. I'd never forgive myself if you gave up because of what's happened between us."

His voice was soft when he spoke. "Andrea, I only ever enrolled to get to you. It's not like I'm giving up my life's dream. Look at me, I'm not cut out to be an academic."

"You can be whatever you want to be," I whispered.

Stu rubbed his neck. "Maybe I don't want to be anything."

I couldn't take the tone of his voice, the self-loathing. Stepping forward, I touched his forearm and stared up into his eyes. "Don't talk like that."

His gaze darkened, his throat bobbing as he swallowed. When his attention fell to my mouth I dropped my hand and took a step backward. "I'm sorry. I shouldn't have come."

I turned to go back to my car, but Stu's voice stopped me. "Fucking hell, Andrea. Wait."

I faced him again, his expression torn as several thoughts flickered across his face. He gripped the back of his neck with both hands and exhaled heavily. I waited for him to speak, expectant.

"What if I said I'd come back?" he asked finally.

"Stu, that would be fantastic. You're making the right decision."

"Hold your horses. I have some conditions."

I bobbed my head. "Okay."

"I want you to give me those extra tutoring sessions you offered a couple weeks ago. If I'm going to do this, I need to tackle my weaknesses head-on."

All of a sudden my enthusiasm waned. This sounded a little too much like a trick to me, a way to spend time alone with me. My expression grew suspicious. "I'll tutor you but no funny business."

One dark eyebrow went up. "Funny business?"

I huffed a breath. "You know what I mean."

"I won't mess you around, Andrea." He paused, his face serious when he amended, "Not again."

"Okay, well, is there anything else?"

Stu levelled me with a serious look. "You have to forget everything that came before."

I crinkled my nose. "What do you mean?"

"I want a clean slate. I'll come back to class. I'll study every day and try my hardest to do well, but you need to forget everything that's gone on between us. Pretend we're meeting for the very first time."

"Stu, I can't just forget—"

"Yes, you can. I can't have you looking at me with those sad brown eyes, constantly reminding me what a shit I am. That's why I couldn't continue coming to class. If you keep looking at me like that I won't be able to concentrate. So it's a clean slate or nothing."

His ultimatum had my heart pounding fast. Truthfully, the idea both relieved and pained me. Even though it hurt to be around him, I had to admit that I missed not seeing him every day. Our time together hadn't just been sexual, it had been emotional—a friendship. We'd laughed together, bantered, enjoyed each other's company, and yes, also had some absolutely mind-blowing sex in between. It was my first real relationship since Mark and though I'd told him it was over, some small part of me was disappointed that he hadn't fought harder to get me to take him back. Maybe I wasn't just angry that he'd given up on his education. Maybe I was angry because he'd given up on *us*.

Were the two so intertwined?

I lifted my gaze to his and finally replied, "Okay, clean slate. I'm not sure I can forget but I promise I won't bring it up. As far as I'm concerned you're just a student and I'm just your teacher."

I held out my hand for him to shake. Stu didn't hesitate to take it, his warm fingers sliding against mine and making my skin tingle. When he could make me feel so much with a single touch, was it even possible for us to have a clean slate? Well, I was willing to try and find out. *For him.*

He smiled down at me. "It's a pleasure to meet you, Miss Anderson."

"It's a pleasure to meet you, too, Mr Cross."

I returned his smile, and when I pulled my hand away it was stained black with motor oil.

***

I was a little wary when I pulled up outside Lee's restaurant a few days later. Stu had returned to class, but this evening was our first private lesson and I wasn't sure what to expect. Normally, I'd just have him stay back after class, but he was working some shifts for Lee so we organised to meet here instead.

It wasn't too packed when I entered, only a few tables occupied with customers. Stu sat at a table at the very back of the restaurant, a laptop opened in front of him and a stack of papers to his left. It looked like he'd been working for hours, his hair standing up in all directions like he'd run his hand through it one too many times.

He was so engrossed in his work that he didn't immediately notice me. I peeked over his shoulder to find spreadsheets full of numbers on the screen.

"Hi," I said and he glanced up.

"Andrea, hey, come sit down. Can I get you anything? A drink, maybe?"

"Some mint tea would be great if you have it," I said.

God, he was beautiful. He wore a T-shirt with the restaurant's name on and a pair of dark blue jeans. Casual, but oh so sexy. He didn't even have to try.

I really needed to stop thinking thoughts like that if I was going to be around him. *Clean slate.* He pulled out a seat for me then walked over to the counter where Lee stood counting money from the till. I busied myself taking the books I needed for the lesson out of my bag. A few minutes later he returned with my tea and a beer for himself.

"Andie," Lee said, "I just made a fresh batch of Guinness bread. You want to try it with my French onion soup? I swear it's the best thing ever."

"No, thank you," I replied. "I already ate dinner." It was a lie but I didn't want to eat anything here. It would feel too much like a date if I did.

"You sure?"

"Have some," Stu urged. "He won't let up until you do. He's like a pushy grandmother when it comes to food."

I chewed on my lip and glanced at Lee. "Honestly, I'm good."

Lee shrugged. "It's your loss."

"A tenner says he'll be back in fifteen minutes. I'm telling ya, nobody comes in here and leaves without eating something," Stu said, closing down his laptop.

"Is that like an OCD thing?"

"Nah. Like I said, on the inside he's a seventy-three-year-old grandmother. You're lucky he didn't make scones today, or he'd be shovelling one down your throat by now."

I laughed. "That's quite endearing. No offence but your brother looks more inclined to be challenging someone to a fist fight than force-feeding them baked goods."

Stu glanced at the books I'd set on the table, his brow arching sceptically. "I hope those aren't for me."

I frowned. "Why not?"

"*The Hunger Games*? Aren't those books supposed to be for teenage girls?"

I shook my head. "Not necessarily. I picked them for you because I think they're a perfect place to start. Though there are many layers to the story, the author has a very simple, pared-back writing style. We can't exactly start off reading Dostoevsky."

"Well, you could've picked something a little manlier is all I'm saying," Stu huffed.

"What's manlier than a reality TV show about teenagers that have to fight to the death?"

Stu's look was incredulous. "That's what it's about? I thought these were the ones with the glittering vampires."

"That's *Twilight*, silly. But if you prefer I'll be more than happy to read those with you instead."

"Nah, fighting to the death is fine by me."

I shook my head, smiling as I pushed the first book across the table to him. We'd gotten through about ten pages when Stu glanced up from his reading.

"Oh, would you look at that. I think that's a tenner you owe me," he said, pleased.

I glanced away from the book to find Lee had placed a selection of cheeses, cured meats, and crackers down in front of us. Stu shot him an expression like he was overdoing the hospitality big time.

"Wow, this looks amazing," I said. "But honestly, you didn't have to."

"Just eat," Lee urged. "Try the gorgonzola with the pastrami."

With that he left, and I stared at all the food, my stomach quietly gurgling. I was starving, but luckily Stu didn't hear. Picking up a cracker, I stacked on some meat and cheese then took a bite. It was delicious, especially since I hadn't *actually* had dinner yet.

"Good?" Stu asked, his gaze fixed on my mouth.

I nodded past another bite. "*So* good."

"Told you he wouldn't let you off the hook that easily."

"I should've listened to you. We're going to have to do these lessons at the college from now on, otherwise I'm going to be two stones heavier by the time we're done."

One edge of Stu's lips curved in a grin as his gaze fell to my hips. "Nothing wrong with that."

His attention had me shifting uncomfortably. I wiped my hands off with a napkin and returned my attention to the book. "Right, well, we'd better get back to work."

Stu didn't protest, and over the next forty-five minutes I'd eaten enough cheese to feed a small army and we'd worked our way through the first two chapters. When it was time for me to go, Stu helped me pack away my things, while Lee wrapped up the rest of the food and insisted I take it home with me.

Two weeks went by in a similar fashion. I went to work in the mornings, tutored Stu every few days, and tried my best to make headway with Alfie. I had no idea what Jamie had said to him, but whatever it was seemed to be working because my cousin was gradually thawing towards me.

It was when I arrived home one evening after my fifth tutoring session with Stu that everything changed. The flat was quiet when I got in and there were some letters on the floor. Alfie must've been stuck in his room all day because usually he picked them up and set them on the entry table for me. I went into the kitchen and dropped the letters on the counter.

Slipping off my shoes, I sat down on a stool, not paying much attention as I tore open the letters, bank statement, electricity bill, dentist's appointment reminder . . . It was when I picked up the last one that I started to pay attention. It was from the loan company, the one who'd sent the burly looking guy in the brown leather jacket to put the fear of God into me. The letter looked more official than usual, and when I tore it open I found out why.

All of my debt had been paid off.

Every.

Last.
Penny.

Twenty-Six

"Alfie! Get out here right now," I said, banging loudly on his bedroom door. I clutched the letter in my hand.

The door opened slowly and my cousin peeked his head out. "What's got you all worked up?" he asked, squinting at me like I'd just woken him.

I shoved the letter at him and waited for an explanation. He unfolded it and scanned the contents before his mouth dropped open in surprise. "Your loans have been paid off."

"Exactly."

"Why do you look so angry? You should be doing a jig on the rooftop right now."

"Alfie, I told you I didn't want a penny of the money your dad sent for that painting. You had no right paying this off for me."

"Okay, well, it's a good thing I didn't, then."

I gaped at him. "What?"

"I didn't pay it, Andie. I didn't even realise my dad had come through with the money. I haven't checked my bank account in a while."

"Then how . . .?"

Alfie rolled his eyes. "Isn't it obvious?"

"Stu? You think Stu did this?"

"Well, it certainly wasn't my father. And I think we're both old enough to know it wasn't your fairy godmother, though it does amuse me to envision Stu in fairy wings and a tutu."

"You definitely didn't pay it?"

Alfie shook his head. "Nope."

I exhaled, running a hand over my face as the reality sank in. "Well, hell."

"What are you going to do?"

"Obviously I can't accept it. I don't even know how he managed to pay it off. It's not like they just let anyone pay another person's loans for them."

"With his background I'm sure he has his ways."

I started pacing, my thoughts frantic. "I'm going to have to make him take the money back. He can't do this."

Alfie came and placed a hand on my shoulder. It was the first time he'd touched me in over a week. "Maybe he needed to. Maybe this was his way of saying sorry."

"He's already said sorry countless times."

"Sometimes actions speak louder than words."

I glanced at him, surprised. "You've changed your tune."

Alfie's expression grew serious. "I've had time to think. I don't blame Stu anymore for what he did. In all honesty I'm not sure I ever blamed him. It's not his fault I was born the son of a ruthless, greedy sociopath. He just got tangled up in all this by chance. In fact, I actually find his actions very noble. He might've deceived us, but there was love for his family at the core of what he did."

"I know but . . . Alfie, I still can't accept this. It's too much."

My cousin patted me on the shoulder. "Good luck trying to convince him to take it back. I don't know him as well as you do, but if you ask me, Stu Cross is as stubborn as they come."

And wasn't that the problem. Alfie returned to his room, and I went to find some wine.

The following morning when Stu arrived to class I was antsy to pull him aside and confront him. Unfortunately, I didn't get the chance until lunchtime, and when the bell rang I found my courage waning. I couldn't settle on an opening statement, couldn't think of a foolproof argument to get him to take the money back. Don't get me wrong, the idea of being debt-free was incredibly liberating, but at the same time I felt trapped. By paying off my loans, Stu had indebted me to him, and I wasn't emotionally equipped to repay, nor did I understand the currency.

The classroom was already empty by the time I came to my senses. Standing from my desk, I grabbed my handbag and went in search of Stu. It wasn't too difficult to find him. He was in the canteen sitting with Kian and Susan as they ate lunch. I hovered in the entryway until I caught his eye, then gestured for him to come over. Once I saw him get up I turned and walked straight out of the college to my car.

Sliding into the driver's seat I waited for him to join me, my nervousness building. Stu opened the door and climbed inside a minute later.

"What's wrong?"

With a shaky hand I dropped the letter into his lap. His dark brows furrowed in concentration as he read it. I saw the moment of comprehension dawn before he turned to me. He exhaled heavily, his gaze softening.

"I paid it."

I folded my arms. "Yes, I know."

His expression tightened. "Are you angry?"

At this I made a very passionate hand gesture. "Of course I'm angry. This was a private matter. You can't just go around paying off thousands of pounds of debt for me, Stu. We're not together."

His jaw stiffened. "I don't need reminding of that, luv."

I blew out air, exasperated. "How did you even manage it? Surely they would've needed some kind of authorisation from me first."

"That's the upside of being indebted to unethical loan companies who send heavies around to threaten the people who owe them money. They don't mind so much who's paying them so long as the money's legit."

I stared at him. "But why?"

Stu's gaze grew heated, his expression intense as he replied, "I'm not sure you want to hear the answer to that, Andrea."

Complete awkwardness descended, and I didn't know what to say. I stared out the window while Stu dropped back into his seat. There were a long few moments of quiet before he spoke.

"Look, by tutoring me and introducing me to your dad you're helping me turn my life around. How about you just look on it as me returning the favour?"

"It's £50,000, Stu. That's more than just a favour."

He ran a hand over his face and I noticed he looked a little tired, like he wasn't sleeping so great. "If I'd done this job three years ago, I wouldn't even be here right now. I'd probably be doing the exact same as Alfie's old man, swanning off to the Seychelles to enjoy all that money. I sure as fuck wouldn't be getting up every morning and going to school, and I wouldn't be breaking my balls studying every night just so I can graduate from this course and go on to do another three or four years of study. But I'm not the same bloke I was three years ago. I've grown the fuck up and it's about time. I don't want to spend the rest of my life going from one dodgy job to the next, constantly trying to avoid jail time. I want something different and that's all thanks to you. So just take the money, Andrea. You deserve it."

What he said made my chest tighten. Suddenly I forgot all my indignant feelings about the loan because I could barely mask how proud I was of him, how happy it made me that he was sticking with education. That he actually *wanted* to. If my estimation was correct there was still another £150,000 sitting in his bank account. He could be anywhere else in the world right now but he was here, attending class.

I reached out and took his hand in mine. "I'm . . . I'm so proud of you," I whispered.

Air rushed out of him all at once; he clearly hadn't expected me to say that. His expression made me think he might kiss me, but he didn't. Instead he tucked a stray piece of hair behind my ear and replied, "This might sound weird, but I'm proud of me, too."

I chuckled softly. "You should be. You're defying the odds, Stuart Cross."

His voice deepened, his eyes tracing my lips. "Well, you know what they say about the right teacher . . ."

At this the bell rang from inside the college, signalling the end of lunch. "Crap," I breathed. "We're late." I looked at Stu again and squeezed his hand one last time. "Come on, we'd better get inside."

He walked behind me down the corridor towards the classroom, his breath touching my ear when he whispered, "So, are we done talking about the money?"

I shivered, unable to help it. "N-not by a long shot."

He stepped by me, smirking. "We're done."

"We are not," I whisper-hissed. His confident expression was sexy and exasperating at the same time. He didn't reply, only turned and stepped inside the classroom, taking his usual seat.

I had difficulty concentrating on the afternoon lesson because something felt different. Something had shifted in the dynamic between us and my entire body was weirdly tense. Sort of like when you're excited for a surprise, but you don't know when it's going to happen.

I was walking up and down between the desks, explaining to the class how they were to complete a new assignment. I held my pen in my hand and dropped it just as I was walking by Stu. I didn't think too much of it when I bent to pick it up. However, when I turned back around I knew he'd been checking out my arse. There was also the fact his eyelids were lowered, his mouth shaped into a seductive grin.

Damn.

We had a tutoring session scheduled for after class, and by the way he was looking at me I considered coming up with an excuse to cancel. He *really* needed to quit looking at me like that, because although it gave me butterflies, my feelings were still very muddled.

On the one hand, I felt like I was dealing with a different Stu, one who finally knew what he wanted from life. He wasn't denying himself the chance to learn anymore. In fact, he was embracing it. But on the other hand, he was still the same person with the same history and background. Even though I'd determined I couldn't trust being with him, especially since I had Alfie to consider, I desperately wanted to. I wanted to believe what he'd said in that note, that he thought me a part of his family. *That he'd defend me.*

I kept myself busy when class ended, chatting with Mary for a while as the students made their way out. Stu remained sitting at his desk, a book opened in front of him. Warmth suffused my chest when I realized he was reading *The Hunger Games*. There was just something too adorable about a big, tough, muscular guy like Stu sitting there reading YA dystopia, not to mention he looked completely engrossed in the story. The fact that I'd converted a man who used to get angry if I even mentioned reading a book into a reader was a reward in itself.

I said goodbye to Mary then walked to my desk. I grabbed a pen and some paper and went to sit by Stu. He glanced up just as I dragged a chair over and placed it so I was facing him. When I took in his expression I noticed he looked a little bit sad.

"You all right?" I asked, tilting my head to study him.

He sucked in a disgruntled breath and frowned at me. "Yeah, why wouldn't I be?"

"You just look sort of upset."

"I'm fine," he huffed.

I glanced between him and the book, then pulled it towards me as I scanned the page. Comprehension dawned. "You just read the part about the burned bread."

"Yeah, so?" Stu tugged the book away from me and back to his side of the desk.

"It's okay to be upset by it."

His mouth firmed as he rolled his eyes. "Piss off."

"Oh my God, you are upset. Don't worry, Stu. I cry over books all the time. It's normal." I smiled widely. It was just so rare to find a subject that made him uncomfortable.

"Andrea, I'm not crying."

"Yeah but, you're not *not* crying either."

"I hate double negatives," he grumped, and I laughed gently.

"If it's any consolation, I cried when I read that part, too. In fact, I'm fairly sure I was bawling my eyes out."

His expression gentled. "It's that soft heart of yours."

"We all have soft hearts when it comes to stories. Come on, even if you didn't cry just now, you had to have cried at least once when you were reading *Jude*. That's the ultimate ugly cry book."

Stu arched a brow. "Ugly cry?"

"You know, when your face goes all red and blotchy, and your nose is running and you're literally a hot mess because you're crying so hard."

Stu shook his head, but he was almost smiling now. "I've never cried like that."

"Liar."

His almost smile turned into a grin. "Now that we're talking about it, I think you might have a bit of sadistic streak making everyone in the class read that one."

"Ah, so you *did* cry," I said, teasing him.

He scowled playfully. "Aren't you supposed to be tutoring me? Because it feels more like I'm being hounded."

I clicked my tongue. "Still avoiding the question. Don't worry. It's okay, I won't tell anyone what a big softy you are."

He sighed heavily and there was a part of me that loved that I was getting to him. "I told you. Lee helped me read most of it, so even if I wanted to cry I wouldn't have in front of my brother."

"Be honest, you both cried," I continued, still goading him. "I can see it now. The Cross brothers holding one another through the heartache."

Stu laughed and I found myself admiring how his eyes crinkled at the edges when he smiled. "Yes, that's exactly right. We hugged it out then ate ice cream in our PJs to console ourselves afterwards. Happy?"

"Did you cosy up on the couch and watch chick flicks, too?"

He shook his head, leaning closer as he briefly stroked my cheek. My skin tingled where he touched me. His voice got lower, huskier. "Yes, Andrea, we watched a chick flick."

"Which one?"

Stu opened his mouth to answer, and I could tell he really had to dig deep to think of a title. "Bridget Jones."

"I love Bridget Jones."

His expression went soft, his thumb stroking my cheek when he blurted, "I love you."

Time stilled. My mouth fell open on a gasp and my heart felt like it was trying to beat its way out of my chest. Had I seriously just heard him correctly?

"What?" I whispered so quietly I was surprised he heard.

His thumb slid down my cheek to my chin, tipping it up so I was looking at him. In that moment I wanted to drown in the gold flecks that glittered in his hazel eyes. His voice was almost as quiet as mine when he replied, "I know you heard me, Andrea."

I pulled away from his touch, standing from the desk so abruptly my chair fell back onto the floor with a loud clack. My cheeks heated and I couldn't look at him anymore. I felt like I was floating underwater. How had we gone from gentle ribbing to this?

I had to get out of there because I seriously couldn't breathe. He couldn't love me. It wasn't safe. He just . . . couldn't.

"I, um, I just remembered I have a thing. I have to go," I blurted.

"A thing?" Stu quirked a brow, not believing me for a second.

"Yes, that's right, a thing," I answered as I hurriedly collected my belongings.

"Andrea," Stu called after me as I turned and fled the classroom like a bat out of hell.

Twenty-Seven

By the time I reached my car I was hyperventilating. Why did he have to go and say that? Why?

We were having a perfectly nice time. Not to mention we'd agreed to forget everything that happened before. I was just supposed to be his teacher and he was just supposed to be my student. Had we been kidding ourselves?

Um, that would a yes, Andie.

I practically dove into my car, already twisting my ring around and around in sheer anxiety and fear. My stomach was all-aflutter, and I couldn't make sense of what I was feeling. Was I sad? Happy? He wasn't supposed to love me. That wasn't a part of the plan. I'd been loved before and I'd lost it. The very idea of going through all that again made me feel vaguely nauseous.

At once I understood exactly why I still wore my ring. It wasn't simply sentimentality.

It was a reminder of the pain.

A constant symbol of all I'd lost. Perhaps subconsciously I thought that if I kept the pain at the forefront of my memory I wouldn't let it happen again. It was self-preservation, plain and simple.

Yet, here I was. A man loved me and . . .

And . . .

I loved him, too.

The realisation hit me like one of those old-school defibrillators shocking me in the chest. My heart literally hurt. Was it possible for emotional pain to turn physical? All I knew was I'd never felt like this before. It was new and strange and terrifying.

315

The door of the college swung open and Stu emerged, looking from left to right as though searching for me. The moment I saw him I sped out of the car park almost as quickly as I'd fled the classroom. When I reached my flat I slammed the door shut and flicked over all the locks. My heart pounded at the thought of Stu following me back here.

Alfie sat on the floor, his legs folded as he sipped on a cup of tea like a little Buddha. He frowned in concern when he saw how worked up I was.

"Andie, what happened?"

I shook my head. "Nothing. Nothing."

Striding down the hallway, I shut myself inside my bedroom. My phone vibrated in my bag, but I didn't need to check to know who it was. I ignored it and flopped onto my bed, burying my face in the pillows as I continued to ride out the anxiety attack. I'd experienced them a time or two in the past, mostly in the months after Mark passed and I was suddenly faced with the reality of a life without him. He was my best friend, and I didn't know how I would be able to go on. *But I had. And I had fallen in love with another man.*

I didn't know how much time had passed when there was a gentle knock on my door. It was Alfie.

"Andie, are you sure nothing happened? You're worrying me."

"Everything's fine, but I think I'm coming down with a bug. I'm just going to stay in bed for a while."

"Oh," he replied, uncertainty in his voice. There was a pause before he continued. "Well I'm going to visit Jamie. He's hosting that Go tournament at the shop tomorrow, and I told him I'd help with the preparations. Do you want me to bring anything back for you?"

"No, thanks," I answered quietly.

"Okay, get some rest," said Alfie and then I heard him leaving the flat.

A little while later there was a knock on the front door. When nobody immediately answered I heard Stu call, "Andrea, let me in. I just want to talk."

My pulse raced as I willed him to leave. I knew I was being horrible, but I hadn't calmed down enough yet to face him. I needed a night to just formulate my thoughts and figure out what I was going to say.

"Andrea! Please." There was a loud bang and then I heard one of my neighbours complaining about the noise. It sounded like they'd gotten into an argument and I groaned. I had to go out there before things escalated further. Climbing out of bed I hurried down the hallway and opened the door. Stu faced a man who lived in one of the other flats, his hands fisted and his shoulders tense as he told him to mind his own business.

I grabbed his arm and yanked him inside before he could say anything else. His body fell into mine as I closed the door, his hand going to my waist to steady our balance. My top slid up a little and I gasped at the feel of his hand on my bare skin. Stu made a weird grunting sound and pulled away, but it seemed like it took effort.

"Sorry."

"No, it's okay. I'm the one who should be apologising. I can't believe I ran off on you back there. It was a truly awful thing to do but I just . . . panicked."

Stu grimaced and reached out as though to comfort me in some way. I froze and he withdrew his hand, rubbing his neck instead. "I didn't say it to scare you. I didn't mean to say it at all. It just slipped out."

I nodded and stared at him, not knowing how to respond.

Stu shook his head and levelled his eyes on me. "No, slipped out isn't the right way to describe it. It burst out, because Andrea, I've felt that way about you for a long time. Every time I see you I want to say it, but I have to bite my tongue. It was only natural that I finally told you how I feel."

I looked away, focusing on the floor. "I thought we agreed to a clean slate. I thought you wanted to forget everything that happened before."

"I did, but I can't forget how I feel for you."

"Stu, please—"

"No, Andrea, you need to listen. I love you. I love everything about you, your kindness, your open heart, your beauty. But look, I'm not an idiot. I know you don't feel the same way yet. How could you after what I did? But I'm going to make you see I'm worth it. *We're* worth it, luv. One of these days you're going to look at me and think, now there's a bloke I could fall in love with."

He stepped forward and cupped my face in his hands, then pressed a light, barely there kiss on my lips before whispering, "Wait and see."

With that he turned and left, and I stood in my hallway, my entire body tingling. *I don't need to wait and see.* I didn't need him to change a thing.

Because I loved him now.

The stark truth of it hit me like a sledgehammer.

I loved him already.

***

The following morning, I tripped over something on the floor when I entered the kitchen. What was a medium-sized wheelie suitcase doing there? It was new, still had the

318

label on and everything. Alfie sat by the window sketching on a pad of paper.

I went to put the kettle on as I asked, "What's the suitcase for?"

My cousin didn't even glance up when he answered casually, "Jamie and I are going on a cruise in a couple of months. I saw they had a sale on in the luggage shop down the street, so I thought, what the hell?"

I swivelled back around. "Hold up. Say that again."

Alfie glanced from left to right, his response sounding like a question. "I bought a suitcase?"

"No, not that. The other part."

"Oh, you mean about going on holiday together? Yeah, it should be fun."

"But . . . you don't travel. You've never even left the UK before, and you hate flying."

"Well, I've decided to face my fears. Jamie's been trying to convince me to join him on one of those Aegean cruises for years. I thought it was about time to bite the bullet."

I tried to hold back my smile. "An Aegean cruise, you say? Sounds very romantic."

Alfie blushed and even in my current state of emotions, I felt a flutter of excitement for him. It was finally happening. The hope I'd been holding on to for years that my cousin would confess his love for his best friend was coming to fruition. He didn't say anything, just continued sketching.

I went about making tea before throwing in casually, "So, when are you going?"

He huffed out a sigh. "Not for another few months. There's still a lot of planning to do."

"For a cruise? Why don't you just let a travel agent take care of everything?"

"We're not using a travel agent. We're . . . designing the trip to cater specifically to our needs."

"That sounds fancy."

"Uh huh. Are you coming to the tournament today?" Alfie asked, a very obvious subject change.

I shrugged. "I dunno. Those things tend to go on for hours, and I can think of a number of far more exciting ways to spend my Saturday."

"You won't be saying that when you hear what the prize is."

"What is it?"

"Well, there's a specially handcrafted Go board, but there's also a collection of signed books, one of which is a first edition copy of *Jude the Obscure*."

My mouth fell open. "Seriously? That'd be worth well over a thousand pounds."

"And it's your favourite book of all time, which is why I signed you up to take part in the competition." Alfie grinned.

"You didn't."

"I absolutely did. Besides, all you've been doing lately is moping and working. You need a day out of the house."

I shrugged, because in a way he was right. I had been moping. And when the likes of Alfie, a man who rarely ventures outdoors, says you need to get out of the house, you know you should listen. The problem? I was still reeling from Stu's declaration yesterday, still trying to decide how to handle the situation.

"You do realise I have no chance of winning. Half the people who compete in these things might as well have starred in their own version of *A Beautiful Mind*."

"You never know," said Alfie. "Lady Luck could be on your side today. And if anyone deserves that book it's you."

And that was how an hour later I was walking down the street to *Novel Ideas* with Alfie. Inside the shop, several shelves had been moved to accommodate the tables for the tournament. The place was packed with competitors and spectators, while Jamie flitted about taking care of all the last-minute arrangements.

"Break a leg," said Alfie, patting me on the shoulder before heading over to offer Jamie some help. I went and took a seat, watching everybody chat animatedly amongst themselves. These sorts of events were few and far between, so for enthusiasts of the game it was a real special occasion. The sense of anticipation in the air actually helped to take my mind off my own issues. Well, that was until the door opened and the source of all those issues stepped inside.

As soon as Jamie spotted Stu he waved him over. It made sense that he'd invite him. Stu had a natural flare for Go. Plus, Jamie didn't know what had gone on between us, unless of course Alfie decided to tell him. I never quite knew what sorts of things those two discussed behind closed doors.

Stu stood and chatted with Jamie. I even saw him initiate tentative conversation with Alfie, and my cousin wasn't blanking him like I expected. In fact, he was being perfectly polite and sociable. This was . . . weird. For once I was the socially awkward one between the two of us, hiding in the corner of the shop and hoping the man I secretly loved wouldn't notice me.

As though sensing my attention, Stu turned, his gaze falling on me. I swallowed and gave him a casual nod. He seemed to take this as an invitation to come over, and a moment later he took the chair next to mine and sat.

"I take it you're here to compete," I said, clasping my hands in my lap. I had this strange urge to touch him, like a ticklish sensation beneath my skin. For some reason it felt unnatural not to. My palms practically fizzled with unspent touching energy.

Stu ran a hand through his hair, and I tried not to fixate on how sexy he looked today. God, who was I kidding? He always looked sexy. "Yeah, Jamie twisted my arm. You?"

"Alfie. Though at least you have a chance of winning."

Stu's expression warmed as his attention moved from my eyes to my lips and back up again. "Well, I've never seen you play so I wouldn't know."

"Oh, you'll see. I'll be eliminated in the first round." My throat grew dry the longer I spent in his presence. What was I going to do? I felt like I was rejecting a puppy, especially with how he was looking at me with such undeserved want and affection.

Could I let myself love again even though I knew the agony it might lead to? Having felt the sheer pain of losing a man I loved with all my heart, it felt foolish to put myself back in that position. I'd be vulnerable again, each day a minefield of possibilities that could steal him away at any moment.

But then, wasn't that how life worked? Any one of us could see our time cut short at any second. And deep in my heart the idea of never being with Stu, of never telling him how I felt, was just as terrifying.

We stared at one another, locked in a moment. My skin felt too hot, my clothes too tight, and all of a sudden I wanted to climb onto his lap, wrap my arms around him and kiss him until we were both gasping for air. The urge must've shown on my face because Stu's expression heated.

"Andrea . . ."

"Okay, everyone, I'd like to say a few words," came Jamie's voice as he stood at the head of the room, holding a microphone. I was relieved for the distraction. "First of all, I'd like thank you all for coming today. This event is the result of months of planning and I'm honoured to have you take part."

Even as Jamie spoke, Stu continued to study me, and I came down with a case of restless leg syndrome. I also couldn't stop fidgeting. Stu placed a hand on my knee, his voice hushed as he leaned in to whisper, "You nervous?"

"Yes," I answered, though I wasn't nervous for the game. I was nervous because I knew I couldn't be without him. And I knew I had to tell him how I felt. The fact that he thought I didn't love him made every organ in my body hurt. The man was incredible. Loyal, thoughtful, intelligent, and drop-dead gorgeous, and I wondered how many people in his life had told him they loved him. I had no doubt he knew his family loved him, because they were amazing. But had anyone else ever told him? I wanted to be that someone.

"You'll be fine. It's just a bit of fun, right?"

I nodded and inhaled sharply when his thumb brushed back and forth, sending tingles all the way between my thighs. It felt like forever since we'd been together physically, and now I was a fizzling bag of hormones and need.

"Yeah," I managed, "just a bit of fun."

"And now that we've taken care of the housekeeping, you can all take your places," Jamie finished, but I'd barely heard a word, too distracted by Stu.

I stood and instantly mourned the loss of his touch. Stu rose with me, his gaze searing into mine as he moved my hair over my shoulders then bent and pressed a kiss on my lips. It wasn't a peck like the one he'd given me yesterday. No, there was far more pressure this time. I made a weird sound of surprise, and he smirked as he stood back up to his full height. He fingered the hem of my blouse, his eyes on the V-shaped neckline. "This is a nice top. Good luck," he said and then moved by me to take his place.

Breathe, Andie, breathe.

When I finally managed to calm down, I sat across from my first opponent, a curly haired woman in a yellow shirt. As luck would have it, I wasn't eliminated from the game right away. In fact, I made it all the way through to lunch. Jamie stood on a chair, writing the scores on a whiteboard. I wasn't surprised to see Stu was almost in the lead. There were just two other players ahead of him. When I checked to see who I'd be playing next my heart stuttered.

"Looks like we're being pitted against one another," said Stu, approaching me from behind. Even though he wasn't even touching me I could feel his heat.

"Yeah, looks like it," I breathed. I was *so* going to lose.

"You coming to lunch?" he asked hopefully.

Most everyone had retreated to the café next door for refreshments. Jamie had made a deal with the manager so we could eat there, since the bookshop didn't have any catering facilities. It was Alfie's favourite, the place where all the good-looking Swedes worked. The ones whose presence he claimed to find *soothing*. Though I wondered if he just enjoyed staring at tall, handsome, blond men while he got his regular caffeine fix.

"Yep. I'm coming," I said and Stu's expression heated. Was this what we'd come to? So starved of one another that even the most ambiguous innuendo turned us on. I certainly felt aroused by the way he was looking at me. Unable to take much more, I turned and headed outside.

I grabbed a sandwich and a cup of coffee before joining Jamie and Alfie at a table by the window. A minute later the chair beside mine moved and Stu sat down. I was blushing already and he hadn't even said anything.

"Andie, are you okay?" Alfie enquired. "You're looking a little flushed. Are you sure you aren't coming down with something? You were feeling under the weather yesterday evening."

"I'm fine. It's just warm in here."

Stu's hand came to rest on my shoulder, his gaze concerned. "Want some ice water?"

I bit my lip. "Um, yeah, sure."

As soon as he left the table both my cousin and Jamie eyed me with interest. I frowned at them. "What?"

"He's a pleasant fellow," said Jamie pointedly.

I scoffed. "I don't think anyone's ever described Stu Cross as a 'pleasant fellow' before."

"Well, they should because he is. And he's clearly besotted with you."

I glanced to where Stu stood over by the service counter, making sure he was out of earshot. "Shut up."

"I'm just saying. It's pretty obvious."

"You need to forgive him," said Alfie. "He's not the villain you've convinced yourself he is."

"If you must know I've already forgiven him. We're friends now."

This time it was Alfie's turn to scoff. "Oh, pull the other one."

I couldn't really argue with him because he was right. I was deluding myself if I thought Stu and I could ever just be friends. He'd affected me since the very first moment he'd stepped into my classroom. When I saw him making his way back over to the table I quickly changed the subject.

"So, Alfie tells me you two are off on a cruise of the Aegean. Fancy."

The two exchanged a glance, and if I wasn't mistaken Jamie looked like this was news to him. Maybe I was just imagining things. Finally, he replied, "Yes, that's right. We're going to drink gaudy cocktails with tiny umbrellas, and soak up the Mediterranean sun while making friends with all the pensioners we can find. It's going to be a roaring good time."

Stu, who had just retaken his seat next to me, didn't look very convinced. He didn't comment though, and I quietly thanked him for the water.

"Well, I applaud you for being the only person able to convince Alfie to go abroad."

"Oh, you know I'm determined once I set my mind to something." Jamie grinned while shooting Alfie another mysterious look. Seriously, what was going on with those two? For some reason I got the feeling I didn't want to know.

Back in the bookshop, I knew this was it. I was going to lose against Stu and be kicked out of the tournament. I took my seat across from him and clasped my hands together. The prize pack sat on a shelf at the other end of the shop and I stared at it, forlorn. Goodbye first edition, signed copy of *Jude the Obscure*. You were a momentary, lofty, idealistic dream from the start.

Stu must've noticed where I was looking because he said, "I can throw the game if you want. I'm not bothered about winning."

I shook my head. "No, don't do that. If I lose it's meant to be. I don't want to cheat."

His expression softened. "All right, then."

Jamie called a start to proceedings and the game began. Somewhere along the way Stu slid his feet around mine, his knees cradling my thighs. I wasn't faring as badly as I expected. In fact, I was beating him and I could tell he wasn't going easy on me. I was genuinely in the lead.

My belly quivered as his legs locked around mine, the position intimate though nobody else in the room could see. "If you're doing that to try and distract me, it's not going to work," I said, biting my lip as I contemplated the board.

Stu's gaze focused in on the movement. "Now why would I want to distract you? I already offered to throw the game."

I shot him a shy look and picked up a pebble. I was black, Stu was white.

Stu tilted his head as he studied me. "You're so beautiful."

I was sure I flushed pink at the compliment and endeavoured to avoid his heady gaze. I could tell he was smiling when he went on, "What? No response."

I sucked in a breath. "Thank you."

He pushed his knees in, holding my thighs tighter. "That's better."

"Shouldn't you be focusing on the game?" I huffed, because the way he was acting was turning me on. I wanted to have sex in the middle of a Go tournament. Bizarre.

"Maybe that's why I can't focus. You're too pretty."

I rolled my eyes, but could feel myself turning redder by the second. Stu leaned closer across the table. "And you're so fucking sexy when you blush like that," he continued. "Makes me want to bite you."

"Shut up."

"But you like it when I bite you."

I shifted uncomfortably in my seat. "That's neither here nor there."

"I like it when you bite me, too."

"Stu," I whispered, glancing around to make sure nobody was listening.

He laughed softly. "What? One of these days, luv, you're gonna let me kiss you again. Everywhere."

"Oh my God," I said, letting out a nervous laugh. "You need to stop."

His gaze was tender as he leaned his elbows on the table. "I can't help it. I love you."

I gasped. My brain became scrambled, and I couldn't think of a single thing to say. I was having heart palpitations to boot. Stu finally focused back on the game, like I'd wanted him to all along. If he kept flirting with me, telling me he loved me, I was in danger of turning into a strawberry right where I sat.

One of these days, luv, you're gonna let me kiss you again. Everywhere.

He loved me. He truly loved me, and despite my discomfort and embarrassment, I knew without a doubt that I was one of the luckiest women in the world because Stu Cross loved *me*.

Needless to say, the entire conversation put me off my game, because over the next twenty minutes he easily gained the upper hand and I lost. I was out of the tournament. All because I couldn't seem to think straight when he was close to me.

I went and sat by Alfie to watch the remaining competitors. My excitement grew the longer Stu remained in the competition, until finally it was just a red-headed guy wearing a Game of Thrones T-shirt and him. Most everyone seemed confused by Stu's presence, because I don't think any of them had ever seen a Go player who looked quite like him before. Tall, dark, and gorgeous, tousled brown hair, effortlessly muscular, and a beguiling smile to make women sigh the world over.

My heart was in my throat as I watched the final unfold. Stu was a force to be reckoned with, a natural even though he'd only been playing a while.

"He's amazing," said Alfie. "I've never seen anything like it."

"I know," I breathed. Stu was amazing. And I was in love with him so much it frightened me. His opponent took the lead for a little while, but soon Stu got the upper hand again, finally winning the game. I cheered way louder than necessary when Jamie announced him the winner and he grinned at me, pleased. He was presented with his prize, and then competitors and spectators alike gathered to congratulate him.

"Not going to go over and give your beau a big sloppy kiss for winning the competition?" Jamie asked coyly, and I shot him a look. He raised his hands in the air. "Just a friendly suggestion."

"Yes well, I've never really been one for public displays of affection," I replied.

"With a man who looks like that, all women like PDAs. If for no other reason than to ward off other females." He chuckled, highly amused by his own joke.

I shook my head at him and approached Stu. His expression warmed as soon as he saw me. I muttered a shy "Congratulations" and he knocked the wind out of me when he pulled me into a tight hug. His lips brushed my ear when he asked, "Want to help me celebrate?"

The question was dripping with sexual undertones and a tendril of desire spread through my belly. I pulled back a little, unable to look at him when I answered, "I, um, ah . . ."

Stu chuckled softly then kissed the edge of my lips. I couldn't tell if he'd been aiming for my cheek and missed, or if it was intentional.

"I'm going to pop open a bottle of wine," Jamie announced once most everyone had gone home. There were just a few stragglers still hanging about.

"Good idea," I said, needing some alcohol. Now.

And that was how an hour later I found myself sitting around a table with Stu, Jamie, Alfie, and three of the other players who'd almost made it to the final. At one point Jamie had popped up to his flat above the shop and grabbed a few more bottles of wine. I was tipsy and flushed, and generally enjoying the conversation and the company. Whether that was down to the alcohol or the fact that Stu kept finding new, subtle ways to touch me, I couldn't say.

His arm rested against mine, his skin warm. I closed my eyes for a minute, enjoying the feel of him.

"Tired?" he asked low enough so no one else could hear. Not that any of them were listening. They were all too drunk and engrossed in their boisterous conversation.

"A little."

"Want me to walk you home?" His breath hit my ear and I trembled. Stu made a noise that sounded a lot like frustration. When I looked at him his eyes were practically glowing.

"Yes."

As soon as the word left my mouth he helped me from my seat and we said goodnight to the others. I was vaguely aware of Jamie's knowing smile as Stu slid his arm through mine and led me outside.

"Wait, I forgot my things . . ." I scrambled to go back into the shop when Stu lifted his other arm on which hung my coat and handbag.

"Oh, you think of everything," I said, a big stupid grin on my face.

His expression was fond and it made my stomach fizzle. "Yeah?"

"Mm-hmm." I glanced up at him. "You're not half as drunk as the rest of us, are you?"

Stu shook his head. "I'm not a big wine drinker."

"No, I remember. You're more of a beer and whiskey sort of bloke."

He chuckled quietly and tipped my forehead. "That's right. Good memory."

"I always remember stuff about you," I slurred just before he dropped his arm and slid it around my waist so I was snuggled against him. The warmth from his body felt delicious, especially since it was dark out and there was a chill in the air. I was almost sad when we reached my flat, because he let go and pulled my keys from my bag for me.

"Thanks, I had a great time tonight," I said, sticking them in the lock and pushing the door open. I turned and stood in the doorway facing him. "I'm glad I decided to compete. It was fun."

"Yeah, me too. You were a better player than you gave yourself credit for."

I shrugged. "Not as good as you ya big . . . winner." I grimaced and smacked my hand over my face. "Oh my God, I really am drunk. I should go to bed."

Stu's gaze was hot and for a second I thought he might kiss me, but he only ran a hand down my arm before stepping away. "Get some sleep, luv. I'll see you in class on Monday."

I swallowed tightly. "Yeah, see you Monday."

A second later he was gone and I went into my kitchen, plopping my bag down on the counter and grabbing a glass of water. I sat on a stool and stared glumly at the room, disappointed that even as tipsy as I was, I still hadn't the courage to tell him how I really felt. My phone buzzed with a text, and I knew it was probably Alfie checking to make sure I got home okay. I pulled my bag into my lap, fumbling for my phone when my hand brushed off something unfamiliar. Upon closer inspection I discovered it was a book, but not just any book.

What the *hell?*

I withdrew the first edition copy of *Jude the Obscure* and emotion swelled within me. Stu. He must've put it in there when I wasn't looking. My eyes started to water as I opened it to find Thomas Hardy's signature on the title page. My fingers skimmed reverently over the inscription. As I did so, something else fell out onto my lap. Actually, two somethings: a note and pretty white-gold chain. I unfolded the note to read it.

Andrea,

Not all stories end sadly. Take a chance on us. I'll be waiting.

Stu.

P.S. If you ever decide to take off the ring, this should keep it safe.

The water in my eyes turned to full-on tears as I held up the delicate piece of jewellery. It glittered under the light of the lampshade overhead. So pretty. My pulse quickened as my attention went to my ring. Without overthinking it, I slid it off my finger and put it on the chain. Next I clipped it around my neck, and somehow it just felt right. It was still with me, because Mark always would be too. But I no longer needed its presence to be a barrier. I didn't need it to protect my heart, because my heart had been given another soul to love. To be safe *with*.

Mark's ring had found a new home and gratefulness filled me, because Stu's kind gesture, his gift, had been what gave me the courage to move forward.

My life wasn't over.

Maybe it had just begun.

I didn't hesitate when I climbed off the stool, grabbed my keys, and headed for the door. Stu's car was still parked outside Jamie's shop, so he couldn't have gone far. I ran outside and onto the street, my heart pounding as I searched for him. I was barely three houses down when I stopped in my tracks.

He stood by the kerb as though debating whether or not to come back to my flat.

Then he looked up.

His eyes wandered over me, but it didn't take him long to see I was wearing the chain. All at once his expression changed from uncertainty to joy to heated possession. He started to smile when I suddenly leapt for him, wrapping my arms around his neck and my legs around his waist. My hands trembled when I cupped his face and pulled his mouth to mine, kissing him with everything I had inside me.

He groaned into the kiss, holding me tight as our tongues collided.

I broke away long enough to whisper, "I love you."

Then my mouth was on him again, kissing, nipping, biting. Stu made a low sound of pleasure and frustration as he tried to catch his breath. "Wait, Andrea. What did you just say?"

"I said I love you. I've loved you for as long as you've loved me. Maybe longer."

At this he clasped my chin in one hand, pulling my mouth back to his in a hot, searing kiss. "Say it again," he growled.

"I love you."

"Again."

"I love you."

His hands cupped my backside, his expression full of sexy promise. "I love you, too, Andrea. So fucking much."

After that everything sped up. Before I knew it he'd carried me back to my flat, into my bedroom, and divested me of all my clothing. His face was between my legs. I arched off the mattress and gasped when I came. Stu crawled up my body. He was naked, too, but I couldn't for the life of me remember how he'd gotten that way. Though there were scratches and bite marks on his neck and shoulders that had to have been my doing.

I couldn't even blame it on the wine, because the strength of my emotions seemed to have zapped away all the drunkenness until it left nothing but stone-cold sobriety.

He pushed inside me and I cried out before biting down on his shoulder again. There was something about Stu that brought out my wild side. I moaned when he started to move, unable to help how loud I was being. We were nothing but sensation and frenzied whispers.

"I missed you."

"I missed you, too."

"Don't ever leave me again."

"I won't."

"Promise me."

"I promise."

"I love the book."

"I love you."

"I love you, too."

Stu gripped my neck as he drew back then thrust into me deep. My eyes closed, a light sheen of sweat covering my body as he drove me to dizzying heights of pleasure. We'd both been so hungry for one another that we'd forgotten to use protection. It felt like we both realised at the same time, but I only caressed his cheek and told him not to stop. I trusted him. Completely. Implicitly. In spite of everything.

It was true what he'd written in that note. I was his family now, and he was mine. I felt it deep in my bones. Our love meant we'd go to the ends of the earth to protect each other. Each of our lists had grown by one.

And sometimes the smallest number could be the biggest in the world.

Twenty-Eight

The letter had been burning a hole in my pocket all day. As soon as class came to an end I walked over to where Stu remained seated and dropped it on his desk. My pulse accelerated as he looked from the letter to me and then back to the letter.

"What's this, luv?"

I already knew. I was nervous for his reaction. I wanted him to be happy and not feel intimidated by the task ahead.

Stu and I had been seeing each other for almost three months. In secret, obviously. I knew that technically it was unethical to be conducting a romantic relationship with one of my students, but we were both adults. So long as it didn't interfere with my work and Stu's studies, then I didn't see anything wrong.

Besides, there was only one month left of the course. After that he wouldn't be my student anymore. I was going to miss seeing him every day.

A couple of weeks ago I'd started helping him with his university application. He applied to the Mathematics BSc programme at King's College, and since Dad worked in the department he'd informed me just yesterday that Stu had gotten in. Stu applied through the college, which meant his acceptance letter had been sent here. And that was why I had it in my possession.

His acceptance depended on his final grades in my class, but I was confident he was going to ace his exams. In spite of his dyslexia, his reading and writing was improving rapidly. He was really trying, and it made me believe he truly wanted this.

"It's a letter about your uni application. Open it," I answered, barely able to conceal my excitement.

Stu smirked and shook his head, his expression warm as he tore open the letter. Obviously, my enthusiasm amused him. Some days I wondered if him studying for a degree meant more to me than it did to him. Our personal relationship aside, as a teacher there was nothing more rewarding than to see one of my students succeed.

He unfolded the letter and scanned the contents. I frowned when I saw his expression falter, his brows drawing together in what looked like disappointment.

What the hell?

"Guess it's not the end of the world," said Stu, shoving the letter aside and folding his arms across his chest.

"What are you talking about?"

He levelled me with a serious look. "I didn't get in. Maybe I can try again next year."

Completely confused, I reached for the letter but he swiped it away before I could pick it up. I looked at him. His face morphed into a giant grin and that was when I knew I was being played.

"You bastard!"

He stood up and pulled me into a hug. "Serves you right for being nosy. I told you not to ask your dad if I got in, but you just couldn't help yourself."

I pressed my face into his chest. "I'm sorry. But I couldn't stand waiting."

He chuckled and stroked my hair affectionately before pulling back to look at me. "I know, and it's adorable."

"Stu."

"Yes, Andrea?"

"You're going to university."

"I know, luv."

I grinned. "And you said this wasn't *Good Will Hunting*."

Now he rolled his eyes, but he was still smiling. "Piss off."

I laughed and stepped away to grab my things. Then I slid my hand into his and dragged him from the classroom. "Your brothers will probably all be at the restaurant, right?"

"Probably."

"Well, let's go and give them the good news."

"Andrea, they're not going to be as excited as you are. They're—"

I turned and held a finger to his lips. "That's enough self-deprecation for one day. We're going to Lee's."

So, obviously, I had an ulterior motive. As soon as I found out Stu was accepted into the course, I called Lee and we put together a last-minute party to celebrate. Everybody was waiting at the restaurant to surprise him, and I was giddy with anticipation.

When we arrived at Lee's, Stu climbed out of his car and came around to open my door for me. I took his hand and together we walked inside. As soon as we stepped through the door everyone was cheering and shouting "Congratulations". I was beaming from ear to ear as Stu shook his head and gazed down at me.

"Completely over the top," he muttered before pressing a soft kiss on my lips. "But thank you."

"You're welcome. We're all so proud of you."

Our entire was family was here, including my mum and dad. Dad and Stu had developed quite a close friendship over the past few months, and surprisingly both my parents were over the moon about my new relationship. They never mentioned the student-teacher thing, and I thought it was probably because they were simply relieved I'd found love again.

Lee came over and pulled Stu into a manly hug. "Congrats, bruv. I knew ya had it in you."

"Thanks," said Stu, looking a little sheepish. He wasn't used to all the pomp and ceremony.

"Incoming," Trevor yelled before jumping on top of Stu and Lee for a group hug. I saw their youngest brother, Liam, standing off to the side and shaking his head at Trevor's antics. Trevor shot him a look. "Get over here, Liam, before I drag you kicking and screaming. One of us is getting a uni degree, and I think I speak for all of us when I say no one expected it to be Stu. This is a momentous occasion."

"Oi," Lee scolded. "That's enough, Trev."

"What? I'm just saying what we're all thinking."

"It's fine," said Stu, raking a hand through his hair as he pulled away from his brothers and came to drape an arm around my shoulders. "If it weren't for Andrea, none of this would be happening."

"Aw, that's so romantic," said Trevor, nudging Liam vigorously. "Isn't it fucking romantic? I think I've got a tear in my eye."

Liam slapped him lightly on the back of the head. "Quit acting like a freakshow."

"What? I'm feeling totes emosh right now. I'm not a robot. I can't hold in my feelings like the rest of you non-feeling shrews."

"Well, try," said Lee before turning and taking Stu's hand. "We're all proud as fuck."

"Can I second that?" came my dad's voice as he approached with Mum.

We spent a few minutes chatting with my parents and then Alfie and Jamie arrived. The two of them had grown even closer these last few months, spending hours and hours locked up in Alfie's bedroom. I couldn't tell if they were getting it on or secretly plotting how to take over the world. Seriously, with those two you just never knew. They still hadn't gone on their cruise, mainly because Alfie kept putting it off. I was beginning to wonder if it was ever going to happen.

The party progressed, and we enjoyed ourselves. Lee made some fantastic food and everybody seemed to be having a nice time. Later in the evening Stu pulled me aside and led me out to his car.

"Where are we going?" I asked curiously.

"I was gonna wait a while to show you, but I don't know, there's something about tonight that feels right."

What he said made me excited, but I tried not to let it show too much. "Okay."

About twenty minutes later he parked on a quiet residential street not too far outside the city. Stu cut the engine and was silent for a minute.

"You don't have to make any decisions right now. I just want you to know the option's there." He sounded nervous, which was way out of character.

"Stu, will you just tell me what's going on?"

He inhaled a deep breath before pointing toward a nice-looking apartment building across the street. "You see that place?"

"Uh huh."

"I just made a down payment on one of the top-floor apartments. I'm moving in next month."

Now I turned to face him, unable to hide my smile. "That's great news." I knew he'd been finding it hard at home, especially with so many people under one roof. "Now you'll finally have your own space."

He scratched at his stubble, before blurting, "I want you to move in with me."

I gaped at him. "What?"

"It doesn't have to be right away. I know everything's still very new between us. But just think about it, yeah?"

I stared over at the building again. It was way nicer than where I was currently living, and the neighbourhood was a lot better, too. Finally, I whispered, "I'm not sure if I can leave Alfie."

"Luv, Alfie is family, so he can live with us if he wants. I'm used to having family around so it's no big deal. There are three bedrooms."

"Oh," I breathed, my heart pounding in my chest. It was just so thoughtful and lovely of him to consider Alfie.

A moment of silence passed before Stu slipped his fingers through mine. I noticed a new set of keys in his other hand. "Come in and take a look around. Maybe it'll help you make a decision."

I let him lead me outside and a few minutes later we stepped off the lift at the top floor of the building. There was a long hallway with doors lining one side and a narrow window running all the way down the other.

Stu slotted his key in one of the doors and pushed it open to reveal a large, open-plan kitchen and living area. There wasn't any furniture yet, but the walls looked newly painted and I liked the wooden floors. Stu pulled me farther inside and led me through all the rooms, giving me the grand tour. It was way bigger than Alfie's and my flat, and certainly a lot bigger than the single bedroom Stu currently occupied in his family home.

I was looking out the window when he came and wrapped his arms around me from behind. His warmth soothed me and I leaned back into the embrace, enjoying the comfort his hugs always brought. He kissed the top of my head.

"Like I said, you don't have to make a decision right away. I just want you to know the offer's there if you ever want to accept it."

I exhaled heavily and twisted in his arms. Stu stared down at me, looking all expectant and handsome, and somehow my decision was clear. I knew what I wanted. Between one breath and the next I pulled his mouth down to mine and kissed him with everything I had in me. Stu automatically responded to the kiss, his arms tightening around me, pulling me close, his tongue sliding along mine in a seductive dance. I broke away on a gasp and announced, "I'll do it. I'll move in with you."

"Don't fuck with me, Andrea," he whispered, his eyelids lowered and his gaze searching mine.

"I'm not fucking with you, Stu. I want to move in with you. I want to wake up with you every morning and go to sleep in your arms every night. Life's too short not to do what feels right in my heart."

"Jesus, I love you," he groaned, his voice husky as he pressed his lips to mine fiercely.

"I love you, too," I replied and for a while we were lost in one another. About half an hour later we were in a state of undress on the floor, trying to catch our breaths.

"Well, at least the place has been christened now," said Stu with a cheeky grin.

I smiled and elbowed him in the side. "Yes, at least there's that. Now all I have to do is convince Alfie to move in with us."

Stu chuckled. "Piece of cake."

He wrapped his arms around me and I lay against his chest, glancing around at our soon-to-be home. I fingered the diamond ring that hung around my neck. It was no longer a symbol of all that I'd lost. Now it represented a part of a journey, one I was still embarking on. I'd been fortunate to fall in love not once, but twice.

And I was ready for whatever else life had in store.

Twenty-Nine

Stu

"Be honest. How do I look?"

Lee sat on the sofa finishing off a bacon sandwich when I came out of my bedroom. He paused mid-chew, looked me up and down, smirked, then swallowed.

Before he could answer Trevor cut in. "You look hot, bruv. A real sexy beast. Rawr."

"Fuck off," I said, scowling and returning my attention to Lee. Unlike Trev, I knew I could trust him to give me a straight answer. He wiped his mouth with the back of his hand. "Why does it matter? Isn't everyone gonna be wearing the same getup?"

"Don't they wear that shit in *Harry Potter*?" Liam piped in.

I shrugged. "Fuck if I know. Feels like a dress."

"They're called *graduation robes*," said Trev, in a fake haughty voice as he produced the stupid hat I refused to put on. "And you need to wear this, too. It's traditional."

"Nope. Not happening. I draw the line at the dress."

Trev sighed. "Again, it's not a dress. And you need to get used to wearing it, because I expect you to have a doctorate by the time you're forty. I wanna be able to go around bragging to everyone that my brother's a doctor."

"Unless it's a medical doctor, it doesn't count," said Lee.

Trev's phone rang, interrupting our conversation. He glanced at the screen, a little secretive smile on his mouth before he answered, "Hey ReyRey, how's it hanging?"

I should've known. Trevor's special little non-girlfriend best friend was the only one who could make him smile like that. Like the cat-that-got-the-cream-who-knew-your-darkest-secret-and-saw-you-naked-and-discovered-your-Internet-search-history all rolled up into one single expression of smug fuck.

"You love it." A pause. "Quit complaining, we both know you love it." A chuckle. "Okay fine." Silence. "Yeah, the graduation's at two. Then we're all heading out for dinner. You coming?" Another pause. "Okay, great. See you then. Smooches!"

Liam screwed up his face while Trev slid his phone back in his pocket. "Smooches? Who are you, Paris Hilton?"

"I'm my own special flavour of exceptional," Trev shot back. "Don't be jealous."

Liam gave him the finger.

"When are you ever gonna stop stringing that girl along?" I asked, frowning.

"Yeah," Lee added, "because you're not fooling none of us with the whole best buds story. I've seen you looking at her tits. A man doesn't look at tits like that and think, *now there's a girl I want to be* friends *with.*"

"Oh, you can all piss off, you big bunch of cynical arsebags," Trev replied snootily. "I don't have to explain our special friendship to anyone." There was a pause and then a glint came into his eye. "But if you must know, that's exactly what I think when I look at tits. I'd much rather be friends with someone with a fantastic rack than some smelly . . . penis-haver."

"Penis-haver?" Lee chuckled. "Now I've heard it all."

"It's a word," Trev went on. "All the cool kids are using it."

I left them to their bickering and went back inside my room. Fuck, I was nervous. Today the college was holding a small graduation ceremony for a few of the adult education classes. I was gonna have to get up on a stage and collect a certificate and shake some posh bloke's hand. It felt surreal to think that less than a year ago I was sitting in a prison cell, just trying to survive and get through one day at a time. I didn't see a future for myself other than one that involved crime. Then I met Andrea and everything changed. She made me want things. Made me want to be a better person, achieve something real. Now I couldn't imagine a world without her in it. *How'd I get so fucking lucky?*

"You almost ready to make a move?" Lee called from the living room. "We need to get going."

"Yeah, be out in a sec."

I took one final breath then headed out. Andrea was already at the college helping get the place ready. I was hoping to steal a minute alone with her before the ceremony started. She was my soft place, and today I was in serious need of the calm she gave me. All it took was one touch, a tender look.

When we arrived, Lee and the others went to find seats while I went to search for Andrea. On the way I bumped into a bunch of my classmates, and yeah, like Lee said, they were all wearing the same robes as me. At least we were in this together.

"Well, would you look who it is," said Mary. "Old cranky drawers himself. You look like you'd rather be having an ingrown toenail removed."

"Ugh, nice visual," Susan complained.

"What? I'm pleased as fucking punch to be here," I said with a grin. "I love dressing up like a twat and parading myself in front of everyone's nearest and dearest."

"It's not about the dressing up," Kian interjected. "It's about celebrating our achievement, and I for one am proud of all of us. Fuck! We've passed our exams and we're getting our diplomas, even if we do have to wear these weird dresses. Bullshit!"

I chuckled loudly and gave his hair a ruffle. What could I say? I liked the kid's optimism, even if he did have a crush on my woman. I knew he was harmless. "I'm glad I'm not the only who feels like they're in drag."

He held his hands out. "Hey, it's the name of the game."

I told them all I'd see them later then continued down the corridor. With clipboard in hand as she went through a list, Andrea was in organisation mode. God, I loved her. She was beautiful without even trying. Her hair hung in long waves down her back, and I had a vision of weaving it around my fist, tugging her neck to the side so I could get a taste. She wore some kind of navy wrap dress and the little tie at the waist had me itching to pull it free. That shit was just too much of a temptation. She was so engrossed in her list that she didn't notice me come up behind her. Letting out a small gasp when I folded my arms around her middle, she hitched a breath then sank into me.

"Hey," I murmured and pressed a kiss just below her ear. "You look gorgeous."

"Hey, yourself," she said and twisted in my arms to peer up at me. "Wow, you look—"

"Ridiculous?" I provided.

She shook her head and blushed a little. "No, strangely sexy." Pausing to run her hands down the silky fabric, she bit her lip and asked, "Is this rented?"

I nodded.

"Damn. I just had a little fantasy of you wearing it at home tonight with nothing else."

I smirked and bent to take her earlobe in my mouth. "Dirty. I like it."

She giggled then sighed when my hand moved over her stomach. I was seriously considering the logistics of a quickie, but then reminded myself there were too many people around. As much as I enjoyed having sex in public places, now wasn't the time.

With a reluctant sigh I let her go and asked, "Is Alfie coming today?"

She smacked her hand to her forehead. "Oh right, I forgot to tell you. He and Jamie *finally* went on their cruise. They left for their flight early this morning."

"The cruise they've been planning for the last few months? I honestly thought that was never going to happen."

She bobbed her head. "Me too. I think they kept putting it off because Alfie's fear of flying was getting to him. He sent a text a little while ago saying they landed safely, so he obviously got over it enough to endure the flight. At least he doesn't have a fear of water, too. If he did we'd be waiting until 2020 for him to finally bite the bullet."

"Well, I'm glad they went. They both deserve a break."

In spite of offering for him to come and live at the new flat, Alfie had surprised both of us by saying no. He claimed he wanted to try going it alone for once, to be completely independent. If I was honest I thought Andrea was more stressed out about the separation than Alfie was.

She loved him though, and I understood her worry because I knew exactly how she felt. I knew what it was like to be fiercely protective of your family.

We shared a look of mutual understanding before there was an announcement over the intercom that proceedings would begin in five minutes. I kissed her and then we both made our way to the function hall.

I took my place next to Kian in the second row from the stage as the ceremony started up. When they called my name I stood and went to collect my certificate. Of course, as soon as I stepped onto the stage my brothers had to make a big song and dance by cheering for me like Arsenal just won the Premiership.

"Go Stu!" Liam shouted.

"Work it, you sexy beast." This was Trevor. Course it was. Half the people in the audience started laughing. Lee let out a rip-roaring whistle, and I couldn't help the smile that spread across my face. Bunch of nutters, but I wouldn't change them for the world. I looked out and saw Sophie and Karla sitting next to them, both shaking their heads in dismay.

I got my diploma, shook hands with the dean of the college, then continued to the other side of the stage. Looking out, I saw Andrea standing next to the other students who hadn't been called yet. As she looked up at me, it reminded me of the first time I saw her face. I'd been gobsmacked. Her expression was one of shock, yet she'd warmly accepted me into her classroom as if seeing a git like me was an everyday occurrence. God, she'd surprised me. Sweet, strong, passionate, real. They were the first four things I thought about her. How any male concentrated in her classes was beyond me. And as she spoke to me, with kindness and encouragement, I realised I had never met anyone like Andrea Anderson before. She was incredible. Now, her gorgeous brown eyes flicked up and she caught me looking. I grinned and held up my piece of paper. She beamed back at me.

Love you, I mouthed. I couldn't have done it without her, none of us could have. She was the most selfless and amazing woman I'd ever known. I'd do anything for her, and I'd spend the rest of my life doing right by her because she'd saved me.

Her smile lit up her whole face, and I could tell even from a distance that she was proud of me. In my gut I felt like the luckiest bastard in the world to be on the receiving end of a look like that.

She glanced across the space that separated us, her expression fierce and full of affection when she mouthed back, *Love you, too.*

And thank fuck for that.

Epilogue

Harry Shields showed up for the night shift, regular as clockwork. He greeted his co-worker, Jerry, like usual and they completed the switchover. When Harry went to start his rounds of the museum, all was quiet. It was always quiet. The presence of so many magnificent works of art seemed to warrant the respect of silence. They hung on the walls as though in slumber, until the sun rose and it was time to be looked at by new eyes.

Harry might've just been an average Joe security guard, but he also liked to think of himself as an art lover. He passed through the Blue room, where one of his favourite paintings was on display, a depiction of a bridge going over the water in Venice by the American artist, John Singer Sargent. Harry had always wanted to visit the Italian city, and he hoped that in a couple years he'd finally have enough saved up to take his family on the trip of a lifetime.

"One day, Venezia, one day I'll see you for real," he muttered to no one in particular. He had a tendency to talk to himself. Sometimes he spoke to the paintings, or even the artists themselves, though he'd never admit it if asked.

How's it going, Raphael? Long time no see.

Working the night shift alone for the past five years had caused him to develop a few . . . eccentricities. Yep, it was just a typical night at the Isabella Stewart Gardner Museum.

Well, that was until he heard an odd scratching noise as he approached the Dutch room. Quickly, he pulled out his flashlight. He shone it around the space, searching for the source of the noise, but it had gone quiet again. Wondering if an animal had found their way in, a wild cat or a fox maybe, he did a brief inspection of the room but everything seemed to be in order. Just a bunch of paintings in frames. He clicked off his flashlight, then stilled. Not all the frames should have paintings. The infamous frame of *The Storm on the Sea of Galilee* had sat empty for over twenty-five years, ever since it was stolen alongside a number of other valuable items on that faithful night in March, 1990. He turned his flashlight back on.

The frame was no longer empty.

Harry let out a string of swear words his mother would've clipped him around the ear for when he was younger and pulled out his walkie-talkie. His co-worker Mick was currently patrolling the courtyard and gardens.

"What is it, Shields?" he answered, sounding bored.

"I'm in the Dutch room, and, uh, I think there's something you need to come see."

***

Meanwhile, sailing down the motorway in a rented Ford Fusion, two best friends celebrated a job well done.

"I can't believe we pulled that off," said Alfie, grinning widely over at Jamie who was smiling, too, as he focused on the road ahead.

"Hey, you're the mastermind in all this. I'm just the one who gave you a little push to go through with it."

"It's not like it didn't take me months and months of planning," Alfie said with a hint of self-deprecation.

"Oh, quit the modesty. You're a genius, and I'm delighted to be along for the ride."

"You're not just along for the ride. If it weren't for you I never would've had the courage to go through with it. I think I might actually be running off your bravery right now, because I'm not sure I ever possessed much myself."

352

Jamie reached across and briefly squeezed his hand. "Nonsense. You've always been brave. You just needed the right person to bring it out of you. That's where I come in, being the crazy, risk-taking son of a gun that I am. Besides, you know I could never resist a good adventure."

"Well, I have always been a fan of your crazy."

They shared a smile then silence fell, miles and miles of road passing them by.

Now Alfie frowned, the reality of what they'd just done suddenly sinking in. "Oh my God, Jamie. We just broke into a museum to return a painting that was stolen over twenty-five years ago. A painting that, if we'd returned it officially, could've seen us being rewarded millions of pounds for its recovery. I think we're both insane."

Jamie tilted his head to the side. "Well sure, but how would we explain having it in our possession? It's not like we could just show up with an almost four-hundred-year-old Rembrandt, and tell them that when you were contracted by an art thief to paint a replica, you actually painted two. And that when the thief agreed to give you a moment alone with the original, you swapped it with the second replica and hid the real painting under your floor boards."

"Well, when you put it like that I guess you're right," Alfie allowed.

"Of course, I'm right. I'm always right. The FBI would have to be involved. They'd want to know who exactly this art thief was and who had the painting all these years. And since your very dear cousin is now very much in love with said art thief, your hands were pretty much tied."

"Andie's going to kill me when she finds out," said Alfie nervously.

"Maybe at first, but once she realises the risk you took to do the right thing, to return a piece of history to its rightful owner, I'm sure she'll find it in her heart to forgive you your deception. Besides, even when the painting's recovery is reported on the news, it's not like this Renfield character will have any recourse, and you said yourself that both Andrea and Stuart used false names and disguises. He doesn't even know their true identities."

Alfie nodded, his confidence bolstered. "You're right. And I spoke with Mum the other day. She wasn't too happy about it, but I reminded her how the sale of my counterfeits provided for the lifestyle she's been enjoying all these years. She owed me. I managed to guilt trip her into threatening Dad with informing the police about the money he hid in Swiss bank accounts before he was sent to prison. There's far more in those accounts than he ever made from the sale of the painting, so I know he'll keep his distance."

Jamie smacked him on the thigh and laughed loudly. "Perfect! I have to admit, I'm quite proud of us. Tonight we've done something that will go down in the history books for years to come. They'll forever wonder who the Good Samaritans were who returned the famous painting, and we'll know it was us. Maybe one day, when I'm old and grey, I'll sit down and tell all my grandchildren the tale of how my best friend in the whole wide world and I embarked on an impossible adventure."

Alfie shot him an amused look. "Grandchildren?"

"Don't look so shocked. Of course I plan to have grandchildren."

"Yeah, but how—"

"When you and I adopt and our little one grows up, I'm sure they'll want to reproduce."

Alfie's mouth dropped open in shock, his cheeks colouring themselves bright red. "You . . . and me . . . adopt?"

Jamie feigned a horrified expression. "Don't tell me you're one of those awful people who hate children? Because if you are, I might have to rethink this whole being in love with you business."

Now Alfie could barely form words. He stared at his friend, his heart pounding wildly in his chest. Of course, he'd secretly held a candle for Jamie for years, always too afraid to tell him for fear of losing their friendship. But he never for a second imagined his feelings were reciprocated.

Jamie glanced back and forth between him and the road. "Well, say something. Don't leave a gentleman hanging."

Alfie flushed all the way down to his toes. "I love you, too," he said in a barely audible mumble.

Jamie grinned, well aware of his embarrassment. "Do speak up, darling. I didn't hear a word you just said."

"Oh for crying out loud," Alfie huffed. "I love you, okay. I've loved you since . . . forever."

Pleased as punch, Jamie pulled the car over onto the side of the road. As soon as they were safely out of the way of any oncoming traffic, he grabbed Alfie by the face and kissed him hard right on the mouth. Alfie gasped, sinking into the kiss like he'd been waiting for it his entire life.

The painting had been returned.

He'd done the right thing.

And now he was kissing the love of his life in the front of a rented Ford something-or-other.

END.

If you enjoyed Trevor and Reya in *Thief of Hearts*, then you might be interested in their short story, *One Epic Night*. To get it for free, please visit L.H. Cosway's website and sign up for the newsletter. You will be sent the story in a separate email after signing up.

One Epic Night

Trevor Cross had been my best friend for the better part of the last three years. He was also the most unique and unpredictable person I knew. Being around him often felt like trying to circumnavigate a minefield, and yet, I wouldn't change him for the world. He was addictive, destructive, frustrating, fascinating. Too full of energy to ever pin down. Our friendship had been on a steady path until one wild and epic night that changed everything. He convinced me to throw caution to the wind, to stay out until the break of dawn and embrace new experiences. I never expected where the night would end, nor how it would alter our relationship for good.

This story is a prequel to Trevor and Reya's full-length book, Hearts on Air, the 6th and final instalment in the *Hearts* series, set for release in 2017.

Thank you for reading *Thief of Hearts*. Please consider supporting an indie author and leaving a review <3

About the Author

L.H. Cosway lives in Dublin, Ireland. Her inspiration to write comes from music. Her favourite things in life include writing stories, vintage clothing, dark cabaret music, food, musical comedy, and of course, books. She thinks that imperfect people are the most interesting kind. They tell the best stories.

Find L.H. Cosway online!

www.lhcoswayauthor.com

L.H. Cosway's *HEARTS* Series

Praise for *Six of Hearts* (Book #1)

"This book was sexy. Man was it hot! Cosway writes sexual tension so that it practically sizzles off the page." - A. Meredith Walters, New York Times & USA Today Bestselling Author.

"Six of Hearts is a book that will absorb you with its electric and all-consuming atmosphere." - Lucia, Reading is my Breathing.

"There is so much "swoonage" in these pages that romance readers will want to hold this book close and not let go." - Katie, Babbling About Books.

Praise for *Hearts of Fire* (Book #2)

"This story holds so much intensity and it's just blazing hot. It created an inferno of emotions inside me." - Patrycja, Smokin' Hot Book Blog.

"I think this is my very favorite LH Cosway romance to date. Absolutely gorgeous." - Angela, Fiction Vixen.

"Okay we just fell in love. Complete and utter beautiful book love. You know the kind of love where you just don't want a book to finish. You try and make it last; you want the world to pause as you read and you want the story to go on and on because you're not ready to let it go." - Jenny & Gitte, Totally Booked.

Praise for *King of Hearts* (Book #3)

"Addictive. Consuming. Witty. Heartbreaking. Brilliant--King of Hearts is one of my favourite reads of 2015!" - Samantha Young, New York Times, USA Today and Wall Street Journal

bestselling author.

"I was looking for a superb read, and somehow I stumbled across an epic one." - Natasha is a Book Junkie.

"5+++++++ Breathtaking stars! Outstanding. Incredible. Epic. Overwhelmingly romantic and poignant. There's book love and in this case there's BOOK LOVE." - Jenny & Gitte, Totally Booked.

Praise for *Hearts of Blue* (Book #4)

"From its compelling characters, to the competent prose that holds us rapt cover to cover, this is a book I could not put down." - Natasha is a Book Junkie.

"Devoured it in one sitting. Sexy, witty, and fresh. Their love was not meant to be, their love should never work, but Lee and Karla can't deny what burns so deep and strong in their hearts. Confidently a TRSoR recommendation and fave!" - The Rock Stars of Romance.

"WOW!!! It's hard to find words right now, I don't think the word LOVE even makes justice or can even describe how much I adored this novel. Karla handcuffed my senses and Lee stole my heart." - Dee, Wrapped Up In Reading